*"You Are ...
Ma...
Trent's Voice Was Low
and Tender.
"Damn, But You Do Tempt Me."*

Why could he not feel toward Amber as he felt about other women, he wondered. On that last night in London when he had rescued the girl and carried her to his ship for an hour of pleasure before sailing, he had not expected her to be as beautiful and as desirable as Amber. So much so, that within only a few hours he had felt this overwhelming desire to have her with him always.

He took a long, ragged breath and whispered, "I'll never let you go, Amber, never!" His words were so low that she barely heard them. Then he straightened and walked quickly from the cabin, closing the door quietly.

Flames of Passion

Sheryl Flournoy

A TAPESTRY BOOK

PUBLISHED BY POCKET BOOKS NEW YORK

An *Original* publication of TAPESTRY BOOKS

 A Tapestry Book published by
POCKET BOOKS, a Simon & Schuster division of
GULF & WESTERN CORPORATION
1230 Avenue of the Americas, New York, N.Y. 10020

ISBN: 0-671-46195-8

First Tapestry Books printing November, 1982

10 9 8 7 6 5 4 3 2 1

POCKET and colophon are registered trademarks
of Simon & Schuster.

TAPESTRY is a trademark of Simon & Schuster.

Printed in the U.S.A.

Acknowledgments

My mother, who is the best friend I ever had or shall ever have. With her love and understanding I have grown. I love her dearly.

My husband, Keith, who has shown me a new kind of love and a different kind of friendship.

Patricia Gallagher, her beautifully written words inspired me. Pat encouraged me and has become a close friend.

And my thanks to a very special lady, *Kate Duffy,* for she is rare. Her steadfast belief in me and in this book mean much more than mere words can express.

Author's Note

In this novel I have used a subject matter that is part historical fact and part fiction. The historical events described herein are as factual in their occurrence as I was able to write them.

The author wishes to thank the following authors and their books for the research that made this book possible. The actual historical events, including characters, dates and locations, were obtained from the following:

Robin Reilly—*The British at the Gates: The New Orleans Campaign in the War of 1812*

Isaac Asimov—*The Birth of the United States, 1763–1816*

Walter Lord—*The Dawn's Early Light*

Perkins and Van Deusen—*The United States of America: A History,* Volume One, Second Edition

". . . love and hate being both passions, the one is never safe from the spark that sets the other ablaze."

"In strong natures, if resistance to temptation is of granite, so the passions that they admit are of fire."

—*Bulwer*

Flames of
Passion

Chapter One

AMBER RAN ALONG THE NARROW STREET IN DESPERATION, fleeing from the two men who ran after her. The storm raged, the rain beat down in forceful fury, the wind blew hard against her small body, pushing her backward, impeding her progress. Still she pressed forward, she had to, the sound of heavy footsteps running behind her gave her the will to struggle on.

She lost her footing, stumbled, fell. Amber sprawled in the street and lay silent for a moment, listening. Had they stopped chasing her? Had they given up? No! She heard the sound of running feet again, closer now. She scrambled to her feet, stepping on the hem of her dress. She heard the ripping of the fabric, felt the downward pull as her body went down once more.

Attempting to crawl, Amber dug her fingers at the street as she tried to move on. Again she found herself on her feet running, running. Her heart beat hard against her breast, and she felt that her lungs would burst. The pursuing footsteps seemed muffled because the blood pounded so loudly in her ears.

A sudden clap of thunder sounded loud and vicious, and Amber felt as if it had reached down and slapped her. The force seemed to whirl her into a cloud of even more terror. Where am I? Where? she thought. Her eyes were wide with fright as she searched for a safe hiding place. But there was none.

Now the voices of the pursuers could be heard clearly.

"Down this wye, Luke. See? There, just a'ead, there she be!" one howled.

"Aye, I see 'er. We got the wench, now," replied the other.

All was lost, she would never escape now, Amber thought, but she ran even faster. She couldn't let them catch her. All the stories she had heard of how seamen used young women, how they sold them when they were finished with them, or even worse . . . killed them! All these thoughts were racing through her frenzied brain. She just couldn't let it happen to her!

Amber wasn't one to give up easily, and even though her legs told her that they couldn't go another step, they did. Her body ached and she felt sick, but still she went on. They wouldn't get her! They wouldn't!

Again she lost her footing, stumbled, fell, got up, stumbled, and fell again. Reaching out to pull herself up once more, her hand gripped an unfamiliar object, and with a sharp intake of breath, she stared at two black boots. Her heart seemed to stop.

Slowly Amber's eyes moved upward to the shadowy form that stood over her. Again the thunder roared and, as the lightning flashed behind the figure, she saw a man dressed in black boots to the knees, black breeches, white shirt loose and open, knotted at the waist, a black cape whipping in the wind, hands on his hips. She thought him to be the devil!

He stood looking down at her, making no move. A shiver ran through Amber's body, the cry that welled within her throat now escaped her lips. It was over! The prey had been captured!

Captain Trent LeBlanc fought his way through the wind and the rain of the raging storm on his way back to his ship, the *Mér Fleur*. LeBlanc was not a man to roam through the streets or to visit the taverns of the towns at which the vessel docked. He nearly always remained aboard because he had seen more than his share of tavern brawls and, though far from being a coward, he did not relish the idea of being robbed or having a knife in his back.

When he wanted a woman, LeBlanc's first mate would have one brought aboard for the evening. In this way his physical needs were satisfied within the confines of his own domain, and the woman was paid and sent from the ship. Rarely had LeBlanc allowed a woman to stay the night. If the *Mér Fleur* was to remain in one port for a long period of time, the woman was paid handsomely to be available to him at all times and was brought to him at his order.

Contrary to LeBlanc's custom of remaining aboard his ship and despite the storm, he had ventured into the town on urgent business. Since he was due to sail early on the morrow, he decided to stop in at a local tavern for a hot meal and a tankard of rum.

Having appeased his hunger, LeBlanc paid the buxom barmaid for his meal and once again stepped out into the stormy night and continued his way toward the harbor.

Suddenly he heard the pounding of running feet, men yelling, and what he thought to be a woman's muffled scream. The sounds came from behind him, and he turned to see a small figure running in his direction. He saw it fall, get up and stumble forward, then fall again, right at his feet. Looking down, he saw the small frame of a woman, wet and muddy. She reached forward and grasped his boot, then slowly raised her eyes to meet his. Her eyes were terrified, and a scream came from deep within her. Then she only stared at him, making no further move to rise, no effort to run. The look of terror was replaced by a look of utter defeat.

The two men who had been chasing Amber now stopped close behind her, she could hear their heavy breathing, but she didn't turn her head to look at them. Her eyes were fixed on the devil-like figure. She saw him raise his gaze from her to the men, his eyes narrowing.

"Gentlemen, has this female committed a crime?" the caped man asked.

The two men looked at each other. "Aye, she 'as. The wench stole our money, she did," said one. "She says to give us a good time, then she makes off w'ile we're not lookin'."

Amber was suddenly aware that the night had become quiet, only the faint rumble of distant thunder broke the stillness, and the rain had stopped.

She heard the men speaking, heard them telling their lies, but she could not deny what they were saying. Her voice refused to come forth.

"How much did the female take?" The question lashed out like the snap of a whip.

"Two weeks' pay, 'ard work's pay," came the whining reply.

The dark figure reached into his pocket, brought out a small brown leather pouch. His lean fingers loosened the tie and took out two small rubies. He handed one ruby to each man. "This should take care of what the wench stole. Now off with you before I change my mind," he snarled.

The men departed hurriedly.

Amber had listened to the exchange of words, but her eyes had never left the cloaked figure. She had watched the display of authority, had noted the arrogance, the insolence of the strong, powerful man. She had begun to feel safe, thinking she had a protector until he looked down at her with haughtiness in his cold eyes. Her heart seemed to leap into her throat.

Pointing a steady finger at Amber, he rasped, "You, wench, will repay me for saving your lovely hide." His tone stabbed at her like a knife. "And I'll be repaid tonight, aboard my ship." Leaning forward, he swept her from the ground and into his arms, arms that were like iron, strong and sturdy, and her weight was as nothing. Purposefully he turned and stalked forward into the blackness of the night whence he had come.

LeBlanc's stride quickened as the rain began to fall in icy sheets and the wind resumed its violent raging.

Yes, he is the devil, thought Amber. He must be, for the rain stopped and the wind ceased when he appeared. And now, now it has started again. She tried to free herself but to no avail. He held her in a vise-like grip as she beat her small fists against his muscular arms, kicking and twisting in vain.

"Let me go! Let me go, I say! Please! You don't understand. I didn't take anyone's money, I didn't!" But her cries went unheeded; he only threw back his head and laughed toward the heavens in wicked mockery. A roll of thunder seemed to echo his laughter.

His hold tightened, his steely eyes darkened, and his black brows arched as he spoke in a sharp tone. "You will be silent, or I will silence you. Now which shall it be?"

Amber felt again the sting of fear and panic, her plea caught in her throat as she admitted to herself that she was entirely at his mercy and that her fate lay in his hands.

They had now reached the waterfront, and she could see the shadowy outlines of vessels anchored in the harbor. Her captor made his way to a small, three-masted vessel, crossed the gangplank, and leaped lightly down to the deck. He carried her down a narrow passageway and stopped in front of a door.

"Jason! Jason!" he shouted.

A man appeared at the end of the passageway. He was clad in dark breeches, shirtless and barefoot with a seaman's cap pushed back on his head. He rubbed his eyes sleepily and yawned as he came forward. The lighted candle which he carried revealed a weather-beaten but kindly face.

"Aye, Cap'n, Jason be here," the older man called as he started down the passage. Drawing nearer, the candlelight showed him Amber's small figure in the arms of the captain.

"Cap'n Trent, sir, is the lass hurt? Would ye be needin' my help, sir?" Jason asked in concern.

"No, Jason, the lady's fine and I can handle this myself," answered the captain with a wink.

"Aye, sir, an' I'm that sure ye kin," Jason chuckled, waving his hand over his shoulder as he turned and started back down the passageway.

"And, Jason!" The captain's call halted the other man's footsteps. "I am not to be disturbed, understand? Not for any reason!"

"Aye, Cap'n," Jason replied as he continued on his way.

LeBlanc turned to the door, and with one swift kick of his booted foot the door burst open. Stepping inside, he caught the door with his foot and another kick slammed it closed behind them, causing Amber to jump with fright. He set her lightly on her feet, turned, and bolted the door with one hand, removing his cape with the other.

Amber stepped away from him, her eyes scanning the room. She saw a large desk scattered with maps and papers, a bookshelf loaded with books, two chairs, and a single bunk. When her searching eyes rested on the bed a sense of helplessness washed over her. Now I know how he means for me to repay him, she thought. Oh, Mother of God! Which fate would have been the worse?

She felt his hands on her shoulders, and he turned her to face him. Her blood ran cold, the impulse of self-protection surfaced, and she pulled back from his reach. Running behind a chair, she stared in terror as he approached her. Laughing wickedly, Trent LeBlanc clutched the arms of the chair as he looked deep into Amber's frightened eyes.

Then his blue eyes darkened with anger as they narrowed dangerously.

"I'll have you in my bed, wench. Now get there!" he gritted through clenched teeth.

Amber made a valiant attempt to bluster her way through. "No, 'Cap'n, sir,'" she said mockingly, "you'll not order me. Nor will I lie in your bed." She stood her ground, determined not to move. Her mind told her, Don't be weak, don't let him see that you're afraid, but his rough voice broke through her thoughts.

"You will do as I say, wench!" he thundered.

Trent's face hardened as he stood upright, his fists clenched at his sides. Amber saw the rise and fall of his chest, heard his heavy breathing as he took a step forward. She quickly pushed the chair, overturning it in front of him. He stopped and for a moment stood as if rooted to the floor, then viciously kicked the chair to one side.

Amber moved to run but was caught in a grip that seemed to tear her arm from her body as he swung her to him, crushing her against his hard body. She struggled, beating at him with her fists, biting and clawing like a wildcat. She tore his shirt, dug her nails into his bare chest before he grabbed her hands, pinning them behind her back.

"The more you fight, *ma petite chatte*, the harder you make it on yourself. For it is I who is the stronger, and it is I who will win!"

"No! No! Please!" Amber pleaded, her defiance replaced by dread.

Trent's mouth tightened, and with a jerk he ripped her gown from her body, letting it fall to the floor. The sight of her own naked breasts gave her a renewed strength that seemed to come from nowhere, and she broke free of his embrace and ran for the door.

She fought at the doorknob, turning it back and forth. It moved freely under her hand, but the door would not open. Then she remembered that Trent had bolted it. She glanced up at the bolt, her hand stretched up toward it, but the bolt was too high for her reach.

Turning from the door, she thrust her weight against it, her hands spread wide at her sides, her eyes tightly closed. Again she heard the deep, throaty laugh and it sent chills cascading through her very soul.

After a moment of silence, Amber opened her eyes to see Trent casually remove his torn shirt, then toss it carelessly to a chair.

"Do not run from me, *ma chérie,* for as you can see, there is no place you can go." His blue eyes glowed like sapphires as they met hers with passion. "You are even lovelier than I had imagined," he said as he came closer.

"Keep away from me," Amber gasped. "I'll . . . I'll kill you!"

Trent only laughed and again he grasped her, his hands around her waist like bands of steel.

"Kill me? Oh, I think not." He closed his mouth over hers, his tongue parting her lips, and kissed her long and deeply. His body shook with emotion, and she heard a moan from deep within him.

Trent lifted Amber in his arms, carried her across the room, and dropped her on the bed. Holding her down with one hand, he shed his boots and breeches. In a moment he was on top of her, his weight crushing her writhing body to the bed.

"Now, wench, my payment," he said harshly.

Pinning her legs with his own he mounted her, seeking his target. Then with a hard thrust he surged forward. A shriek of pain escaped Amber's lips and Trent flinched, then braced himself. In astonishment he stared down into Amber's lovely face. Tears rolled down her cheeks; her green eyes were glazed and shocked. She lay unmoving but for the trembling of her small body.

Tenderly he brushed tears from her face and, cupping one firm, ripe breast in his hand, gently caressed it. An all-too-familiar twinge cut through his body, and his unsatisfied passion grew as he moved back against her, deeply. He was no longer in control, his physical need overcoming his conscience.

His passion satisfied, Trent rolled off her and lay close to Amber's warm, trembling body. Putting his arms around her, he pulled her closer to him. She made no resistance. The fight seemed to have gone from her; the brave spirit was no longer there.

His breath came fast and heavy. He nestled his face in her hair, and with his lips against her ear he whispered, "I'm sorry. I did not know."

Amber lay quietly in his arms, too spent to move. The night had been too much for her. She felt his body relax gradually as he lay against her. His breathing became slow and peaceful. She thought him to be asleep and stirred slightly, but he tightened his hold.

"Sleep, *ma petite chatte,* it will be better in the morning." Trent spoke softly, just above a whisper. Gently he kissed her cheek and moved his finger lightly over her lips. "I'll not disturb you again tonight, *ma chérie.*"

Amber lay sleepless, mentally reviewing the staggering events of the day. It was her nineteenth birthday and the day she was to be wed to Sir Michael Windom—a marriage of convenience arranged by her Uncle Edward. She had never seen Sir Michael, but she knew him to be a man thirty years her senior. He was reputedly one of the wealthiest men in England, and there was no doubt that she would be envied by many.

Though she loathed the thought of a loveless marriage, Amber had agreed for Uncle Edward's sake. She felt a deep sense of loyalty and gratitude to him for having given her a home twelve years before. He and Aunt Alice had taken the homeless child at the age of seven, following the sudden deaths of her parents. Having no children of their own, they had become father and mother to the lonely Amber, had taken her into their home and hearts as their own.

Uncle Edward had appeared to be a man of wealth, and she had been reared in comfort and luxury. But in the past few months Amber had learned that her uncle had borrowed much money from Sir Michael and had heavily mortgaged his home and business.

Sir Michael had heard of Amber's beauty and, having questioned Uncle Edward extensively, had thereby determined her to be a virgin of marriageable age. Although she had many admirers, she had taken none seriously.

So the two men had contrived the marriage: Amber in exchange for full payment of all of Uncle Edward's debts.

This morning as she rode in her uncle's carriage from the Inn through the unfamiliar streets of London where she had been brought for her wedding, her thoughts had returned to the conversation she had overheard.

"Sir Michael has agreed to cancel the mortgages and to consider paid any and all debts owed him in exchange for Amber's hand in marriage," Uncle Edward had told Aunt Alice.

"Oh, Edward," she had gasped, "that's terribly unfair to Amber! Surely you wouldn't . . ."

"There is no other way, Alice. That is Sir Michael's final word. Either he gets Amber, or he forecloses on the mortgages and we lose everything."

"Why Amber, Edward, why must it be Amber?"

"Sir Michael has had many mistresses, Alice, but never has married. He knows Amber to be not only beautiful but a virgin as well. He means to have her."

Amber had known from that moment that she must sacrifice her future to save what Uncle Edward had worked for so many years.

As the carriage had rounded the curve and stopped before the steps of the church, Amber had taken a deep breath as she stepped out. Turning to the driver she had said, "Thank you, Wells, please tell Uncle Edward that I wanted to come early. He'll understand."

"Very good, mum, and the best of luck," he had answered.

She had watched as the carriage clattered down the street and out of sight. The best of luck to me, he said, the best of

luck, she remembered thinking. Slowly she had started up the
wide stone steps as if on her way to the gallows. Her heart
was heavy and she had fought back the tears.

A few steps away from the door she had stopped and stood
staring up at it. Suddenly she had felt as if she were turned to
stone, and Amber stood motionless, her feet unable to move
forward.

I'll not go in there . . . I can't! Why should I marry a man I
don't love? A man I don't even know! A man I've never seen!
Her thoughts had run wildly through her mind. "I can't do it!
I can't!" she sobbed, and she had turned and run back down
the steps.

Where could she go? The town was new to her, she had
never been there before, but she knew that she had to get as
far away from the church as possible. She was not going to
marry Sir Michael Windom, and Uncle Edward would just
have to understand. So she had run . . . and run . . . and
run! She had made up her mind and there was no turning
back!

Wandering aimlessly through the streets Amber had
watched children at play, peered into shop windows, and had
gone into one shop to look at the bolts of fabric.

Stepping from the shop she had glanced at the darkening
sky, noticing the coldness of the air. A sudden clap of thunder
jolted Amber, causing her to realize she must get back to the
Inn.

Uncle Edward and Aunt Alice will be frantic, she had
thought. And Sir Michael! I must explain.

Then the rain had begun to fall, and Amber walked swiftly
down street after street. Where am I? she had thought.
Which way is the Inn? Then came the realization that she was
lost. The streets were now deserted; there was no one to ask
for help.

The rain pelted down and the wind whipped her skirts as
she made her way with difficulty toward a lighted doorway.
Stepping inside, she had found to her consternation that she
was in a tavern, which she knew was no place for a lady, but it
was warm and dry.

"Well, well, well! What we got us 'ere?"

Amber had turned to see a grubby-looking man standing
behind her. His beard was long and dirty, his hair matted. He

wore gray breeches which were torn in several places, no shirt, and a red scarf knotted about his neck.

"'Ow much, girlie?" the man asked in a grating voice.

"I beg your pardon?" Amber replied with a shudder.

"I said 'ow much. I'll pay yer price." The man smelled of grog and tobacco, and his nearness made her uneasy.

Amber stepped away, edging closer to the door. But the man had followed, had laid his heavy hand on her shoulder, causing her to flinch.

"What be the matter, wench, ye maybe don't like ol' Ben?" His grin had showed yellowed teeth. "'Ey, Luke, come see what I got," the man yelled.

Across the crowded room the man, Luke, picked up his mug and headed toward the doorway.

Amber had been seeking help but was finding herself in a most unpleasant situation. By now she was thoroughly frightened.

"Please, I must find my way back to the Yardage Inn. Can you tell me where I may find it?" she had implored.

Luke had ambled up, and his beady black eyes traveled over her. His breath was foul; he was dirty and smelled of sweat.

"Sure, I'd be knowin' where the Inn might be," Luke answered. "Ye say ye be needin' to go there, aye?"

"Yes," Amber had answered, hopefully. "You see, my aunt and uncle are there waiting for me. I went for a walk and . . . well, I got lost. If you would be so kind as to tell me how to get there? Or, perhaps, to get me a carriage . . ."

"We'll do better than that, girlie, we'll take ye, won't we, Luke?" Ben said as he winked at him.

"Aye, Ben, we be not far from the Inn. 'Tis right around the corner."

Instinct had warned Amber that the men were not to be trusted; she had seen the wink and had noted the undercurrent in their voices. As the nearest man reached for her, she had given him a swift kick on the shin and bolted from the doorway.

His yell had followed her. "Why, ye little bitch! Ye'll be sorry ye done that," he had bellowed. "Grab 'er, Luke! Dammit, man, ye wanta pay fer a wench when ye don't got to?"

Amber had not looked back as she had fled into the night.

LeBlanc awoke and found that he still held Amber in his arms. Very carefully he slipped his arm from under her, resting her head lightly on the pillow. He eased into a half-sitting position and stared down at the young face, a face lovelier than any he had yet seen, the face of a child but yet a woman. As he watched, a tremor ran through Amber's body, and from beneath her closed eyelids a single tear glistened on long, red-gold lashes, escaped and rolled slowly down one pale cheek.

Gently he brushed back the curls that framed her face, exposing an ugly bruise on her forehead. A frown crossed his brow, and he silently cursed the abominable men who had chased the frightened girl.

"You are very lovely, little one, too lovely," Trent whispered, his lips against her soft hair. "You'll no doubt one day capture some man's heart and he'll never be free of you."

Still deep in exhausted slumber, Amber stirred, and the movement brought her body close against him. His body responded. Aroused, he felt his need of her. Every nerve, every muscle, his very being awakened.

"No, *ma petite chatte,* not even in your sleep will I allow you to tempt me. I hold true to my promise that I will not disturb you again this night." With these whispered words Trent eased himself from the bed, stepped quietly across the cabin, and took a blue silk robe from his trunk. He pulled it on, tying the sash about his waist as he moved to his desk.

He poured a glass of brandy and sat on the edge of the desk, his eyes drawn like a magnet to Amber. He observed her small frame, her beauty.

"*Mon Dieu!* A virgin!" Trent exclaimed in a low voice. "A virgin, and I took her as if she were a common whore! No . . . worse! Damn you, LeBlanc, you raped her!" He groaned aloud.

Trent was angry with himself, yet he tried to make excuses for what had happened. But there was no excuse; he knew that he had not given her a chance. His jaw tightened with anger.

"Blast it! What in hell were you doing in that part of town?" he scolded the sleeping Amber. She stirred and Trent caught his breath. If she wakes up now, he thought, there'll be hell to pay!

He sat gazing at Amber, his eyes tender, wondering what could have brought her so near the waterfront. A light rap on the door roused Trent from his wandering thoughts and jolted him back to the present.

"Cap'n? Cap'n, sir?" came a hushed voice from outside the door.

Briskly Trent crossed the cabin, slid the bolt, and opened the door. Stepping into the passageway he quietly closed the door behind him and turned to his first mate, who stood looking up at him uneasily.

"Damn you, Jason! I told you that I was not to be disturbed . . . not for any reason . . . remember?" Trent's voice showed his irritation.

"Aye, sir, I 'member. Only, sir, my orders has allus been to remind ye of the time. I mean, when ye got a woman wit' ye, sir," Jason said nervously, "so she kin leave the ship, sir. Ye said ye didn't want no woman sleepin' aboard."

"Yes, Jason, those were your orders, but I've changed my mind tonight." Trent smiled and the expression on his face was one Jason had not seen before.

"Ye have, sir?" Jason asked in surprise. "Changed yer mind, I mean . . ."

"Damn it, Jason! That's what I said. I am the captain of this ship, man. I can change my mind if I choose," Trent bellowed, then quickly opened the door to his cabin to see if his loud voice had awakened Amber.

He thought, Why am I so worried about her waking? and again found that he was holding his breath. He released it with a sigh of relief when he saw that Amber was still sleeping and that his outburst had not disturbed her.

Quietly he closed the door again and turned back to see Jason staring up at him, a puzzled look on his face.

"Well? What else do you want?" Trent asked the anxious Jason.

"Then, sir, what time ort I to wake ye? I mean, so the . . . uh . . . lady can go ashore? We sail at dawn, sir, and . . ."

"The lady won't be going ashore, Jason. She'll be sailing with us."

Jason's eyes widened and his jaw dropped. For a moment he didn't speak, only stared at Trent in disbelief.

"But, Cap'n, sir! Ye never afore . . ."

"Blast it, Jason! I changed my mind about that, too!" Trent ground out, trying to keep his voice low. Then the corners of his mouth tilted upward, and he chuckled at the look of anxiety on Jason's face.

"Jason, close your mouth," Trent laughed, "and stop looking at me like that. I haven't lost my mind." Leaning down from his greater height, he spoke in a low voice. "I've just found something I like and I want to take it with me, that's all."

Jason drew himself up and squared his shoulders as a grin split his homely face. "Cap'n Trent, sir, ye didn't go and git yerself a wife now, did ye?" He figured that was the only way Trent would allow a woman to remain on board. To himself he thought, That's it! He's gone and got hisself wed. That's why he left the ship. He don't hardly ever go ashore and tonight he did and that's why he was so furious 'cause I knocked . . .

"No, Jason," Trent's words broke his thoughts. "I didn't get married! *Mon Dieu!* What ever gave you a fool notion like that?" The words wiped the grin from Jason's face. "Go back to bed, Jason, I'll not need you again tonight."

"Aye, Cap'n." He shifted his weight from one bare foot to the other but made no move to go.

"That is all, Jason. I'll let you know about breakfast. I'll call for you," Trent said, dismissing him.

Though the words were not spoken, his meaning was clear. Jason knew that he was to stay away from Trent's cabin.

Entering his cabin, Trent closed the door softly behind him and stepped near the bed, watching Amber in the soft glow of the lantern which lighted the room. How beautiful she is, he thought as he moved closer, his eyes lingering on her breasts. Leaning over, he gently stroked her soft skin. His body was aching, calling out for her. His blood ran hot, and his hand shook so that he pulled it away and sat down on the edge of the bunk, his eyes never leaving Amber.

Why did this slip of a girl affect him this way? He had never had a woman who could stir him in the way she did. When he had realized that she was a virgin, he had not yet taken her completely and had tried to break free, tried to leave her, but he didn't. When he had looked down at her lovely face, had felt the warmth of her perfect body, his desire had mounted to uncontrollable passion and he had taken her.

The irony of the situation was that he knew he had to have her again! That was why he had told Jason that she wasn't going ashore, that she was sailing with them. He had known that he had to take her with him.

Trent removed his robe and slipped back into bed beside Amber, pulling her close. He drew the sheet up over them, resting his head against her hair and bathing in the warm softness of her naked body. There was an aching in his loins, but he restrained himself, controlling the animal reaction which surged through his mind and body.

At length sleep came to Captain Trent LeBlanc.

Chapter Two

TRENT AWOKE TO THE SOUND OF HEAVY FOOTSTEPS POUNDING overhead and the deep, rumbling voice of his bosun, Drake Monrow, who was shouting orders to get underway.

"Look alive, you bastards! Get a move on or I'll kick your dead arses overboard! . . . You, there! What might you think you're doin'? . . . This ain't no time to play! . . . Move! Move! . . . If we ain't out of this port when the Cap'n comes topside there'll be hell to pay!" Drake's yells went on and on.

Trent chuckled. "Drake, you old son of a sea dog! Is to threaten them with the captain's rage the only way to get your men moving?" He laughed aloud now, amused at the threats Drake was still yelling to the men, knowing full well that they would never be carried out. It was a well-known fact that the *Mér Fleur* had an excellent crew and that Captain Trent LeBlanc was well liked and highly respected, despite his quick temper.

The sun was slowly creeping into the sky, finding its way through the porthole of LeBlanc's cabin. He knew that he must rise and see that his ship was ready to sail. The voyage would be a long one, with stops all along the way to Havana, their final destination.

16

Then Trent felt Amber's body snug against his. It brought back the memory of the previous night and the beautiful maiden he had roughly swept from the ground and had carried, kicking and screaming, through the streets to his ship. He remembered her in his arms, how soft and feather-light she had been.

Trent pressed his hand over his eyes as if to close out the memory of his taking her by force and learning that she was still a virgin. But he had mistaken the girl for a prostitute. How was he to know? She didn't tell him who she was. "Damn it, LeBlanc, you didn't give her a chance, remember?" he again scolded himself.

Anyway, it didn't matter now, she was his. Call it "booty," "prize," or whatever, he had rescued her from the hands of two drunken gutter rats and had probably saved her life. He dreaded the thought of that soft, innocent young body in their hands. But he had saved her and she was indebted to him, was she not? So the fair-skinned beauty was his, and she would just have to accept it! Besides, there had not yet been a woman who had rejected him, and this one would be no different, he mused.

During the wee hours of the morning Trent had realized that this woman was one he could never let go. Now he lay watching her as she slept in his arms, her head lying peaceful-ly on his chest, her red-gold hair veiling her creamy white shoulders and cascading down her smooth silky back. Her slender fingers were enlaced in the dark mat of hair that ran along his hard, flat belly.

Trent grinned as he thought of her reaction should she awake and find her body molded perfectly to his, after her fierce battle for her virtue some hours before. His arms tightened around her, again he wanted her.

"No time, LeBlanc," he reminded himself. "You have a ship to get to sea. And, as Drake Monrow would say, 'This ain't no time to play!'"

Rising from the bed, Trent stretched his long, lithe body, then turned to cover Amber, his gaze lingering on the soft curves of her small frame, her lean thighs and young, firm breasts. God, but she was beautiful! Would she ever be able to care for the likes of him, he wondered, the man who had robbed her of her virtue? "Ah, yes, my sweet. You are now

Captain Trent Darnell LeBlanc's woman, and you'll come to like it!"

LeBlanc dressed quickly and slipped from the cabin, locking the door behind him. For when she awoke she would remember the events of the night and would hate him. She would, without a doubt, attempt to escape.

Amber lay half awake and relived one morning of the previous week when she had run lightly down the stairs and into the kitchen of her Uncle Edward's home. Her old governess, Abby, had sat at the end of the long table drinking a cup of tea.

"Good morning, Abby! Isn't this the most beautiful day?" Amber had spoken cheerfully.

"*Oui,* my pet, 'tis lovely," Abby had replied.

"Mmmm, is that your tempting scones I smell? I'm starving!" Amber had said, hugging her arms around her middle. "Is Aunt Alice up yet?"

"*Non,* pet, she isn't feeling well this morning and says that she will be down later. I'm to bring her breakfast tray up." Abby had gone to the oven and returned with a plate of hot scones, which filled the room with a rich aroma.

Sitting down again, Abby had looked into the small white china teacup. She was silent as she studied the leaves in the bottom.

"What do you see in the tea leaves, Abby? Can you really see into the future?" Amber had asked, her green eyes dancing with excitement. "Tell me, Abby, tell me what you see!"

Abby had continued to sit quietly, her eyes never leaving the cup.

Amber had sighed and sat back in her chair, tucking her slim legs under her. "Oh, I don't really believe in such stuff, anyway," she pouted. Then putting a hand to her mouth, she giggled. "You know, I did when I was little."

Still Abby had made no move, nor had she spoken.

Amber had tried again. "Do you remember that Uncle Edward gave me a little dog, Tippy, on my tenth birthday? And the next day he ran away. I cried and cried, I thought I would never see him again. You were sitting right there, right where you are now, looking into your teacup. Remember?

You said, 'Do not worry, my little pet, he will be home by morning. It's here in the leaves.' Don't you remember, Abby?"

"*Oui*, I remember, and it was so. He came home the next day, did he not?" Abby had answered. "I also remember many other things," the old woman went on, "I see something now, something in your future, not so far away." Abby's face had worn a worried frown.

Sitting forward in her chair, cheeks flushed, eyes shining, Amber had urged, "What, Abby? What do you see?"

"I'm not sure I should tell you, my pet, perhaps it would not be best," the old woman had warned.

But Amber had coaxed, her dimples flashing, "Oh, please, Abby, please tell me!"

"I see a black cloud that won't go away. Each time it seems to clear, it only drifts back again. There is evil, evil all around; and faces, all faces I've never seen. You, my pet, are in the midst of a storm . . ." Abby had stopped short and looked up at Amber's gentle face, the green eyes wide with interest as she listened to the old woman.

Turning her attention once again to the tea leaves, Abby's kindly face had suddenly paled. She had placed her hand over the cup and closed her eyes tightly.

"What else, Abby? Don't stop now, tell me what else you see!" Amber's excited voice had broken into whatever thoughts were worrying Abby.

The old woman laughed half-heartedly, trying to hide her emotions. She loved this sweet, vibrant young woman who had been her charge for the past twelve years. But Abby also believed in her own gift of reading tea leaves and seeing into the future. What she saw ahead for her innocent, tender Amber, she feared.

With a troubled sigh, Abby had continued. "I see a man, tall, dark, and handsome. This man . . ."

"Oh, Abby," Amber had interrupted, "'you always say that. Ever since I was this high!" She measured with an outflung hand.

"Amber, I have really seen such a man," Abby had reproved sharply, "and if you doubt me, then I shan't say another word!"

"No! No! I don't doubt you, please go on."

"This man," Abby had repeated, "he will play an important part in your life, my pet, but I see darkness around you both, a darkness caused by many things . . . and a storm of uncertainties."

Amber had started to speak, but the old woman had looked straight into her eyes with an expression that was unnerving. Then, in a voice so grim that it seemed to Amber that her heart would stop its beat, Abby had said, "It will be your doing, this eerie darkness. Yours! For you have dormant qualities which will surface as rebellion and temper. And, my pet, don't be too soon to judge, for this man will tame and govern your temper and will teach you willing submission! Beware the changing of blues in the sea of his sapphire eyes and never stare into their depths unless you are ready to surrender all!"

The words were so forceful that Amber had found herself trembling. Springing from her chair, she had felt a cold chill run through her body and had shut her eyes, afraid to open them.

"Oh, Abby, no!" The cry came as she opened her eyes to find a gray mist all around her. Where was she? "Abby! Abby, where are you?" she screamed. Now fully awake, Amber realized that she was in a bed. What bed? Whose? Oh, God! Everything was coming back, now. Uncle Edward . . . Sir Michael . . . the marriage . . . Amber running through the streets . . . the mighty giant of a man in black. He had towered over her as she had fallen in her flight to reach safety.

Amber choked, and tears ran down her cheeks as she remembered how the man had carried her to his ship. Ship! That's where she was, on board the ship, and he had raped her, made demands on her body! She clutched the sheet to her still naked body.

Had Abby been right, after all? Was this the man, the evil? Amber had run in the darkness, run in a storm. . . .

"Oh, merciful God! What will happen to me, now?" Amber cried aloud. She scrambled to her feet, wrapping the sheet around her, and ran for the door. It was locked! Why? Why would anyone want to lock her in?

She felt a gentle rocking beneath her feet. *"No!"* she yelled and ran to the porthole. "My God! Water! Miles and miles of water!" she gasped. "We're at sea and I've been kidnapped!" The word boomed in her ears. "Kidnapped! He has taken me prisoner!"

In a panic Amber ran back to the door, but as she reached it she tripped on the cumbersome sheet and fell to the floor.

Just then she heard the scrape of a key in the lock and the door opened. Trent strode in, stumbling over Amber. He braced himself against the door jamb and looked down at her. "Good God, woman!" he roared, closing the door behind him. "What are you doing down there? You damn near caused me to break my neck!"

Walking over to his desk, Trent shed his damp shirt and tossed it atop his sea trunk. He stood watching Amber as she struggled to her feet, the ivory-colored sheet still clutched to her body.

Now on her feet, her face distorted with anger, Amber glared at Trent.

"How dare you! You . . . you . . ." she fumed, unable to get her words to come forth. "Where are my clothes, my shoes? Why am I on board this ship with it at sea?" she demanded, sparks shooting from her green eyes.

Trent was watching the flames of anger in her eyes and the clenching of her teeth as she spoke in her fury. He casually leaned against the desk, stretching his long legs. Folding his arms over his chest, he watched and listened, trying not to laugh. He tightened his lips to keep control, but the corners of his mouth kept threatening to give him away. He was amused at the display of temper.

Failing to get an answer from the silent man, Amber stamped her little bare foot in helpless rage.

Trent bowed arrogantly and smiled sarcastically, revealing perfect white teeth. "And a very fine morning to you, too, *Mademoiselle*. Now that you seem to be finished with your ranting and can find no way to address me other than 'you,' permit me to introduce myself. Captain Trent LeBlanc, at your service." Again he smiled devilishly. "And you, my lovely, what might your name be?"

"Do you make a habit of raping a woman before you know

her name, Captain?" Amber's words were scornful. "I really see no need to tell you 'what my name might be.' It is no concern of yours!" she finished, her chin tilted upward.

"Damn it, woman! I asked your name!" Trent bellowed as he hit the desk with both strong, massive fists, then held them clenched at his sides.

Amber jumped. This man was not one to push, he indeed had a hot temper. He reminded her of a wild bull readying to charge. She swallowed hard, her body shaking from the harshness in his voice. She found that she could not look into his eyes.

"Amber," she whispered, her voice cracking, her lips trembling.

"Speak up! I can't hear you!"

"Amber," she said louder, "Amber Lynn Kensington."

"Amber, is it? Very well, Amber, you shall call me Trent."

She was trying desperately to put up a bold front, her head was held high, and though her chin quivered slightly, Amber said nothing.

"And for the answers to your questions," Trent went on, "Ah, yes! Your shoes! If you will look, you will find them at the end of the bunk. And for your clothes . . . that's another matter, I'm afraid." He grinned wickedly as he looked at Amber still clutching the sheet to her naked body. "You had the misfortune of having them torn from that lovely body of yours. Now for the last question. Why are you on this ship? Well . . . we sailed very early this morning, ma sweet, and I just had not the heart to awaken you." Trent chuckled at the exasperation on Amber's face.

"I insist that you take me back, Captain," Amber said hotly.

"Oh, you do now! I'm afraid you don't understand, Mademoiselle, you see you are on this ship because I chose to bring you here. And you will go where this ship goes because, again, I choose for you to do so. Now, if what I have said is beyond your comprehension, I shall attempt to explain further."

"I understand, Captain, I understand all too well! You've kidnapped me! Well, it will do you no good, there isn't anyone to pay you what you might ask. I have no family, no one. So it is your loss, Captain," she laughed, "you have nothing to gain by keeping me."

"But, *non, ma* sweet, I have everything to gain. This will be a very long voyage, and a man can find himself lonely. My need for a woman will not be denied, not on this voyage," Trent said as he stepped toward Amber, his hand touching her soft cheek. He ran his thumb over her parted lips. "Yes, I have everything to gain," he repeated softly.

Amber stepped back, out of his reach. "Don't you touch me! You'll not ever again touch me, not after last night!" she sputtered, "I hate you! Hate you! I'd die before I ever let you touch me again!"

Trent stood quietly before her verbal onslaught, waiting for her wrath to subside. When he made no further move, no effort to speak, Amber resumed her attack, "Now turn this ship around this minute, or . . . or . . . you'll answer to Sir Michael, my . . ." Amber broke off, placing a hand to her mouth. But it was too late, Trent had heard and his eyebrows shot upward in surprise.

"Oh? But *Mademoiselle,* by your own words, you just said that there was no one. So, who might this 'Sir Michael' be?" he inquired.

"I'll not tell you one thing more, Captain. You'll find out soon enough," Amber bluffed. He'd think about that, she told herself, but her bluff was short-lived as he threw back his head in laughter.

"No doubt I will, and since you choose not to tell me at this time, I see that I will just have to dismiss the thought completely," Trent answered, "and now that my ship is underway, I have a few entries to make in the log. If you will excuse me?"

Without waiting for an answer, Trent walked around the desk and drew the large, leather-bound book toward him. He sat down and began to write, as if unaware of Amber's presence.

Amber turned angrily and padded back across the cabin to sit on the edge of the bunk. What was she going to do? This man was going to keep her aboard his ship. He had no intention of turning back! "Oh, Abby, why didn't you warn me? If you could see all this, why didn't you warn me?" she murmured.

"Did you say something?" Trent asked, raising his head to look at her. But Amber only glared at him, her green eyes full of hatred. He studied her in silence for a moment, then returned to his chore.

After what seemed like hours, LeBlanc still sat at his desk. He now had a map spread before him and was working with measure and quill.

Amber sat quietly with her feet tucked under her, elbows braced on her knees and her chin resting in her palms as she studied Trent's handsome face. She noted the deep-cut features and his now unreadable expression. Was there no way to reach this man? No, she decided. He was an arrogant bastard who lived by his own rules.

Tilting her head as if to look at him from a different angle, Amber said to herself, "A noble brow, strong straight nose, high cheekbones, and powerful jaw. He has the look of stubborn pride, and there is a sadness about his gentle face." Gentle face? Had she actually thought that? Then her thoughts ran on. His mouth was full and sensual, and in his cheek a little muscle twitched. And there were hints of laughter lines at the corners of his eyes.

Sensing her intent scrutiny, Trent glanced up and his eyes met hers. The look he gave her was almost like an embrace. Amber blushed and lowered her head.

"Go ahead, *ma* sweet, it is all right for you to look. You can learn much about a person when they are unaware that they're being watched. Expressions, the fine details of a face, the look in the eyes—these things can tell one a lot about someone. Why, I learned much about you last night as you slept in my arms. Such things as how you tighten your lips, exposing the whisper of a dimple, or cling to me and whimper during a bad dream. No, no! Do not be ashamed that you were so observed. There is no reason to be shy, for after last night we are intimate friends, are we not?"

"No, we are not!" Amber stormed as she raised her small clenched fist at him. "You raped me and you shan't get another chance to watch me sleep, not here nor anywhere! Do you hear? I am not your woman! I'll never . . ."

"Such a little wildcat you are, but I must say a very pretty one," Trent broke in, knowing full well that it would only

make her angrier, "and I do like my women with spirit. You
are my woman, Amber, like it or not. As of last night, you
belong to me. You will find that I am a possessive man, and I
shall not beg one single favor from you, *ma* sweet! If I choose
to have you, then I will have you, and if you are unwilling,
then I'll just have to take you by force. Understand?" His
words were cold and his eyes never left hers.

Amber had begun to tremble with fear.

Trent rose from his chair and stood over her, his blue eyes
taking in the length of her body. The slightest of smiles hinted
at his lips as he placed his hand under her chin and tilted her
head upward.

"You are a most desirable woman, Amber, and I find that
my need for you grows stronger by the moment," he said
huskily.

"I'll not do your bidding, Captain, I'll not ever allow you to
force yourself on me again!" Amber spoke with a vengeance.
But hardly had the words left her mouth before Trent had her
in his arms, crushing her to his breast. The sheet was flung
from her bare body, his eyes, dark with passion, flashed a
warning, and her heart seemed to shoot upward and catch in
her throat.

Amber struggled as Trent's hot lips came down on hers. He
ran his hands lightly down her smooth back and in another
moment had laid her on the bed. He knew that later he would
regret his action, but the effect which Amber had on him was
awesome. All he could think of now was of having her in his
arms and of making love to her.

And once more Trent took Amber by force.

Trent eased himself from the bed and began to pull on his
breeches, but already regret had begun to wash over him. He
glanced back at Amber, who lay huddled on the far side of
the bunk, her face turned to the wall. Her small body was
shaking with anger and humiliation.

Trent tied the drawstrings at his knees and put on his soft
black leather boots.

"Amber," he called softly. There was no reply. "Amber!"
he thundered, and she started as her name was flung at her in
anger. Slowly she turned her face toward Trent and raised her

eyes to his. Standing with feet apart and hands on his hips, he delivered his ultimatum. "You will share that bed with me as long as you are aboard this ship, do you understand?"

"Then I shall leave this ship, sir, for I will not . . ." Amber started.

But Trent had swooped down from his great height and had grasped her shoulders with hands of iron. Flinching from the pain, she met his fiery eyes and they seemed to burn through her.

"I am your lover and you my mistress! You will go nowhere! By the time this ship reaches its destination you will have learned submission!" Then, releasing her, Trent turned and stormed out the door, slamming it in rage behind him. Amber heard the key turn and knew that she was again locked in. She drew the sheet up to her chin and buried her face in the pillow to drown out her cries.

When next she heard the key turn, Amber gazed at the door apprehensively. But it was only Jason carrying a tray. Tucked under one arm was a small bundle.

"The Cap'n, he said ye might be hungry," he stated, "so's I brung ye a little sumpin' to eat." He set the tray on the desk and continued. "An' he says fer ye to put on these." He handed the bundle to Amber. "'Tain't much, but it be sumpin' to cover ye so's ye kin go topside. The Cap'n, he says ye to be ready in 'bout a half-hour."

Two burly crewmen entered, carrying a wooden tub partly filled with water. They set it down in the middle of the cabin and withdrew without a word.

Jason was leaning over Trent's open sea trunk, a towel in one hand, as he searched the depths of the trunk. Straightening, he laid the towel and a bar of scented soap on a chair and crossed the cabin to the doorway. On the threshold, Jason turned and looked back at Amber. "And, missy, the Cap'n—he ain't sitch a bad man, ye'll see," he said, apologetically. With that, he closed and locked the door behind him.

Amber ate the slices of beef and biscuit and drank the tea. When the last crumb was gone, she picked up the towel and soap and stepped quickly into the tub for her bath.

After she had completed her hasty toilette, Amber pulled

on the tan knee breeches, tying them around her small waist with a piece of heavy cord which she found in the sea trunk. She donned the wine-colored shirt and knotted it at the waist. Retrieving her black satin slippers, she found that one heel was broken off. Tossing them aside, Amber looked down at her small bare feet and shrugged. "Who needs shoes, anyway?" she muttered.

After combing her slender fingers through her long, damp hair, Amber tied it back with a silk scarf from Trent's trunk and sat down to wait for him to return.

How she hated him! He'd not touch her again, she vowed. She wanted to scratch his eyes out, slit his throat—she wanted to kill him! But knowing that she could do Trent no real harm, she came to the conclusion that her only way out of her dilemma would be to kill herself. Anything would be better than returning to this cabin to have her body violated again and again. So she'd just jump overboard. "That's it!" she said aloud. "I'll wait for the right time, and then I'll jump overboard!"

Minutes later Trent entered the cabin and Amber sprang to her feet. He looked her over, noting the baggy breeches, the too-large shirt, and realized that they in no way detracted from her unusual beauty.

"Ah, *Mademoiselle,* I am flattered that you have donned your best clothes for the likes of me," he said teasingly. Seeing the sparks of anger which kindled in her green eyes, he hastily continued. "I must say that Fitz, my cabin boy, never looked that good in them. But he was the only one whose clothes would be small enough for you, and even he at sixteen is larger than you."

"Thank you, Captain, for the hot bath and the food. I was in need of both. And I trust that you don't mind—I took the liberty of taking a few necessities from your trunk."

"Oh, *non, non, ma* sweet. The trunk is at your disposal. You will no doubt find several items that may be of some use, as well as a few trifles you may find to be of interest. Now, if you will come along we'll go topside for a walk. This will be a long voyage, and we will make a habit of walking on deck sometime of each day, except in bad weather, of course."

As he talked he was leading her from the cabin and down

the companionway to the deck. She saw the activity of the crew, spotted Jason talking to a man at the ship's wheel and, looking up toward the masts, glimpsed two men working with the rigging high overhead.

The bright sunshine was a welcome sight to Amber, and the salty sea air was bracing. Under other circumstances than those in which she now found herself, she might have enjoyed a sea journey, she thought.

But she could not enjoy it, she must refrain from thinking that there could be any pleasure for her. LeBlanc had made it plain that she was here for his pleasure.

Then she remembered that a little earlier, as she waited for Trent to bring her up to the deck, she had faced the alternatives: either remain here as Trent's unwilling mistress and be subjected to the humiliation of having her body ravished, or escape by jumping overboard. As she stood looking at the beauty of the sea, feeling the warm sunshine as well as the gentle breeze that lifted the curls which had escaped the confinement of the bright silk scarf, she breathed a deep sigh. She knew that she could never be self-destructive.

But then an idea struck her mind. Perhaps I can pretend, she thought, perhaps I can make him think that I'd rather die than accept his terms.

The opportunity came on the heels of her thoughts. Trent's attention was claimed by one of the crew, and she broke free of his hold and ran to the railing. Hoisting herself quickly to the top of the rail, she stood looking at Trent, who had run after her.

"I'll jump," she screamed, "I swear I will!"

Trent stood rooted to the deck. Was she mad? Surely she wouldn't jump! He slowly took a step forward, watching Amber closely.

"Amber, come down from there!" His voice was deadly calm, yet demanding. If I could just reach and grab her quickly, he thought irritably, I'd break that pretty little neck! What in the devil did she think she was doing?

In an attempt to distract Amber, Trent laughed easily and said, "Ah, now, *Mademoiselle,* I can appreciate your desire to command a better view, but you should know that it's a bit

dangerous up there." Taking a careful step closer, he extended his hand. "May I assist you in stepping to the deck?"

"Don't come any closer, Captain," she snapped. "I mean
it, I'll jump!"

"Then, *ma* sweet, I suggest that you get ready to jump,"
Trent said as he leaped to the rail and reached out for Amber.

She moved quickly away, her eyes fixed on Trent. Noting
the coolness of his eyes, she thought, Why, he doesn't for one
moment believe that I would jump! Well, I'll show him. If he
takes one more step, I will jump, or at least I'll make him
think I will.

Suddenly she was falling, down . . . down . . . down—and
with a splash she was going under, deep into the sea. She
gulped for air, but there was none. It was dark, wet, and
eerie. Then blackness everywhere.

Trent stood transfixed upon the railing. The little fool! She
actually did it! Mother of God, she jumped! Trent could not
believe what he had just seen happen. Amber had indeed
done as she had threatened!

"Damn, Cap'n, 'er jumped," came Jason's shocked voice
at Trent's feet. "Just lak 'er says 'er would!"

Jason's voice jolted Trent to action. Kicking off his boots,
he cut the water in a clean dive. The crew watched as their
captain emerged without the girl. A second dive . . . then a
third. . . . The minutes seemed to drag by as the watchful
men waited breathlessly.

Fearful for their captain, Drake and another crewman
dived into the sea to help. Then Trent surfaced with Amber,
and the men in the water helped the two back to the ship and
over the rail. Trent fell to the deck exhausted, then raised
himself to his knees and looked down at Amber's lifeless
body.

"*Mon Dieu,* what have I done?" he asked himself. "I might
as well have pushed her overboard. She warned me and I
didn't believe her. I laughed at her!" He shook his head in
self-disgust. Then he laid his head on Amber's breast and
listened for a heartbeat. Yes, it was faint, but it was there!

"Is the lass dead, sir?" Jason asked unsteadily. "I just
didn't think 'er 'ud do it. I heered 'er threatenin', but I didn't
think 'er 'ud do it!"

"No, Jason, she's alive," Trent answered, relieved. "But, by God, I'll kill her when she comes around!" he roared as he lifted Amber in his arms and started for his cabin.

Once again Captain Trent LeBlanc kicked open the door of his cabin and entered, carrying a wet, bedraggled Amber in his arms. This time he laid her tenderly upon the bunk and knelt beside her. Gently he pushed her hair back from her forehead, then holding one small hand in his, he whispered fervently, "Thank God, you're alive!"

Then he arose and went to the trunk for a blanket, knowing that he must remove Amber's soaked clothing.

Amber stirred slightly, and in a semi-conscious state raised a hand to her brow. Am I alive? she wondered. What happened? She remembered standing upon the rail. And then she had told Trent that she would jump and he had answered that she should get ready. . . . Mother of God! Did he push me? No, he wouldn't. But she remembered going down into the water . . . and the blackness. . . .

"Trent!" Her scream sent a shuddering chill up Trent's spine. He spun around to look at the distraught girl.

"Oh, God! I'm drowning! Trent!"

He ran to the bed and cradled her cold, wet body in his arms. "Shhh, it's all right, *ma chérie*, you are safe and I am here," he whispered.

Frightened and trembling, Amber still clung to Trent. Gradually his words of assurance penetrated her mind. I am alive, she thought, I'm all right. And he saved me. Then the blankness vanished like fog dissipating in the sunlight, and she realized that she was clinging to Trent, whom she was supposed to hate!

She pulled free of his embrace and her green eyes flashed as she stared at Trent. "I warned you," she said, "I told you that I'd jump and I did!"

Leaping to his feet, Trent stormed at her. "Blasted woman! You little fool! Haven't you a brain in that lovely head?" He paced the floor, pounding his fist hard against the palm of his hand. His eyes were dangerously dark, his face was filled with anger. "What in hell did you think you would accomplish by drowning yourself?"

For a moment Amber was silent, not sure how to answer. She remembered now that as she had backed away from Trent

on the railing she had misstepped and had fallen, not jumped.
But she had no intention of allowing Trent to know that. Oh,
no! She would never give him the satisfaction of knowing. He
must always believe that she had made no idle threat. She
might have to use threats again, and she would want him to
take them seriously.

"Damn you, Amber! Answer me! What did you think you
would accomplish?"

Trent's furious voice brought Amber to her feet, her eyes
every bit as dark and as dangerous as his. With her hands on
her hips and her bare feet planted firmly, she faced him with
hostility.

"I'd be free, that's what! Free from the likes of you! Free
from being raped night after night! I'd be free . . . free . . .
free!!" she screamed.

Trent's face tightened, growing harder as she spoke with
venom. He saw the fury in her face, the trembling of her
small chin, and eyes blurred with angry tears.

"I should have let you drown," Trent said disgustedly, his
eyes burning into hers. Then he turned and strode quickly
across the cabin. At the door he turned and smiled maliciously. "But then, perhaps I'll get another chance, eh, *chérie?*"
He left the cabin, slamming the door hard behind him.

Furiously, Amber picked up the water pitcher and flung it
at the departing Trent. But it only smashed against the closed
door.

"Damn you, LeBlanc! Damn your soul to hell! I'll kill you,
do you hear? I'll kill you!"

Trent's reply was a hearty laugh from the other side of the
closed door.

Chapter Three

AMBER PACED THE FLOOR IN A FIT OF ANGER, CLENCHING AND unclenching her small fists, trying to think of some way she might get revenge. She had never hated Trent more than she did at this moment!

She spent the entire afternoon sulking in the cabin, thinking Trent would return. And if he did return, what course of action she should take. After rejecting several ideas, Amber decided that she should pretend to be humble since she had gained nothing by her antagonism.

Attempting to reason with herself, she thought aloud. "You're not going about it the right way. . . . The more you fight, the worse off you'll be. . . . Why not admit you are wrong. . . . Just tell Trent, 'I'm sorry, Captain, please forgive me for my ill temper and my bad behavior. From now on I'll try to be good and to comply with your wishes. It is really much better than our constant battling, and the results are always the same, anyway. All it does is to prove your point. . . . For as you told me in the beginning, it is you who is the stronger and it is you who will win. . . .' *No!* I won't do it! I'll die first!"

When the knock came at the door, Amber turned expec-

tantly. At the second knock she realized it could not be Trent
as he would never knock, he would just walk in as always.

"Who is there?" she called.

"'Tis Charles Fitzgerald, mum, the cabin boy."

Amber pulled on the door, and to her surprise it was not
locked.

"Oh, you must be the one they call Fitz, whose clothes I am
wearing."

"Yes, mum. I come ta clean the cabin, mum. The Cap'n, he
told me ta put it ta order. I brung clean sheets and towels."
Looking down at the shattered fragments he continued. "And
the Cap'n, he said I wus ta pick up the . . . uh . . . pieces of
glass. . . . He said as how they wus a accident."

"Of course, Fitz, I was just leaving. Would you happen to
know where I might find Jason?"

"Yes, mum, I seen 'im in the galley afore I come here. He
mought still be there," the boy answered.

"Thank you, Fitz. And thank you for the use of your
clothes," Amber said as she walked past him. Then she
paused, "Oh, Fitz, where is Captain Trent?" she asked, as if
it were an afterthought.

"He be at the wheel, mum, took over 'bout half-hour
ago."

As Amber walked down the passageway she remembered
that the cabin door had not been locked, and once again
anger swept through her. She raised both clenched fists and
shook them at the absent Trent. Through gritted teeth she
rasped, "You arrogant bastard! You didn't lock the door. You
always locked me in! I stayed in that blasted cabin all
afternoon thinking I was locked in! And I could have gone up
on deck. I could even have jumped overboard!"

Then Trent's words came rushing back. "I should have let
you drown. . . . Perhaps I'll get another chance."

Fury burned through Amber at the memory. Why, she
thought, perhaps he thought I would jump overboard. . . .
Maybe he hoped I would! Well, I'll show him! I'll stay around
now just for a chance to get even. She smiled at that thought.

Jason was in the galley, as Fitz had told her, and when
Amber entered the old man looked up.

"Evenin', missy, is there sumpin' ol' Jason kin do fer ye?"

"Yes, Jason, I found the cabin rather lonely and thought I'd join you . . . that is, if it's all right?" Amber said in a soft voice.

"Shure, 'tis fine. I kin use the company," he replied kindly. "Are ye all right? I mean, after this mornin'. Ye shure give us a fright, why, the Cap'n, he was plumb aside hisself. Ye just orta seen 'im." Jason chuckled to himself.

As Amber sat in silence, Jason continued. He told her how Trent had gone to her rescue, that the crew had watched anxiously, and when Trent emerged time and again without her that Drake and a crewman had dived into the sea to help. He related how Trent had finally surfaced with Amber, his strength almost gone, yet he clung to her, the mighty effort it had taken to boost her over the rail, then falling exhausted to the deck.

Amber listened in wonder at the story, then shrugged indifferently.

"He would have done that for anyone," she said coolly.

"Shure 'e would, missy, but 'tain't so much what 'e done, as how 'e acted an' the look on 'is face when 'e seen ye layin' on the deck an' 'e didn' know if ye wus dead or 'live." Jason shook his head as he remembered Trent's expression. He had never seen that look in Trent's eyes, not for any woman.

Amber felt an uncertain tug at her heart at Jason's words. She knew that she should find Trent and thank him for saving her life, but she also knew she wouldn't. She sighed and pushed the thought from her mind.

Then she changed the subject. "Jason, do you think I could have something to eat? I've been in the cabin all afternoon. I didn't feel like . . . I was . . . I mean . . ."

"I know, missy, ye just set right there. Ol' Jason'll git ye a bite and mebbe a bit 'a tea?"

"Yes, Jason, tea would be nice, I feel a little chilled," she replied.

While she ate, Amber listened to Jason tell about his life on the high seas and wondered if he would tell her anything more about Trent LeBlanc. He seemed to know Trent well, and she knew that Trent liked the older man. I wonder if Trent has ever confided in Jason, she thought, and if so, would Jason disclose anything he knew.

She wondered how Trent would treat a woman he loved. Would it differ from the way he treated her? Amber had felt that there was a gentleness in him, for had he not comforted her after her fall overboard, even though he thought she had jumped? And had he not shown remorse after he had robbed her of her virginity?

"Has Captain Trent ever been in love, Jason?" Amber blurted the words out before she could stop them.

"The Cap'n in love? Why, me lass, I don't rightly know fer shure. I've been with 'im fer goin' on seven years now and I ain't knowed 'im ta be in love. Afore that . . . oh, 'im's had women, lots of 'em, but love, missy? No, no love." Jason seemed sure of what he was saying. "The Cap'n, he ain't never took time fer love."

"Jason, you can't mean that! A man like Captain Trent has never been in love. . . . Why, I don't for one moment believe it," Amber said in surprise.

"'Tis true, missy, fallin' in love fer Cap'n Trent . . . well, it ain't no easy thing for 'im. . . . Ain't shure he knows how ta love. . . . I ain't shure he's ever loved nobody."

"But what about his mother? His father? Surely he loved them?" Amber pressed. She found that she wanted to learn as much as she could about this man in whose hands lay her destiny.

"Nobody knows where the Cap'n come from ner nothin' about 'is past. The only person the Cap'n has ever showed any real feelin' fer is Casey Reed. He be cap'n of the *Sea Dog*. She lays anchor in the same ports as us 'bout three ta four times a year."

"Then this 'Casey,' he would know something about Trent . . . I mean, Captain Trent." Amber flushed as she realized how easily Trent's name had slipped from her lips. She saw the faint smile that crossed Jason's face. She went on. "What do you know about this Captain Reed?"

"Aye, missy, I know 'im. He be a fine man, handsome and smart, and 'e knows as much 'bout the sea as Cap'n Trent. When Casey Reed be aroun', why the Cap'n, he's a changed man, he is, and when he laughs it be lak music. There be a deep frien'ship atween them two all right, a deep frien'ship."

"Then this Captain Reed, he should know about Captain Trent's family, his home and where he comes from, right Jason?" Amber had become most interested.

"Aye, missy, only he don't talk 'bout it. No, he don't talk

at all." Jason shook his old head as if he could not understand it.

"Well, Jason," Amber sighed, "I wish I knew more about your Captain so that I could better understand him. One minute he can be kind and gentle and in the next he can fly into an awful rage. Please tell me what you do know."

Jason thought briefly as if considering how to answer her. Then he said slowly, "The Cap'n, he be a hard man, only he ain't no bad man. Me, I've seen both sides of 'im, too, missy. He be a proud man and respected. . . . 'Is men they fear 'im fer he's got a quick temper, but they like 'im and they respect 'im 'cause they know 'im to be a fair and honest Cap'n."

"And you, Jason, how do you feel about him?" Amber insisted.

"Well, missy, I ain't never had to put my feelin's 'bout the Cap'n in words, but I reckon he be my choice of a cap'n to sail with, no matter what other folks got to say 'bout 'im." Jason was firm.

"What do you mean, Jason? What do 'other folks' say about him?"

Jason hesitated, wondering if he had said too much. But the old man knew that Amber would insist on an answer, and he decided that perhaps she should be told by him, rather than to hear rumors and superstitious remarks from others of the crew.

Taking a deep breath, Jason spoke slowly and clearly. "Some say he be the devil's own son. They say he come in from the night on a death ship that drifted in on the tide with no man's hand on the wheel. They say that as the ship cut through the fog, the Cap'n he stood in the bow clad all in black with his feet wide apart and his hands clasped behind his back." Jason stopped for a moment, looking at the wide-eyed Amber. She was completely engrossed in the story and merely waited in silence for him to continue.

"Men fear him," he went on, "and I seen many a man cower from just one look of his fiery eyes. There be a dark side of that one, a dark side. Ain't nobody ever ventured into it, they be too afeared."

Amber had lingered until late into the night, thinking Trent would come to look for her, but he had not. Knowing that

Jason must have his sleep, she bade him good-night and made her way back to the cabin.

A single candle burned on the desk, and Trent was sound asleep in his bunk. On the floor he had spread a blanket, and a pillow was placed at one end. There could be no doubt that the pallet had been prepared for Amber.

She stared down at the makeshift bed in disbelief. How could he expect me to sleep on that hard thing? she thought angrily.

Remembering Trent's ultimatum, "You will share that bed with me as long as you are aboard this ship," Amber wondered if perhaps he no longer expected of her that which she could not willingly give.

She stretched out on the pallet and tried to get comfortable, but it was impossible. The floor was hard, and the blanket was too thin for Amber to relax. The rope belt seemed to cut into her waist, and the knot prevented her lying on her stomach. After shifting her position several times and finding the situation intolerable, she rose from the floor and made her way to Trent's sea trunk.

The candle had burned out, and the only light was from the bright moonlight which filtered through the porthole. Delving into the trunk she found a shirt made from a soft silk fabric. Untying the bothersome rope belt, she stepped out of the breeches and removed the shirt belonging to Fitz and laid them both across the back of a chair.

Slipping into Trent's shirt she found that it made a suitable sleeping garment. The silky fabric felt cool against her body, the shirt tail reached just atop her knees, but the sleeves hung far down over the tips of her slim fingers, making it necessary for her to roll the sleeves over her wrists.

Amber looked over at Trent who lay sleeping peacefully across the room in the bunk, then glanced back down at her place on the floor.

"You lecherous bastard," she hissed. "You seek to further humiliate me. You lie there nice and cozy on your soft bed, while I am expected to lie on that . . . that thing!" She pointed a finger at the detestable pallet. "You think I'll give in . . . share your bed. . . . Well, I won't! The tables will soon turn, Captain, just wait!" And she returned to her

wretched pallet only to twist and turn for the remainder of the
night.

At daybreak Amber still lay wide awake and miserable, but
when she heard Trent stirring she closed her eyes and
pretended to be asleep. He rose from his bunk and began to
dress. Amber lay motionless so that he would not realize that
she was awake.

On his way out of the cabin Trent paused beside the pallet
and stood staring down at the "sleeping" Amber.

"She slept," he said to himself. "She stayed on that
damnable pallet after all."

When he had made the crude bed last night Trent had
assured himself, "She won't stay long down there. *Non,* she
will be climbing into my bed within a few minutes." But she
had not done so.

It angered him that she had remained on the floor throughout the night, but at the same time he laughed at himself for
being so confident of himself and so sure of Amber.

"Touché, Mademoiselle," Trent said in a low voice. He
clicked his heels together and gave her a mock salute. "Score
one for you."

Amber lay on her stomach, her loose hair cascading over
her shoulders with the tiniest whispers of red-gold curls
caressing her face. Trent leaned down and brushed them
gently from her cheek, ran his finger lightly along her jaw and
over her lips. Amber was puzzled at the emotions that surged
through her body at his touch. Her heart lurched, her pulse
quickened, and she felt suddenly breathless.

"You are most beautiful, *ma* sweet," Trent's voice was low
and tender. "Damn, but you do tempt me."

Why could he not feel toward Amber the same as he felt
about other women? he wondered. On that last night in
London when he had rescued the girl and carried her to his
ship for an hour of pleasure before sailing, he had not
expected her to be as beautiful and as desirable as Amber. So
much so that within only a few hours he had felt this
overwhelming desire to have her with him always.

"Never should I have left the ship," Trent scolded himself.

He took a long, ragged breath and whispered, "I'll never
let you go, Amber, never!" His words were so low that she

barely heard them. Then he straightened and walked quickly from the cabin, closing the door quietly.

Amber sat upright, staring in dismay at the door through which Trent had gone. "Never let me go!" she repeated aloud. "Dear God! What does he want with me? He could have any woman, so why should he choose to torment me?" She choked back the fear that threatened to overcome her.

"It can't happen, I won't allow it!" Amber assured herself. Scrambling to her feet she stood stretching her tired, sore muscles. How she missed her nice, soft bed and her pretty room at home. She longed to walk through the gardens where she had so often cut roses and gathered fresh flowers.

But with a deep sigh she brought her mind back to the present and knew that she felt a great weariness through her entire body. Utter fatigue from the trying experiences of the past two days plus a sleepless night on the hard floor had taken their toll, and she knew that she must have sleep.

The cabin was uncomfortably warm, and Amber decided to remove Trent's shirt, but before she disrobed she knew that she must bolt the door so that no one could enter and find her unclothed. So she dragged a chair across the room, placed it in front of the door and, standing in the chair, drew the bolt.

Replacing the chair, Amber removed the shirt, climbed into the bunk, and slipped between the sheets. "Trent won't be back for hours," she told herself. "Jason said, 'The Cap'n, he take 'is turn at the wheel early in the morn',' so I should have time to nap and get dressed before he comes back."

So she closed her eyes and tried to relax but found that it was not easy to fall asleep. The bed seemed to be still warm from Trent's body, and his scent filled her nostrils. He seemed very near and it was as if he embraced her naked body, but it was only the sheet which covered her. She tensed as the sheet slipped lightly over her skin, then a tingling sensation enveloped her as she remembered the times Trent had run his fingers over her body.

Had her own flesh deceived her? Had she wanted to respond to his lips, his touch, his passion? Could it be that her moral upbringing had caused her to resist Trent's lovemaking and that her true emotions had been submerged by her sense of propriety?

"No! I won't accept that! It isn't right," Amber reproached

herself. Then she closed her eyes and channeled her thoughts toward home . . . Uncle Edward . . . Aunt Alice . . . Abby. . . . She fell into a deep, dreamless sleep.

LeBlanc stood at the wheel of the *Mér Fleur* in the quiet of the early morn as the sun peered over the horizon. He filled his nostrils with the fresh sea air as a light breeze played across the bridge. He could taste the salt on his lips as he listened to the gentle slap of the waves as the sloop moved smoothly through the water.

How Trent loved the sea! As a mere lad he had dreamed of sailing the seas and of one day being captain of his own vessel. Now those dreams had become reality. At the age of one and thirty he was not only captain of his own vessel but the proprietor of one of the most successful shipping companies in the business.

Trent LeBlanc was a self-made man, having achieved success unaided, and had become quite wealthy. He was happy with his life and would have no time for a wife and a family for a long time. He had thought he had his life planned out, but prevailing circumstances warned Trent that his plans would be drastically altered. "One *Mademoiselle* Amber Lynn Kensington being the prime reason," he mused.

He had warned himself that Amber was no ordinary woman. This one—she is different, very different, LeBlanc, had been his thought. But he had not heeded his better judgment and had allowed her to remain on board.

"Which was a mistake, my man, a very definite mistake! *Mon Dieu*, LeBlanc, you should have put her ashore," he reproved himself.

But it was too late. He knew now that it had been too late from the time when he had felt her body beneath his and had experienced the passion which she stirred within him. And he had fallen asleep with Amber in his arms, just as if she belonged there! Trent recalled the sensation of having her lean smooth thighs pressed against his, the abundance of her soft, red-gold hair, the sweet taste of her lips, and her full appealing breasts. His loins suddenly tightened at the memory.

"What am I to do?" he groaned. "What have I gotten into? What kind of web has she begun to weave?" Amber was in his blood, burning hot through his veins and, he admitted, she had found her way into his very soul.

Why did he have this uncontrollable need for Amber? Why this urgent desire to possess her? *"Mon Dieu!"* Trent roared into the wind. *"Mon Dieu!"*

It was nearing the time for Drake's turn at the wheel, and Trent was becoming impatient. His thoughts of Amber had aroused desire, and he was eager to return to her.

"Monrow!" he yelled to the man who had appeared on the deck below.

"Aye, Cap'n," Drake answered, heading toward the bridge.

"Take the wheel," Trent ordered. "I have something to attend to."

"Aye, sir." Drake took a firm grip on the wheel as Trent strode away. With a knowing smile, Drake shook his blond head and murmured, "Oh, to be the Cap'n and to have that treasure in my cabin." His gray eyes twinkled.

Trent walked along the passageway, his mind on Amber. He would have her and she would like it. This time he would be gentle, he told himself, would not be so insensitive to her feelings. She must be taught to respond to his passion, to feel her need as well as his.

Halting at the door of the cabin, he smiled in anticipation. "Yes, *ma* sweet, this time it will be different!" Turning the knob, he pushed the door.

It didn't open . . . he pushed again . . . the knob turned freely in his hand but . . . then realization dawned on Trent. "She slid the blasted bolt! She's locked me out!" he said in surprised confusion.

"Damn you, Amber, open this door!" he yelled irritably. There was no reply. *"Amber!!"* He beat his clenched fist on the door in fury. She had done it now! Fighting him was one thing, jumping overboard was another. But locking him out of his own cabin . . . well, that was too much!

"I won't have it! Do you hear me, Amber? *Open the damn door!!"* He was furious, his face had turned brick-red, and the veins stood out on his neck. "I'll kill her! I'll strangle her with my bare hands!" Trent ground out.

He thrust his strong, muscular shoulder against the door,

hitting it with great strength. The door did not budge. Again he beat on the door and let out a string of oaths. His anger rose to a hot-tempered peak, and he again lunged against the door. This time as his shoulder collided with the wooden barrier it burst open with a violent crash, slamming hard against the wall, the wood splintering around the bolt.

Trent stood on the threshold with his chest heaving, eyes dark and murderous and his mouth pressed into a thin determined line.

But his wrath was short-lived. His anger melted like snow in sunshine as he beheld Amber, curled up like a kitten on his bunk, sleeping peacefully. Trent's face softened, and a smile lit his sapphire eyes as he tread quietly across the cabin and knelt beside the bed.

"Poor lamb," he murmured, lifting Amber's unresisting hand to his lips. "You have had a harrowing two days, and God alone knows what happened before that, and it has all caught up with you. So sleep, little one, sleep."

Amber stirred slightly and began muttering in her sleep. Trent leaned over, placing his ear close to her lips but found it difficult to grasp the meaning of her jumbled words. Most of it was incoherent, but he understood enough to know that Amber seemed to be pleading with someone. Some of her words were clear, but they were interspersed with unintelligible mumblings.

"I love . . . Michael . . . no! . . . cannot marry . . . another . . . please . . . do not make me . . . pl——" The words faded into a soft moan.

Trent rose and went to sit behind his desk and, drawing the log forward, took the quill from the inkwell. But his mind was not on the task. He was thinking of Amber and the disjointed monologue he had just heard.

Was "Michael" the "Sir Michael" Amber had mentioned before, and was he possibly the one she loved? Was it he whom she wanted to marry and was someone trying to force her to marry another? A pang of jealousy rose within him.

"Well, neither 'Sir Michael' nor 'another' shall have you," Trent spoke softly as he looked across at the sleeping girl. "You are mine, Amber Lynn Kensington, and no other shall have you!"

But the nagging reminder that he knew nothing about

Amber bothered Trent. Who was she? From where had she come? And who in the hell was "Michael"? It was the latter question that bothered him most.

After a moment Trent replaced the quill, rose, and left the cabin.

Amber rested her arms on the rail as she stood in the stern watching the trail of turbulence left in the ship's wake.

"Farther and farther from home," she whispered with a deep sigh.

She remained motionless for several minutes, then straightened and began to walk slowly toward the bow.

As she neared the bridge, she glanced up and saw LeBlanc at the helm. His strong bare back glistened with sweat in the bright sunlight, and his handsome head was held proudly. His breeches were not baggy like Amber's; they seemed to be molded to his muscular thighs.

Amber stood quietly watching the display of Trent's powerful muscles as he turned the ship's wheel. As much as she hated him, she had to admit that he had a magnificent body and that he was truly too handsome.

Trent seemed to sense her gaze, and he turned to see Amber watching him from below. She immediately lowered her head, turned, and walked swiftly away. With a wave of his hand Trent signaled Jason, and when the older man climbed to the bridge, Trent gave him the wheel and went in search of Amber.

He found her leaning dejectedly against the rail, an aura of sadness about her. He felt a quick sympathy for her, knowing she must be lonely and homesick and that she surely felt her situation to be hopeless. I could show her more tenderness and understanding, he thought as he neared her.

"Lovely!"

Amber started at Trent's deep, husky voice so near her, and she turned quickly to stare up at his handsome face. He was so close that his breath fanned her cheeks, his deep blue eyes held hers, and her heart shook in panic against her breast. She realized that this man had the power both to excite and to frighten her.

"W-what?" she stammered nervously.

"I merely said, 'Lovely,'" he replied.

Amber, growing more uncomfortable at his nearness, turned back to gaze at the sea. "Yes, it is lovely," she agreed. "The sea . . ."

"I wasn't speaking of the sea." Trent smiled warmly. "Although the sea is lovely, I can of a truth say that your beauty gives her a great deal of competition."

Amber blushed and turned to Trent, pleasantly surprised at the unusual gentleness in him. The man amazed her with his ever-changing moods. She wondered what there was deep inside him that could cause him to be so callous and unfeeling, yet could change him into a kind and gentle person.

Thinking that while he was in this genial frame of mind would be a good time to make her request, she said quickly, breathlessly, "I want to go home, Captain." Her eyes were soft and pleading, and the look tore at Trent's heart. "Please, Captain, we're only two days out and surely—"

"*No!*" he exploded. "I told you that you will go where this ship goes! And I further tell you that you will go wherever I choose for you to go! Is that clear? Not that it would particularly distress me to lose four days and put me behind schedule, because I own this vessel and the company that transports the cargo she carries. So you see, *Mademoiselle,* I don't give a tinker's damn as to whether or not you want to go home! Ah, *non, ma* sweet, this ship stays on her course to Havana. And with you on board!"

"But I want to go home, Captain." Tears started down Amber's cheeks, and she continued in a small voice. "You don't understand. I have to go back. I have to get back to—"

"To Michael?" Trent broke in angrily. "That is his name, is it not? Your love?" He stood relentlessly before her, his jaw tight.

Amber gaped at him, shocked at both his words and his tone. His sapphire eyes smoldered like banked fires.

"Michael?" Amber asked in astonishment. She had not expected him to remember the name she had thrown out unthinkingly in her early attempt to have him return her to London.

"Come now, Amber." Trent was impatient. "I haven't the time for games. So tell me, who in hell is Michael?"

Amber did not answer. Her mind was in a turmoil. How could she answer without telling him everything . . . the

arranged marriage . . . Uncle Edward . . . the unpaid debts.
. . . How will I get out of this? she thought. As panic
threatened her, she turned away.

But Trent reached out and grasped her shoulders in a firm
grip, his lean fingers biting into her soft flesh. He spun her
around to face him, and she instinctively raised her hands to
his chest in an effort to push him away. He grabbed both her
wrists and pulled her close against him, his strength assuring
her that she could not pull free.

With his face close to hers he ground out through clenched
teeth, "Do you love him, Amber? This Michael?" As she
hesitated, Trent tightened his hold, unaware that he had done
so. "Well, do you?" he demanded.

"You're hurting me," she gasped. But he made no move to
free her. The more she twisted, the harder he gripped. The
fleeting thought struck Amber that there was certainly no
gentleness in him now.

She stopped struggling and stood before him with tears
streaming down her flushed cheeks. In a low voice she asked,
"Why are you doing this to me, Captain, why are you hurting
me? Why do you wish to always hurt me?"

Remorse swept through him, and he loosened his powerful
grip but did not release her. "Hurt you, little one? Is that
what you think I want to do?" Her tears moved him more
than he cared to admit. He felt an uneasiness caused by a
sense of guilt. *"Mon Dieu,* Amber, it is not my wish to hurt
you," Trent answered contritely as he gently drew her small,
trembling body into his arms. He stroked her soft hair and
held her close. "It is only that you are so impossible! You fight
me at every turn, and I do not seem to be able to make you
understand that I desire to have you with me, always!"

Amber was silent, making no move. For the first time she
felt safety and security in his embrace. She had become
tranquil as Trent spoke, and now she felt herself responding
to his tenderness.

Brushing his lips lightly over her hair, Trent felt the
suspicious ache in his loins, his whole body, and even his
heart. Amber had become as necessary to him as breathing,
but he had not yet admitted it to himself. At the same time,
Trent was creeping slowly into Amber's heart, though neither
of them was yet aware of it.

"Will you tell me, Amber, tell me something about yourself? Why were you out that night in the storm? From what, or from whom, were you attempting to escape? And were the men who chased you sent to bring you back? Please tell me, Amber. Perhaps I can help," Trent almost pleaded.

Amber stepped back, out of the circle of his arms, and looked into his earnest face and his blue eyes, tender with concern. Perhaps he will understand, she thought. Perhaps when I explain he will see that I must go back.

Looking out over the wide expanse of the sea, she began. "I will have to go back a very long way, Captain, so that you will understand. Back to the time when I was a lonely, orphan child of seven years. Both my parents were killed, and I was left with no one save my father's brother, Edward. He and Aunt Alice had no children, and they took me in and reared me as their own. They were apparently quite wealthy and I wanted for nothing. I grew up in complete luxury."

Trent listened in absorbed attention while Amber told in detail the story of her past twelve years. He did not interrupt or ask questions but learned who she was, that she had lived in a small village some thirty miles outside of London, that Edward Kensington was a merchant and, until very recently, a seemingly wealthy man.

Amber related how she had overheard the conversation between Edward and Alice Kensington and had learned of Uncle Edward's current financial difficulties, how he had borrowed heavily against everything he owned, and how his creditor, Sir Michael Windom, had demanded full payment within ten days. And how, knowing that it would be absolutely impossible for Edward to get that much money in so short a time, Sir Michael had refused to allow him more time but had graciously offered to cancel all Edward's debts and to give him paid in full receipts if Edward, in exchange, would give his niece, Amber, in marriage to Sir Michael.

Poor Edward really had no choice, and Amber had agreed to the arrangement out of a sense of loyalty to Edward and gratitude to both Edward and Alice for having given her a lovely home and the luxuries she had enjoyed, as well as the love and feeling of belonging which she could never have had without them.

Amber told of how she was to have been wed on her nineteenth birthday, how she had realized at the last minute that she could not go through with her agreement, and how she had fled from the church just before the ceremony. Her encounter with the two men had been the result of Amber's being unfamiliar with her surroundings, the storm, and her attempt to find shelter. When he heard how the men had offered Amber money in exchange for her favors, Trent's blood boiled. "And to think I gave the bloody buggers fine rubies when I should have given them my cutlass in their gut," he said savagely.

Amber turned eagerly to Trent and, lifting her tear-stained face, she said, "Do you see, Captain, why I must go back? I must fulfill my part of the agreement or my uncle will lose everything. Everything! I can't do that to him, not after all he has done for me. You can see that, can you not?"

As Trent stood looking down at Amber he thought how beautiful she was. She would give herself, forfeit her chance of any happiness, for those she loved. She was begging him to take her back to repay a debt that was not hers. She was asking him to take her back to another man. Another man! That he would never do! No! He wouldn't give her up to this man, not to any man! She would no doubt hate him for what he must do, for the hurt he would cause her, but it must be done.

Taking a deep breath, Trent reached out and took Amber's face in both hands, stroking her cheeks lightly with his thumbs. His heart wanted to give in to her, but he knew that if he did, he would surely lose her. And he had no intention of allowing that to happen!

"Amber," he began, "your story is a sad one, and I am sorry that you were placed in such a position. But as I have told you before, I'll not turn this ship around for any reason." He could not bear the look in Amber's eyes, the hurt and keen disappointment. "Please excuse me, *Mademoiselle,* but I must see to my ship," he said brusquely as he turned on his heel and strode away.

Amber stood in utter confusion. The man is insufferable, she thought as she watched him slip out of sight. She had been a fool to think he would understand, a fool to bare her heart to him. Another rush of tears stung her eyes and she ran from the deck, and Trent, watching her from the bridge, knew that her heart must be breaking. And he felt an acute stab of conscience.

LeBlanc leaped from the rail of the *Mér Fleur* to the deck of the vessel which had drawn up alongside. He landed, feet solid and sure, his cutlass gripped firmly in his hand.

"Defend yourself, you cunning bastard!" he yelled to the man who ran toward him. The man was clad in tan breeches and black boots and was bare-chested save a leather strap that ran from his broad shoulder down his deeply tanned chest and around to his back. The strap held both a dagger and a pistol. His face, although ruggedly handsome, wore a wicked smirk. He stopped short and drew his cutlass, and the two men slowly began to circle. Deep blue eyes met steel-gray eyes in a challenging glare, their cutlasses ready to do battle.

"I'll take pleasure in cutting you into little bits, you heartless pirate, but first I shall make you crawl on your belly and beg for your life, worthless as it is," the man taunted Trent.

"You'll not have the chance, you swine, for I shall have your heart out before you can make the first swing of your cutlass," Trent boasted.

Then with quick, powerful swings by both men, the sound of steel against steel rang out and bounced across the water. Again and again the blades met and then locked in a deadly hold over the men's heads, neither giving an inch, their eyes locked as were the blades they held over their heads.

"Had enough, you bastard?" Trent gritted through clenched teeth. The steel-gray eyes narrowed as they looked deep into Trent's cool eyes.

"Enough?" came the reply. "Why, you arrogant bastard, are you so sure of yourself?" Then the man threw back his head and roared in laughter and Trent joined in. The cutlasses dropped to the deck with a clang as the two men embraced each other in friendship.

"Reed! You ugly mongrel, damn, but it's good to see you!" Trent said affectionately. His white teeth gleamed in a wide smile.

"Ah, yes, my friend, it is truly good to see you, too," Casey Reed replied enthusiastically, guiding Trent toward Reed's quarters.

"Brandy?" Reed asked as they entered his cabin. He motioned Trent to a chair.

"Of course," Trent replied, sinking into the chair and stretching his long legs before him, crossing them at the ankles. His blue eyes studied Casey who was pouring their drinks. Casey stood tall, a muscular man whose copper-colored hair was sun-streaked and whose boyish good looks had sent many a woman into a swoon.

"Tell me, Trent, how have you been?" Casey inquired. "And why did I not see you in Nassau in April as usual? Did you have a problem?"

"*Non, non* problem. I had business in Spain and from there I went on to Izmir," Trent answered lazily.

"Izmir! Why the hell Izmir?" Casey asked in genuine surprise.

"Cargo," Trent replied casually, watching Casey's face closely.

"Cargo? From Izmir? Why? Since when do you do trade with the Turks?"

"I was not the buyer of the cargo, I only intercepted it before it reached London. Our mutual acquaintance who hires the frigate *Sea Glory* on occasion owned the shipment. As you know, he has been the subject of some underhanded dealings for some time now. Well, Simmons's men have been watching him closely, and when he made his move and arranged for the shipment, Simmons sent word for me to come to Spain.

"When I arrived in Spain I learned that the *Sea Glory* was to receive a cargo of women slaves who would later be sold in France and England. I was given official authority to follow, wait, and intervene because the main cargo was opium," Trent concluded.

"Opium!" Casey shouted, almost choking on the swallow of brandy he had just taken.

"That's right, opium," Trent said calmly. "So I set a course for Izmir the next morn and waited for the *Sea Glory*'s return and intercepted her before she made her way back into

Atlantic waters. From there the women were taken back to Simmons in Spain, where arrangements were made to transport them to the New Colonies to be freed.

"I put a torch to the vessel and sent her and the opium to the bottom of the sea along with the cargo that I chose not to keep for myself. The crew, those who were still alive, were left with Simmons."

"And our 'friend' in London? What of him?" Casey asked as he poured another brandy for himself.

"Oh, he knows only that the ship was attacked by pirates. He does not know what really happened to his cargo." Trent took the last sip of his drink and smiled. "I'm more than sure he believes the story that reached London. I was there long enough to see that it was told." Trent laughed a pleased, assured laugh.

"I'm sure," Casey chuckled and ran his lean tanned fingers through his sun-streaked hair. "Now, tell me, how was London?"

"Wet! Rained for most of the two days I was there. Made it damn hard to load my cargo," Trent growled as he held his empty snifter for Casey to pour more brandy.

"What about the women? Is that little redhead still at Madame La Roy's? A feisty wench, that one. And those hips!" Casey rolled his eyes upward as he whistled through his teeth. "You've had her, haven't you?" He waited for an answer from LeBlanc, but it did not come.

Trent sat staring into his brandy snifter as he swirled the brownish liquid around in the glass, the fingers of one hand tapping lightly on the chair arm.

Casey tried again. "You have had her, have you not?"

"What? Had whom?" Trent asked, shaking his head as if to clear his thoughts.

"Val. The redhead at Madame La Roy's. You know, Trent, the one who purrs like a kitten and scratches like an alley cat. Damn, I carried the marks for a week afterward. But she was good." Casey smiled, remembering, and he leaned back in his chair lacing his fingers together behind his head.

"You're lucky that that's all she did," Trent assured him. "She bit me, drew blood, the little bitch. Why, I had to tie her mouth with a bandana, even had to put my damn shirt back on to keep her from ripping the hide off my back with those blasted nails." Trent tried to keep his amused expression unnoticed, but a devilish grin kept playing across his face.

"Not to mention that you tied her hands, too!" Casey replied and laughed heartily as Trent's mouth dropped open.

"How did you know that?" Trent demanded, sitting forward and slamming his glass down on the desk.

"She told me!" Casey answered amused. "I have yet to hit London or any other port after you've been there that the wenches aren't clamoring about the handsome Captain LeBlanc. And it does bore me how they're always comparing the two of us. And Val"—Casey waved his hand airily—"she forever talks about you, and the things she says, well . . ." He left the sentence in midair.

"What things? And damn you, Casey, don't lie to me!" Trent stormed.

"Ah, my friend, but you do have a temper! Let me put your mind to rest on that score. Any man should be pleased to know that a woman, even a whore, would speak of him in such a way. But no man enjoys being compared to another while he lies in that woman's bed!"

Trent settled back in his chair, a smug look on his face. It did him good to hear that women desired him, to know that his lovemaking was satisfying. His thoughts turned to the young woman who at that moment lay sleeping in his bed on the *Mér Fleur*. He chuckled with self-satisfaction as he thought that Amber would one day enjoy his passion, would know and desire him as other women had.

"The price men have to pay for not measuring up!" Trent boasted, laughing at the scowl on Reed's face. "Oh, come now, I was not speaking of you, *mon ami*. In every port that you lay anchor half the women know Captain Casey Reed and the lover he is."

"Every woman!" Casey corrected sternly.

"Right!" Trent agreed. "And now that we have that little matter nicely settled, I have something I wish to discuss with you. Something of the utmost importance. In two days' time you should be in London's port. I want you to check on something for me as soon as you arrive there. If it proves to be the situation that has been told to me, then I shall expect you to conclude the matter according to my instructions. *And not a word to anyone, understand?"*

Casey had watched Trent's face as he spoke and knew that he had never before seen such an earnestness about him.

"Of course, Trent. You know that I will do whatever you ask," he promised with deep sincerity as he settled himself to hear Trent out.

Amber had run to the cabin with tears flooding her eyes. Slamming the door behind her she had thrown herself on the bed, beating her fists on the pillow in frustration. She had cursed Trent LeBlanc and wished him dead many times over before she had finally cried herself to sleep.

Now she stirred and woke slowly, the memory of her entreaty to LeBlanc still with her. Suddenly Amber's eyes opened wide and she sat upright. Something was wrong! Very wrong! There was no sound coming from overhead, no laughter, no singing, no shouting of orders. And the ship! It wasn't moving! A chill ran through Amber, and she was afraid to move. "But I must," she said to herself. "I must see what is wrong!"

Springing to her feet, she went to look through the porthole. A ship! There was another ship alongside the *Mér Fleur*. What is going on? Amber wondered. Had they been seized by pirates? No, she thought, LeBlanc was a pirate, an arrogant, callous cutthroat himself, and pirates didn't attack other pirates. Or did they?

Amber crept slowly and quietly out the door and down the passageway toward the deck. Once on deck she could see the shadowy figures of men as they walked around the ship. It was now dark, and she could barely make out anything she saw. Moving among the barrels and wooden boxes, Amber made her way to the side of the *Mér Fleur* nearest the other vessel.

Hearing voices close by, Amber stopped short, her heart beating fast and hard against her breast. She hid herself behind one of the large barrels.

"The Cap'n, he will be havin' 'is dinner aboard the *Sea Dog*, Fitz," came Drake Monrow's voice. "He wants to visit with Cap'n Reed, and he's only got a while. The *Sea Dog*, she's headed for London, and they'll be movin' on before long. You're not to disturb the lady. Cap'n says she's sleepin' and you're to take her a tray when she wakes."

"Aye, sir. And will you and Thomas be havin' your supper

on deck or in the galley, sir?" asked Fitz. "Cook wants to know, sir."

"We'll be down shortly, Fitz," Drake told the boy.

So it's the *Sea Dog*, Captain Reed's ship, Amber thought. She sighed in relief. It wasn't pirates and they were safe, after all. And the *Sea Dog* was on her way to London. London! Could she sneak aboard the other vessel, stow away until they reached London? She could, she decided, and she would!

Amber hurried back across the deck and down the companion ladder to the passageway. As she made her way down the dark companionway she already had her plans in the making. Once inside the cabin she paced the floor, her bare feet moving swiftly across the polished wood planks from one side of the room to the other. She had to make her plan work so she could get back home and explain everything.

"Oh, dear sweet God, please let me get safely aboard the *Sea Dog* and don't let anyone find me. Please let me get back to London," she whispered softly as she closed her emerald eyes tightly.

Hearing voices in the passageway, Amber quickly crossed to the bunk and slipped into bed, pulling the covers over her. There was a light rap on the door, then when she did not answer there came a second rap, somewhat louder this time.

"The missy, she still be asleep," came Jason's low voice. "I come to see if'n she be ready fer her supper. Poor wee one, she be fer shure wore out. Never even heered the Cap'n when 'e come stormin' through that there door this morn rantin' an' snortin' lak a bull, 'e was, an' beatin' on the door a-yellin'! Whooee! 'Im was fierce mad, 'im was, an' 'im bust this 'ere door open, 'im did!" Jason chuckled in pure amusement. "The missy, she locked 'im out, she did. That little lady, she be a handful. The Cap'n, 'e don't rightly know 'ow to 'andle that one. Makes 'im awful mad, it do."

"Beggin' yer pardon, sir, but why is Cap'n Trent a-keepin' the lady aboard when 'e never afore let a woman stay aboard the *Mér Fleur*? That be 'is rule, it be law! An' the lady, she don't wanta be 'ere, I kin see it in 'er face. She be wantin' to go home, back to England. Why is this lady different, sir?" Fitz's young voice showed great concern.

"Don't know, lad, don't know. But ye be right 'bout 'er not wantin' to be 'ere. That was the Cap'n's doins', it was, an' I ain't the one who be a-askin' 'im fer reasons. An' ye askin' 'bout 'er bein' different, well, that she be. An' I 'as me own idees as to the Cap'n's reasons fer keepin' 'er aboard," Jason replied, his tone soft.

"Jason! Jason! Where the hell are you, man?" came Trent's voice from overhead. "Jason!" the yell was insistent.

"Oh dear," Amber gasped, "how will I ever get out of the cabin and to the *Sea Dog?* I thought Trent would be aboard the *Sea Dog* for the better part of the evening. But now he's back and my plan has been spoiled." She groaned aloud, feeling defeated in her purpose.

"Aye, Cap'n, I be down 'ere. Do ye be a-needin' sumpin', sir?" Jason's call was loud and clear.

"Aye, Jason, 'I be a-needin' sumpin,'" came Trent's mocking reply. "Blast it, Jason, why are you forever asking me if I need something? Can't a man call a body without needing something?"

Amber now stood at the door, and she heard Jason say to Fitz in a hushed whisper, "The Cap'n, methinks 'e 'ad a bit too much of the good Cap'n Casey's brandy. I kin 'ear it in 'is talkin'. 'E never—"

"Damn!" Trent's oath came ringing down the companionway. "Jason! You blasted old coot, where the hell are you? I can't see a damn thing!"

"'Ere I be, Cap'n," Jason answered, moving toward the companion ladder. "Sorry 'bout the light, sir, but I didn' know ye was a-comin' back so soon."

Amber ran back to the bed, her face flushed and her heart heavy in her breast. My God! He's drunk! What am I to do? her agitated thoughts ran. Her mind began to race, and she knew that she could not get off the *Mér Fleur* unless she took drastic measures.

She scrambled for the bed and pulled the blanket to the floor, spreading it quickly and reaching for a pillow. I will be on my pallet when Trent comes in, she thought. He will think I'm asleep, and surely he won't bother me. Amber remembered him standing over her that morning, thinking her to be asleep, and he had not bothered her then.

Just as she knelt to the pallet, Amber bolted upright and stared down at the dreaded thing on the floor. She looked from the bunk to the pallet and back again. A sly smile crossed her pretty face as she turned and with light, rapid steps she moved back to the bed.

"Ah, Captain, tonight you shall have the pleasure of that hard, miserable floor. And when you wake at dawn to find your bones aching and your muscles taut and sore, then the tables will have turned, just as I predicted." Amber smiled at the thought. "And when you find that I have gone in the night with the *Sea Dog* . . . oh, sweet revenge," she purred as she slipped back into the bunk and made herself comfortable.

She heard them at the door, heard Jason asking, "Ye shure ye be all right, Cap'n?" The door swung open and Jason continued, "I mean, sir, ye look a mite wobbly, if'n ye don't mind me sayin' so."

"Blast it, Jason, who appointed you my keeper?" Trent snapped waspishly. "*Mon Dieu*, man, leave me alone! And yes, I do mind you saying anything to me right now. Go on, old man, I'm back in my cabin and it's not yet midnight. So go! Go!" Trent ordered, motioned Jason off with his waving hands, and leaned against the door jamb for support.

But Jason stood his ground, not moving from the dimly lighted passageway.

"Well? What are you waiting for?" Trent asked, his words slurred.

"The missy, 'er . . . well, 'er ain't 'ad no supper, sir. 'Er ain't been outa the cabin, sir. 'Er's been dead asleep all evenin'. Don't ye think I oughta 'ave Fitz bring 'er a bite to eat an' . . . well, mebbe ye'd be a-likin' some 'ot coffee, sir. I'd be right pleased to bring—"

"Jason!" Trent stormed, "I don't want any coffee! And if the lady is asleep"—he glanced quickly at the bed—"and I believe that she is, then she won't be eating. If you would like, you may have Fitz bring a tray of cheese and dried beef and leave it outside the door. Now, if you'll be so kind, I bid you a good night, sir." With a somewhat unsteady bow, Trent added, "I'll be going to bed now."

Trent closed the door in Jason's face and left the old man standing in the dim passageway. Jason slowly shook his head and went in search of Fitz. He was sure the missy would awaken hungry.

Locking the door with shaking fingers, Trent weaved his way across the room. Amber lay very still on the bed, not daring to breath, in the hope that he would believe her to be asleep.

God, but his head was pounding, Trent thought. He had known he should have stopped drinking after Casey had poured him the sixth . . . or was it the tenth? . . . brandy. But Casey was capable of downing brandy after brandy and never blinking an eye, and even when Trent's head began to spin, he would not allow Casey to get the better of him and would match him drink for drink, his deep blue gaze fastened on Casey's steel-gray eyes.

Of course, Casey would be just as drunk as LeBlanc, but when each had reached his own cabin with head pounding and feet unsteady, his masculine pride would tell him that no man had bested him! But the only soothing each head would get was the softness of a pillow beneath a throbbing skull that often felt as if the ship's anchor had been dropped upon it.

"Ah, bed!" Trent murmured as he staggered toward the bunk. But suddenly his foot caught on the pallet and he almost lost his balance. He looked down at the blanket and pillow on the floor and then to Amber lying in his bunk.

"Oh, *non, non, ma* sweet," Trent spoke, shaking a finger at the girl. "Playing my own game, are you, little one? Well, I shall not be put out of my own bed, oh *non.*" He bent down to retrieve the blanket and pillow and found that he had to brace himself with an outstretched hand as the floor threatened to come up to meet him. Straightening, he laughed low and fiendishly, sending chills shivering up Amber's spine.

He tossed the blanket to a chair and laid the pillow lightly on the bunk. Then sitting on the edge of the bed he pulled awkwardly at his boots. Removing them, he let them drop aimlessly to the floor and stood to shed his breeches and silk shirt. They, too, found a place on the floor.

Trent crossed the room, slightly swaying, and found the water basin. The water pitcher which Amber had smashed had been replaced, and he poured water into the basin, splashing it over his face and chest. He ran his fingers roughly through his black hair and again splashed water over himself.

Amber lay quietly watching through half-closed eyes as Trent moved about the room. Even though somewhat unsteadily, his sun-baked torso moved with pride and grace. In the faint light of the cabin she could make out his tall powerful body and found herself wishing for more light. Her face flushed with excitement, and she felt a strange kindling warmth in her loins. What was it? What was wrong with her? she wondered. She was becoming confused because her body seemed to be calling out to Trent's.

Stop it! Amber demanded of herself. Stop! My God, what is happening to me? She despised him, loathed him, did she not? And she had made plans to slip off this ship in a very short time, away from this man whose body she craved at this moment.

Amber took a deep breath as Trent returned to the bed, pulled up the sheet, and slipped beneath it. Reaching out, he pulled Amber to him. She could feel the lean taut muscles of his arms embracing her, and the crisp mat of hair on his chest teased her neck as he nestled his head against her hot, flushed cheek. Trent placed a tender kiss on her temple and Amber's body trembled slightly at his touch. He felt the tremor as if it had flowed from her warm body into his, and he tightened his hold, pressing closer to her silken body.

"Amber," Trent whispered in a ragged, husky voice, "you are an exciting creature." He took a long, uneven breath. "I ache for you, little one. *Mon Dieu*, if you only knew how much!"

As he stroked the softness of Amber's face with his, the tiny stubbles of Trent's unshaven face grazed her flesh, but not unpleasantly. Her breath came in short, heavy gasps despite her vain effort to control it. And her body was reaching out for his touch as she unconsciously kneaded her frame to his. Loosening the cord belt, he slid her breeches down the length of her soft, silky legs. As his hand moved, ever so slowly, up her smooth thigh, Amber felt a threatening moan well up in her throat, and she bit her lip trying to suppress it. But as his hand found its way to the soft flesh of her inner thigh, the moan escaped her lips along with a rushing shudder of her body.

Trent's mouth sought Amber's and his lips crushed hers. She parted her lips willingly to receive his searching tongue, and he tasted the warm sweetness of her kiss. Amber heard Trent's low groan as he slipped his hand inside her shirt, moving the palm of his hand over her swelling breasts. She felt the hardness of his body against hers, and as he entwined his leg around her, Amber started at the bulge of his manhood as it lay hard against her, searing her with the heat of his passion.

"Oh, God, no!" Amber cried against his shoulder. What was she doing? She was letting herself be caught up in this man's passion. Then she realized that it was her own passion, as well. She stiffened and tried to push away, but Trent's grip became more demanding as she struggled against his embrace.

"*No!* Please, no!" she pleaded.

"*Mon Dieu,* Amber, don't stop me now!" Trent's voice was hushed with emotion as he looked down at her. "Let me make love to you, Amber. You tell me 'no,' but your body, little one, is saying something else. Damn you, Amber, don't deny me the passion you now feel!"

"Oh, please understand, Captain! It is only my flesh that wants you, wants your touch, not me," Amber cried as tears ran down her sun-kissed cheeks. Even as she pleaded with Trent, her eyes were so full of passion that it tore at his heart. Why was she doing this? Why? Did she hate him so much? Trent stared down at her for a moment, his heart beating wildly against his strong breast. Then he closed his eyes tight and gritted his teeth so hard that Amber heard the grinding sound come forth, and he rolled away from her.

Amber lay stunned as she listened to Trent's ragged breathing. She felt the jerking shudders as they ran through his body. Finally he spoke in such a tender, yet cutting tone that it stabbed Amber's heart no harder or deeper than if he had plunged a knife into it.

"Amber . . . why? Why did you tease me so?" There was a wistfulness in his voice. "You have your revenge now. You have shown me how very much you hate me. And now I know that I am truly repulsive to you!" Trent sat up on the side of the bed. Amber could see the fine film of sweat glistening on his body and even in the dim light of the cabin she could see the dying flame in the sapphire of his beautiful eyes. They seemed to become as black as the midnight sky, and there was a grim expression on his handsome face.

Yes, Amber thought, she had wanted revenge! Yes, she had hated him, had detested him and wished him dead. But now! After the fire Trent had kindled within her, the emotions that were so new, so truly wonderful, she wondered if revenge was so sweet, after all! She chilled at the feelings that still held her body in sweet yearning for Trent.

Suddenly he spoke and Amber saw that he stood staring out the porthole. "Was your revenge as sweet as you had hoped, Amber? Does it taste like the sweetness of the bee's honey? How it must thrill you to know that a man has desired you to the point of becoming a mumbling fool!" His words were now becoming cold and seemed to come from far away. Amber shivered at the iciness. "Damn it all! I begged you, *begged* you! Damn you, Amber, for ever coming into my life! Damn you for being so beautiful and so desirable! And damn my soul to hell for wanting you!" Trent's words had the ring of steel as they came forth, and he slammed a clenched fist against the wall in helpless rage.

After a long, poignant silence Trent turned back to the bed and, without so much as a glance at Amber, with his back to her he reached down and picked up his breeches. As he put one foot into the breeches leg, Amber's quivering voice broke into the cold grayness of the room and he stopped.

"Trent," she choked. But he did not speak, nor did he turn to look at her. She tried again. "My revenge is not as sweet as honey, nor is it as sweet as the gentle touches you just laid on my body. The taste, it is as bitter as gall and I can find no pleasure in it." Trent remained silent, making no move as he listened in stunned surprise to her words. "Trent?" Amber gasped as the tears began to trail down her cheeks.

Trent heard the rustle of the sheets as Amber came to her knees on the bunk behind him. Reaching out a trembling hand, she touched his rigid back and felt the taut cords of his muscles as they rippled across his back at her warm touch. Amber rested her wet cheek against his back and whispered, "You are all any woman could ever desire, Trent LeBlanc, everything!" Then she placed a soft kiss at the bend of his back as she slid her arms around him.

After a moment Trent turned to Amber and as he looked down into her soft, emerald-green eyes his heart seemed to stop in his breast and then began to beat frantically. But the damage had already been done and he mistook Amber's gentleness as pity.

"Spare me your sympathy, *Mademoiselle!* I'll not have your

pity, never your pity! And I'll not come into that bed and lie with you just because of what you are now feeling. Oh, *non!* Neither my pride nor my dignity will I exchange for a romp with a woman aroused only in an attempt to alleviate her own teasing mistake or to salve her conscience.

"I am a man, Amber, not a schoolboy, and one day you will come to realize this fact. And when you cease to behave like a spoiled child and become a true woman, you will not only want but will need a real man—such as I! There is no doubt that I still want your ripe young body and I still want the taste of your lips. But the game has not yet been won, and you are not to forget that the rules are of my making.

"Yes, I shall have you again, but not now. When the time comes, it will be on my terms, and there will be no turning back, no stopping me. This unfinished matter will be resolved at my convenience!"

And with that, Trent pulled on his breeches and left the cabin.

Chapter Four

AMBER SAT ON A TACK BOX IN THE STERN OF THE *MÉR FLEUR*, HER bare feet tucked beneath her. Across her lap lay a piece of frayed rope, and her fingers idly knotted it. But her mind was drifting back over the days and nights since she had been aboard the vessel. It had been a fortnight since she had been taken from London, and the time had been spent in a far different way than she would ever have expected.

The crew, to a man, had become Amber's friends, and each was eager to help teach her the things she wanted to know about the operation of the ship. They answered her questions, and she knew every inch of the *Mér Fleur*, from bow to stern. It was a familiar sight to the crew to see Amber's slight figure high up in the rigging and not uncommon to find her at the ship's wheel, when Jason or Drake was on watch.

Tossing the rope away, Amber rose and made her way to her favorite spot at the rail. All was quiet and the sea was calm, a warm breeze blew over the deck and upward through the sails.

As she looked out over the vastness of the blue-green water with its unseen horizon, Amber remembered something Jason had told her.

"The sea, 'er 'as many moods, as do the Cap'n. When ye kin understan' 'er moods, each and every one of 'em, if'n 'er be peaceful an' tranquil, or angry an' deadly. When ye understan' 'er, missy, then ye'll understan' the Cap'n."

The memory turned her thoughts to LeBlanc and the night he had returned to his cabin after having too much brandy following his visit with Casey Reed. When Trent had stalked from the cabin, hurt and angry, Amber had begun to realize that her feelings for the man whom she professed to hate so intensely were not those of hatred at all. They were in reality the stirrings of love and passion, and they warred with her sense of decency and good breeding. She had fought her emotions, but with each passing day her frustrations had lessened, and she now readily admitted to herself that she had truly fallen in love.

Amber's love for him was apparent to everyone but LeBlanc himself. It was only because he was blinded by his own stubborn pride that he was not made aware of it. He had held true to his final words to her. He was playing the game by his own rules. And Amber? She was subdued and passive, although she was the opponent.

Lying with Trent on the nights he wanted her, Amber never showed the passion that ate at her. Time after time she had caught her trembling lip between her teeth to hold back the moans of her passion. She would lie with her mind miles away in an effort to keep her wanton body from responding. Often she had dug her nails into the palms of her hands, sometimes drawing blood, to prevent herself from throwing her arms around Trent and clinging to him. And when he was satisfied, his own desire fulfilled, he would fall asleep while Amber lay awake, staring into the darkness with hot, saline tears scalding her eyelids.

Amber wanted the love of this wonderful, mysterious man, and knowing that she did not have it was breaking her heart. When did it happen? When had she fallen in love with Trent? Amber asked herself these questions many times. But yet she knew! It was the night that she had responded to his touch, to the love he had offered her. He had pleaded, "Amber, don't stop me now! . . . Let me make love to you, Amber. . . . Don't deny me the passion you now feel." It was the night that her own body had awakened to the need that a woman feels for a man. She had been afraid and had tried to suppress those emotions, but when she could not and the passion had begun to surface she had acted like a fool, like a child.

Trent's words had come back to plague her. "I am a man . . . not a schoolboy, and one day you will come to realize this . . . when you cease to behave like a spoiled child . . . become a true woman . . . you will not only want, but will need a real man—such as I!"

Amber groaned aloud. "I *do* want a man, I *do* need a man, but the man I want and need is you, Trent. *You!*" Lifting her head defiantly, she proclaimed to her friend, the sea, "I am a woman! I am! And I'll show him. I'll be the woman he wants me to be, I swear it. And you, Captain Trent LeBlanc, shall reap the harvest! The seeds of passion that you planted have taken root and are growing. Each time you touch me, Captain, they grow stronger as do the crops in the fields at the touch of the sun and the kiss of the rain. Oh, yes, 'Cap'n Trent, sir,' you shall reap what you have sown for I am a woman ready for the harvest!"

Now that Amber had made her declamation and was ready to start anew, she would show LeBlanc that she had learned well her lesson. "You will be dealing with a 'true' woman, Trent, and she will make a few rules of her own." She smiled at the thought. "I shall have your very soul, Trent LeBlanc, and you will love me the way a man loves a woman. You shall have lust and passion, but in return you will give the one thing you have refused to give to anyone, my dear Captain, and that is *your love!*"

For the first time in days Amber felt almost lighthearted, and she gave a ripple of laughter that was caught by a gentle breeze and wafted out across the wide expanse of the beautiful, serene water.

Amber had never realized the beauty of the sea, but now she could truly understand why Trent loved it as he did, why it was the fulfillment of all his dreams, his way of life. His heart must beat with the swell of the waves. Was the sea to be her competition for Trent's love? "No," Amber protested, "there will be no rivalry because I would never attempt to separate them for I have learned to love the sea and all her mysteries almost as much as Trent does. I want to share them with him."

She lingered at the rail for several minutes longer, her mind busy with thoughts and plans, completely oblivious to her surroundings.

"Sail ho!" came the warning call. "Sail ho!"

LeBlanc ran for the bridge and grabbed the spyglass from Drake who was at the helm. "What's her flag?" he yelled to the man high in the rigging. "Can you see her flag, man?"

"Cap'n, sir, she's not flyin' her colors," the man called back.

Trent stiffened as he looked through the spyglass. "Pirates!" he hissed. "All hands on deck! . . . Prepare for battle! . . . Move, men!" he shouted.

Amber stood frozen to the deck. Pirates! This was something she certainly had not expected! She raised her eyes to the bridge and at the same moment Trent turned to see her on the deck below, standing tansfixed, her eyes big and filled with a mingling of fear and excitement.

Leaping from the bridge, Trent rushed to Amber's side and grasped her arm, pulling her along toward the companion ladder.

"Get below!" he ordered. "Go to the cabin and lock the door! Do not come out for any reason!" Thrusting his hand deep into his pocket, he produced a key. "Lock the door and do not open it to anyone except me! Do you hear?" he instructed. But Amber did not seem to hear him. She stood as if in a daze.

"*Amber!*" Trent shouted as he shook her in exasperation. "Do you hear me? Go to the cabin and stay there! I will come for you when it's safe!"

But Amber shook her head as she stared up at him. "No! No, I won't go! It is my fight as well as yours and I won't leave you!" she assured him. So he tugged at her arm in an attempt to help her down the companion ladder, but she planted her bare feet firmly and refused to budge.

"I said 'no,' Captain. I will not go!" Amber said stubbornly.

"Yes, you will go!" Trent yelled and he picked her up, throwing her small frame over his shoulder. Amber kicked and screamed as he carried her down the ladder and to the cabin. He pushed the door open and swung Amber from his shoulder and dropped her to the floor with a thud. Before she could get to her feet, Trent had slammed the door and locked it from the outside. Amber ran to the door and beat her fist vainly against it.

"No! No! Trent! For God's sake let me out! *Trent!*" Amber screamed. She sank to the floor, her very being filled with a mixture of fright, anger, and love for the man whose pounding footsteps she heard running back along the companionway to the deck. "He'll be killed!" she sobbed. "Dear God! I have to get out of here!"

Just as LeBlanc emerged from the companion ladder, the first broadside was fired from the pirate ship's guns and sought its mark, making its way to the bow of the *Mér Fleur*. The force of the impact caused Trent to reel off balance and crash to the deck. He rolled quickly to his feet and ran to the ship's wheel.

"Bring her around!" he called to Drake. Turning in the direction of the cannons, Trent cupped his hands around his mouth and shouted the command, *"Fire!* Send the bloody bastards to hell!"

The *Mér Fleur*'s cannons belched, sending forth brilliantly burning orbs.

The pirate ship returned her fire, hurtling spheres of red-orange fire ripping through the rigging to the sails. The sound of cracking timber soared across the *Mér Fleur,* and a flaming mast came crashing down like a mighty bolt of lightning. Blood-curdling screams of death rang out across the waters as the burning sail and timber collapsed on the deck enveloping several men in leaping flames of hell. Others rushed to put out the fire before it spread.

As the pirate vessel drew nearer, the sounds of cannons roared, and the deadly burning cannonballs volleyed between the expanse of sea to both ships. LeBlanc, wielding a pistol in one hand and a cutlass in the other, stood firmly on his deck, ready for combat. The pirates swung from ropes and the rigging to the deck of the *Mér Fleur.* Trent cut his way through man after man and they fell to the deck injured or to their deaths.

When the first rumble of crashing timber roared overhead, Amber sprang to her feet and ran to Trent's desk. Pulling out the desk drawers one by one she searched for another door key, and when she could not find one, she fell to her knees, burying her head in her hands.

"I have to get out. I have to! I must fight for my life, I cannot just wait for them to come and take me!" she cried. She knew that Trent had locked her in for her own safety, knowing full well what the pirates would do to her. What they would do to any woman!

"I will not just sit and wait!" Amber muttered. She ran to the sea trunk and in desperation began rummaging through it. There was a small gold box and she opened it quickly. Inside the box were hairpins and a comb. Gathering up her hair in both hands she twisted it into a coil and wrapped the cord of hair around her head, pinning it in place. Then she pulled out a wine-colored bandana and tied it over her bright hair.

Perhaps she could pass herself off as a boy, she thought. At least she might have a better chance of survival.

Amber grabbed a hairpin and ran for the door. Inserting the pin into the keyhole she moved it up and down, from side to side, in and out, in a futile attempt to spring the lock.

The roar of the cannons, the firing of pistols, steel clashing against steel, men shouting both in anger and in pain—all these sounds drummed in Amber's ears, and her panic made her desperate. One last effort to unlock the door and, wonder of wonders, the lock released and Amber jerked open the door and ran out into the passageway, headed toward the deck.

Once on deck Amber could see that the battle was raging. Men were fighting in every part of the ship. Her eyes frantically searched for LeBlanc, but she could not see him. Her heart seemed to stop, and she felt sick as she wondered if he had been killed. "Oh, dear God! No!" she shrieked as she ran toward the bridge. Stumbling over a body, she plunged to the deck. She stared into the unseeing eyes of the dead man and at the blood spilling from his chest.

Amber fought back the nausea that welled up in her throat. She must be strong, she told herself, since she had asked for this unpleasantness. Reaching for the cutlass that lay in the dead man's hand, she pried his fingers from the hilt.

With the cutlass secure in her own hand, Amber rose to her

feet and stepped forward. Lifting the weapon, she swung at the first pirate that came near her. She advanced with a forceful motion and with speed and grace she cut down her attacker. Onward she fought, two more men, one more, and she cut, slashed and jabbed her way to the bridge. Then she saw LeBlanc, his powerful arm swinging his cutlass at first one pirate then another as he and Drake Monrow fought side by side in the heat of the battle.

Suddenly Amber spied a pirate headed toward Trent's back and she stifled a scream. Before she could call out a warning, Drake had turned and cut the man down. Amber released her breath in a deep sigh of relief.

Climbing to the bridge, Amber took her stand behind Trent, her weapon ready. She would make sure that no other man had the chance to come up behind him again. She was ready to die for him and would do so before she would let another bloody cutthroat have opportunity to harm him.

As Trent turned and saw Amber, he only had time to exclaim, "Hell and damnation, Amber!" in anger and astonishment. But the look in his deep blue eyes would stay in her memory forever! Even if she lost him in this battle, she knew now that he must truly care for her!

They fought back to back, Amber and LeBlanc, each helping the other. She showed a skill with the cutlass that many a man could not. When Trent fell injured to the deck with blood oozing from his wounded shoulder, Amber's protective instinct surged forth. As the pirate readied to plunge his cutlass into Trent again, Amber leaped forward and with a deadly swing of her cutlass she knocked the weapon from the man's hand, giving Trent the time he needed to raise his pistol and fire. The pirate fell dead to the deck below.

The battle raged on for what seemed like hours to Amber, but in reality it was only minutes. Things were happening so fast that she barely had time to ward off one attacker before she faced another. Her arms grew weary and she felt ill at the sight and smell of blood, but she fought on.

A blow from her cutlass knocked a pistol from the grip of a pirate, and Amber quickly retrieved it. No sooner had she done so when, from high over her head, a pirate swung down from the rigging behind Drake. Realizing that Drake was about to lose his life, Amber raised the heavy pistol, steadied her aim, and gently squeezed the trigger. Her aim was sure, and the pirate fell dead at Drake's feet. Drake gave her a fleeting smile of gratitude.

Because of his shoulder wound, LeBlanc was now fighting with only one hand while the other hung limply at his side. As Amber turned back to help him, he was desperately fighting off two men, and she came to his assistance, evening the odds. Trent's opponent was not long in meeting his death, and as the other was felled by Amber's blade he reeled forward, toppling her to the deck. In a moment she was back on her feet and stared in horror as she saw Trent knocked from the bridge by a pirate swinging from a rope. Trent crashed to the lower deck, striking his head on the rubble of the fallen mast.

Another pirate saw the fall and stepped toward Trent, his cutlass raised. Amber leaped from the bridge and with a blood-curdling scream she ran toward the man. As he turned to face her, Amber stopped short.

"Why slay a man when he's down and without a weapon, you whoring bastard? Step forward and fight a man who is on his feet and armed!" she challenged.

Thereupon the pirate struck out, his blade meeting Amber's. The steel blades hung in the air over their heads. That was the last thing LeBlanc remembered as he fought back the cold, clammy hand of darkness that reached out and swallowed him.

Amber's adversary was strong and she was tiring of warding off his blows, but she held her own. Her steps were sure and quick as she moved to avert blow after blow of the man's cutlass. When she felt a sting of pain and saw the crimson of her own blood staining her sleeve she experienced a violent surge of fury, and with it came renewed strength. She had felt the bite of his cutlass, and she vowed that she'd not give him a second chance.

With a sudden vengeful lunge Amber thrust her weapon into the belly of the pirate. He looked at her in shock, his eyes bulged at the gash in his flesh but before he could cry out or move Amber pulled the bloody blade from his belly and with a savage brutal stab she drove the blade deep into his throat.

As his body sagged downward, Amber watched unfeelingly, and in her emerald-green eyes was a triumphant gleam.

The battle was over! The pirates were victorious! Amber turned to see the remaining crewmen of the *Mér Fleur* being lined up against the starboard rail. A pirate strode toward Amber and motioned with his blade to the line of men. "Move, boy," he bellowed, "get over there with the rest of the swine!" Amber hastily joined the line. LeBlanc's crew stood waiting.

The burly captain of the pirate ship leaped onto the deck of the *Mér Fleur,* and Amber wondered where he had been during the battle. He had let his men do the fighting, now he had come forth to reap the spoils of battle, unscathed and haughty. "You dirty, yellow bastard!" Amber whispered under her breath.

The pirate captain was tall and grubby, his brown matted hair hung down past his shoulders, and he had a heavy beard. He wore only dirty white knee breeches that were tattered and torn. A ragged scar from temple to chin gave him a wicked look, and a hush seemed to settle over the ship at his appearance.

"Who be the captain of this scum of a ship?" he bellowed. He swaggered forward and spat upon the deck. His insulting attitude caused Amber to seethe with indignation. "I say who be the captain?" Grabbing a cutlass from one of his men he thrust it hard into the wooden planking of the deck. Its point embedded in the wood while the hilt swayed vibrantly. "Step forward, Captain, and prepare to die!" the pirate leader roared as he laughed mockingly.

Where was Drake? Amber wondered, and Jason? Why didn't someone say something? LeBlanc lay wounded and unconscious but somebody should act. But no one spoke. Amber's thoughts were of Trent and his beautiful ship, which was now in jeopardy. He had fought bravely for the *Mér Fleur* and for his men. Why could he not have been the victor? It was unfair, Amber was thinking, when her attention was drawn by the boastful words of the pirate captain.

"I do not wish to kill any more of your men, Captain. I can find a use for them. But I will kill them, one by one, until you

step forward or until one of your men tells me who you are."
He strutted a few steps up and back down the deck as he
waited for an answer. "Come now, Captain, my patience is at
an end! Which is it to be, your life or theirs?" And he drew
his own cutlass from his sash, pointing it at LeBlanc's
crewmen.

With a courage Amber had not known she possessed, she
took a deep breath and with her head held high and fire in her
green eyes, she boldly stepped from the line. Planting her
bare feet solidly, wide apart as she had seen Trent do many
times, Amber stared defiantly up into the cold eyes of the
swashbuckling pirate.

Then with a rapid movement of her hand she reached up
and snatched the bandana from her head and shook her hair
loose, letting the red-gold tresses fall free about her shoulders
and down her back.

"I am captain of this ship, sir!" she declared. "There is no
reason to murder any more of my men!" Amber's words were
crisp and authoritative.

The pirate leader stared in shocked amazement, first at
Amber, then at the *Mér Fleur*'s crew. Not one showed
surprise; their expressions remained unchanged. LeBlanc's
men stood straight and proud. They had seen Amber in the
thick of the battle fighting by their captain's side. They had
seen her save the lives of both LeBlanc and Drake Monrow. And even though they would like to spare her whatever she was to face, not one spoke. LeBlanc had his men
well trained, had taught them never to speak out or give
information for any reason. "Not even if my life or that of
one of your mates is at stake," he had told them many
times.

Staring down at Amber, the pirate captain thought, Surely
not! Not a woman! Yet he had heard of female captains, but
they had always commanded pirate ships. And these men,
they were looking at her with pride and . . .

"To the death, Captain?" Ambers words rang out.

"What?"

"I said 'to the death?' You have asked for the captain of
this ship to step forward and prepare to die. Well, I have
stepped forward and I, sir, am prepared, only . . ." She
stopped with a wicked grin crossing her lovely face.

Reaching out Amber grasped the hilt of the cutlass tightly in her hand and pulled it free of the wooden plank. Raising it, she touched the end of the blade with the tip of her long, slender finger and tested its point.

"It seems that you have dulled the point, sir. That means that it will hurt all the more when it pierces your filthy hide!" she hissed. "Now I do trust that it is you, sir, that is prepared to die, for I shall take pleasure in ending your murderous life!"

And in the next moment she had raised the cutlass and with a flash it met the blow of the pirate's weapon. He lunged, Amber sidestepped, he lunged again, the tilt of his blade nicking Amber's hand and blood trickled down her fingertips, making it difficult for her to keep a firm grip on the hilt of her weapon. Again fury raged within her, and Amber returned the pirate's blow, her blade ripping along the length of his left arm. Around and around they went, neither giving the other time to make their mark.

The crew of the *Mér Fleur* watched Amber proudly but with anxiety. They knew that she was tired from previous fighting, while the pirate leader had come fresh to the duel. There was a collective groan from the crew as the pirate suddenly lashed out with his foot and knocked Amber's feet from under her. It would be the end, they thought as the pirate thrust his cutlass downward with awesome power. But Amber rolled quickly to one side, and the blade grazed her back, ripping her shirt, and tiny beads of blood soaked the fabric.

Beyond feeling the pain, Amber's body seemed to be numb while her mind concentrated on vengeance. She was on her feet in a flash, and the flames of hatred that lit her green eyes were like luminous masses of burning phosphorus. With speed and deadly force Amber knocked the cutlass from the grip of the pirate, sending the weapon flying to the deck. Stepping forward, she placed her foot firmly upon the hilt of the fallen cutlass and raised her own in readiness. The pirate leader stood uncertainly under Amber's malevolent stare.

"I will not kill a man who is unarmed! I am not the yellow, murdering bastard that you are!" Amber rasped. "You shall have a weapon in your hand when you die. But before I kill you, I shall draw blood from your miserable body until you have paid for every drop of blood that was drawn from my men!"

With a quick movement of her foot, Amber kicked the cutlass to him. "Pick it up!" she ordered. "Pick up the weapon, you cowardly bastard!"

Amber took a step backward as the pirate reached down and picked up his cutlass. Again they circled, blades ready, while Amber's green eyes noted every move of her opponent. Calm but alert, she was like a panther readying to pounce on her prey. When he raised his arm to strike out, Amber's blade bit into the pirate's thigh. He yelled in pain as the blood poured from his wound, but he continued to fight.

Again Amber marked, and the tip of her blade ripped a nasty gash across the pirate's belly, laying open the flesh. Staggering, he grabbed his belly as his blood spilled through his fingers.

"And now!" Amber declared victoriously, "Justice will prevail when the final bite of my cutlass is felt as I drive it through your malicious heart!" And with those words she thrust the blade into the pirate's breast, and as he fell forward, blood gushing forth, Amber quickly withdrew the blade and again thrust it deep into his heart as she had promised.

Standing over him, her bloody cutlass in her hand, Amber met the pirate's eyes as he stared up at her, choking in his own blood.

"May your worthless, yellow soul rot in hell, you dirty bastard!" she hissed as she spat upon the crumpled, bleeding body of the ruthless cutthroat who lay on the deck, his cutlass still in his hand.

The dying pirate opened his mouth as if to speak, but only his blood spilled forth.

There was a sudden flurry of movement and LeBlanc's men overpowered the band of pirates who stood in awe at the sight of their dead leader, dead at the hands of a mere woman!

A roar of victory rose from the crew of the *Mér Fleur.*

Amber turned to see Trent making his way toward her, but before he reached her she swayed, dropping the bloody cutlass to the deck. Her knees gave way, and she saw the deck coming up to meet her.

* * *

When Amber fainted, Trent had caught her as she fell, sweeping her up into his arms and, carrying her to his cabin, had placed her tenderly upon his bed. Stripping off her bloody shirt he had called for warm water and had washed and cared for her wounds. Although suffering from his shoulder wound and from his fall from the bridge, Trent would allow no one else to care for Amber. He had not left her, even when Jason had attempted to cleanse and care for Trent's wound. He was adamant.

"I must take care of Amber!" he had told Jason. "Damn it, I have lived through worse than a blasted bump on the head, man! Now damn you, Jason, let me take care of Amber!"

LeBlanc had been so concerned about Amber that he had knelt beside her for several hours, not caring about himself. When Fitz, at Jason's command, had slipped in to see if he might sit with Amber while Trent rested, he found Trent asleep with one arm across Amber's unconscious body, his head on her breast and his wounded arm still unattended. Fitz had gently shaken his captain to awaken him and Trent had risen, flexing tired muscles.

"Cap'n, ye need yer shoulder fixed up, sir. Ye hafta take keer uv yerself. If'n ye don't, sir, ye won't be no help ta the missy, sir," Fitz had told him. Then looking down at Amber, who lay white-faced and still, Fitz had noted that her only color was that of her red-gold hair streaming over the pillow.

"Cap'n, will she be all right, sir?" the boy had asked in concern. "The crew, sir, we all seen what she done. She wus fightin' fer allus!" A tear had escaped the boy's eye, and he wiped it away. "Please, sir, if'n I kin help?"

"But you are helping, Fitz," LeBlanc had assured him. "I am sure that she can feel our anxiety. Do not worry, lad, she will be fine!" His words were positive, but Trent was terribly worried, though he did not want Fitz to know.

Amber had lain unconscious and with a fever for days, while the crew had gone about their duties of repairing the *Mér Fleur*. At the times when Jason or Fitz emerged from Trent's cabin, there was always one of the crew asking about Amber. All the men kept a prayer for her in their hearts and waited for word that she had rallied and was out of danger.

LeBlanc had not left the cabin once in the three days since

the battle. Just as he always had, Jason entered the cabin on the fourth morning with food, and as Trent picked at his breakfast, Jason watched him gravely.

"Ye go topside, sir. Ye be needin' fresh air. 'Tain't no good ye settin' 'ere day an' night, sir," Jason urged. "Jason'll call ye if'n there be any change in the missy."

But Amber's condition had remained unchanged from the time Trent had brought her to his cabin following her collapse after her duel with the pirate leader. The wound on her arm refused to heal and had spread infection through her body. It was the wound she had received when she had saved LeBlanc's life, and he felt bitter regret that she should suffer so when he had been solely responsible for Amber's presence on the ship.

"I want to be at her side when she awakens, Jason," Trent answered the old man's plea. But after several minutes Jason convinced him that he should go up and see what progress had been made toward restoring the *Mér Fleur* to her former state, and Trent, after a long tender look at Amber's lovely face, made his way up the companion ladder and once again walked the deck of his beloved ship. He looked out over the sea and breathed the salty air.

An hour later Trent was on the bridge when Fitz came running along the deck. "Cap'n! Cap'n, sir! The missy, she be askin' fer ye," he called.

Trent leaped from the bridge and started for the cabin in a run while the entire crew stopped whatever they were doing and waited breathlessly.

Jason met LeBlanc in the passageway. "Cap'n, 'er's been a-callin' fer ye. Only 'ers not knowin' it, 'er not back with us, yet," he warned.

Trent brushed by the old man and swiftly crossed to Amber's side, taking her hand in his. "Amber," he whispered, "Amber, it's Trent! Can you hear me?"

She made no answer but lay unmoving with eyes closed, still unaware of her surroundings. Trent looked up at Jason who stood waiting behind him.

"I will stay with her now, Jason. I wish to be here if she rouses." The first mate smiled at his captain and, with an "Aye, sir," he left the cabin.

Trent sat beside Amber, his heart heavy as he remembered

the battle with the pirates. When he had seen Amber on the bridge behind him he could have killed her for being there. He had been so sure that she couldn't take care of herself and then to see her wielding a cutlass and doing a good job at it had shocked him. Oh, he had still worried about her, but she was holding her own. Not only had she saved his life on two occasions but she had saved Drake's life as well. What a fighter, he thought.

Then when he had been knocked out the last thing Trent remembered seeing was Amber running toward a pirate with murder in her green eyes. And if that were not enough, when he had regained consciousness he had looked up to see her in the bloody duel with the pirate captain. And she had won! Amber had killed the worthless bastard and had cursed him as he lay dying at her feet, then as a final gesture had spat upon him!

Trent looked at Amber's pale, lovely face. "So kind, so feminine, yet you fought like a bloody cutthroat," he whispered. "You are truly a woman, Amber Kensington! How could I have been so blind?" And with these thoughts Trent knew that Amber was very much a part of him and of his life.

Suddenly Amber sat up in the bed, eyes wide and staring. "They're dead," she screamed. "God! *No!* Everyone is dead!" Trent grabbed her shoulders and tried to push her back down on the bed but she fought with all her might. "No, let me go, you bloody coward! Let go of me! You killed them . . . they're dead . . . all dead!" she wailed. And she stared up at Trent with eyes so full of hatred and pain that it cut at his heart. Then he realized that she was not seeing him, she was seeing someone else, the pirate captain, he would guess.

"You will pay for this, damn you! . . . I'll kill you! . . . Do not make the mistake of turning your back on me for I will kill you!" Amber raved as she tried to get free of Trent's hold.

"Trent, oh Trent!" she continued. "Please, God, don't let him be dead, too! . . . Don't take him away from me! . . . Drake! Look out! . . . Papa? Papa, where are you? . . . I hurt, please stop the hurt, Papa . . . stop the hurt. . . ." Then Amber slumped to the bed, making no further sound nor struggle.

"Jason! *Jason!*" Trent yelled loudly, pressing his palm to

Amber's brow. Her brow was hot to his touch, and he knew
that her fever had risen and caused her to be delirious.

Jason burst in, a worried look on his kindly face. "Cap'n,
what is it? Is it the missy, sir? What be the matter?" he asked.

Trent turned quickly back to Amber as she screamed
out. He held her to the bed, her head thrashing from side to
side.

"Her fever!" he answered Jason's query. "It has gone
higher and is making her out of her mind! Bring fresh water
and towels. I have to bring the fever down. And hurry!"
Trent ordered as Jason hastily departed.

"Abby? . . . Are you there, Abby? . . . I'm burning . . .
stop the pain . . . please make the pain go away . . ."
Amber moaned.

Trent's heart went out to Amber and he cradled her in his
strong arms. "Shhh, little one, it is all right," he spoke softly
in her ear. "I am here and I am going to take care of you. I
will make the pain go away." His gentle words seemed to get
through to Amber, and she nestled her head against his chest
with a deep sigh. "I'll not leave you, little one, not ever!"
Trent vowed as he pressed his lips against her fevered brow.

Amber's fever finally broke, and Trent bathed her brow
with cool damp cloths until late in the night. When he was
satisfied that she was all right and was sleeping naturally, he
climbed wearily into bed and lay with Amber in his arms until
he fell asleep from sheer exhaustion.

Waking weak and confused, Amber opened her eyes to see
the cabin alight with the soft glow of a candle. Then she
realized that Trent lay beside her and that she was encircled
by his strong arms.

"Trent!" she whispered hoarsely. "Trent, are you awake?"

He woke at her hushed words and tightened his embrace.
Pushing her damp hair from her brow, Trent said softly,
"Welcome back to the world, little one." His voice was filled
with emotion. "You had us worried! How do you feel?"

"I am tired. W-what happened? I don't remember much."

"I shall tell you all about it after you are better, *ma* sweet!
Right now I am going to call Jason and have him bring down a
tray. You need to eat. And I have a crew that will mutiny if I

don't have good news about you soon!" Trent declared. "You don't know how important you have become to us all!"

"How long have I been asleep?" Amber asked.

"Asleep! You have been unconscious for damn near five days! *Mon Dieu,* Amber, we thought you were going to die! You had no business coming on deck in the midst of a battle! Do you not know—"

"Please, Trent, don't yell at me. I cannot bear it. If you should hate me for . . . well, for . . ." She choked on the words.

"Hate you! *Mon Dieu,* Amber, how could I ever hate you? I am sorry, *ma* sweet, I should not have yelled. But I have been so worried about you!"

"You have?" Amber asked in genuine surprise.

"Well, of course! We all have been, Jason, Fitz, Drake— the whole crew."

"Oh!" Amber was disappointed in his reply. She was glad that the crew cared enough for her to worry about her, but she had wanted Trent to express a more personal concern. "Are Jason and Fitz all right?" she asked. "And how about Drake? I do not recall seeing them at the last."

"They are all fine," Trent assured her. "I lost quite a few men, but we are getting back to order. The ship will have to have repairs when we reach the islands. Right now we are just limping along, but we will be all right. We are only about a day out from land."

"And you, Trent, are you all right? I th-thought you were dead!" Tears welled up in her beautiful eyes. "But you are alive!" she breathed.

Trent chuckled. "Yes, I am very much alive, as you can see. It is amusing, though."

"What is?" Amber asked indignantly. "I certainly see nothing amusing. We could all have been killed!"

"I did not mean that the danger was amusing. I simply meant that it was amusing that you should worry about me being alive. After all the times you have vowed to kill me, when there was a real chance of my death, you stepped in and saved my life. Not once, but twice! Oh, Amber, I shall never understand you, never!" Laughing softly, Trent pulled her closer in his embrace and tenderly kissed her.

A moment later Trent started to rise from the bed, but Amber stopped him in panic. "Where are you going?" she asked anxiously.

"I am only going for Jason. You need food, little one. I shall not be gone very long," he promised. "Now rest until I return."

"No! Please do not leave me! Please, Trent!" Amber pleaded as she clung tightly to him. Her tears spilled over, and he knew that it was from her physical weakness. Attempting to compose herself, Amber looked up at Trent, her eyes soft and imploring and her lips trembling. "Please, I'm not hungry!"

Trent settled back in the bed and drew Amber close. "I'll not leave you, Amber, although you have not eaten for days and you have no strength. But Jason will no doubt come in soon and until then, *ma* sweet, you must rest. Never fear, I shall not leave you." He was glad she wanted him with her, glad that she needed him. She was still weak from her ordeal and soon fell asleep.

When Jason made his appearance Trent told him that Amber's fever had broken, that she had awakened, and that she had talked with him. He asked Jason to bring some broth and tea so that it would be there when next Amber awakened. With a wide grin and a fervent "Thanks be to me Lord!" Jason went in search of the others to tell them the good news and to prepare food for Amber.

On the following day they dropped anchor at a small island in the Azores and began making the badly needed repairs on the *Mér Fleur*. Although the crew had made emergency repairs following the battle, there were major repairs that could only be done in port.

Trent spent his time working on the ship and seeing after Amber. He made a few trips to the island but was never gone for long.

After two days Amber had regained much of her strength and was growing tired of the cabin. She wanted to go on deck and breathe the bracing sea air and feel the warmth of the sun. She wanted to visit with the crew, none of whom had been allowed in the cabin except Fitz and Jason.

But Trent was being cautious and told Amber to remain in

the cabin for at least another day. Although she was greatly disappointed, she did as she was told. "It is for your own good, little one," Trent had said.

The next morning, shortly after LeBlanc had left the cabin, Amber arose and ate her breakfast from the tray Jason had left for her. She dressed herself in a shirt and breeches belonging to Trent. They were far too big for her, but that didn't bother her in the least. She rolled up the shirt sleeves and breeches legs and emerged from the cabin.

Trent looked down from the bridge and saw Amber gingerly crossing the lower deck, and placing his hands on his hips he shook his head and smiled.

"Good morning, Miss Kensington!" he called cheerfully. "I see that you have disobeyed the Captain's orders. I also detect that you have not yet regained your sea legs." He chuckled as she looked back at him impudently.

Imitating Trent's stance and pretending shyness Amber replied, "Begging your pardon, sir, but unless I misunderstood the Captain yesterday, he said I was to remain in that awful cabin for only one more day. And since there are only twenty-four hours in a day, my time of confinement is ended." Then she flashed him a coy smile and curtseyed politely.

"I see that there is no arguing with you, *Mademoiselle*, therefore I stand corrected." With a suave bow Trent added, "I now invite you to join me on the bridge." Extending his hand, he assisted Amber to the bridge.

She spent the entire morning on deck, happy and thankful to be alive. She missed a few familiar faces and was saddened by the knowledge that those men had been killed in the pirate attack. She had come to know and to like all the men and shed tears at their fate.

Later in the day Trent told Amber that he must go to the island and that he would return in a few hours. She watched as the longboat pulled away from the *Mér Fleur* and wished that she could have gone with them. But Trent had said "no" when she had asked him if she might go.

She turned from the rail as Jason hailed her. "The Cap'n, 'e says ye mighten want to 'ave a bath, missy. 'E laid out a shirt fer ye an' I washed yer breeches real nice an' clean," Jason informed her. "An' the men, they be takin' the tub down fer ye. Ye be needin' anythin' more, ye jest let ol' Jason know, missy, an' 'e'll see to it fer ye."

Amber thanked Jason and returned to the cabin and waited for the men to bring the tub. When they brought it, Fitz brought buckets of warm water and poured it into the wooden tub.

When the men had gone, Amber stripped off her clothes and tied her hair with a piece of ribbon she had found in LeBlanc's trunk. Fetching a towel and the scented soap, Amber slid gratefully into the warm, soothing water.

Amber sat in the tub letting the warm water cleanse and relax her body. Closing her eyes, she thought of the nights before the pirate attack, the nights Trent had taken her, had made love to her. She missed being in his arms, she longed for his kisses.

And now, this very moment, she could almost feel his strong arms around her, holding her to his warm body. On the nights Trent had stayed on deck while she recovered she had lain awake, wanting him, feeling lost without him next to her. Those nights had been long and lonely, and often in her sleep she had reached out for him, only to awake disappointed that he was not there.

Amber longed for Trent and her body called for him, for his touch, for his kisses. She had long ago realized that she loved Trent and had set out to show her love, to be a "true woman" and to win his love. But her plans had been interrupted. Now that her health was improving she was ready to fight again, only this time the battle would be for love.

"Oh, Trent," she whispered, "how very much I love you!"

Amber finished her bath and, stepping from the wooden tub, she reached for her towel. She stopped short, her heart pounding. Although her back was to the door she knew that Trent was there. She could sense his presence, and she turned to face him. He stood leaning casually against the door, a smile on his face. Straightening, he walked slowly toward Amber, his body aching for her.

Trent reached out and touched her cheek, his eyes burning into hers. She made no move to cover herself, just stood looking at him. There was something happening between them in that moment, and they were both aware of it. A spark leaped from one to the other and the fire began to rage.

Trent's blue eyes were gentle, they held Amber spellbound and helpless. Then his gaze swept over her comprehensively. And now she was sure! She wanted his arms around her, his body loving hers. She wanted his lips on hers and she knew that he wanted it, too. Amber took a long, quivering breath, knowing what would happen next. Her very soul cried out for Trent to take her.

"How proud and beautiful you are," Trent spoke in a low voice that had difficulty coming out. He rested his hand momentarily on Amber's head, then pulled the ribbon from her hair letting it fall free about her shoulders. He lovingly stroked the fine, silky curls, and Amber felt her knees weakening.

"Amber, I mean to have you! Here! Now!" Trent's voice was husky with emotion. He leaned down and brushed his lips across her cheek, then, slipping his fingers through her hair, he pulled her face up to meet his.

"Put your arms around me," Trent whispered hoarsely. His breath was coming fast and raggedly, and she felt it hot against her brow. Amber felt a tremor pass through his body as he crushed her against him.

"Do as I say, Amber, and do not be foolish this time. You will see that it is right." Trent's voice was passionate. "Now, at this moment, you want me as much as I want you. Tell me, Amber, tell me that you do!" he urged.

Amber knew that he was right, knew that there was only one thing for her to do. Willingly she put her arms around his neck and raised her lips to his. Trent's lips came down to cover hers and she welcomed his kiss. He kissed her wildly, wantonly, and the excitement welled up from deep inside him. Amber's fingers dug deep into Trent's shoulders as she pulled him closer to her. She felt as if she could not get close enough, she wanted more.

Trent responded to her touch. Her sudden, unexpected passion made his need even stronger, her clinging grip had a powerful effect on his own passion. Running his skillful hand over Amber's swelling breasts, Trent felt her shiver at his touch, and her kisses became more demanding. His hand was like fire on her cool skin, and Amber molded her body to his, a soft, sweet moan rising in her throat. He knew she felt the same aching he did, felt the same hunger.

Stepping back away from Amber, Trent looked at her beauty. Her cheeks were flushed, and the look in her green eyes was that of passion. Trent's heart leaped in his breast, and the stirring in his body was somehow different. This lovely creature wanted him. He had waited so long for her to want him in the same way that he desired her. And now she did! He could not believe it!

Again Trent crushed Amber against the length of his hard body. This time he kissed her deeper and with more meaning. Her lips were tender and yielding. After a moment, Trent spoke in a soft low tone and said, "Now you will learn the fine art of making love. You will learn how to please a man, me! And the pleasure will be all mine. *Mon Dieu*, Amber, how I have waited for this!"

Trent felt the fire in his body and the aching in his loins. He tasted the sweetness of Amber's mouth and felt the warmth of her body. And in that moment, in the fever of his passion, Trent knew that none would ever compare with Amber. Never had he desired any woman so much.

He kissed her with a passion that made her dizzy and took her breath away. Amber clung to him and he picked her up, still kissing her, and carried her to the bed. Then Trent removed his boots and shed his breeches and shirt, standing naked before her. Amber took in the sight of him, his tall, straight frame, his bronze skin, the broad shoulders, the dark mat of soft black hair that ran across his chest and down his smooth, flat stomach and rested at his manhood. Amber stared at Trent's naked body, amazed at the sight of him. He was indeed exciting and seductive. He was a magnificent creature.

She felt the sweet yearning in her body, the yearning a woman feels for the man she loves. Trent drew nearer and Amber held out her arms to him. She reached up and pulled him to her. He saw her moisten her lips slowly with the tip of her tongue and she parted her lips as Trent took them with his. She pressed her slim, shapely body to his as she drew him down on her.

Her heart and body were ready to accept him. She was ready to love him. With her eager hands on Trent's body,

Amber shyly explored his searing flesh with virgin knowledge as Trent's skillful hands guided hers. She yearned to know all and was overwhelmed at the power of her caresses as he responded to them. And when she had yielded all, her body beckoned his.

Amber felt Trent's lips warm and gentle as they moved over her whole body. They found their way to the firm soft mounds of her breasts and his tongue flicked over the tender nipples, teasing her, leading her deeper and deeper into a passion she never knew existed. His hands ran along her body causing every nerve to cry out for more. Her body was burning with passion and desire and she wanted him. Wanted all of him!

"Trent!" Amber breathed. "I want you. Please, I want you now!" She looked up into his handsome face. There was a smile playing about his lips, his eyes were anxious but he was biding his time.

"All in due time, little one, in due time," he told her as he kissed her cheek lightly and whispered against her throat so low that she almost did not hear the words. "I want no other man with you, ever!"

Amber's passion was at its height and her pulse quickened as Trent's embrace tightened, pressing her close to him, and his hot flesh burned against hers. Again his lips took hers, and each drank the sweetness of the other. His hands again roamed over her body, and he fondled each breast until its rosy crest became taut and erect.

Trent positioned Amber beneath his ready body, her new-found passion luring him on. Their bodies were wet and fire raged within them. He kissed her fevered skin and sought her smooth lean thighs. Trent devoured Amber with his mouth, his body, and his passion. Raising her hips to meet his, she moved rhythmically with him.

And the sweet warmth of surrender engulfed Amber, and she found the pleasure of bathing in the waves of passion as Trent slowly and tenderly took her to the peak of ecstasy.

When the storm of passion had calmed, Trent lay relaxed on her and Amber ran her fingers along his back and kissed his cheek. They clung to each other, their breathing hard; unwillingly they returned to reality. Trent looked down at her and she parted her lips to speak, but he covered them with his hand.

"The desire I have for you is unsettling," he told her in a hushed voice. "And with your desire matching mine . . ." Trent broke off, shaking his head. Amber lay quietly listening and after a moment he continued. "I knew you would be like this. It has been torment! Knowing that there was so much passion in you and you not letting it out. *Mon Dieu*, what torture!"

Rolling away from her, Trent lay back on the bed lacing his fingers behind his head, his eyes closed.

"Trent?" Amber spoke just above a whisper. "Trent?" she said again, but there was no answer. He lay still and silent. What was he thinking about? she wondered. She felt unsure about it all. She had responded to him, loved him, and now she wondered if she had been wrong. Her eyes burned with threatening tears while she lay still, afraid to move, her mind asking questions.

Amber knew that she loved this man who lay beside her with a love that she had been afraid to face. And she had desired him as much as he had lusted for her, only Trent had been truthful about it! But Amber? She had been too proud to admit to herself that she could lust after Trent, or any man!

Trent raised up, resting his weight on his elbow, and with his chin cupped in his hand he stared at Amber. Her heart jumped and she blinked back the unshed tears, her chin quivering. She looked wide-eyed at Trent, and her heart ached. He was about to speak, but before the words could form on his lips she reached out and pulled him to her, burying her head on his chest.

"Love me, Trent!" she whispered brokenly. "If you can't love me, then use me! I do not care!" Her breath was hot against his flesh, and she raised her mouth to his. This time Amber was the persuader, it was she who demanded.

Trent's entire being stirred, and the fire in his loins was rekindled and rose to Amber's demands. Her touch was soft and smooth as her fingers ran down along his ribs to his stomach, and he shuddered as a fiery twinge spread along his belly to his manhood arousing him to his full extent.

And the flames of passion blazed once more.

* * *

Amber paced the deck of the *Mér Fleur,* her mind in a turmoil. She had not been herself for days and it bothered her. She had lost her temper with Trent several times and on occasion had found herself trying to start a fight with him.

And Trent had been different since the battle with the pirates and her fight for her own life. He was still the proud, arrogant man at whose feet she had fallen on the London street many weeks ago. But he was kinder and more gentle with her, and had been from the time she had begun to share his bed willingly. Their lovemaking had been all that one could ask for.

On many mornings Amber had awakened with a queasy stomach and felt too sick to get out of bed. Then upon rising she had been nauseous and, most times, to the point of vomiting. At first she could not understand this and wondered why she should become seasick after so many weeks at sea when she had not been so at the outset of the voyage.

Something was definitely wrong, Amber told herself as she paced the wooden planking of the deck. She tried to remember when things had started to go wrong but she could not.

Everything bothered her. It was too hot in the daytime, it was too cold at night, and the food tasted bad. She was completely miserable, and she was ashamed of herself for letting these things bother her so. Never before had she complained about them, so why now?

Once when she was especially irritable, Trent had attempted to comfort her and she had turned to scream out at him, "I am tired of being on this damned ship!" Then she had fled to the cabin in tears.

But perhaps she had been right, Amber thought. She *had* been at sea too long. It helped her feelings to know that they were now nearing Havana. At least there she would be able to go ashore. LeBlanc had not allowed her to go ashore on any of the small islands on their route from London to Havana.

"It is too dangerous," he had told her. "When we get to Havana I will take you ashore, *ma petite chatte,* and if you are good and patient until we arrive there, I will buy you clothes. Clothes that will fit you."

It had been a long time since Trent had called her *"ma*

petite chatte," Amber reflected. That brought back the memory of the time she had asked her friend, Jason, the meaning of the phrase. He had chuckled at her question, then had answered, "Well, missy, it means 'my little cat.' An' from what the Cap'n tole me, ye shure done some fightin' the night 'e brung ye to this ship. Accordin' to the Cap'n, ye wus fair a-spittin' an' a-scratchin' with all yer might." And now, Amber thought, Trent had again called her his little cat and knew she deserved it, with her attitude and temper of late.

Amber sighed and thought, I do not care about clothes, I just want to feel solid ground under my feet!

Finally Amber faced the facts and admitted that all her bad moods and sick feelings were the result of one thing! And she was scared!

Amber Lynn Kensington was with child!

Chapter Five

As the *Mér Fleur* entered the harbor in Havana, Amber became anxious. She was finally going ashore after weeks at sea. There had been a time when to visit London would have been the greatest thrill she could imagine, but since then she had been far and had seen much. She had seen islands in the Atlantic and had seen natives come to meet the ship when it stopped near their island. And now she was finally going to set foot on a new land.

Amber had dreamed of Havana and of all the things she wanted to see and do. Trent had warned her, "It is not London, Amber, and I am afraid you may be a bit disappointed. The shops are very different." But she had told him that she would not care how different they were, so long as she could visit them.

Amber stood leaning over the rail, trying to get a better view of Havana. Her cheeks were flushed with excitement, and she could hardly wait for Trent to take her ashore. But he had to supervise the unloading of the cargo, he had told her, then he would be free to accompany her. "You will not go ashore without me," he had instructed her, so she would have to be content to watch from the deck and wait for him.

"LeBlanc! LeBlanc!" a shrill voice called from the dock below, and Amber turned quickly to see a woman waving a red bandana in her hand. She was young and very pretty. Her raven black hair hung freely down her back, and Amber gaped at the way she was dressed. Her skirt came only a little below her knees and had a slit on one side that revealed her tanned thigh. The skirt was tied loosely and hung low on shapely hips. A strip of bright multicolored fabric had been wrapped around her upper body and tied across her breast, leaving her shoulders and midriff bare. "Why, she is barely covered," Amber gasped.

And as she watched, Trent leaped from the vessel to the dock and the dark-haired beauty ran forward to meet him with outstretched arms.

"Maria!" Trent greeted her and before he could say more, the girl threw her arms around him and kissed him long and passionately, rubbing her slender body against him.

Amber stiffened and gritted her teeth as a new and dangerous emotion swept through her. She watched as Trent returned the girl's kiss in what she considered to be the same display of desire. Amber had never before experienced raw jealousy, but now she did and she recognized it for what it was. Her quick temper began to smolder, and she saw that her fingers were digging into the wooden rail and wished savagely that the rail were Trent's throat!

And down on the dock below, the girl still stood close against Trent with her hands clasped loosely around his neck.

"Oh, my darling! It is good to see you! It has been too long!" Maria gushed. "How long are you to be here?"

"Only a week this time, Maria. I have to unload cargo here and reload with a cargo of tobacco and return to London. How have you been? And where is your brother?" Trent asked.

"Carlo will be here shortly. I could not wait! When I saw the *Mér Fleur* arriving, I knew that I had to be here to meet you! Oh, Trent, but I have missed you!" Maria purred as she again pushed her body close against LeBlanc.

Amber heard her words and slammed her fist hard on the rail. Why, the dirty bastard! she thought hotly. Her green eyes darkened as she watched the two. I am carrying his child, and he stands there with another woman as if I do not even exist! How dare he! How dare he do that! And with that she wheeled around and stalked back to the cabin.

Amber had stormed off without witnessing all of the scene on the dock.

Annoyed, Trent reached up and pulled Maria's arms from his neck and set her aside, none too gently. She looked up at him questioningly.

"But what is wrong, Trent? Are you not glad to see Maria? You forget the times we have been together?" This was a Trent she did not understand.

"I am sorry, Maria. I have no wish to hurt you, but you must know. I am not the same Trent LeBlanc. There have been some changes. I am not the same man who was anxious to bed you. There is a woman who belongs only to me, and I shall keep her with me always. She is here with me now, aboard my ship, and I need none other," Trent explained matter-of-factly.

Maria heard but could not believe. Captain Trent LeBlanc had long been known for his reputation with women. None had ever so much as dented his heart, and it had been said that LeBlanc would never belong to only one woman!

"Do not tease Maria," the girl cooed, believing him to be jesting. She stepped close to him and raised both arms to encircle his neck, but Trent caught her wrists and pushed her to one side.

"No, Maria, I speak the truth. Let us not invite attention. I have work to do." Trent's words were deliberate, his voice cold.

"But, Trent," she insisted, "why could it not have been Maria? I would go with you. I would stay with you on your ship. It is not too late, Maria knows how to please you!"

"But it *is* too late, Maria!" Trent was becoming irritated. "I have the one woman for me, the only one I shall ever desire. And she is truly the only woman who has ever pleased me! Do you not know, Maria, that had I wanted a woman like you," he laughed unpleasantly, "there are many in every port. Now we are done with the subject!" And with that Trent strode off to direct the unloading of his cargo, leaving an unbelieving Maria staring after him.

Waiting long enough to make certain that Trent was absorbed in his work, Maria decided to take matters in her

own hands. She had not believed Trent's story and, determined to find out for herself, she walked up the gangplank to
the deck of the *Mér Fleur*.

This was not her first time aboard the ship, and she knew
her way to Trent's cabin. On the way there she wondered
what she would say or do, just in case he had told her the
truth and there was a woman there. Oh, well, she thought, I'll
think of something, if I have to.

She stopped at the door to Trent's cabin to decide whether
or not to knock on the door. Rejecting the idea of knocking,
she quickly opened the door.

Amber was sitting on the bunk leafing aimlessly through
one of LeBlanc's books, and when the door opened she
looked up expectantly, thinking it to be Trent. She stared at
the intruder without a word.

Maria returned the stare in utter disbelief. It was true! But
perhaps it would be possible to put an end to his involvement
with this pretty copper-haired girl if she could plant some
seeds of doubt in her mind about LeBlanc, let her know that
he had other women, tell her that he was fickle.

"Oh, please forgive the intrusion." Maria smiled sweetly.
"Trent told me that he had a passenger on this trip. I am
Maria, Trent's woman." Then she walked over to the desk,
pulled out a drawer and took out a bottle of Trent's brandy
and a snifter. She poured herself a drink and settled comfort-
ably in Trent's chair. As she lifted her drink to her lips she
said, as an afterthought, "Oh, would you like a brandy? Trent
would be furious if he thought I had neglected a guest."

So that's what I am, a guest! Amber thought angrily.

Amber had not spoken a word since Maria had entered but
had watched the girl move about the cabin with familiarity.
Now Amber answered the question with a brief "no!" She
was trying to suppress her anger.

"So you are going to Bermuda," Maria said. "I have never
been there, but I am told that it is a lovely place." She paused
for a sip of brandy, giving Amber opportunity to speak, and
Amber said nothing but thought to herself, Bermuda, huh! So
that's what Trent told her!

Maria tried again. "It must be an awful inconvenience for
Trent to have to carry a passenger. You know, the *Mér Fleur*

is a cargo ship and is not at all suitable for passengers. Poor Trent!" She stopped and took another sip of brandy, but Amber remained silent. Poor Trent, indeed, she was thinking. Just wait until "poor Trent" returns!

"Poor darling!" Maria purred. "It must be terribly hard on him to share Drake's cabin while you are aboard." Still nothing from Amber. "But as he told me, 'Maria, do not be disturbed about it. It will be for only a little longer.'" She drained her glass and Amber found herself thinking, I hope you strangle on "poor Trent's" brandy, you black-haired bitch!

When Amber continued to remain silent, her narrowed green eyes fixed on the trespasser, Maria began to feel uncomfortable and rose hurriedly.

"If you will excuse me, I think I will wait for Trent on deck. You need not come with me, I know my way," Maria said, crossing the cabin. Stopping in the doorway, she looked over her bare shoulder and fired her parting shot, "I do hope you will have a pleasant voyage. And I'm sure that your husband will be happy to have you with him again." The door closed quickly behind her.

Unaware that Amber had seen him with Maria or that Maria had been aboard the *Mér Fleur*, LeBlanc went about his work of supervising the unloading of his cargo, spoke with various traders about shipments, and attended to his business matters. Finishing up with his affairs for the day, Trent hurried back to Amber so that he could take her ashore as he had promised.

As he entered his cabin, Amber was standing by the desk and she whirled around and hurled a book at him. Her aim was poor, and the book hit the wall with a bang, falling to the floor with fluttering pages.

"How dare you!" Amber spat. "You whoring bastard! I despise you, Trent LeBlanc!" Her green eyes flamed as she stared at him.

Trent stood with mouth agape. What in hell is wrong with her now? he thought. What have I done this time? Why is she so angry—oh, no! Maria! She saw me with Maria!

"Amber, what the hell is wrong with you?" he asked as he

started toward her. But Amber picked up Maria's brandy
snifter and sailed it across the room. Trent ducked as it soared
over his head and shattered against the door.

Laughing softly to himself, Trent thought, Why, she is
jealous! And he took another step in her direction.

"Stay away from me! Do not touch me, you—you wom-
anizer!"

"In God's name, woman, are you mad?" Trent shouted.

"Yes! Yes, I am mad, but not in the way you are thinking!"
Amber shouted back. Her fists were clenched at her sides,
sparks leaping in her eyes, and her lovely face had darkened
with an angry scowl.

Trent smiled disarmingly and said in amusement, "Why,
Amber, you are jealous! *Ma petite chatte* is jealous!" He
chuckled at her evident frustration.

"Jealous! I am not jealous, and I am not your *petite ch*——
whatever it is! Do not call me that, ever again!" she rasped.
"I am not your anything! Oh, I am sure that all of your
women praise you and your lovemaking. I am sure that they
all fall at your feet! Well, I, sir, will not!"

"But you have fallen at my feet, and on more than one
occasion, do you not remember? And you *are 'ma petite
chatte,'* and I shall call you that as often as I like. As for being
jealous, little one, you are just that—jealous! But I must say
it becomes you, Amber," Trent said with a devilish grin.

"Why, you arrogant bastard! Damn you! You detestable—"

But Trent had gripped her shoulders with both hands, and
his fingers bit into her flesh as his frosty glare held her. He
spoke with deadly calm.

"Your wrath is most unladylike, Amber! Were you not
reared as a gentle-bred woman! You are a willful and
stubborn young beauty, you have a nasty temper and a
vicious tongue. And you have the audacity to call *me* names!"

Trent's blue eyes smoldered warningly as he continued.
"Oh, you are the one to be calling names, *ma petite chatte!* I
must say you are sorely vexing me!" Dropping his hands from
her shoulders, Trent swatted Amber's backside gently but
firmly and walked away.

Trent went to his trunk and pulled out clean shirt and
breeches, then began to undress. Amber stood where he left

her, seething inwardly. She vowed to herself that this was not the end of the matter, but restrained her anger.

Oh, no! This is not finished, she mused to herself. She would not be made a fool, she would not be abused, not again! If Trent thought her a fool he would surely learn differently. And he could have all the whores in Havana and elsewhere, she thought as she dropped wearily to the bed, for she would not be there to know about them.

Why had she ever thought she could possibly hold a man like LeBlanc? her thoughts ran on. What a foolish dream! And now she carried Trent's child, and if he did not love her, then he would not want her child, his bastard child! Suddenly she felt that she must talk to someone, but who would understand? There was no one, she must bear this alone!

"Amber! Do you hear? I asked if you were ready to go ashore!"

Amber had heard Trent's words, but she had no wish to go anywhere. She wanted to be alone. Her heart was breaking, she wanted to cry.

"I am not going. I think it would be best if I stayed here since I do not feel well, Trent. You go, I will be all right here," she told him.

"Not well enough to go ashore? When all you have talked of for days is getting off the ship, of setting foot on solid ground!" Trent said in surprise. "Really, Amber, I do wish you would make up your mind!"

When Amber made no reply, Trent added, "You were feeling fine a short time ago, and downright energetic, it seemed to me!" He grinned as he remembered her attack on him.

"I said I do not feel well and I choose to stay here for now," she snapped. "You will be going ashore again, will you not? I shall go another time."

"As you wish, *Mademoiselle!*" And with a sweeping bow, Trent left her.

Amber turned and burying her head in the pillow she began to cry. She had been swept from the London street like a piece of discarded rubbish, had been placed on a ship bound for unknown regions and imprisoned by a madman. And, as if her situation were not bad enough, she had fallen in love with that man and was now carrying his child!

If only he cared for me just a little, Amber thought, sighing heavily. But he does not. He has only used me for his own pleasure and will no doubt cast me aside when he tires of me. And he has already told Maria it will be for only a little longer. He has told Maria not to be disturbed about it!

Amber cried out in desperation, "Only a little longer for you, Trent LeBlanc, but it will be a lifetime for me! I love you! I need and want you! I will never love another! Oh, dear God, my child will never know his father!"

"Missy?" Jason's voice startled her and she sat upright on the bunk. He was standing in the middle of the room. "'Scuse me, missy, but I heered ye cryin' an' I knocked on yer door, only ye didn't heer me." The kindly old man came over and sat down on the edge of the bunk. He reached out and placed his hand over Amber's. "Ye be talkin' out loud, missy. Kin ol' Jason help?"

"Oh, Jason! What am I to do? Please help me! I must get back to London, get back home! My family, they will help me. They love me and I want to go home, Jason, home!" Amber was sobbing wildly while tears streamed down her lovely face. Jason felt a great compassion for her.

"Ye love 'im, missy, I knowed it! I sees ye lookin' at 'im an' I sees lots more. Like the way the Cap'n looks at ye, an' 'e do keer! 'E jus' don't know 'ow to let ye know it. The Cap'n, 'e ain't a-tryin' to hurt ye, missy!"

"But Jason, you don't understand," Amber choked. "He does not love me! And you are right! I do love him and I can never have him, never have his love! Right now he is with another woman—do not look at me like that, Jason. It is true. She was here to meet him when the *Mér Fleur* docked. I saw them . . . saw her run into his arms and kiss—oh, Jason! It hurt to see him in another woman's arms and that is where he is now! In her arms!" Amber wailed, breaking into tears again. She laid her head on Jason's shoulder and sobbed brokenly.

"No, missy, I don't think the Cap'n be with no other woman. 'E 'as ye an' 'e ain't a-goin' to no other woman with ye 'ere! Ye be diffrunt, ye be a real lady an' the Cap'n, 'e ain't a-wantin' none o' them wenches on shore, not with ye to come back to!"

Always before, when they were nearing port, LeBlanc had given Jason instructions to procure a woman for him during their stay. In Havana, it had been Maria as first choice and, if she were not available, a wench called Isabella. But this time Trent had not so much as mentioned a woman, and Jason felt that he knew why. He knew his Captain well, knew that if he would admit it, LeBlanc was falling in love with the missy! But he also knew that Trent was too stubborn to acknowledge that he loved anyone. He had boasted that he would never belong to one woman. And now this beautiful young woman was very much in love with his Captain, Jason thought, loved him the way no other ever could. And when he had entered the cabin he had heard Amber mention a child!

"Missy?" Jason called softly. "Do the Cap'n know 'bout the babe? Do 'e know ye be nourishin' 'is seed?" he questioned.

"Oh, no! And, Jason, you are not to tell him! Promise me, Jason! You must promise that you will not tell him! He must not know! He will never love me, not even if he knew about the child. He would never want a—bastard child! This must be our secret, Jason, mine and yours alone. Please, you must swear to me that Trent nor anyone will ever know. Swear it, Jason!" Amber begged as she stared at him, wide-eyed and frightened.

Even though Jason believed that Trent would want to know, he had no wish to cause Amber more pain. She had been through enough. "My child will never know his father," Jason had heard her cry aloud in anguish.

"Jason! Promise me!" Amber demanded after moments had passed and he had not given her his word that he would remain silent about the child.

"'Tain't right, missy," Jason replied doubtfully. "A man 'as the right to know 'e 'as a child. The Cap'n, 'e orta know, an' 'e'll be right mad if'n 'e wus to fin' out I knowed an' didn' tell 'im." He paused for a moment, then went on. "But I won't, if'n that be what ye want. Ol' Jason, 'e won't tell, missy!" he promised Amber. "Now, ye jus' lay 'ere an' git some rest. I be back to see 'bout ye in a bit. There be sumpin' I kin git ye afore I go, missy?"

"No, thank you, Jason. You are a dear! Thank you for

being here. Yes, I will rest for a while. I have a lot of thinking to do."

And Amber did. As soon as Jason left the cabin, she made up her mind that she would leave the *Mér Fleur*. She would run away and find a way back to London. She loved Trent LeBlanc, but it would be better for her to leave of her own accord before he should grow weary of her and put her off his ship.

Her decision made, Amber rose determinedly, removed her shoes from the trunk, and put them on for the first time since she had been aboard the ship. One of the heels had been broken during her flight in London, she remembered, but she thought it better to wear shoes than to be barefoot. Amber braided her beautiful red-gold hair, pinned it up, and pulled a soft blue silk scarf from the trunk to tie over her head. There were no other preparations to be made, and she started for the door.

A thought struck Amber's mind and she turned back to the desk. Seating herself in Trent's chair, she drew paper from a drawer and took the quill from the inkwell. With a heavy heart, she began to write.

> *Captain,*
>
> *I am truly sorry that I, a mere passenger, have caused you any inconvenience while aboard your ship.*
> *I shall not be going to Bermuda, as you had planned. It seems that my husband has returned to London.*
> *I have gone to book passage on the first ship leaving for London, where I will join him.*
> *And you may tell "Trent's woman," Maria, that she no longer need be disturbed—your "guest" has gone!*
>
> *Mademoiselle Kensington*

Amber placed the note on the pillow, so that Trent would be sure to find it, and left the *Mér Fleur*.

Walking along the dock, Amber questioned several seamen and dockhands in an attempt to locate a ship bound for London. Finally she boarded the vessel *Wind Bird* and asked to speak to its captain. She was taken to his quarters and introduced herself to the short, stocky man with red hair and beard. He told her that he was Captain Boyd and asked what he might do for her.

"I wish to book passage for London, sir. I was brought here against my will by the captain of the *Mér Fleur*. He abducted me in London and sailed with me on board his ship. I have no money at this time, but I am certain that if you take me back to London, my uncle will pay well, not only for my voyage, but a reward for bringing me home." Amber spoke earnestly.

The Captain sat politely listening as Amber told her story. He was studying her lovely face and expressive eyes and knew that there was character and good breeding in this young woman.

"My dear Miss Kensington," he began, "I am truly sorry that you find yourself in this situation. But there is no way that I can possibly help you. No, wait," he told Amber as she started to rise. "You see, my ship is not due to leave Havana for at least three days, at which time I will not be going directly to London. I shall have stops all along the Bahama Islands.

"Besides which, I know of Captain LeBlanc and, although he is an unusual man, I cannot believe that he would take you . . . or any other woman, for that matter . . . against her will. From what I know of him, he would never have that problem!" Captain Boyd chuckled. "Are you sure that perhaps the two of you did not have a lover's quarrel and you want to leave him?" he asked.

Amber rose to her feet. "I am sorry that I have wasted your time, sir. I shall try and find another ship on her way to London. Perhaps the captain of *that* vessel will not have heard of Captain LeBlanc's reputation and will believe my story!" she snapped hotly.

"I doubt that. Your captain is known far and wide. He is a man that many fear, all respect, and most envy. And if you plan to get passage out of Havana I suggest that you do not mention that the ship upon which you were brought here was the *Mér Fleur*. There is not one ship in port that will take Trent LeBlanc's woman aboard her. Not one captain would take that responsibility without LeBlanc's knowledge and permission.

"No, miss, I would not mention that you even know LeBlanc if you wish to leave Havana on any other vessel. I know not one man that would want Captain Trent LeBlanc as an enemy! You must not truly know the man. I would as soon deal with the devil himself as to deal with his son!"

Amber knew that the redheaded man must be right. She had heard many tales about LeBlanc from Jason and the rest of his crew and knew that, although they liked him tremendously, they stood in awe of him. She remembered something Drake Monrow had told her. "LeBlanc is a man to fear, missy. He has a power in him and his eyes carry a glint of danger. His look can make the best of men uneasy. There are many who are afraid to speak to him for fear that one wrong word could cause LeBlanc to call them out at dawn!"

Back on the dock again, Amber stood uncertainly. Suppose no one would let her book passage on their vessel?

"Damn!" she hissed. "Damn you, Trent LeBlanc! I cannot get away from you even when I try!"

"Pardon us, miss, but our Cap'n, he said ya was tryin' ta fin' a ship ta London. Is that right?" a tall lanky seaman called out to Amber as she started along the dock.

Amber turned to see the skinny man and his friend coming up behind her. They were dressed in seamen's garb and seemed to be pleasant enough. The tall man smiled and bowed slightly.

"The name's Klein and this here is Fulton. The Cap'n— that is, Cap'n Boyd of the vessel *Wind Bird*—he asked us to ketch up ta ya an' ta tell ya of somebody what might be some help in gettin' ya ta London," the man Klein said.

"And who might that be, please?" asked Amber. "Where is this person?"

"His name be Dingwell, Jack Dingwell, ma'am. He can get things done when nobody else kin. An' Fulton an' me, we're offerin' ta take ya ta him. That is, miss, if'n ya want ta go see him?"

"Well, of course I do. I want to get back to London as soon as possible. Could I see this Mr. Dingwell today?" Amber was interested in the possibility.

"Sure, miss, we'll take ya ta him right now," Fulton assured her.

And they did. Unknown to Amber, Jack Dingwell was a man engaged in the business of buying and selling. And Klein and Fulton had been right when they had told her that he could get things done. Jack Dingwell bought and sold human flesh! Slaves! And the two men sold Amber Kensington to Jack Dingwell.

Amber had considered herself a prisoner on the *Mér Fleur*, but she had not known how fortunate she had been. Now she was thrown into a small bare room, hardly large enough for three people, yet there were twelve. They were all females of various ages, some were black, some were dark-skinned, and only one white, save herself. The room was filthy and smelled of sweat and human waste.

She remembered sitting outside Jack Dingwell's office while Klein and Fulton had gone in to "make arrangements." When they had come out of the office they had assured her that everything was taken care of, wished her a safe voyage, and said goodbye.

When Jack Dingwell came and stood before her he looked her over like she was a piece of merchandise, Amber recalled. He was a man of about forty years and short, fat, and bald. She found him unpleasant before he even spoke. And when he did, she knew that she disliked him immensely.

"Skinny little thing, aren't you!" he said in a flat tone, and it had been a statement, not a question. "But you've got big enough tits, and from what I can see in those clothes you are wearing, your body isn't too bad. Doris!" he yelled and a young black girl ran into the room. "Take this one to Evans and tell him to put her with the ones to be sold Friday." Turning back to Amber he snorted, "You got a name, wench?"

Amber stood shocked and unable to speak. She did not understand. She had been brought here to speak to this man about finding her a way back to London. How dare he speak to her this way. As the black girl took hold of her arm, Amber pulled away abruptly.

"How dare you speak to me in that manner, sir!" Amber stormed indignantly. But before she could say another word Dingwell had raised his plump hand and slapped her across the mouth.

Reeling and stumbling backward, Amber tasted blood in her mouth, and as she touched her fingers to her stinging lips she felt the warm wetness of her blood. She lunged at Dingwell's throat and dug her nails in. He tried to swing her off but could not.

"Evans! My God, man, get in here!" Dingwell screamed. "Evans!"

Amber had raked her nails across Dingwell's cheek and small beads of blood were appearing along the scratches. That was the last she remembered. She had felt strong hands on her, a sudden, throbbing pain in her head, then there had been blackness.

When Amber revived, she had found herself in this stinking room!

LeBlanc returned to the *Mér Fleur* after a few hours on shore and went straight to his cabin. He was very pleased with himself, having bought new clothes for Amber. He visualized how she would look in the new attire. Never had she complained about having to wear the ill-fitting garb belonging to Fitz or himself. She had been content with them, and Trent knew she would be highly pleased with his purchases. Perhaps, he thought, it would help to appease her. LeBlanc would have liked to have bought pretty dresses and slippers for Amber as he had never really seen her in feminine attire. On the night he had found her, she had been clothed in a gown, but as a result of the storm and fleeing from those two scoundrels the dress was torn, wet, muddy, and bedraggled. But knowing that he intended to keep Amber with him aboard the *Mér Fleur*, Trent realized that pretty dresses and slippers would not be proper attire for her.

So his purchases consisted of soft, black, leather knee boots, three pairs of breeches, an array of brightly colored shirts, and various personal items.

Pushing the cabin door open and with a pleased smile on his handsome face, Trent entered his quarters, his arms laden with parcels. But the smile died when he saw Jason's agitated face instead of Amber's lovely one. Jason seemed to be very disturbed about something, and he jumped to his feet as his Captain stopped abruptly, just inside the door.

"Cap'n, sir, it be the missy! 'Er be gone! I come to see if'n 'er needed anythin' and I foun' this 'ere note!" Jason said, extending the note to Trent.

Dumping his parcels onto the bunk, Trent grabbed the note and began to read. After the first few lines, he looked at Jason with a puzzled frown.

"But this does not make any sense!" he exclaimed. "What does she mean by saying that she is going back to London? Or that she will be joining her husband?" Trent shook his head as if trying to clear it. "Why, Jason? Why would Amber do this to me?"

"Mebbe ye better read the rest, Cap'n, sir. It might 'elp answer them questions ye're askin' me," Jason told him.

Returning to the note, Trent read on. Suddenly he crushed the note in his fist and with a bellowed oath he roared, *"Maria! Mon Dieu! Maria* has talked to Amber! The little bitch came on board the *Mér Fleur,* knowing that Amber was here!" He mopped his brow that had beaded with sweat and dropped heavily into his chair. "That's what this is all about, Jason. The lying bitch told Amber something which upset her enough to cause her to run away!"

Jason said nothing. He knew that it was best to let his Captain ponder the situation without interference from him. And as he watched Trent spring from his chair and pace the floor, a muscle twitching in his cheek, there was no doubt in Jason's mind that LeBlanc loved Amber, even though he would not admit it. He had been right, Jason thought, when he had assured the missy that the Captain cared for her.

"Maria means nothing to me, Jason. Nothing! Amber should know that. She must know that it is she whom I want! Not Maria, not any common whore!"

"Beggin' yer pardon, sir, but 'ave ye ever told the missy what ye be a-tellin' ol' Jason?" the man asked. "The way I sees it, mebbe ye ain't. An' Cap'n, sir, the missy, 'er tole me— Ye know, Cap'n, if'n that Maria comed 'ere an' seen the missy, then 'er musta tole 'er sumpin' real bad to upset 'er this a-way." Jason had broken off as he remembered his promise to Amber not to reveal to anyone that she was with child.

"From this note, I would say that Maria said plenty," Trent replied as he smoothed out the crumpled paper and reread it, studying each line. "'A mere passenger' . . . 'your guest' . . . 'Trent's woman,'" he read aloud, and suddenly it all fell into place. *"Mon Dieu,* Jason, I think I have it! Maria must have made Amber think that I told her that Amber was a guest, a passenger. And 'Trent's woman, Maria,' must mean that she told Amber that she, Maria, was my woman!" As he met Jason's eyes, Trent remembered that the old man had been about to say something that Amber had told him but had broken off and spoken of Maria, instead.

"What were you going to say, Jason? When you said that Amber had told you, and then you stopped and said something else. Now what did Amber tell you, man? Come, if you know anything about this, out with it! It may help to find Amber!" Trent's words were more command than request.

When Jason did not answer, Trent stood looking at him with narrowed eyes. "Jason! I have asked you a question and you are to answer! That is an order!"

"But, Cap'n, sir! The missy, 'er made me swear! I be a-goin' a-gin' 'er wish if'n I tell—Cap'n, I be a-goin' back on me word if'n I do!" Jason pleaded.

"Blast it, Jason! I am your Captain and I have given you an order! Do not stand there with knowledge that could help me with this problem and not tell it to me! Now, Amber could be in trouble and need our help. You know the danger of a lady out alone in a place like this. Now, for the last time, Jason, tell me what you know!" LeBlanc was not to be denied and Jason was aware of it.

"Aye, Cap'n," Jason began reluctantly. "Ye see, sir, I come to see if 'er wanted anythin' an' when I got to the door, I heered the missy a-cryin'. An' I knocked on the door, only 'er did'n' 'ear it. Sos I opens the door an' comes in 'cause 'er wus a-cryin' sumpin' awful an' 'er wus a-talkin', Cap'n. 'Er wus a-talkin' right out loud an' nobody 'ere but 'erself." Jason hestitated, unwilling to betray Amber's confidence, but knowing LeBlanc's wrath when his orders were not obeyed, he took a deep breath and went on.

"Well, Cap'n, sir, what I heered 'er say, wus—Cap'n, sir, ol' Jason, sir, 'e did promise the missy 'e wouldn' say it to nobody, least of all to ye, Cap'n!" Jason shifted uneasily from one foot to the other, staring at the floor.

LeBlanc had waited long enough and he exploded. "Damn your eyes, Jason! *Mon Dieu,* what in hell did she say?" In his exasperation, Trent grabbed the old man by the shoulders and shook him. Jason's head rolled from side to side and he realized that Trent would make him tell, or else!

"Aye, Cap'n, sir!" Jason blurted as LeBlanc released him. "Ol' Jason'll tell ye, sir!" He stopped and gulped, then went on. "The missy, 'er said 'er wanted to go home, sir. 'Er said 'er family, they loved 'er. 'Er said 'er family'd 'elp 'er. An' then—an' then 'er said—" Jason paused but LeBlanc impatiently demanded that he continue. "Cap'n, 'er 'ad seed ye an' Maria on the dock an' 'er wus a'kissin' ye. An' 'er said ye wus in another woman's arms, right then, an' Cap'n, 'er said, 'My child will never know 'is father,' that's what 'er said!" Jason had finally divulged all he knew.

"*Mon Dieu!*" LeBlanc cried out with great emotion. "*Mon Dieu,* Jason. My suspicions are confirmed! Amber is with child, *my* child!" He sank to the bed as if suddenly his knees had given way and stared into space. Abruptly, he leaped to his feet and grabbed Jason, whirling him around and patting the old man on the shoulder. "*Mon Dieu,* I am to be a father, Jason! *Me! Trent LeBlanc! A father! Mon Dieu!*"

And just as suddenly he realized that Amber was missing and that he may never again see her! That possibility sobered him, and he looked at Jason with a plea in his blue eyes. "Help me find her, Jason. She cannot be far. No vessel is due to sail before three days." But the look in Jason's eyes stopped his flow of words. "What is it, Jason? What are you thinking?"

"Well, 'er left, Cap'n, 'cause 'er said ye did'n' keer 'bout 'er," Jason said sadly. "'Er said ye'd not want a bastard child."

"What? A bastard child? What does she mean? He'd be no bastard child! I am his father!" LeBlanc was indignant.

"But, Cap'n, the missy, ye ain't wed to 'er! That be what 'er meant. An' the babe, 'e would'n 'ave yer name, sir!" Jason explained.

"Oh!" LeBlanc said, lamely.

Jason decided that this was as good a time as any to probe the depths of his Captain's feelings for the missy.

"Then, Cap'n Trent, sir, do ye really keer fer the little missy?" he asked anxiously.

"Care for her! *Mon Dieu,* Jason! She owns my very soul!" Trent said with feeling. But it was not the answer the old man wanted. He had not said that he loved Amber, he could not admit to *loving* anyone!

"But Cap'n, 'er be gone. What if'n ye can't find 'er?"

"I will find her, Jason!" Trent declared as he started for the
door. "I will find her, never fear." He looked back over his
shoulder at the faithful old man who followed him. "If it takes
a lifetime, damn it, I will find her!" LeBlanc spoke fervently.

Havana was crawling with LeBlanc's men. The entire town
stirred with the news that LeBlanc's woman was missing.
LeBlanc had sworn to tear the city apart until he found her,
the word spread, and those who knew the man were certain
that he would do so. They devoutly hoped that he would find
her soon.

No man spoke to Trent unless he had something to report.
LeBlanc's rage was worse than any had ever known it. It had
been two days since he had last seen Amber, and with each
day, Trent's concern for her welfare increased.

Captain Boyd came to Trent and related how Amber had
visited him and asked passage to London aboard the *Wind
Bird.* He told how he had refused her request without both
LeBlanc's knowledge and permission and that he had informed Amber that no other ship's captain would give her
passage if it were known that she belonged to Trent LeBlanc.
Captain Boyd knew LeBlanc's reputation and took no gamble
that LeBlanc would learn that Amber had been aboard the
Wind Bird and come looking for Boyd.

"Thank you, Boyd," Trent said, rising to his feet. "I am
truly glad that you came to me with this information. Miss
Kensington is a very headstrong young lady. She was much
distressed when she left the *Mér Fleur,* but I believed that she
would return when her anger had subsided. Then, when she
did not—well, I can only conclude that harm has come to
her." Although LeBlanc seemed outwardly calm, there was a
sharpness in his voice. "I have posted a reward for any
information that might be helpful in finding her or to the one
who returns her to me."

"But I will accept no reward for what I have been able to
tell you, LeBlanc. I have been no help in locating the lady,
only to report that I did speak to her. And that was two days
ago." Boyd was very much in earnest. "I am only willing to
help you find your woman. Pretty little thing, she is. Of a
truth, I can see why she is so important to you. Anything that

I can do, I will." And Boyd, too, rose to his feet. He extended his hand to LeBlanc, who shook it warmly.

"Again, I thank you," Trent said as the two men walked to the door. Stepping into the passageway, they saw Jason running toward them.

"Cap'n Trent, sir," Jason called, "there be a young man 'ere, 'e says 'e knows where the missy be! 'E won't talk to nobody 'ceptin' ye, sir!"

"Where is he, Jason? Bring him to my quarters at once!" LeBlanc turned to Captain Boyd and again shook his hand and thanked him.

When the knock came at the door, Trent prepared himself for yet another false trail. Ever since he had posted the reward there had been a stream of seamen, beggars, and waterfront doxies with "information" as to where the copper-haired beauty had been seen or where she might be found. None of them had solid information, but they were hoping for a portion of the reward. The few leads that had seemed possibly legitimate had proved to be futile.

"Come in!" LeBlanc called as he seated himself behind his desk.

A young man entered. He was of medium height, his complexion a tanned bronze, and his blue-gray eyes searched LeBlanc's face nervously.

"You wish to speak to me?" Trent's words seemed harsh, and the boy became uneasy. He had heard stories about the feared and infamous Captain LeBlanc, and the tales were many. And the tale that was uppermost in the mind of the lad was that LeBlanc was "the devil's own son," and now that he stood face to face with LeBlanc, he was certain that all the stories were true.

This was indeed a strong and powerful man, a man with authority, and the boy reached up and respectfully removed his dirty cap releasing a mane of sooty-black hair which fell onto a broad, intelligent brow.

The newcomer stood nervously twisting his cap in his hand. Finally he took a long, uneven breath and spoke.

"Captain LeBlanc, sir, I know where your lady is. If it is the same lady, and I believe that it is. No one have I seen more beautiful, sir." The words were simple but sincere.

"You say that you know where this woman is? And that

you believe her to be the same woman that I seek?" LeBlanc questioned.

"Yes, sir, I know where the lady is and, as I have told you, sir, I believe her to be the same lady," the lad assured Trent.

"You refer to her as 'lady' when I said 'woman,'" Trent remarked. Leaning back in his chair he placed his booted feet on the desk and thoughtfully regarded the young man.

"I refer to her as a lady, sir, because that is what she is. She is not like the usual women he gets."

Trent's feet met the floor as he sat forward in his chair, his blue eyes burning into the boy's clear eyes. "Like *who* gets?" he demanded.

"Jack Dingwell, sir. The lady was sold to him two days ago. You see, sir, I work for him, although it is not of my choosing. I was given to him by my uncle when he sailed to France three years back because he did not have the means to take me with him. So I work for Jack Dingwell for my keep, sir, and that is where I saw the lady. She is sick—well, not really sick, sir. She had been knocked on the head and hard, by Evans. He is one of Dingwell's men. When she learned that she had been sold, the lady attacked Dingwell and tried to get away. That is when Evans hit her, knocked her out cold. Then when the lady fell on the floor, Evans, he—" The boy's words faltered.

"He *what?* Tell me, boy!" Trent was now standing impatiently. His coolness was completely gone as he waited for the young man to say more. *"What?"*

"Well, sir, Evans, he's a mean man. He kicked the lady when she fell and he bruised her ribs. When she did not come around, he jerked her up and slapped her across the face. He busted her lip and left a bruise on her cheek. Sir," the boy said feelingly, shaking his head. "Sir, he didn't have to do that!"

Trent was furious. If the "lady" proved to be Amber, he would kill Jack Dingwell, and this man, Evans, he would take care of in his own way, Trent swore to himself. Amber had suffered enough without this.

"Can you describe the lady?" LeBlanc asked.

"She is beautiful, sir, with long copper-colored hair and eyes as green as the brightest emeralds. Her skin is a tawny tan and smooth as the finest silk. You see, sir, I took care of her until they came and threw her in that room. And she was still unconscious, sir, when they took her away. That's where she is now, sir, and all this time . . . she is hurt and sick. Evans, he would not even let me bring her food. And today, sir, the lady goes on the block at the private auction, at noon. I would have come sooner, sir, only I did not know who she was. But when I saw the notice that you posted, I came straight here!"

From the description of "the lady" Trent felt almost certain that it was Amber of whom the boy spoke. But so that there would be no doubt in his mind, he asked, "What was the lady wearing? The color of her dress, her shoes?"

"She was not wearing a dress, sir," the boy replied. "She was dressed in tan breeches and a man's shirt, both were too big for her. And her shoes were made of satin but they were stained and a heel was broken off one."

"Amber! *Mon Dieu!* It *is* Amber, there is no doubt!" Trent was at the door in a flash and opening it he yelled, "Jason!" There was no need to call a second time for Jason was already at the door.

"Aye, sir," he replied anxiously.

"Get the men together! This lad knows where Amber is, and we're going after her! Hurry, man, she is to be sold at auction at noon!" Trent's words were barely spoken before Jason turned, leaving on the run. Looking back at the young man, LeBlanc spoke.

"You are helping me to find the most important thing I have ever possessed. For that I am deeply grateful. I stand true to my word on the reward." As he spoke, Trent reached his desk and pulled a box from a drawer. When he opened it the lad saw that the box contained coins of both gold and silver. And there were jewels—rubies, emeralds, pearls, amethysts, sapphires, and jade. "Your choice, my lad," Trent told him.

The young man stood looking down at the sparkling contents of the box but made no move. Then he lifted his blue-gray eyes to Trent's and slowly shook his head. In a clear voice and with complete honesty, the boy spoke.

"Neither money nor precious jewels can pay for a life, sir. My reward is that the lady will be returned her freedom and

not be sold as a slave. You see, sir, freedom is priceless."
Replacing his worn cap, the boy turned to the door and
added, "If you will follow me, sir, I will take you to where the
auction is to be held."

"One moment, young man," Trent's words halted him.
"What is your name? And how old are you?"

"My name is Rual, and I am seventeen, sir," was his
answer.

"Where are your parents, Rual?" Trent queried.

"My mother is dead, sir, and I never knew my father.
When my mother died I had no one but my uncle. He was not
really my uncle, he was not even kin. But he was the only real
friend we had, and he took me in. I helped him in his shop,
but when he had saved enough money for his passage to
France he left here and turned me over to Jack Dingwell,"
Rual explained.

"Well, since you refuse to take money or jewels, Rual, is
there any other reward you might accept?" Trent asked. "I
will grant it, Rual, all you need do is ask."

Rual stood straight and proud, his broad shoulders
squared, his head held high as he met LeBlanc's questioning
eyes.

"I would like to sail with you, sir, on the *Mér Fleur!*" Rual
answered without hesitation. "As you can see, I am strong. I
have learned to take orders, I can use a weapon and I can
fight. That, sir, would be all that I would ask!"

"Rual," Trent began, watching the boy with narrowed
eyes. He saw himself, Trent LeBlanc, at the age of seventeen,
remembered his sincere wish to belong to the sea, his earnest
efforts to make his way in the world. He, too, had had no
parents, not from the age of thirteen. The comparison
between the early lives of the two of them caused Trent to
weaken as he was about to refuse the boy's request.

Then, as he looked into the clear depth of the blue-gray
eyes, they locked with his keen, sapphire gaze without
wavering. Trent could recall only one man who could meet his
own domineering stare without faltering. That man was
Casey Reed. Now there was another, and in that moment of
self-recognition in the eyes of this young man, LeBlanc made
his decision.

"Granted! Your request is granted, Rual," Trent stated.

Only then did Rual's eyes leave the other man's.

"Thank you, sir," he answered humbly. "You will not regret your decision, sir, I promise you."

"But there is one thing that you must know, Rual. On the sea, the Captain's word is law. To *my* men, my word is law always, whether at sea or on land. Is that clear, Rual? And can you accept this without question?" LeBlanc's words were strong and positive, and Rual knew that there would be no leniency.

"Aye, sir!" Rual answered with a smart salute and a companionable grin.

After a long moment, Captain Trent LeBlanc turned away, sighing deeply. *"Mon Dieu*, LeBlanc," he murmured to his inner self, "you have just met yourself at age seventeen!"

"Cap'n Trent, sir," Jason interrupted LeBlanc's thoughts, "the men are all ready, sir."

Straightening his shoulders and looking down at Rual, Trent motioned him toward the door. "Shall we go?" he asked and followed Rual down the passageway.

Amber stood awaiting her turn. Dingwell had brought her along with ten other women and six men to the large warehouse where the auction was to be held.

"We are to be sold at a private auction," one woman said to the waiting group who stood apprehensively where they had been herded.

"At least we will be going to a rich master," added a tall, young black girl.

Strange, Amber thought, how the others seemed to accept all this. But I cannot, I will not, accept a "master," her thoughts ran on. Then she almost laughed at her contradictory thoughts. Had she not had a master all these weeks? Had she not been a slave to Trent LeBlanc's demands? Yes, of course, she had already had a master. And she had run away. She had run away from what she considered an unbearable situation to an impossible fate.

Amber leaned weakly against the wall and closed her eyes. A mental picture of LeBlanc's face seemed to swim before her as it had each night since she had left the *Mér Fleur*. Her hands moved to her middle and she lightly stroked her stomach. My child will never know his father, never know his heritage, Amber thought sadly, and he will not be born free. She wondered if her child might one day despise her for what she had done.

"Oh, Trent, my love," she breathed as tears welled in her dull eyes. The sparkle had gone from those beautiful emerald-green eyes, and her buoyant spirit had diminished greatly.

"He will be selling you as a maiden," someone whispered in Amber's ear.

She opened her eyes and stared at the young girl at her side. Her name was Neva, and she was older than Amber by only a few months. She is lovely, Amber thought, with her dark coffee-colored hair falling freely about her shoulders, her eyes the color of chestnuts, the small rosebud mouth, and her smooth olive skin. This was what Amber had seen when she first opened her eyes after hours of unconsciousness following the blow to her head. Neva's lovely face, the face of an angel, Amber remembered thinking.

"A maiden?" Amber brought her thoughts back to the present.

"Yes, a virgin," replied Neva, "the same as me. The same as the two girls over there." She pointed to the two young women who stood huddled together. "They are sisters," Neva went on, "they do not wish to be separated."

"But, Neva, I am not a virgin!" Amber replied.

"I know, but do not say otherwise," Neva advised her. "Dingwell will get a high price for one as beautiful as you, Amber. And he will get even more by selling you as a virgin. Your new master will not mind that you are not a virgin, for once he has bed you, it will no longer matter."

Amber blushed hotly at Neva's frank words. She was unaccustomed to such bold remarks from another woman. But then she remembered that she was no longer in her untarnished little world with its loving fortress to ward off the pain and uncertainties of the harsh outside world. She must accept this different world and fight to survive therein.

"Why, oh why," Amber groaned, "did I ever leave the *Mér Fleur*? Why did I flee from Trent and the safety of his strong arms?"

Uncertainties? she thought, and then a name flashed into her mind. Maria! It was all because of that black-haired bitch. I should not have allowed her to agitate me, I should have confronted Trent with all my doubts and uncertainties. And about Maria.

"The child, Amber," Neva's voice jolted Amber. "You will have to pass off the child as belonging to the man who buys you. You must make him believe that it came early and swear on your life that it belongs to him. A man never takes to another man's offspring. They have their pride, you see."

"Neva!" Amber gasped in astonishment. "How did you know about the child?"

"You were unconscious when they threw you into that room with the rest of us, and I took care of you as best I could. You spoke of your unborn child and you called the name of your lover many times. Trent, is it not? You love him very much, yes?" Neva's rust-brown eyes were clouded with concern.

"Yes, Neva," Amber replied softly. "I do love him very much, only . . . well, he does not love me. And he knows nothing of the child which I carry."

"I do not believe that any man would not love you, Amber. You are a very special lady, and it would take a strong man to keep from falling in love with you. And an even stronger man to win your love. No, I cannot believe that what you tell me can be true." Neva's words were firmly stated.

Amber made no reply. She retreated to her thoughts. Nothing seemed to matter now. It was too late to hope for a life with LeBlanc; he was lost to her forever. She would be sold and taken away, never again to see Trent LeBlanc.

Amber stared down at the white dress she wore. Suddenly she understood why Neva, the two frightened sisters, and she herself were dressed in white. They were to be sold as virgins, as Neva had pointed out to her. All the rest of the poor slaves-to-be were still wearing the same clothing in which Amber had first seen them. Only the four "virgins" had been allowed to bathe and had been given the clean white garments.

The dress was made of a thin, cotton fabric and clung to the soft curves of Amber's body. In the bright light of noonday, one could plainly see the outline of her beautiful body and of her fine, shapely legs. There were no sleeves, and her softly rounded arms were exposed to full view. The hem of the dress came midway between ankle and knee, and the low-cut bodice revealed the swelling mounds of her young breasts. Jack Dingwell's intent was to expose Amber's beautiful body in the flimsy gown, to parade her before the lustful eyes of rich, potential buyers, to make them bid against each other for this copper-haired beauty until he could raise the price for a substantial profit.

"Move, bitch!" Evans's harsh voice startled her. His rough, calloused hand grasped her naked upper arm, his dirty fingers digging into her soft flesh as he jerked her forward. "It be yer turn on the block!" he hissed. "Might even buy ye fer meself, if'n the price it don't go too high. I wouldn' pay more'n ten gold pieces fer the likes uv ye." Evans laughed harshly, showing broken yellow-brown teeth. "'Sides, yer all bruised up." He laughed again, cruelly.

"Only four virgins did I have, and two are already gone!" Dingwell's voice rang loudly as Amber walked slowly up the steps to the small platform. "Now this one, my friends, she is my best! She is strong, beautiful, and ready to be picked. I had her brought over from England," Dingwell barked as he stalked to Amber's side. "Hair of soft texture, gentlemen," he said, lifting Amber's red-gold hair, "and a body made for the sole purpose of bedding. She is young and can be easily molded. Now, what is the first bid?"

Amber felt ill and she fought back the tears as she heard the first bid, then a second. The third bid came from Evans and her heart almost stopped. She would kill herself, she thought desperately, if Evans were the high bidder. Then came another bid and Amber breathed easier. After that she closed her ears and her mind to the bidding, and her eyes to her surroundings. Until she heard Dingwell's shout.

"Sold! Sold to the highest bidder!" Dingwell slammed a wooden hammer on the table before him. "And now, sir, you may claim your purchase, one golden-haired wench!"

"The wench belongs to me!" The voice was clear, resonant, and authoritative. With a start, Amber recognized the familiar voice and raised her green eyes to see LeBlanc in the warehouse doorway. His lean body casually rested against the door frame, his arms were crossed over his broad chest, and on his handsome face was cold fury. Amber stared in utter disbelief. Was Trent here, she wondered, or was she dreaming?

"Not true! I bought her fair," sputtered a pudgy, red-faced man as he jumped to his feet. "I bid the highest and she be mine!" He raised his fist and shook it toward Trent. Then, turning to Dingwell, the man showed him the money clutched in his pudgy fist. "I'll be takin' her now!"

"She will go nowhere!" LeBlanc thundered, "not with you or with any other bastard!" Now in full stride and in a towering rage, he crossed to the would-be purchaser and, looming over him, grabbed the man's upraised fist in his own strong hand. "Buy yourself another wench with your money," rasped LeBlanc as he pushed the man's fat, money-filled fist into the pudgy red face. "This one is not for sale!" The words lashed out razor-sharp, and his steely eyes were hostile.

"She has already been sold," the man said, as he tried to maintain his composure. He straightened his shoulders and raised his eyes to meet the stare of cold, sapphire-blue eyes. Seeing the hostility and the determination in those of LeBlanc, his own eyes fell and he stepped away. "However," he blustered, "if you wish to buy the wench from me—"

"I will not buy what is already mine!" LeBlanc roared. His eyes narrowed dangerously, a muscle twitched in his firm jaw and his breath came raggedly. Stepping forward with fists clenched at his sides, he spat out, "I have told you that the wench belongs to me! She carries my child within her belly!"

The silence that held the warehouse caused LeBlanc's words to ring out. They filled the large room, rolled across it and bounced back again. The pig-faced man looked surprised, and the color drained from his face as he glanced from LeBlanc to Amber, who stood wide-eyed, her gaze fixed on Trent.

"Is this true, wench? Does this man speak the truth?" the pudgy man questioned, unaware that the man who towered over him was one of little or no patience, not realizing his peril in daring to question this man's word.

Amber parted her lips to speak but closed them in silence at LeBlanc's upraised hand. Seeing this display of submission and knowing that this small gesture was understood by the young female, the man watched her lower her eyes meekly. She has obeyed this man before, he thought, the man speaks the truth. It is so that this tall stranger is already her master.

"You are right, sir, the woman shows that she belongs to you, that you are, indeed, her master." Turning to Dingwell, the man declared, "I will not purchase damaged goods, Jack! The wench is with child, yet you claim that she be a virgin! You will not get my money for her!"

Dingwell had stood by during the verbal exchange between his prospective buyer and the stranger. Yet the aggressive authority exhibited by this unknown person and his absolute fearlessness caused Dingwell to be nervous and unsure. Now, in an effort to regain control of his business affairs, he spoke to Trent with an outward show of confidence which he did not possess.

"Just a minute, you! This is a private auction, my good man!" Dingwell blustered. "Who do you think you are, that you can barge in here professing to be the owner of this wench? She that I bought and paid for!"

With deadly calm LeBlanc approached the platform upon which Dingwell stood with Amber. Impaling him with blazing sapphire eyes, Trent answered Dingwell with an exaggerated bow.

"Who do I think I am? Why, I *know* who I am, sir," he said mockingly, "and I think *you* should know, too. The name is Captain Trent LeBlanc, master of the *Mér Fleur!*"

The name struck terror to Dingwell's heart and caused a hushed murmur to sweep over those assembled in the warehouse. It was obvious that LeBlanc's reputation was well know, even though his face was not. Amber saw Dingwell's face blanch and noted the fear which leaped into his eyes as he visibly began to tremble.

"And now, if there are no further objections to be overruled, I shall take what is mine and depart your stinking premises!" With these words LeBlanc reached up and swung Amber from the platform and into his arms. She met his warm gaze and their eyes held for a moment. She was safe! Trent had found her and it was not a dream. Clinging tightly to him, her head resting against his chest, Amber wept quietly. But when he turned to leave, she roused.

"No, Trent, wait! Please! We cannot leave Neva! We have to take her away from here! She is my friend, she helped me when no one would. Please!" Amber begged as she stared at the young girl who was waiting to go on the block. As LeBlanc hesitated, Amber whispered to him. "Please, Trent! You have to!"

"I truly have no choice," Trent told Amber. "If I leave her, you would never forgive me." But she knew that it was not the only reason. LeBlanc had often talked about the slave traders, and she knew how he hated the business. No, he would not have left Neva, but Amber saw that he wished her to believe that he would take the girl along just because he wanted to please Amber. So she smiled and kissed him lightly on the lips, lingering a little longer than he had expected.

"Mon Dieu, woman," Trent breathed, "you would tempt the devil himself!" Then turning to the hopeful girl who hovered nearby, he said, "Neva, you are coming with us."

The anxious Neva looked fearfully at Dingwell, afraid to walk away.

"Never mind him," LeBlanc spoke curtly. "He will not attempt to stop you. He would not dare! So come along."

As Neva darted to his side, Trent stared at Dingwell in open contempt. "You, sir, I shall deal with very soon. You may expect to see me at the most unexpected time." He chuckled aloud at the duplicity of his own words, then added mysteriously, "As for your man, Evans—well, you should not concern yourself about his absence as he has been dealt with already."

LeBlanc's parting words hung in the air as he strode from the warehouse with Amber held tightly in his arms and Neva trotting along close behind him. Outside the warehouse the three were joined by Jason, Monrow, and a few of the crew from the *Mér Fleur* who had accompanied LeBlanc to the auction but had been ordered by LeBlanc to remain outside. "I shall handle this alone," had been the words of their captain. "Do not interfere unless I signal for you."

The group walked in silence through the narrow streets toward the harbor. Trent still held Amber securely in his arms. God, but he was glad he had found her, glad that he held her in his arms once more. Then he felt a sudden surge of anger, anger for the hours that she had put him through pure hell!

"I can walk, Trent," Amber told him. "You can put me down, now."

LeBlanc stopped so suddenly that Jason, walking behind, stumbled against his broad, rigid back. Staring down at Amber, Trent's blue eyes flashed fire as he exploded, "Put you down? For all in God's name that is holy! Damn it, Amber, do you not realize that you are damned near naked? *Mon Dieu*, woman, do you think that I would allow you to walk through the streets dressed only in that—that—that thing you are wearing? Christ! Do you not know that it is damned near next to nothing? Why, you can see right through the flimsy thing! Put you down? Let you walk? Hell and damnation, woman, are you daft?"

As Trent's words spluttered to a halt, the humor of the situation struck Amber. Her green eyes lit with amusement, and she clapped one hand over her mouth in an attempt to suppress the unbidden bubble of laughter that threatened.

LeBlanc strode forward with Neva and the crewmen stepping up their pace to keep up. No word was spoken, but Amber, looking over Trent's shoulder, saw Neva clutching her filmy garment close around her. Then Monrow shed his shirt and gently laid it over the embarrassed girl's shoulders. She flashed him a shy but grateful smile. It was obvious that LeBlanc's outburst had caused Neva to feel even more self-conscious, though apparently he had not given a thought to Neva's scantily clad person.

Walking along in silence, Trent remembered the nights that Amber had been gone. How he had worried about her! How he had missed having her beside him! How he had needed her! Ached for her!

As the little party stepped aboard the *Mér Fleur*, LeBlanc felt as if a great weight had been lifted from him. Amber was safe. She was back with him, back where she belonged.

"Jason!" Trent called as he headed for the companion ladder.

"Aye, Cap'n, sir," replied the faithful Jason, hastening to catch up with LeBlanc. "'Ere I be, sir."

"See that the young woman is properly cared for. I shall leave her in your hands, Jason, I know that you can be depended upon to do the best possible for her." Jason stood at the top of the companion ladder, and as his captain disappeared from view, his words floated back. "And Jason, I am not to be disturbed. Understand? Not for any reason!" Jason chuckled as he remembered that he had been given that same order before. It was the night that the Cap'n brought the missy aboard for the first time.

LeBlanc entered his cabin and crossed to the bed where he gently placed the nervous Amber. She was unsure of just what Trent's next move would be. Would he lash out at her for running away? Would he be angry that she was now with child? That he would be his usual, unpredictable self, she was certain.

Amber had not long to wait to learn which direction his temperament would take. "Why, Amber?" Trent asked in a controlled voice. "Why did you run away? Did you not care that you worried me?" He sighed heavily. "Do you not know what would have happened to you had I not found you? *Mon Dieu!*"

Trent began to pace the floor as he ran his strong fingers through his hair impatiently. Amber remained silent, not knowing how to reply. After a brief silence LeBlanc spun on his heel to face her.

"What did you think you were doing?" he roared as he beat the air with a clenched fist. "Did you really think that you could get back to London? And even if you had, did you not know that I would come for you? Or did you think that I would just forget about you?"

Amber sat quietly under LeBlanc's rage. She was still frightened, but now the knowledge of what he had saved her from was rapidly sinking in, and she was appalled at the possibilities.

"Amber, answer me!" LeBlanc's words cut through her thoughts. "Did you think that I would not come looking for you? Did you truly believe that I would let you go?"

Amber raised her bottle-green eyes and looked deep into Trent's dark blue ones. Tears began to cloud her eyes and her chin quivered. "I do not know what I thought. I do not know anything anymore. At the time I thought I was doing what was best." The tears spilled over and ran down her cheeks and she caught her lower lip between her teeth to keep it from trembling.

They stared at each other as silence engulfed the room, neither seemed to know what to do or what to say. Then Amber broke the silence with a stifled sob.

"Trent," she choked in a small voice that stabbed at LeBlanc's heart. "Please let me go, please! Have you not hurt me enough? Why do you go on?" Unbidden, the picture of Maria in Trent's arms flashed through Amber's mind. "Why do you keep me? I have had more than my share of shame and hurt. You do not really want me, so why?"

"You carry my child in your belly!" Trent stormed. "That is reason enough to keep you. *Mon Dieu,* Amber! I am not the animal you believe me to be! Of course I care what happens to you, to my child!" As he reached out to Amber she jerked away, her wide eyes shooting angry daggers.

"And would you have come for me had you not learned of the child?" her words were barbed. "Now *you* answer *me,* Trent LeBlanc! Is it only the child for whom you have concern? Were I not with child, would you have come for *me?*"

"Hell, yes!" Trent roared. "Have you not learned that I do not easily part with what belongs to me? And do you not know that *you* belong to me?"

"And Maria? Does she not also 'belong to you'? Is she not one of your 'possessions'? Is she not 'your woman'?" Amber demanded hotly.

"*Maria!*" LeBlanc spat the name as if to rid his mouth of a bad taste. He had completely forgotten that Maria must have been the reason for Amber's flight. Now it all came back to him, meeting Maria on the dock, Jason telling him that Amber had seen Maria kiss Trent, Maria's apparent visit to Amber, and the blasted note Amber had left behind.

"Maria means nothing to me, Amber! Absolutely nothing! Oh, she has been convenient to my needs in the past, but that is what it is, Amber, *the past!*" Impatiently thrusting both hands through his black hair, Trent continued, "She is a whore! A waterfront doxie! And I do not need Maria any more, Amber, now that I have *you!*"

Instantly Amber was on her feet, her face white with rage.

Trent saw the flash of violent fury in her darkened eyes and felt the fiery sting of her open palm as it met his cheek.

"*Whore!*" Amber screamed. "Is that it? *So now I am your whore!* Therefore you no longer need Maria or any other *whore* now that you have *me!*" She gave a short, sarcastic laugh. "Now that I am at your convenience!"

"*Mon Dieu,* Amber!" Trent rubbed his hand across his smarting cheek. "That is not at all what I mean. Why do you persist in twisting my words to a meaning other than that which was intended?" He spread his hands in exasperation, then his voice softened as he went on.

"Come, little one, do not make this situation more difficult. Please understand, Amber, that I have never thought of you as a whore. As my woman, yes! But as a common whore, absolutely not! You are many things to me, *ma* sweet, but never that!" As he spoke, Trent moved to Amber and stroked her red-gold hair, gently caressing the long silken locks. He felt the fire of passion flow through his body at the touch, and his arms closed around Amber's slender body.

"Never run away from me again, Amber. Never!" he said huskily, and his lips crushed hers in a bruising kiss. His mouth was demanding and Amber felt it warm and inviting. Trent parted her lips, his tongue searching, yearning for hers. Amber stood unyielding for a moment. She had resolved not to give in to him too easily but she knew that her resolves were weakening, and she felt her body begin to respond to LeBlanc's tenderness. She had missed his embrace and had longed for his caress.

During the long nights while Amber was away from Trent she had ached for him, had dreamed of being in his arms. Now she was where she had longed to be, so why fight it? she asked herself. Why deny yourself the pleasure this man gives to you? You want him, you want him to want you, so show him that this is your desire! Go ahead and show him, Amber, she urged.

So when LeBlanc picked her up and gently laid her upon the bed she gave no resistance, her body supple and yielding.

Trent's lithe body came down on Amber, pressing her deep into the softness of the bed. He was hungry with desire and she felt the proof of his need pressed hard against her. The hot throbbing pulse of his manhood hammered wildly against her thigh, sending a warm current of craving throughout her own eager body and a tightening in her loins. Her own hunger became so intense that she wrapped her arms around Le-Blanc's neck and clung tightly to him.

Trent kissed Amber wildly and deeply, then pulled his lips from hers as she fought to remain locked in the embrace. He stared down at her, his blue eyes dark with passion watching the rise and fall of her firm white breasts as they heaved against her bodice. Reaching down, LeBlanc methodically untied the tiny ribbons which fastened the bodice, allowing Amber's breasts to spill forth. His breath was ragged and came in short gasps as he slowly ran lean, tanned fingers over her soft flesh, down between the mounds of her breasts. Amber shivered in anticipation under Trent's tender touch and molded her pliant young body to his.

"Ah! God, Amber!" Trent groaned, his voice hoarse with emotion. "I should hate you for the hold you have over me! You are a witch, Amber, a damn, bloody witch, and I cannot get enough of you! Damn me, but I cannot get you out of my blood!" And he claimed her lips once more, tasting the sweet poison of her kiss. The poison that spread through his body like a sickness little by little, slowly taking possession of him until one day he would no longer belong to himself.

LeBlanc was aware of all this but could not find the power to stop or to control his need for Amber, his obsession for her. She flowed within his veins like hot, molten lava from an angry volcano. Trent LeBlanc had always been his own man, master of his emotions, and never had *anyone* dominated him. Would to God, he thought, that I could eject Amber from my being as easily as the volcano spat forth its own fire and fury!

Moving away from her, Trent stared deep into Amber's passion-glazed eyes.

"You are mine, Amber. You will never belong to another. I will not give up what is mine. And what you feel now, you will never feel with another. The flames of passion that burn so strongly between the two of us will never be extinguished. They will exist in a suppressed state, smoldering, waiting to burst into a raging flame that no one but I will be able to ignite. Only then will they again blaze as they do now."

LeBlanc's eyes held Amber's, burning through her, and her heart drummed in her breast. She loved and feared him at the same time. She knew that the words he spoke were true, that there would never be anyone for her but Trent. Not as a lover, not as a man.

I love you, Trent LeBlanc, can you not see? her mind cried out. I love you. But Amber could not bring herself to speak the words aloud for fear that he would not wish her to *love* him, only to want him as he desired her.

"Make love to me, Trent," she whispered, tracing the outline of his firm jaw with the tip of her slender finger. "I have missed being in your arms. I have missed all of you!" Amber arched her body upward against his as she pulled LeBlanc to her. "Please make the memory of the last few days go away, Trent, love me—"

Amber's words were lost as LeBlanc's eager mouth closed over hers. Only a soft moan rattled in Amber's throat as their bodies became one.

Trent lay peacefully, holding the sleeping Amber close to him. His mind idly wondered on his feelings and about his future. Caught up in his thoughts, he did not hear the knock on the cabin door, and when the door opened slightly he turned his head and saw Jason. The old man's face was flushed with embarrassment, but LeBlanc smiled at Jason's discomfort and motioned for him to come in. Trent pulled the sheet close around Amber's body before he spoke.

"Yes, Jason, is there something that I can do for you?" he asked, chuckling at the red-faced man. "If Amber were awake, Jason, I am afraid that you would be in a great deal of trouble. She would not like to be found in this particular situation, but I shan't tell her." Then he added, "If *you* won't!"

"Oh no, sir, Cap'n, why ol' Jason would'n tell the missy, no sir! An' beggin' yer pardon, sir, but I did knock on the door, sir, 'cept'n ye never heered me," Jason assured LeBlanc. "But there be a message for ye, sir, an' the man 'e says ye was ta get it 'immediately.' 'E said, 'Waste no time, ol' man, yer master 'as important business.' An' then 'e give me this 'ere note." Jason handed the slip of paper to LeBlanc.

"Thank you, Jason. And so long as you are here, you might tell me if the young woman, Neva, has been cared for? And the lad, Rual, has he been advised of his duties?"

"Aye, sir. The girl, 'er be in Monrow's quarters, an' 'e be sharin' wi' me. An' the lad, sir, 'e 'as been tole. A good lad 'e be, sir."

"Fine," LeBlanc replied as he opened the note. "Have the crew ready to get underway, Jason, I have a feeling that we will be sailing soon." His eyes scanned the message and he chuckled aloud. "Yes, Jason, I was almost sure of it. It is well that the cargo has been loaded. See that all our supplies are on board by late afternoon. We may sail on the night tide or early dawn."

"Aye, sir, it will be done," Jason assured as he headed for the door.

"Wait a moment, Jason," Trent stopped the man, "I shall be leaving the ship for a while, and you are to see that neither of the young women go ashore. That is an order! And ask Drake to meet me topside, I shall be there shortly."

"Aye, Cap'n," Jason answered and took his leave.

When the door had closed behind the first mate, LeBlanc again read the message, slowly and carefully.

LeBlanc:

   Urgent that I speak with you immediately! Also, must know if the Mér Fleur can be ready to sail on short notice, perhaps as early as the morrow.
   Developments between families are cause for concern, the matters requiring attention as soon as possible. Need your assistance to intervene.
   Four o'clock, La Habana Tavern. Important!

                                                           Simmons

After studying the contents of the note at length, LeBlanc glanced down at Amber as she slept peacefully on. With a deep sigh, he quietly slipped from the bed and began to dress.

What does Simmons want this time? Trent wondered. Blast it! It had damned well better be important, he fumed as he gazed at Amber who lay naked between the sheets. Her russet-gold hair fanned out across the pillow, her tawny smooth shoulders peering from beneath the upturned covers, soft gold-tipped lashes caressed her fine cheeks.

"Ah, yes, it had better be important!" LeBlanc whispered, tugging on his boots and shaking his head in frustration.

He had been summoned from his bed just when he was readying to nudge that silken-skinned beauty awake, ready to seduce her thoroughly. He had thought that he had nothing more to do that afternoon but to share the comfort of a soft bed with Amber and her enjoyable charms.

Chapter Six

DAN SIMMONS SAT AT A SMALL TABLE IN THE BACK OF THE LA Habana Tavern, his dark brown eyes alert as he studied the room and each man that entered. His ale had become flat, leaving a bad taste in his mouth. His fingertips drummed nervously on the table, and he squirmed impatiently in his chair. Simmons's current assignment was not to his liking. "God! How was LeBlanc going to take this?" Simmons groaned.

Many times before had he sought LeBlanc's assistance, but never had he asked the man to spy on one of LeBlanc's own friends. He will not like this, Simmons assured himself, no, he will not like it at all! This meeting was one that Dan Simmons wished heartily that he could cancel, but he knew the importance of the needed information. He also knew that Trent LeBlanc was the only man who could obtain it.

The tavern door swung open, and a man of about fifty stepped in wearing a gray tailcoat, white ruffled shirt, and gray jersey knee pants. One by one he dusted his black, buckled slippers by rubbing them against his white-stockinged calves. His pale eyes searched the large room as he removed his gloves and a black cocked hat. Dan Simmons's gaze met that of the dandily dressed man, and a slight smile crossed the aging but still handsome face of the latter.

The newcomer crossed the room to Simmons's table. With a tight-lipped smile, Simmons greeted him. "Tanner," he said, rising and extending his hand. Then with a curt nod of his graying head, added, "Please sit down," and resumed his own seat.

All this looked innocent enough to anyone who might have been observing the scene—two gentlemen meeting in a local tavern for a few drinks and a chat. It was done all the time, and this meeting, on the surface, was no different.

But to the man who sat hidden in the shadows of a darkened corner, watching the two men with keen interest, there was more to this casual meeting than met the eye. The stranger slowly leaned back, making himself comfortable in his chair, as he rested one booted heel on his knee and lit a cheroot. His sharp eyes missed nothing, noting every detail.

Indeed, there is something going on here, and I shall soon learn what it is, he mused as he watched the scene with lazy amusement. There was an almost ruthless slant to his mouth as he drew on the cheroot, his gaze never leaving the two men who sat on the other side of the dimly lighted, smoke-filled room.

"I have been waiting for well over an hour," Simmons was saying irritably as he consulted a large gold-cased pocket watch. "Did I not understand that we were to meet at two o'clock? Was there a problem?"

"Not really a problem, Dan," William Tanner replied with a sigh. "I was detained at an earlier meeting." Leaning forward conspiratorially, Tanner said in a low voice, "Mischief is brewing in New Orleans, Simmons, and it seems to have something to do with the barbaric Lafitte. Damn! Will Claiborne never give up? He hates those Lafittes, especially Jean, to a dangerous point." He shook his head and continued. "Claiborne has set many traps for the man but has yet to catch him. Now this thing with the British! Do you know anything about it?" Tanner questioned.

"A little," Simmons replied, "but I am not at liberty to discuss it. Orders, you know."

"Oh, of course, orders!" Tanner smirked. "I understand."

Simmons reached out his open hand toward Tanner. "You

have papers for me, I believe?" It was both a statement and a question.

"Oh, yes," said Tanner as he reached into his inside coat pocket and removed an envelope. As he laid it in Simmons's palm, Tanner asked, "And what is this scheme you are working on?"

Simmons merely looked back at him with narrowed eyes and said nothing.

"Orders again?" Tanner asked sarcastically.

"That is right! Orders!" Simmons answered shortly.

Realizing that acquiring information from this man was going to be difficult, Tanner decided to change his tactics, and, after a brief silence on the part of both men, he tried again.

"I understand that you will be meeting with the infamous Captain LeBlanc to negotiate a deal," Tanner ventured.

"True," Simmons said. "I do have an appointment with LeBlanc." Under his breath he added, "I hope."

"I hear that he is a strange person, that one," remarked Tanner. "I would not wish to have any dealings with that pirate!" he grunted in dislike.

"Captain LeBlanc is a private merchantman, Tanner, not a pirate," Simmons's voice rose in anger. "He is also a valuable agent, one who has worked with our government for seven years. He has always been available when we needed his assistance, and, no matter what the task, he has never failed us," Simmons went on. "LeBlanc is a good man, and you will do well to remember that!"

"Oh? I had heard rumors to the effect that your 'valuable agent' does not perform for our government simply because he is patriotic or has nothing better to do," Tanner snorted. "It seems that he and a fellow pirate captain named Reed attacked an American ship on her way home. And in her own waters!"

"Did your informer also tell you that the ship fired on them first? Did they tell you that LeBlanc's vessel was flying a pirate's flag and that Captain Reed's vessel was flying the flag of France? That the two were pretending to be in battle in order to divert an English brig of war to prevent it reaching American shores? No, I can see that they did not. Christ! Why cannot people get their stories straight before they repeat them?" Simmons roared, slamming a fist hard on the table.

More calmly, Simmons continued in patient exasperation. "My God! LeBlanc was only protecting his ship and his crew. He was not out to fight a battle with anyone, unless it was the British brig." He paused, running a hand through his graying hair. "He has been spying and fighting bloody battles for our own, and his adopted, country. He has been helping *us*, working for Claiborne in New Orleans, for Jackson, and for President Madison himself. LeBlanc has been able to accomplish things which our own men have not. Including Naylor!"

"It has come to my attention that Naylor has tried to get information on Lafitte for Claiborne but, as yet, has been unsuccessful. I hear that he can not get anywhere near Lafitte. Do you believe that this LeBlanc can succeed where Naylor, our best man, has utterly failed?" Tanner queried.

"I do!" Simmons stated flatly.

"And why is that?" Tanner inquired in surprise. "Do you truly think that LeBlanc is so much the better man? Do you believe him to be a god or a wizard? You must think that the man can just walk up to Jean Lafitte, slap him on the back goodnaturedly, and say, 'Jean, my good man, I need some information on your activities that Governor Claiborne would like to know.'" Tanner laughed in derision. "Simmons, either you are dreaming, or you are getting old!"

"Neither, Tanner. It is just that Trent LeBlanc is a very unusual young man. I do not know that I have ever met anyone quite like him. He is a man of means, a man of quality and of rare ability—" Simmons broke off, and a wide grin spread across his pleasant face. "Besides all this, LeBlanc is a personal friend of Jean Lafitte! No, he will have no trouble, none at all!"

"Friend! Of Lafitte! And you trust him?" Tanner was aghast. "My God, Simmons, are you mad? What are you thinking? Suppose LeBlanc chooses to take sides with Lafitte? What if—"

"He will not," Simmons broke in. "LeBlanc can be trusted. If I had even the smallest doubt about him I would not ask him to take this assignment. You seem to forget, Tanner, I know the man, I have worked with him for a long time. Not once has he ever given me any cause to distrust him!"

Simmons chuckled. "Oh, he has not always been agreeable, and he often loses that damnable temper for which he is so famous, but I repeat—the man is reliable and is to be trusted." The words harbored no dispute.

"Then it will be on your shoulders, Simmons, you remember that! I shall have nothing to do with the matter," Tanner hissed through clenched teeth as he pulled on his gloves and pushed his chair back from the table. "I do not like this man, LeBlanc, and I feel very strongly that you should find another man for this assignment."

Rising to his feet, Tanner put on his hat and looked down at Simmons, who had remained seated. The two men stared at each other for a long moment before Tanner rasped out, "Never say that I did not warn you! This LeBlanc character is known to be a strange and unpredictable man. He will turn on you or anyone else, for the right price. You remember that!" And with those final words Tanner turned and stalked across the room.

As Tanner disappeared through the door, the watchful man in the darkened corner drew deeply on his cheroot before dropping it to the floor. He stood to his feet and crushed the smoldering remains beneath one booted foot. Then with long, even strides he crossed to where Simmons still sat.

"Afternoon, Simmons. Mind if I join you?"

The smooth, arrogant voice brought Simmons's head up with a jerk.

"LeBlanc! What the devil!" Simmons sputtered. "How long have you been here? I did not see you come in."

"Very true, for it was *I* who saw *you* come in. I have learned to be vigilant. I am trained to observe, am I not? Furthermore, I know why you have sent for me, and I must tell you, Simmons, I do not like it!" LeBlanc asserted, his dark blue eyes piercing into Simmons's brown ones. Anger flickered in the blue eyes, the brown eyes betrayed Simmons's attempt at self-confidence.

"Ah, my young friend, you are always so sure of yourself? How could you possibly know why I need you?" Simmons chuckled, hoping to humor the tall, dark LeBlanc who still towered over him.

"Am I not to meet with Jean Lafitte? Is that not your plan?

And what is the information which I am to obtain? Or is that not to be made known to me until after I have accepted the assignment?" Trent asked hotly, his eyes never leaving Simmons. "Why in hell did I ever let you talk me into this damnable spying? Damn!" Trent cursed, swinging one long muscular leg over the back of the chair to sit down. "I will not promise *anything* when it comes to Jean, Simmons. He is *mon bon ami* and I will not deceive him. Why do you get me involved in these things?"

Simmons laughed softly before he replied. "My young friend, it is truly of your own doing. If you do not remember, allow me to refresh your memory. Did you and Casey Reed not stand before Andrew Jackson and me and ask if there might be *anything* or *any way* that the two of you might amend the trouble that you two young pups got yourselves into? So you see, your being 'involved in these things'—I really did not have to 'talk you into it.'"

Sighing heavily, LeBlanc said, "You are right, as usual, Simmons. So will you tell me the plans, or are you going to go on reminding me of my 'foolish, younger days,' as you so often call them?" Leaning back in his chair, Trent laced the long fingers of both hands behind his neck and rested his head firmly against them. "I would like to know what is ahead of me. First of all, I want to know if, by any chance, I might lose my life. I am somewhat fond of myself, you know, and it seems that there are others that are, as well. I do not wish to deprive anyone of my person by ceasing to exist." LeBlanc smiled smugly.

"Ah, LeBlanc, you conceited young devil!" Simmons jested, obviously much relieved that Trent's attitude was changing. "I am sure that the ladies will continue to have the pleasure of your company for a long time to come. After all, you are indeed too 'fond of yourself'—*your* words, not mine—to allow anything to happen to the one and only Captain Trent LeBlanc." Simmons laughed heartily. "Why, who would the young lads pretend to be? And the young ladies dream about? No, you would never let it happen!"

"All right, Simmons, you have made your point," LeBlanc said coolly. "Now what information am I to extract from *mon bon ami*, Jean Lafitte?"

Simmons studied LeBlanc's unreadable expression for some time before he answered. Then, with a deep sigh, he reluctantly began his story.

"We have received word that a few days ago a brig of war lay anchor outside the Barataria Bay. She was flying the flag of Great Britain. Early on the following morning Lafitte and a few of his men took a small boat to the mouth of the strait, where they were met by a gig from the British vessel. It was reported that the British gig was manned by three men, perhaps officers. There were shouts from the gig, asking to see Jean Lafitte.

"Lafitte and his men led the gig back to the island. Now, we know what took place on that island and why the British were seeking Lafitte. Within twenty-four hours a messenger arrived in New Orleans with a letter from Lafitte, along with letters and documents from the British government. They included a request for Lafitte's services in exchange for a captaincy with full rank and honor, plus thirty thousand dollars. The packet was delivered to Jean Blanque, a member of the legislature and a man of influence in New Orleans, who read them and immediately took the packet to Governor Claiborne.

"Lafitte made certain demands of Claiborne, demands that Claiborne could not meet within the time limit set by Lafitte. Therefore, Claiborne believes that Lafitte may sell out to the British," Simmons concluded. "You see now, LeBlanc, why we must have your help. We believe you to be the one person who can learn Lafitte's intentions, whether or not he will betray our country." Simmons paused, then looking deep into Trent's sincere blue eyes, he said, "I know that Jean Lafitte is your friend, LeBlanc, but if he is a traitor—for God's sake, do not hesitate to inform us of the fact. There are many lives at stake!"

"I do not believe Lafitte to be a traitor, but I will find out what I can. If what I learn is important, I will relay it to you." LeBlanc rose to his feet and, leaning forward, laid his hand upon Simmons's shoulder. "You, too, are *mon ami,* Simmons. And this information you require is truly important to our country. I will be ready to leave early on the morrow. Is that satisfactory?"

"Yes! Yes, that is fine. And thank you, LeBlanc, I knew that we could depend on you!" Simmons gave him a tired but grateful smile.

Amber awoke slowly, reluctant to open her eyes. She stretched her arms lazily, high over her head, then turned, dreamy-eyed, on her side. Her warm smile faded, and she wrinkled her button nose in disappointment when she saw that Trent was not there. Amber had expected to awake and find LeBlanc close beside her. Her hand gently glided over the pillow that still held the imprint of his head, and a warm tingle ran over her body.

"Mmmm," she purred contentedly and closed her eyes again. Gracefully she stretched her lovely, slender frame like a satisfied feline after a long, enjoyable nap. Safely snuggled in Trent's bed again, Amber allowed her mind to drift back over the days just past, days of fear, pain, and humiliation brought to a climax by Trent's rescue, and her homecoming this afternoon. Trent had been worried about her, then he had been angry with her and she with him, but nothing had seemed to matter once they had found themselves in close embrace.

Opening her eyes again, Amber studied the cabin, feeling the warm, gentle emotions that lingered, the emotions she shared with LeBlanc. There were many memories here for her. Some of them were not so pleasant as others, but she refused to think of the unpleasant ones. Not now! She would not wonder how many women had shared the bed in which she now lay so peaceful and contented. Nor would she think of all the fights that she and Trent had had. No, all that was "in the past," as he had said.

Amber's gaze strayed to a pile of boxes which lay abandoned in the far corner of the room, boxes that she did not remember having been there before. Curious, she slipped from the bed and crossed the room. Dropping to her knees, Amber moved her hand lightly along one box as she pondered whether or not she dared explore the contents. But her curiosity outweighed her better judgment, and she lifted the lid from the box.

Her green eyes widened with pure delight at the sight of a

vivid, emerald-green shirt of rich silk with soft, fine lace bordering the deep V of the neck and the cuffs of the long sleeves.

Breathlessly Amber pulled the shirt over her head, the smooth silk whispering down her arms, across her shoulders to settle on her shapely body. The light fabric clung to the peaks of her breasts and flowed downward, the sides nestling at her tiny waist, the back draping over her nicely rounded bottom.

Thrilled at the possibilities of the remaining boxes, Amber eagerly opened them, hastily spilling out the contents and examining each article with childish enthusiasm. "They are beautiful!" she trilled, "just *beautiful!*"

Amber was still kneeling on the floor marveling at her unexpected discovery when a knock at the door startled her. She stared at the closed door apprehensively, thinking that if it were Trent he might be angry with her for meddling. She felt like a child caught in mischief. Suppose the clothing was not meant for me, she thought frantically, suppose they had been purchased for another?

A second knock brought her to her feet, then she heard Neva's uncertain voice. "Miss Amber? Are you there? It is Neva, Miss Amber, may I come in?"

Amber released the breath that she had unconsciously held. "Yes! Oh, yes, do come in, Neva!" she called out, relieved.

Neva entered the cabin, closing the door behind her as she saw that Amber was clad in only a bright green shirt.

"Mercy sakes, Miss Amber!" Neva stifled a giggle. "But you do look funny with nothing on but a shirt!"

Amber shrugged and turned back to the pile of open boxes and her pleasure in the new-found garments.

"Oh, Neva! Come and look at all the beautiful things! Trent must have purchased them the day that he wanted to take me shopping, the day that I ran away! Come!" Amber urged the girl who stood just inside the door. "Come and see all the lovely things!"

As Neva slowly crossed the cabin, Amber saw that the girl still wore only the flimsy, white dress from the auction and the shirt which Monrow had placed about her shoulders on the way back to the *Mér Fleur*. Compassion for the unfortunate young girl rose in Amber's heart as she realized the similarity of their situations. Both had been brought aboard the vessel with nothing more than the clothes on their backs, which, in both cases, was not much.

"They are indeed most beautiful, Miss Amber!" Neva's warm brown eyes lighted at the gaily colored garments, and the joy that Amber evinced caused Neva as much happiness as if the clothing had been her own. "I can see that your man took much time choosing them—undoubtedly each item was selected with special care."

Looking at Neva in surprise, Amber questioned, "What do you mean, Neva?"

"Well, miss, I am certainly no authority, but my guess is that those were men's shirts," Neva explained, "and your Captain has had someone put feminine touches on them. They went to a lot of trouble, too." The girl was studying the handiwork on one of the shirts. "See here, miss! See how the lace has been added?"

"Do you really think so?" asked Amber, "I mean do you really think that all this finery was added, just for me?"

"I do, miss. No shop in this town has this type of merchandise because all the women wear the native dress. Truly, miss, I have never seen shirts such as these. No, I feel certain that your man had these touches added," Neva stated firmly.

Amber felt as if her heart would burst with pride and happiness. Neva had shown her with those few words that Trent did care for her. Why else would he have been so particular about his purchases, she thought, when he could just as well have brought the garments to her in their original state? But he had cared enough to make them special, special enough that she would still feel feminine, though clothed in men's attire.

There was one last box and as Amber removed the cover her astonished eyes fell on the soft, black leather knee boots.

"Oh, Neva, look!" she gasped. "They are absolutely perfect! They are just like the ones Trent has!" Amber carried the treasured boots across the room and sat on the bed to pull them on. They fit snugly on her small feet and the soft leather hugged her calves.

"I like these best of all!" Amber voiced.

Neva laughed at the copper-haired beauty who danced around the cabin dressed only in a green shirt and black knee boots.

"But why would he buy boots such as those?" she asked. "I mean, why did he not buy slippers for you? You are a lady, Miss Amber, and ladies do not wear knee boots. And where are the skirts and shifts that go with these shirts? You cannot go around like that, miss!" Neva's voice was scandalized.

"Skirts? Trent did not buy skirts, Neva. He bought breeches, see?" Amber pointed to a box half-hidden beneath the pile of clothing. "Why would he buy skirts?"

"Breeches! But, Miss Amber! A lady does not wear breeches!"

"*This* lady does! Why, that is all that I have worn for weeks! That is all I had to wear, only they were not mine. And *these are!*" Amber exulted. "Besides, I could not possibly wear skirts aboard the ship, Neva, because they—well, they are just not suitable, that is all!"

"Whatever do you mean, 'they are not suitable'?"

"Why, one cannot climb up into the rigging, nor fight a battle, nor can one 'man' the wheel! *That* is what I mean!" Amber explained patiently.

Neva leaned forward to pick up an armful of the new clothes and began to fold them, stacking them in neat piles, while her mind tried to absorb what she had just heard.

Never had it entered Neva's head that this beautiful, fragile-seeming girl was anything other than a lady, a gentle, well-bred *lady!* One of wealth and society. It seemed incredible and poor Neva was shocked.

"You have done these things?" she finally asked. "You have actually done battle?" Neva's face was a mixture of emotions.

"Of course, I have," Amber answered casually, holding out one booted foot in admiration. "We fought a battle with pirates only a few weeks after I came aboard the *Mér Fleur,*" she continued, her attention more upon her boots than on the conversation.

Neva's brown eyes widened with excitement.

"Did you actually fight? *You?* And did you kill anyone? Oh, Miss Amber, it makes my blood go cold, just thinking about it! Were you not afraid?"

"Yes, Neva, I actually fought. We *all* fought, the entire crew! And yes, I suppose I was frightened—only at the time I really did not think about being frightened. I was much too angry for that. Trent had locked me in this cabin—for my 'protection,' was what he said—but I got out because I wanted to help. And when I reached the deck there was so much going on that I had no time to be afraid."

Neva had placed all the carefully folded garments on the bed, and now Amber lifted a shirt of russet-brown satin from the neat stack, thoughtfully regarding it.

"But did you—uh—did you *kill* anyone?" Neva pursued the subject.

"Yes," came the brief, matter-of-fact reply.

Neva paled. Nervously refolding the brown shirt that Amber had laid back on the bed, she asked in a hushed, unsteady voice, "How many?"

"Oh, three. Maybe four, I am not sure," Amber replied offhandedly. Then, upon seeing Neva's pale face, she laughed and said, "Do not look so shocked. I am no less a lady for having done so. You would have done the same. Besides—" Amber broke off, smiling almost ruthlessly, "It was terribly exciting! The battle, I mean. And if it should become necessary, I shall do it again!"

"Mercy, Miss Amber! I would have plumb near died of fright! No, miss, you are wrong. I could never have done what you did." The girl sighed. "I am not as brave as you." After a brief pause, she added in admiration, "You are a very special lady!"

"One is only as brave as one must be, Neva, and I have no doubt that you, too, are brave," Amber assured the girl. "You are my friend; you were there when I needed someone. And I shall always be here for you. You see, you *too* are special!"

"Thank you, Miss Amber," Neva replied meekly, "I am most pleased that you feel this way."

"And stop calling me 'miss,'" Amber scolded, "we are equals, Neva, and we shall always be so!"

"Yes, miss. Now put on these breeches before someone comes in." She held out a pair of tan knee breeches. "Here we are on a ship full of fit men, and you walking around half naked!" Neva reproved gently, her warm smile removing any criticism from the words.

"Ah, do not be such a goose," Amber jested fondly. "No one would dare to enter without knocking." She twisted her head over her shoulder, straining to see the backs of her leather-encased legs. "Damn!" she blurted, then giggled at the expression on Neva's face. "You will become accustomed to that, too. There is an awful lot of swearing aboard the *Mér Fleur*. Ohh—I cannot see my boots! Tell me, how do I look?"

"Lovely!" came the deep, throaty answer, and both women whirled about in surprise. Trent LeBlanc was leaning lazily against the door, arms crossed, in his usual arrogant manner. "I must say, Amber, that it seems that you are forever tempting me! Although I would never allow you on deck dressed as you are, in my cabin it is indeed a pleasure!" he chuckled.

Removing his cape, LeBlanc hung it on a wall peg and turned back to the two girls, neither of whom had moved. Brown eyes were lowered hastily in embarrassment, green eyes flashed half-apprehensively, half-defiantly.

"Well, little one," Trent broke the silence, "are you not pleased with my purchases? Is there anything not to your liking?"

"Oh, Trent, they are beautiful! Just beautiful!" Amber shrilled as she ran to him, throwing her arms about him. She tilted her head upward and her green eyes were dancing with joy. "Thank you! Oh, thank you!"

"Well! I am most pleased that you like them," Trent voiced as he encircled Amber's small frame in his arms, crushing her to him. He felt the warm softness of her body, brushed his lips lightly over her brow, then his lips met hers in a long, deep kiss.

Neva stood watching, a gentle smile on her pretty face. You are wrong, Miss Amber, she thought. This man *does* love you, even though he hides it deep within him. Then she slipped quietly from the room, softly closing the door.

The kiss was warm and tranquil. Amber found herself lost in the peace that claimed her. Then of a sudden she pulled from Trent's embrace, her face flushed with embarrassment. "Ohh—I forgot—Neva?" she stammered, her bright eyes searching the room.

"She has gone," LeBlanc said softly, smiling down at her. Then sighing deeply, he pulled Amber back into his embrace. "It seems that we are alone, *ma petite chatte*. You managed to stir my blood when first I walked in." His hold tightened and his voice became husky. "You looked damned inviting, kitten, and I find myself quite hungry for your charms. I dare say, woman, if you are to make a habit of running around as you now are, I shall never find the will to leave my cabin!"

At that Trent swept Amber into his arms and strolled across the cabin.

Chapter Seven

NEW ORLEANS CLAMORED WITH EXCITEMENT, AND THE JUBILANT
sounds from the enchanting city rang out.

As the carriage clattered along the waterfront into town,
Amber found herself caught up in a whirl of delight. Turning
her head this way and that, she fluttered about the carriage
seat trying to absorb her new and fascinating surroundings.

She found New Orleans altogether extraordinary. The
dock was astir with seamen in brightly colored attire, shouting
orders and cursing as they loaded or unloaded cargo.

Negroes rolled cotton bales and loaded them on flatbed
wagons. The streets were alive with men of every nation, or
so it seemed from the mixture of languages that reached
Amber's ears.

The public market was crowded, and merchants sold to
men and women, rich and poor, young and old.

Children ran and played, and Negro slaves shuffled by,
carrying baskets on their heads.

And far away, over the bustling sounds of the city, tavern
music and the shouts of brawls, one could hear the low, sweet
melody of a Negro's song.

LeBlanc smilingly watched Amber's enthusiasm, pleased

that she appeared to like the atmosphere of this new world. When he had first told her that they were going to New Orleans she had not been happy at the prospect. And she had again asked him to take her home, back to London.

But now they were here and would remain here for at least four weeks. Or so LeBlanc had been told by his contact, with whom he had met shortly after their arrival. Information concerning Lafitte was to be given to Wells, Trent's New Orleans contact, who would, in turn, relay the vital facts to Simmons.

LeBlanc's instructions were to settle in his home at Travinwood and to go about life as he normally would do. Upon completion of the Lafitte assignment, he was to mark time and wait until he received further orders, so this is what he would do.

"Well, *ma* sweet, what do you think of New Orleans?" asked LeBlanc. "Are you still disappointed that we did not go back to London?"

"I find the city fascinating! I never believed all the stories that I heard," Amber replied breathlessly. "How long are we to be here? Will I be able to see everything? May I go to the markets and visit the shops? Will—"

"Slow down, kitten, one question at a time. We will be here for some time, I have business to attend to. And since that is to take some—ah—weeks, then I think we can manage one, maybe two visits to town. That is, only if you behave yourself!" Trent warned sternly, but with a smile.

"Now sit back and stop fluttering around like a worrisome little chit! We have a few miles yet to go before we reach my home. I sent Neva and Jason on ahead to let the household know that I am coming so that everything will be in order for our arrival."

Amber gasped. The words "my home" had startled her.

"Your home? But I did not know that you had any home other than the *Mér Fleur!* You never mentioned 'home!'" Amber's green eyes mirrored astonishment.

"No? It must have slipped my mind," was his cool reply. "Perhaps it slipped your mind to answer my question. I asked if you are still disappointed that we did not go back to London?"

Amber's eyes sparkled as she answered, "Had we returned

to London I should have missed all this! We can go back to London later, can we not?" Then she grew somewhat subdued, as if lost in thought. "I do sometimes wonder about Uncle Edward and Aunt Alice, and I am sure that they have been sick with worry. And I truly would like to see them again," she said wistfully.

"All in good time, little one," Trent soothed her. "I make a promise to you that you shall see them again."

The carriage rumbled along, its wheels stirring the reddish-brown dirt from the road, leaving behind ghostly clouds of dust.

Gracing each side of the road were massive, moss-draped oaks with gaunt, finger-like branches that arched low over the narrow lane that seemed to go on endlessly.

And through the shadowy under-sky of moss-laden branches, the mellow glow of golden sunlight sifted through the gray, veil-like shadows. Overhead, luminous blue sky with heavy melting white clouds washed by.

Far ahead, as if sprouting forth from the very depths of the earth, rose great white columns, bringing with them the splendor of Travinwood Manor.

There, enveloped by trees from enchanted dreams, Travinwood stood proud and elegant in her shroud of breathtaking beauty. And it was then, at first sight, that Amber fell in love with her, fell beneath her magical spell.

"Welcome to Travinwood, little one! Welcome to my home!" LeBlanc spoke with pride. "She is a grand place, with charm running throughout her timber, grace within her structure, and holds profound memories!"

"Why, she is magnificent, Trent!" Amber said in a hushed voice. "I have never seen anything so beautiful!" She was spellbound by this mysteriously beautiful place, which almost took her breath away. "Tell me more about her!"

"Travinwood has a special character, all her own. She has a gentle, sensitive nature—just like Trisa." LeBlanc's voice tightened with a hint of sadness as he slowed the carriage, his eyes intent on the great house ahead.

Amber turned to Trent, a frown on her pretty face. "Trisa?" she whispered. She noted the emotion in his voice and saw his sincere expression, the tenderness in his blue eyes.

"My mother!" he said softly. "My father built Travinwood for her and it took four years. There are twenty-four rooms in the main house, and later a wing consisting of four rooms was added. There are coach houses, stables, a small cottage, and a smokehouse.

"There are two formal gardens with fountains, ponds of crystal-clear water and marble sundials. The ground floor is graced with a great ballroom and a magnificent library filled with fine rare books." LeBlanc finished with, "This shall be your home now, kitten—for a while. I trust that you will like her."

As the carriage rolled to a stop, a young Negro boy scrambled to his feet and ran down the wide stone steps. The boy was no more than eight or nine years old, and his face bore a wide grin that seemed to fill his entire face with flashing white teeth.

"Massah Trent!" the youngster shrilled in pure delight. "Oh, Massah Trent, we's ben awaitin' fer hours an' hours!"

With a happy laugh LeBlanc swung down from the carriage and stretched his long legs to relieve his stiff muscles. The excited lad squared his shoulders and held out his small black hand to Trent.

Smiling, Trent shook the hand and said, "How are you, young Kane? You have certainly grown since last I saw you!" He bowed low and the boy returned the bow. "And where are your shoes and stockings?" LeBlanc asked, looking down at the bare, black feet.

Kane threw back his curly head and burst into gleeful laughter.

"Sho ain't agonna be de same 'roun heah now dat you's back, Massah Trent, no suh, sho ain't!" he stated.

LeBlanc lifted Amber from the carriage and set her on her feet.

"Kane, this is Miss Amber. She will be mistress of Travinwood while we are here. Amber, this is Kane. He is my shadow when I am home, but if you should need him for anything, I am sure that he will be at your service. Is that not right, Kane?" Trent asked the boy.

"Yas*suh*, Massah Trent, ah sho *will!*" came the enthusiastic reply as Kane stared at Amber, his black eyes shining. "Sho gotcha a purty lady, Massah Trent, yas*suh*, sho 'nuff!" He grinned widely, and with a wave of his hand he ran to lead the horses away, the empty carriage rattling behind.

Amber giggled. "He is darling, Trent. How old is he?" she asked.

"He will be nine years old in three days. He thinks that I have come home for his birthday," Trent told her. "I was here when he was born, and I have somehow managed to be at Travinwood on each of his birthdays. Not that it has ever been planned for that reason, it just happened. But he does not know that, nor do I wish him to know." LeBlanc laughed heartily. "One would almost think that I am his father."

"Well, are you?" Amber blurted, the words coming out before she could stop them.

"Of course not!" Trent roared, his blue eyes wide, dark and stormy.

"You need not look so shocked, Trent. I have heard of such things, you know. Men *have* fathered children by their slaves," Amber retorted.

"You may rest assured that *I* have not! There are many things which I have done, Amber, but that is not one of them. True, I have lain with many women, but to my knowledge I have never fathered a child!" Suddenly his white teeth flashed as he smiled proudly. "That is, other than the child that now grows within you, kitten. Never before have I known a woman whom I would want to bear a child of mine." Trent kissed the tip of Amber's nose as she tilted her head upward to meet his gaze. "Not until now," he said tenderly.

"I am sorry, Trent," Amber said contritely. "I just thought —well, it was just that you seemed so fond of Kane and—"

"I am fond of him, as I am of all the children that Mattie has brought into this world. And at last count there were ten, I believe."

"Ten!" Amber's voice was shocked.

"Well, eleven, counting me." Trent chuckled at the bewildered expression on Amber's face. "Mattie was the midwife who helped to bring me into the world, little one. She was my 'mammy,' that is what they are called in the South." Shaking his head, he went on, "And Mattie still thinks she is my mammy. To her I will never be more than 'young Master Trent.'"

Placing his hands on Amber's shoulders, Trent looked deep into her green eyes and said, "Mattie will be thrilled to learn that there is another LeBlanc on his way. But we must be very careful, lest she spoil him as she did me."

Then with one arm encircling her slender shoulders, Trent walked with Amber up the wide, stone steps toward the massive double doors of Travinwood. When those doors swing open, Amber thought, I shall be entering into a part of Trent's life that I have never known, the part that holds his past, his mystery.

LeBlanc pushed open the wide door and Amber, taking a deep, unsteady breath walked past him, stepping into the entry and thereby into a whole new world.

She stood transfixed, entranced by beauty far beyond what she had expected. The great entry hall was of ivory-colored marble with swirls of jade-green. High overhead, suspended from the second floor, hung a silver chandelier dripping with hundreds of tiny crystal tears.

Ornate silver candle brackets hung on walls covered with hand-painted wallpaper, and a mahogany staircase with ornamental balustrades and marble-topped steps rose gracefully to the second floor.

A place such as this is one found only in dreams, thought Amber.

"Massuh Trent!" The deep, vibrant voice came from behind them, and Amber turned to see an elderly Negro man wearing a stylish cutaway coat of mustard-yellow adorned with black braid. The collar and wide cuffs were black, as were his shoes and stockings. His breeches and waistcoat were the same mustard-yellow, and he wore a high-necked, ruffled-front shirt.

"Suh, ah wus jes' on ma way ta fetch ya ta da house," the man said, and as he walked toward them Amber noticed that he walked with a slight limp. His hair was speckled with gray, and in his hand he carried a black tricorne with braid which matched the braid on his coat. "Mattie ben moughty worried 'bout ya, suh," he finished.

"Morgan!" Trent greeted the older man as he strode across the entry to meet him with a warm handshake and a brief embrace. Amber watched this exchange, puzzled, and Trent turned to her, his hand still on the black man's shoulder.

"This is Miss Amber, Morgan. She will be staying with us for a while," LeBlanc said. "Anything she wants, see that she gets. We want to make her feel as if this were her home."

"Miz Amber," Morgan acknowledged the introduction with a bow. "We sho gonna do our best. Sho is gonna be nice ta have a mistress in Travinwood agin. An' Miz Amber sho do make a purty one!"

"Why, thank you, Morgan," Amber accepted the old man's compliment. "I am sure that I shall enjoy my visit. Travinwood is a most beautiful place!" She smiled her rare, dimpled smile.

"Massah Trent, yo room is ready when ya wanta go up, suh. Mebbe Miz Amber would lak ta rest a bit. Mister Jason done brung y'alls baggage, an' Mattie, her's ben a-flutterin' 'roun all da mornin'."

"Yes, thank you, Morgan. I feel sure that Miss Amber would like to rest for a while. And I am certain that she would enjoy a nice, warm bath after the journey. I trust that the young lady, Miss Neva, has been taken care of? And the cottage, Morgan, has it been readied for occupancy?" Trent questioned.

"Yassuh, Massah Trent, evahthing is ta orduh, suh, jes' lak ya asked," the old man nodded his head vigorously as he assured Trent.

"Then I shall take Miss Amber upstairs and see that she gets settled in. Have hot water sent up for the bath, Morgan, and send up some cool drinks—"

"Lawdy mercy, young Massah Trent! Ya young rascal, ya done s'pose ta ben heah," the strident call rang out from the top of the stairs. "Chile, ya git yorself on up heah an' give yo ol' mammy a hug! Cum on now, quitcha dallyin'. Dese heah ol' laigs cain't make dem dere stair lak dey useta."

LeBlanc and Morgan looked up the stairs, then at each other, and began to laugh.

"Mattie, you have not changed a bit, still ordering me around!" he called up to her. "Look out, here I come!" And with long strides he mounted the staircase, taking the steps two at a time. The old woman held her arms wide as she met him, and he clasped her in a swift embrace.

"For da Lawd's sakes, jes' looky at ma baby!" Mattie crooned. "Why, ya young debbil, if ya gits any bettuh lookin' ya gonna break mo hearts dan ol' Mattie kin keep up wif." And she caught Trent to her ample bosom in a bear-like hug. Holding him with a hand on each shoulder, she stepped back and looked at him proudly. "Jes' look at 'im, Morgan, ain't he da handsomest young buck ya evah did see? Ma chile, ma Massah Trent!" Mattie said happily.

"Now, Mattie, I was thirty-one last July. I am not—" LeBlanc had begun.

"Ah knows how ol' ya is!" Mattie stopped him, indignantly. "Ah wus heah w'en ya cum inta de worl', jes' a-cryin' an' a-lettin' evahbody know dat anuthah LeBlanc wus heah!" Mattie's voice rose higher as she talked. "Ah's yo mammy, ah raised ya, so's don'cha go a-tellin' ol' Mattie how ol' ya am. An' ya don't need ta think ya evah gonna be too big fer me ta whup, chile—dat is, if ya needs it!"

"Oh, Mattie, Mattie! You are a dear!" Trent said through his laughter as he squeezed the soft, plump hand that still held his. "Now, if you are finished with my 'coming-home lecture,' there is someone I want you to meet," he told her as the two of them descended the stairs at a leisurely pace. "I am sure you will like her," he continued, then, leaning down, he whispered in Mattie's ear, "*I do!*"

In the entry Amber had stood with Morgan, watching the tableau at the top of the stairway. There is much affection in this lovely home, she thought. I wish that I had known Trent as a child, could have known his family. And she wished that her child could be reared in this loving atmosphere, wished that she could have someone like Mattie to help rear him and love him.

"Mattie, this is Miss Amber," LeBlanc said as they reached the main floor. He tenderly placed one strong arm around Amber, pulling her close to him.

"Yassuh, she jes' lak Mister Jason say she wus," Mattie stated flatly. "'Ceptin' ah couldn' 'magine nobody bein' as purty as he say she wus." Her bold eyes raked Amber from head to toe, then she nodded her grizzly head in approval. "Cum, chile, give ol' Mattie a hug, lemme welcum ya ta dis home," the old woman coaxed as she held out both hands and smiled her warm, toothy smile. Amber moved slowly from Trent's side and into Mattie's open arms.

Mattie felt that she knew her young master better than any living soul, and she had not seen him so elated since his mother's death. She had seen the light go out of those sapphire-blue eyes and, until now, had never seen it rekindled. But the way those startlingly blue eyes lit up when they rested on this young woman confirmed the story she had pieced together for herself from the things Miss Neva and Mister Jason had told her, ably abetted by her own questions.

Having been sent on ahead to inform Morgan and Mattie that LeBlanc was in New Orleans, Jason and Neva had brought the news that he would be coming home for awhile and that there would be others with him. Arrangements were to be made for Jason, Drake, and Rual to stay in the cottage and for two ladies who would be guests in the main house.

But all the baggage that had been brought was sent either to the cottage or to Master Trent's suite, and Mattie learned that the young woman, Miss Neva, had no baggage. In answer to her questions, Jason told her that Miss Neva had been saved from the slave auction by LeBlanc, therefore she had no belongings. And, "The missy's, that is, Miss Amber's things are in the Cap'n's trunks," had been Jason's words.

This gave Mattie reason to raise her eyebrows and ask further questions. So Jason stammered through the story, beginning in London, to the present, being careful to omit the fact that the missy was carrying the Cap'n's child. He thought it best to leave out that part, feeling that he would be in trouble enough for what he had related.

And, of course, Mattie drew her own conclusions as to the situation between her master and the lovely young woman she was yet to meet.

Pulling her thoughts back to the present, Mattie patted Amber on the arm. "Honey-chile, ya kin jes' relax an' feel at home, heah," she told the girl. "We gonna take real good keer uv ya. Ol' Mattie knows how. Ah gotcha a nice, hot bath a-waitin' for ya in yo room. Now, ya jes' cum along wif Mattie an' ah'll show ya ta it." The words were spoken in a gentle tone and gave Amber reassurance as she was steered up the stairs. "Ya gonna lak it heah, honey, an' ah put ya in one uv de purtiest rooms in da whole house!"

Mattie's words drifted down to Trent, drawing his attention from Morgan's attempt at conversation with him. "Put ya in one uv de purtiest rooms in da whole house!" was what he had heard.

"Mattie!" LeBlanc's sharp call halted the steps of the two women.

"Yassuh?" Mattie said, turning to look down at LeBlanc's stern face.

"Just what room did you put Miss Amber in?"

"Well, suh, ah put her in de green room on de wes' side, same's de uthah young lady," Mattie explained, holding her breath as she waited for his reply. She knew that he might very well be angry with her arrangement, but she meant to learn what the relationship was between the master and this young woman. She wanted to know just how much he cared for her. However, this was the first woman he has ever brought to Travinwood, she remembered, and she wanted to see just how far from him the master would allow Miss Amber to stay. If not having her in his bed meant that she was too far from him, then—

"Oh, no! Miss Amber is to be in the master suite, Mattie!" he said firmly.

"But, suh! Whar *ya* gonna—"

"Am I not the master of Travinwood, Mattie?"

"Yassuh, but—"

"Then, as master of Travinwood I shall be in the master suite! *With Miss Amber!* Comprehend?"

"Yas*suh*, Massah! Ol' Mattie unnerstan's. She unnerstan's jes' fine!" Mattie replied aloud. She chuckled to herself, thinking, Away frum de Massah's bed *wus* too fur, yassuh, *too* fur. Mattie smiled knowingly.

Chapter Eight

LEBLANC HAD JUST DESCENDED THE STAIRWAY WHEN THE FRONT door knocker sounded. He glanced at the tall clock in the corner of the entry and smiled. Seven o'clock, he thought, he is right on time as I knew he would be. I have never known him to be late.

As he crossed to open the door, Trent heard the shuffling footsteps and called over his shoulder.

"It is all right, Morgan, I will answer." Then, before opening the door, he added, "And Morgan, I shall be in the study for quite some time. See to it that no one interrupts as I have an important conference."

"Yassuh, Massah Trent, anthin' else, suh?" asked the servant.

"No, that will be all," LeBlanc replied, pulling open the heavy door.

On the stoop waited a man clad all in black, from the boots on his feet to the hat on his head. The man was tall and of medium build, his skin was pale tan. His slow smile revealed straight white teeth, and lights danced in his dark, almost black eyes. The man was not much older than LeBlanc, and his sooty-black hair was worn long. Dark shadows played

148

about his handsome face. He swept his hat from his head as
he made a low bow.

"Ah, Jean, *mon bon ami,* it is good to see you," LeBlanc
greeted the newcomer, his hand extended in a warm welcome. The two men shook hands heartily. "Come," and
Trent stepped back to allow Jean Lafitte to enter. As Lafitte
stepped inside, LeBlanc slapped him genially on the shoulder, then led him toward the study.

"Mon ami, it is indeed a pleasure to see you after such a
long time. I came as soon as I received your message. But tell
me, how did you know where to find me? And how did you
know that I was in New Orleans?" Again the lazy smile
lighted the man's handsome features.

"Ah, but I know many things. I have ways of obtaining
information, just as you do," LeBlanc laughed, closing the
study door behind him.

Seating himself in a large, leather chair, Lafitte asked, "Tell
me, Trent, how has it been with you? Still up to your
mysterious goings and comings? I understand from Casey
Reed that the two of you are still working for the
gouvernement. You are doing many things for *le gouverneur,
oui?* And how is the honorable *Monsieur* Claiborne?" Jean
chuckled wryly at the amused look on his friend's face.

"You never cease to amaze me, *mon ami!* So you have no
time for an idle chat, is that what you are telling me? And you
already know why I sent for you, my message gave you that
information. Whether or not you accepted this appointment
was your decision, I only requested that you come," Trent
said.

"Then I am the reason for your being back in New
Orleans?"

"Yes! You see, I have been asked to extract certain—ah—
information from you," LeBlanc laughed truthfully. "So! Are
you going to make it easy for me? Or will I have difficulty in
accomplishing my mission?"

"So you have asked me here to reveal all my secrets, eh?
All right, what is it that you seek? No," he raised a hand to
check LeBlanc's reply. "Let me guess! Claiborne received my
letter and the papers sent to one Jean Blanque. Now he sends
you, as his *spy,* to learn if it is a bluff, eh? Well, I need not tell
you, mon ami, that Jean Lafitte does not bluff. The papers

that Claiborne received were given me by the British and are genuine! I am truly weary of playing games with that pompous bastard! I presented him with my demands and I stand by them!" Lafitte struck his open palm with his fist.

"What were those demands, Jean?" LeBlanc asked in a quiet voice.

"Surely you jest!" Lafitte blurted, studying the face of his friend.

"No, *mon ami*, I truly know nothing of them. I was in Havana to deliver cargo when I received instructions to come here, and I have only arrived this day. I was told only that you were visited by the British and that they were allowed on Grande Terre, and that you later sent certain demands to Governor Claiborne. Demands that he could not meet!" Trent explained.

"Then your mission is to drill me, to learn what you can of my intentions and to discover my future plans." Lafitte's voice held a tinge of bitterness. "Then when you report your findings to *le gouverneur*—then he will decide what is truth, eh?"

"Jean, I would never disclose any information concerning your plans that you gave me in confidence. I will report only that which you give me your permission to relate." LeBlanc was earnest. "Do you have so little faith in our *amitié*? Have I not proven myself to you many times in the past?"

"*Oui, mon ami,* and you must forgive my assumptions. Only because I *do* trust you, LeBlanc, did I come here. Your message clearly indicated what you wanted of me, and I choose to make you aware of my intentions and to assure you that I am no 'traitor,'" Lafitte stressed. "And you do have my permission to relate what I am about to disclose, although I have already made it quite clear to Claiborne. It is not my fault that he chooses to question what is truth!"

"I know that you are no traitor, Jean, but it is my assignment to make sure of all the facts. You do understand, do you not?"

"*Oui, mon ami,* I do understand and I do not blame you. So, here is the full story," Lafitte began. "Early on the morning of September the third . . ."

And Lafitte related the full story, omitting nothing.

Trent heard him out, without interruption and without questions. Then at the conclusion of the tale he rose from the corner of his desk where he had sat throughout the conversation.

"I shall make my report, Jean, just as you have conveyed the information to me."

Lafitte also rose from his chair and again the two friends clasped hands.

Trent continued, "I thank you for your trust and for your help. But most of all, Jean, I thank you for your continued friendship."

A brief embrace, customary of the French, and one last handshake before the two men stepped from the study and walked to the front door.

"Keep in touch, *mon ami*," LeBlanc said to his friend in parting.

"I shall. And may you keep in good health!" Jean Lafitte replied.

"Dat Satan, he Massah Trent's hoss," Kane told Amber as he pointed a small grubby finger at a sleek, black stallion which stood some distance from the other horses.

"Ohhh, Kane! He is magnificent!" Amber breathed, looking out across the clover-blanketed field at the exquisite animal. He was black as midnight, and the sheen of his coat glistened richly, reflecting the bright sunlight.

Yes, she thought, Trent would indeed possess such an animal, for how very much like his master was Satan. He held his head proudly, arrogantly, as if he dared another to cross him. The strong, lithesome body moved with brash self-assurance. His powerful, lofty legs provided him with an imposing height.

As Amber and Kane neared the fence, the animal watched their approach, and then, as if daring them to come closer, he reared back on his hind legs and danced backward. With his fore hooves pawing the air, Satan tossed his great, majestic head back and forth, his black mane flying wildly, and snorted in a defiant manner.

Of such beauty was this superb animal that Amber knew that he must certainly have been carefully selected. Satan's unusual attractiveness and his "one-of-a-kind" character well matched the manner and temperament of the suave and domineering nature of Trent LeBlanc.

"Kane, it has been so long since I have gone riding. I should like to go, now. Is there a saddle horse suitable for me? And will you ride with me?" Amber's enthusiasm seemed to overflow to the youngster.

"Yassum, ya kin ride Moon," Kane told her. "Moon, he be gentle 'nuff fer ya ta ride. 'Cept if'n he ain't han'eld gentle, den he git sorta skittish. But bein' a lady, ah knows ya'd han'el 'im right."

"Fine, shall we go?" Amber said as she turned toward the stables.

Kane trotted along beside her, talking as he went.

"Ah got ma own hoss, missy." At Amber's quick look, Kane grinned and said, "Ah gonna call ya 'missy,' 'cause dat's what all de folks frum Massah Trent's ship calls ya." After this explanation, Kane went on as if he had not digressed from his subject. "Massah Trent give 'im ta me fer ma birfday las' year. He named 'Storm,' 'cause he wus borned on a stormy night."

Entering the stables, Kane hurried to get a saddle for Amber but she stopped him, "No, Kane, no saddle for me. I shall ride bareback."

Kane grinned at her with great admiration. "Jes' lak me, missy, ah don't ride wif a saddle. An' ah laks de way ya dresses, too. Ya know, plain lak me. Ya be a real lady an' all, 'ceptin' ya don' dress all fancy," he explained. "Ya lak Miz Trisa wus."

"What do you mean, Kane, 'like Miss Trisa'?" Amber questioned.

"Wal, Miz Trisa, she was purty an' gentle, jes' lak ya are. She made ya happy an' made ya laff all de time. She wus a good lady an' never made ya feel lak she wus better'n ya wus. An' she even wore britches sumtimes. Ah sho did lak 'er, jes' lak ah laks ya."

Kane smiled up at Amber, then shook his head. "Only diffrunce 'tween ya an' Miz Trisa is dat ya laks ta go 'roun barefooted, lak me," the boy said as he kicked the dust-covered ground with the heel of one bare foot.

* * *

As Amber and Kane returned to Travinwood after a leisurely ride, they heard the sound of trotting hooves and the rattle of a carriage. Rounding the side of the house, they saw the carriage draw up to the front steps. A tall, slim black man leaped down from the driver's seat and extended a hand to assist a lady from the passenger's seat.

"Uh *huhhh!*" Kane muttered, "Ah knowed she'ud be heah soon's she heered de Massah be home!"

Amber saw the dislike in the boy's face. "Who is she, Kane?"

"Dat Miz Kathleen Fulton, an' she'll be 'roun heah lots, now dat Massah Trent be home," and Kane sighed disgustedly.

Through narrowed eyes Amber watched as Kathleen stepped from the carriage. She saw slim ankles exposed as the haughty lady lifted the hem of her light-blue silk gown above the tops of her kid slippers to ensure that the gown did not touch the ground. Taller, by far, than Amber, Kathleen's slim frame was gracefully curved, and the tight-fitting, daringly low-cut bodice revealed a goodly portion of her voluptuous breasts. Her skin was creamy-white, and her blond hair was arranged atop her head in ringlets.

Amber admitted to herself, though grudgingly, that Kathleen Fulton was a lovely young woman. And Amber also knew at once that she thoroughly disliked Kathleen Fulton.

"You may return for me in an hour," Kathleen told her driver, who promptly climbed upon the carriage and picked up the reins.

"Yassum," the black man replied. Then he slapped the reins against the rump of the gray horse and headed back down the lane.

As Kathleen turned to the steps, she heard the whinny of another horse and looked to see Amber and Kane riding slowly toward her. She moved a few steps in their direction and, closing her dainty parasol, smiled sweetly.

"Kane, is your master at home?" she asked in a honey-dripped voice. "I do hope I have not missed him." Lifting a tiny, jeweled pendant watch she checked the time of day then sighed, "Oh dear, it is his usual riding time."

"No ma'am, Massah Trent he ain't ben out, yit, 'cause ah jes' seen Satan still in de pastuah whar he wus w'en we lef heah."

Kathleen's silver-blue eyes swept over Amber's slight form. She wrinkled her small nose in displeasure at the sight of the figure dressed in black knee breeches and loose white shirt. Amber had tucked her russet-gold hair under a black cap which she had found in Trent's room. She sat astride a golden-tan palamino whose broad back caused her small bare feet to dangle just short of the animal's stomach.

"Are you new here?" Kathleen asked Amber, "or did you come from Captain LeBlanc's ship?" Without waiting for a reply, she continued, crossly, "He is always taking in runaway lads. I tell him that he should not do so, for one never knows what sort—" Shaking her blond head, she babbled on, "But he does not listen. I am sure that he will continue to do as he pleases, as usual!"

In the presence of the stylishly dressed Kathleen, Amber was painfully aware that she, herself, looked like a dirty stable boy. But the fact that this snooty, pale-skinned snob looked at her with contempt made Amber furious. She has no right, Amber fumed, no right at all to speak to me in this manner!

But she held her temper and her tongue. Her mind went back to Havana, the scene with Maria, how she had jumped to conclusions based on the woman's words without giving Trent a chance to explain and thought, *but not this time!* She would learn who Kathleen Fulton was and what she was to LeBlanc before creating problems for herself.

So Amber made no answer to Kathleen, and Kathleen seemed to expect none, for she turned abruptly back toward the house.

"Mattie!" LeBlanc called as he stepped from the stairs. "Mattie!" the call was repeated as he strode across the marble entry, the heels of his riding boots clicking loudly.

"Suh?" Mattie answered, coming from the dining room and wiping her flour-covered hands on her apron. "Did ya need sumkin, Massah?"

"Do you know where Miss Amber is, Mattie?"

"Yassuh, she wif Kane. Dey ben a-runnin' 'roun dis heah

place all de mornin'," the old woman laughed. "Dat Kane, he jes' as much taken wif Miz Amber as he evah wus wit' ya, suh!" She shook her head and smiled fondly. "Dat litta lady, her sum kinda speshul, sho is!"

Trent smiled, pulling on a pair of brown kid gloves that matched his boots and breeches. He tied a soft, white scarf around his neck and tucked it into his tan, silk shirt.

"If I do not see Miss Amber, tell her that I shall be back for dinner. And see to it that she does not overdo, Mattie, she—well, she is fragile."

"Yassuh! Ol' Mattie'll tak keer of Miz Amber, don'cha worry none 'bout dat!" she assured Trent as he headed out the door, waving a hand to her.

Stepping onto the porch LeBlanc almost collided with Kathleen, who had just reached the doorway. He grabbed her by the shoulders and steadied her as she stumbled.

"Kathy! What are you doing here?" Trent asked in surprise.

Kathleen's arms went around his neck and her thin, pink lips pressed upon his open mouth. She moved closer to him before he could recover from this unexpected encounter.

From where Amber watched, it appeared as if Trent had pulled Kathleen into his embrace. She had seen Trent come through the door, had seen him clasp the woman's shoulders, had noted the quick movement which had brought Kathleen close to LeBlanc and, of course, the kiss.

Amber sat tensely astride Moon's bare back, her angry green eyes boring into the back of the despised, blond head. She nudged Moon's flank, urging him closer to the porch and laid her forefinger across her slightly puckered lips, cautioning Kane to remain quiet so that she could hear the two on the stoop.

"Darling, I came as soon as I heard you were here," Kathleen was saying. "I was at Madame Dunlap's having a dress fitted when her son ran in shouting that the *Mér Fleur* was in port. 'You know what that means, Maw?' he yelled, 'that means Cap'n LeBlanc is home!' He was really excited that his hero was in town, but no more so than I! So I got in my carriage and came right over!" she cooed, running her finger along Trent's chin.

Amber clenched her jaw in fury, her eyes shot sparks of

green fire. Unconsciously she jerked the reins taut, Moon was startled, and in a liquid movement he reared dangerously. Amber clung to the palamino's wide neck as he danced nervously.

"Miz Amber!" Kane's terrified scream met Trent's ears. "Hang on, missy! Whoa, Moon, *whoa!*"

LeBlanc leaped from the steps and ran to Amber's assistance. Kane had managed to grab the reins of the frightened horse and was pulling desperately.

Trent's long arm reached high and yanked Moon's bridle. The animal stood quivering while LeBlanc patted and soothed him. Then looking up into Amber's ashen face he saw her gazing down into his enraged face.

"What in the hell do you think you are doing?" Trent stormed. Amber only stared wide-eyed, biting her underlip, and said nothing. "Get down from that damned horse this minute!" he commanded as he reached up and swung her down from the horse. Setting Amber on her feet, LeBlanc shook her by her shoulders. "Damn you, Amber, are you trying to kill yourself? Do you not ever think before you do fool things? Suppose—"

"Oh, stop yelling at me," Amber shouted, jerking free. Her cap fell from her head, releasing her abundance of red-gold hair, which tumbled about her shoulders. "All you ever do is yell at me, Trent LeBlanc!" She choked as the tears stung her eyes.

Mattie had heard the commotion and had run outdoors in time to see Amber clinging to the horse and had stood watching the scene, her hands clasped in front of her. Then she saw the master shake her young mistress, heard him yell at her, and decided at once that this was just too much.

"Massah Trent," Mattie's voice was loud and reached LeBlanc before the panting Mattie rushed up. "Now, don'cha go hollerin' at dat chile lak dat! An' a-shakin' her dat way, shame on ya!" she scolded, holding out her short, pudgy arms to Amber. "Come heah, honey chile, ya cum heah ta Mattie an' lemme see if ya's awright!"

Amber took a step toward the kindly old servant, but suddenly she felt dizzy. Her eyes would not focus on the woman, and she put one hand to her brow and the other to her stomach.

"Massa Trent!" Mattie shrilled as Amber swayed. But Trent had seen the unsteadiness in Amber's step and quickly swept her into his arms.

Kathleen had been shocked at the sight of the beautiful, russet hair falling from beneath the cap of the small person she had thought to be a boy. Now she stood watching in confusion as Trent had first lashed out at the creature, then had clasped her to his bosom, holding her tightly in his strong arms. And there was Mattie, clucking around like a mother hen while Kane had swiftly slid from Storm and run yelling toward a man who was coming from the cottage in a full run. What is going on, here, she thought, and who is this person?

"What happ'n, Cap'n?" Jason asked breathlessly, his weathered face full of concern. "Is the missy all right? Is she hurt?"

LeBlanc carried the unconscious Amber up the front steps, striding along as if he had not heard Jason's questions, with Mattie and Kane trailing behind him. Jason fell in line and the procession entered the house, leaving Kathleen unheeded.

Trent mounted the winding stairs, calling for Mattie to follow. But his order was unnecessary, for Mattie was close behind him. Kane dropped to the bottom step of the stairway, while Jason paced the length of the entry.

Kathleen stood in the open doorway, bewildered and forgotten.

"What happened, Kane?" Jason asked the worried boy.

"Well, Miz Amber, she wus on Moon . . . he got skeered . . . he bolted . . . he jes' 'bout throwed de missy . . . den de Massah, he cummed a'runnin' at us," Kane swallowed hard, "well, he pulled de missy down off'n Moon—" The boy paused, catching his breath, then went on. "Well, de Massah, he shook de missy an' talked ta 'er real mean lak . . . an' den she jes' up an' fain'ed!"

As Kane concluded the story, Jason stood for a moment, uncertainly. Then he seemed to reach a decision and told the youngster, "Tell the Cap'n that I 'ave gone ta fetch a doctor!" Jason bolted past Kathleen in the doorway, almost knocking her down.

Silence filled the entry where only Kane and Kathleen remained. Kane was busy with his own thoughts and concern for his 'missy,' and Kathleen still stood in bewilderment.

Finally she could stand it no longer, and Kathleen stepped further into the entry. Placing her hands on her hips, she stood looking down at the boy.

"Kane, who is that woman? What is she to everybody? More important, what is she to Master Trent?"

Kane slowly raised his black eyes, then he stood up.

"Dat be Miz Amber an' she be a very special lady." Then his eyes twinkled and he smiled broadly. "Miz Amber be Massah Trent's lady," he said proudly. "He brung her all de way fum sum place called England!"

Upon obtaining this bit of information, Kathleen raced up the stairs in high dudgeon. She walked along the upper hallway, opening and closing doors, as she searched the rooms for those who had preceded her. She had expected to find them in one of the guest rooms but as she neared the master suite she heard voices. Slowly Kathleen approached the door to Trent's rooms, and she entered quietly, surveying the scene before her.

The golden-haired woman lay upon Trent's bed and he sat beside her, tenderly bathing her brow with a damp cloth. Mattie hovered at Trent's shoulder as she murmured endearments to 'de missy' and gentle scoldings to 'Massah Trent' for 'treatin' de missy lak dat,' interspersed with encouragement and comforting words for her master that 'de missy'll be awright, ye jes' wait an' see.'

Kathleen moved swiftly forward.

"What is that woman doing in this house? Why is she in your room, Trent? And in your bed?" Kathleen's voice was venomous. "Why did you bring your whore home with you?"

LeBlanc leaped to his feet and crossed the room with long strides. When he reached Kathleen, he grabbed her arm roughly and pulled her back out into the hallway.

"Amber is not a whore and you will not regard her as such, do you understand?" he stormed.

Propelling Kathleen rapidly toward the stairs, Trent told her, "You will do well to leave this house, Kathleen! And now!" his voice was laced with warning.

Jerking free of his hold, Kathleen sped down the stairway shouting over her shoulder, "She *is* your whore, Trent LeBlanc, you do not fool me, not one bit!" LeBlanc heard the great front door close with a heavy thud.

He stood in the hallway breathing heavily, attempting to gain control of his temper before returning to Amber. Then he heard Mattie shuffling toward him and turned toward her.

"Massah Trent, ya gonna let dat woman git by wif callin' Miz Amber dat name?" Her arms were crossed over her bosom, and her chest heaved with indignation. "Ya gonna let 'er talk ta ya lak dat an' do nothin' 'bout it?"

"No, Mattie, I am not! She will answer to me, but right now I am more worried about Amber than I am about that vicious woman."

As he reached the door, he stopped and said in a low voice, "She should have revived by now. Where is Miss Neva? I may need her help."

"Miss Neva went inta town wif Mistah Monrow and Morgan, suh. But don'cha worry none, suh. Ah'll be heah, dat kitchen kin jes' wait. Miz Amber, her be more importan'."

LeBlanc gave the old woman a quick hug and said, "Thank you, Mattie."

"Massah Trent, suh!" The urgent whisper came from the stairway, and they both turned to see Kane's curly head appear as he bounded toward them soundlessly on bare feet. "Mistah Jason say ta tell ya he's went fer a doctuh!"

LeBlanc's sigh of relief spoke volumes to Mattie. She knew that not only had the master not thought of a doctor but also that he was fully aware of the fact that there could be complications due to Amber's condition.

"Thank you, Kane," was his simple reply to the boy. "Watch for Miss Neva and ask her to come up, right away," Trent instructed Kane, knowing that the youngster wanted to help out in the crisis and giving him a definite and, to Kane, an important commission.

Returning to Amber's bedside, LeBlanc resumed his place and again began to bathe her brow while Mattie sat heavily in a leather chair near him. Lacing her fingers together in her lap, the old servant asked softly,

"Massah, why din'cha tell ol' Mattie dat de young mistress wus wif chile?"

Trent's gaze never left Amber but he stopped bathing her brow and touched her pale cheek with the back of his hand.

"I had no intention of trying to keep it from you, Mattie, I just had not found the right time to tell you," he replied.

Then turning his head to look at Mattie, he smiled lazily. "How did you know? Did she tell you?"

"Nawsuh, Massah. Ah's ben 'roun too long not ta know. Ah only laid eyes on dat one two days ago, but ah knowed she wus. An' jes' befoah she fainted, Miz Amber grabbed 'er belly, lak she had a pain."

"She will be all right, but she must have lots of rest and quiet. And she must eat right. Now that she is carrying a child, it is necessary that she eat better than she apparently has been," Doctor Holmes told Mattie as he replaced his stethoscope and other medical instruments in his worn black bag.

LeBlanc entered in time to hear the doctor's last few words.

"I have given her a sedative and she will sleep for awhile."

"Doctor Holmes, how is she? Will she be all right? And the baby?" Trent questioned, his voice husky with emotion and concern.

"If she is well cared for, she will be fine," was the answer. Then, as if an afterthought, Doctor Holmes asked, "Are you the father, Captain LeBlanc?"

"I am!" LeBlanc replied unhesitatingly.

"Is this her first child?" was the doctor's next question.

"Yes, it is. Why? Is there a problem? Is the child all right?" Trent's voice was tight with anxiety.

"The child is fine," Doctor Holmes assured him. "I can foresee no problem . . . that is, if she takes care . . . there were some signs . . . but not much . . . still, I feel that she should take it easy for a few days. And I will come back in a day or so to check on her. In the meantime, should you need me, just send me word." And the little doctor rose to his feet.

"Thank you, Doctor, we will see that Amber is well cared for. I shall see to it, personally," Trent assured him as they left the room together.

Mattie stayed by Amber, patting the girl's hand and crooning softly.

After LeBlanc had seen the doctor out, he returned and crossed to the bed. He stood gazing at Amber's pale face, his blue eyes soft and tender. Reaching down, he stroked the red-gold hair gently.

"Mattie," Trent's voice was almost a whisper. "You feel that I was too rough with Miss Amber this afternoon, do you not?"

"Yassuh!" Mattie answered him without a qualm. "She didn' go ta make Moon shy lak dat. She didn' mean no hahm." There was no doubt how the old woman felt about the situation. Her young mistress had been treated unfairly, to her mind, and she had no misgivings about letting the young master know it.

"Damn it, Mattie! Amber should not have been on that blasted horse in the first place! She never thinks, *never!*" Trent's voice rose in frustration. "She should have known better! Damn her, she has to learn the hard way. She will not listen to me, she fights me at every turn!"

"Captain Trent? Is Miss Amber all right?" Neva asked as she entered the room with Morgan right behind her. "Kane was sitting on the front steps waiting for us and he said—" her voice broke as tears threatened.

"She will be fine, Neva. The doctor has just left, and he said that she must have a lot of rest and good food. And she will get that here," Trent told her. "She will just have to take it easy for awhile and she will be as good as new."

"But Kane said something about her riding a horse. Why was she on a horse, anyway?" Neva persisted.

"Damned if I know! But, knowing Amber, she will come up with a good reason, or one that she thinks is a good one. I could wring her skinny, little neck!" LeBlanc steamed, running his fingers through his hair.

"Suh?" Morgan spoke for the first time. "Miz Kathleen, she in de liberry, suh. She say she not a-leavin' dis house 'til she talks ta ya."

"What? I thought she had gone. I told her to!"

"Yassuh, she lef', 'cept Kane say she cum back. She in dah waitin' fer ya, suh." Morgan was clearly uncomfortable about the problem.

Clenching his fists at his sides, LeBlanc let out a string of oaths as he stormed out the door. The only way to handle Kathleen, he decided, was to throw her out of his house. She had been a thorn in his side for too long, always showing up when he was at Travinwood, trying to trap him into marriage.

Once she had gone so far as to arrange for her father to catch her and Trent in a compromising situation in the stables. But LeBlanc had stood his ground and had told her father that Kathleen had come to him willingly and that he would not marry her under any circumstances. Furthermore, he had told the irate father, he had not been the first to lie with Kathleen. And that had been the end of it.

But that was not the end, so far as Kathleen was concerned. She continued to come around, continued to be available to him. Trent had tired of her long ago, but he knew that when he was at Travinwood he never had to go to the trouble to find a woman to fulfill his need with Kathleen so readily accessible.

All these things Trent was thinking as he made his way down the stairs and across the wide hall to the library. And he had decided to approach Kathleen in a clam, matter-of-fact manner, then he would throw her out. For good!

Entering the library, LeBlanc closed the double door behind him and turned to Kathleen, giving her a long, level look. Then, without a word, he crossed to a small cabinet laden with a variety of decanters.

"Why are you here, Kathleen?" he asked harshly, pouring brandy into a crystal goblet. "Did I not tell you to leave this house?"

"But, Trent, darling! I know that you did not mean what you said," Kathleen purred. "I know that it was because I lost my temper in the presence of your servant, and for that I am sorry, my love. It was when I saw that—that woman in your bed—well, I just—"

"The lady's name is Amber Kensington," Trent broke in. "And she happens to be one of the most genuine ladies that I have ever had the pleasure to meet." LeBlanc spoke carefully, not yet ready to show his hand.

"Lady! A 'lady,' is she? Why, she does not ride like a lady, she does not talk like a lady, she does not even *dress* like a lady!" Kathleen said heatedly. She was too caught up in her own storm to care what she said. "You have the nerve to call that—that whoring little bitch a *lady?*"

So enraged was Kathleen that she did not see Trent's expression, did not see his hand tighten on his glass, nor did she see him flinch at her words, 'whoring little bitch.' Had she done so, Kathleen would not have dared to go further. "Why, I am quite sure that she has slept with any and every man who beckoned her. She is obviously the kind of woman that could not be satisfied with one man. And you, Trent LeBlanc, a man with your background, to bring her here!" Kathleen waved her hand expansively. "To allow that woman in the beloved home of your dear father and your darling mother! Thank God they were spared seeing it!" And she rolled her blue eyes heavenward.

LeBlanc gulped down his brandy and poured another while trying to frame a fitting reply. Before he could do so, Kathleen rushed on.

"Darling," she twisted her hands together as if pleading, "You must see what this woman could do to you, to your reputation. Why, a man of your wealth and means—" Kathleen paused and looked around the grandly furnished room. "Can you not see that all of this is what she is after? Your money, darling, not you!"

Trent's words were slow and deliberate. "I am quite sure that you believe everything you have just said. But there is no reason for you to fear for the safety of my wealth in regard to Amber—Miss Kensington. For, you see, she had no knowledge of my wealth, nor had she ever heard of Travinwood until she arrived here. She is much too honest and is far too outspoken for me to ever distrust her."

Placing his empty glass on the liquor cabinet, LeBlanc folded his arms across his chest, and, planting his feet widely apart, he looked straight into the depths of Kathleen's eyes and stated,

"You will never again speak of Amber in the manner in which you have taken the liberty during this conversation, Kathleen! And that, my dear, is not a mere threat! You will not speak of her in any way, except with utmost respect! Amber is young and still somewhat innocent. She is as pure as any virgin maiden, and I know not one man worthy of her!"

"Virgin!" Kathleen screamed. "First you call her a lady! Now, a virgin! Why she is no more either than—than—"

"Than you are, Kathleen?" Trent's words were like ice.

"Trent!" Kathleen gasped, her hand fluttering to her breast. "Whatever do you mean by saying such a thing to me?

My goodness! The woman has already poisoned you!" Suddenly a thought struck her, and she covered her open mouth with her hand as she cried out.

"Oh, darling! You have not—surely, you would not—" She stopped, staring wide-eyed at LeBlanc.

"I would not—what, Kathleen?" Trent asked blandly. "Go ahead and ask what you were about to." His smile was cold.

"Well—you did not marry her, did you? Oh, darling, not someone like her!"

"No, I am married to no woman, nor will I be! You, of all people, should know better than to ask such questions!" Trent looked at her with distaste.

"But you brought her here! And she now lies in your bed! Why? If you are not wed and if she means nothing to you, why did you bring her here?"

"I did not say that Amber means nothing to me. And I brought her here because I chose to. Amber belongs to me!" Trent's words brooked no argument.

"Then she is your slave? You bought her, is that it?" Kathleen showed her relief. "Oh, darling! I should have known!" But her relief was short-lived as LeBlanc quickly set her straight on the matter.

"Amber is *not* my slave, neither did I *buy* her! But she *does* belong to me, she will *always* belong to me!" Trent was speaking more to himself than to Kathleen. "I *made* her mine and she will never be touched by any other man! Amber is pure and untarnished!"

The words left Kathleen speechless for a moment, then she recovered.

"Your Amber is no virgin, Trent LeBlanc! Have you not lain with her?" she asked. Then she laughed aloud. "Trent LeBlanc has not lain with this woman? *That* I find hard to believe!" Then angrily she spat out, "You have lain with her! She has spread beneath you! Your 'Miss Pure and Innocent' is no virgin!"

"What you say is true, Kathleen, and I should know. For it was I who took her virtue some months past. It is my bed, and mine alone, that she has shared. No other man's arms has she lain in, no man save myself has ever touched her!" He spoke gently, then suddenly his voice rang like steel. "But *you,*

Kathy! Oh, you are a completely different story! Your virtue was gone long before I lay with you!"

"Trent, darling, whatever do you mean? You—you knew that I was not a virgin. You knew that I had—had been raped!" Kathleen's voice softened and her silver-blue eyes searched Trent's.

"I know that is what I was told, after I let you know that I was aware that you were not a virgin. Do you not remember, Kathy? When we first lay together you were very upset that I knew that I was not the first," Trent laughed without humor. "Then you began to weep and told me the story of how, at the age of fifteen, you had been raped. But I have always found your story a bit hard to believe, especially when you seemed to be so experienced.

"You knew far too much for a woman who had never spread beneath a man save for rape!" Trent poured another brandy and lifted the drink, slowly swirling the liquid around in the glass, then took a sip.

Then pointedly, but ever so sweetly, he said to the silent Kathleen, "It is *you*, my darling, lovely Kathleen, who is the conniving, whoring bitch, not Amber! No!" he said, when she opened her mouth as if to reply. His command checked any rebuttal, and she remained silent.

"You see, I know that you have been with many men, both before me and after. And you made the mistake of bedding my closest friend, and when Casey Reed drinks . . . well, he talks a lot. That was before I ever met you, and you have lain with him many times since then. It seems that when Casey and I are in town at the same time, Kathleen Fulton hops from my bed to his, and that she has done so on more than one occasion."

LeBlanc raised his drink in mock salute, then drained it. He appeared to have nothing more to say, and the silence lengthened. Kathleen had listened in dismay, unaware that Trent knew so much about her actions. Now she found her tongue and made a feeble attempt to refute the accusations.

"No, Trent! You do not understand! It is not like you think!" Her words stumbled to a halt as she tried to think of a way out of this trap into which she had walked. "You see, darling, I was not aware that you knew Casey Reed. When I learned that you were friends, I knew how it would affect you should you ever find out that I had lain with Casey."

She hesitated, but when Trent did not speak, went on, "Do you not see, my darling, I know your temper! I know how you are about what belongs to you and I told Casey—"

LeBlanc's abrupt, sarcastic laughter stopped Kathleen. "My poor, deluded Kathleen! Do you really believe that I ever thought of you as belonging to me? Do you honestly think that knowing that you shared the bed of Casey Reed would bother me? Pray allow me to enlighten you! You are wrong on both counts!"

His scornful words and mocking laughter shocked Kathleen. A look of disbelief crossed her face, and she opened her lips to speak, but Trent spoke first.

"Oh, yes, my dear! You are dead wrong! I must say, in all honesty, that the knowledge of your conquests never bothered me. Not in the least! With whom, or with how many men, you spread yourself, I do not care! And you see, I have known for a very long time what you are. Quite frankly, I shall be glad to be rid of you. You have been like a pebble in my boot. I have known that it was there and that it was a source of irritation. But I just had not the time to dispose of it!"

"No! I do not believe you! You have come back here, you have come back to me every time! You made love to me, you know you did! You had to love me, you had to care!" Kathleen protested.

"Yes, I came back here. I came back to Travinwood, to my home. But never to you, dear Kathleen, never to you! As for making love to you—what man would not fall into bed with a willing woman? But as for *love*, no! No, love had nothing at all to do with it," Trent assured her as he strode to the door.

Opening the door with a flourish, LeBlanc bowed mockingly, and with a swift, sweeping motion of his hand, he said,

"I believe you know your way out. I shan't detain you longer!"

Chapter Nine

TRENT LEBLANC SAT AT THE TABLE WHICH HAD BEEN PLACED IN the curve of a large bay window in the kitchen. He absently stirred his coffee as he gazed out the window into space. Beautiful red geraniums in clay pots were placed on the wooden ledge and provided a bright spot in the spotlessly clean kitchen. But LeBlanc saw nothing of their beauty as he continued to stir the steaming black liquid with a monotonous motion.

On the other side of the kitchen Mattie sat on a high stool peeling potatoes and watching her master. She saw him yawn and rub his tired eyes, then stare down at his cup. The spoon made a rhythmic, high-pitched tinkle as it met the sides of the cup, and the annoying, nerve-wracking ting . . . ting . . . ting . . . was becoming too much for Mattie.

"Massah Trent, ah thought ya took yo coffee black."

"I do, Mattie."

"Den why ya a-stirrin' yo coffee lak dat?" the old woman asked.

"What?" Trent replied, then looking down at the spoon he removed it, and, placing it thoughtfully on the table, he tilted back his chair, resting his arms behind his head.

After a long moment of silence, Mattie asked, "Ya still be worried 'bout Miz Amber? Yo mind be on 'er all de mornin', ain't it? Now doncha know dat she a-gonna be jes' fine, Massah? De doctah, he say so!"

"Yes, Mattie, I know what he said and I believe him. Amber has been doing fine these last two days, and Doctor Holmes says that she will be able to get up tomorrow. No, Mattie, that is not what is bothering me."

Pushing away his coffee cup, Trent stood and slowly crossed the kitchen to gaze out the window on the other side of the room. Mattie watched him with concern. She had seen the disturbed look on her master's face and had noted his restlessness during the past few hours.

"Suh, kin ol' Mattie hep? Ya know dat when ya wus a little scamp ya useta tell me all yo problems." Mattie set aside her bowl of potatoes and laid the paring knife down, ready to listen.

After a few moments Trent turned and retraced his steps, sitting heavily in the chair. Mattie said no more until it was apparent that her master was reluctant to speak.

"Ah got all yo confidences, all yo secrets locked up right heah," Mattie pointed to her heart with a backward motion of her thumb. "Don' nobody know mo 'bout ya den ol' Mattie do, chile!"

With a long sigh, Trent pulled out a chair and said to the old servant, "Sit down, Mattie, here by me." When she made no move, LeBlanc chuckled softly and continued, "Come on, you have sat at this table before, with my mother and me."

"Yassuh, ah knows dat! Only, suh, dat wus when ya wus a young'un, befoah ya wus de Massah of de house," was her firm reply.

"Being master makes no difference, Mattie. You are much more than a servant, you know that! Now, sit down!"

Mattie obediently sat on the chair Trent indicated and, folding her hands in her lap, waited for him to speak.

Leaning forward, Trent placed his elbows on the table and cupped one hand over the other, pressing the doubled fists to his lips as if in deep thought.

"Mattie, am I truly such a terrible man? Do you feel that I have been so unfair with Amber? Keeping her with me, I mean?"

"Massah Trent, ah don' thank ya really wants me ta answer dat!" Mattie replied firmly and without hesitation. "As fer ya bein' a bad man—nawsuh, ya ain't bad. But why ya askin' dese thangs, anyhow? Ya nevah afoah keered 'bout what folks thought 'bout ya. Ya allus ben de way ya want ta be."

"But maybe I was wrong, Mattie." Trent stretched back in his chair and crossed his long legs before him. "Just never thought much about it—well, not until Amber came along. She has a way of bringing out the worst in me!"

"An' de best!" Mattie blurted. "She brangs out a side o' ya dat ah ain't seen since ya wus a wee one. But dat ain't whut's a-worryin' ya, Massah. It go deepah den dat."

Trent remained silent, his gaze resting on the old woman's kind face. He had never been able to hide anything from Mattie, he remembered. She seemed to always see right through him, right through to his heart, and sometimes he had felt that she could read his thoughts.

"You are right!" he finally said. He ran his finger along the spoon that lay on the table, toying with it. "You are always right, Mattie, how do you do it?"

Mattie's wise old eyes locked with Trent's blue ones.

"Ah's not always right, Massah, not always. But ah has ben wit' ya evah since ya wus a babe, 'ceptin' dem few yeahs whin de pirates took ya," Mattie sighed deeply at the memory, then continued, "An ah knows ya, Massah, dat ah do! Now, whut be de mattah dis fine mornin'? Whut is it gotcha so skiddish?"

Trent ran his strong, tanned fingers through his black hair, as was his habit when frustrated.

"It is Amber, Mattie! Is it not always Amber—" Trent left the question in midair. He pounded his fist on the table, causing the spoon to jump, and the cup and saucer rattled loudly as coffee spilled over the cup rim. "Damn! but she infuriates me! Why can she not just give in?" he thundered.

"Gib in? Massah, whutcha mean, 'gib in'?"

"She wants to go back to her blasted sweet England! She asked me again this morning. There she was, looking lost in that big bed, her face pale as sheep's wool, her damned enticing green eyes clouded with despair and her little chin quivering—damn!

"Damn, but she was pitiful, Mattie! And, fool that I am—"

Trent stopped and rolled his blue eyes heavenward. "I almost
gave in to her!" He shook his head in disbelief. "She is a
witch, Mattie, a damned witch! Underneath that lovely,
innocent, child-like woman, lies one shrewd but sensual
hellion! Christ! She had my heart near breaking and she knew
it! Knew it!"

Trent rose from his chair and began pacing the floor. Mattie
sat watching, a hint of a smile on her aged face, as he raged
on. Oh, but de young Massah wus in a tiff, she thought. Then
she decided that now was the time to bring up a subject which
she had been meaning to discuss with him.

With Trent's temper already to the boiling point, Mattie
felt that it was just as well to get it over now. He could not
possibly get any angrier, or at least she hoped he would
not.

"Why don'cha do jes' dat?" Mattie's calm voice broke into
Trent's rage.

"Why not do what?" he demanded, wheeling around to
stare at her.

"Why don'cha let de chile go? Let Miz Amber go home?
Back to England?" Mattie twisted her hands nervously. "If'n
dat whar Miz Amber want ta be, den why don'cha let de chile
go?"

"Like hell I will! *Mon Dieu,* woman! What are you saying?
No! Amber is staying here! *Right here!*" Trent roared,
stamping his booted heel against the kitchen floor in fury.

Mattie smothered a chuckle as she remembered that as a
small boy he had often beat his heel against the old kitchen
floor in fits of temper. She was reminded that the young
master had always come here to ride out his storms of anger.
But now she brought her attention back to the present as her
master continued his tirade.

"I do not give a damn whether she likes it or not! Amber
will do as I say!"

"Will she, Massah?" Mattie countered. "Beggin' yer pah-
don, suh, but how ya gonna mak Miz Amber do dat? Ah
means, if'n she wants ta go she will, one o' dese days. Ya
cain't keep de chile heah if'n—"

"I can!" Trent cut in angrily. "I can and I will! She has no
money, no way to leave! There is not one ship that will take
her aboard! Not one! I have seen to it!" At the knowledge

that he had been able to thwart any escape attempt, Trent smiled slyly.

"Trent LeBlanc! Shame on ya!" Mattie blustered, shaking her finger at him as if he were still a child. "Shame!" Then, forgetting her place as a servant, the old woman scolded, "Now ya ortant ta a-done dat! If'n dat fine littah lady want ta go home, den ya orta let 'er go! Miz Amber be a genteel, well-bred lady, not jes' sum purty no-count ya picked up on a dirty street!"

"But I *did* pick her up on a dirty street, Mattie, and I have paid for doing so. She was not 'a genteel, well-bred lady' when I found her sprawled in the mud and stench of a London back street!"

Now Mattie was becoming angry. She liked the mistress, and, although she loved her young master, she had no intention of allowing him to speak this way, even in anger.

"Now, ya listen heah, ya young pup!" Mattie was on her feet, hands on her hips, her ample bosom heaving with indignation.

"*I beg your pardon!*" Trent turned in surprise, a mixture of anger and puzzlement on his face. "Mattie! Have you forgotten your place?"

"Ah have not! But *you*, suh! Ah sho thank *you* has! Ya talkin' 'bout Miz Amber in a no-respec' way! Ya wouldn' stan' fer it frum dat Kathleen woman, ner frum no othah, ah'm thankin'. But dar ya stan', heah in yo own house, a-talkin' 'bout de chile lak 'er wus dirt 'neath yo fine feet!" Mattie's words carried the sting of a scorpion, and she bristled with resentment.

Trent stood staring at the once humble servant. Never had he seen Mattie's wrath as he now witnessed it, never had he fallen prey to her fury. Oh, she had scolded him many times, had even spanked him as a child, but never anything like he was now experiencing! Speechless, Trent listened as Mattie held forth.

"Miz Amber, she be wif yo chile, Massah. An' dat come frum ya own words! De way ah sees it, mebber she orta go! Mebber she be bettah off away frum ya!" Mattie stopped to catch her breath. "An' futhahmo', ah mought jes' he'p her git away!" she concluded hotly, her arms now crossed over her bosom.

"*Mon Dieu*, Mattie! What has gotten into you? Speaking to me like that when I was a child may have been excusable, but I am a man now, Mattie! And I am master of this house!"

"Is dat right?" Mattie queried, her faded eyes narrow. A sarcastic smile touched her lips as she waited for Trent's reaction.

"*Mattie!*" His voice was drenched with warning, but Mattie chose to ignore the fact.

"Mastuh of Travinwood, dat's true. But as fer bein' a man . . ." Mattie's words trailed off, and she stood her ground as she stared at the dumbfounded LeBlanc. "A real man would let go of sump'n dat wahn't his!" she finished.

"*Amber is mine!*" Trent returned angrily. "Mattie, curb your tongue! And that is a warning!"

"Awright, Massah, Ah has ben warned." Mattie's chin tilted a trifle. "But ah ain't done wif ma say! Ol' Mattie ain't nevah a-foah spoke a-gin' ya, suh, but ah is now! Ya be wrong! Miz Amber, she don' b'long ta ya, no suh. She be her own mastah. An' de chile in 'er belly . . ." Mattie let the words hang for a moment before she continued, "de chile be 'er own, too. It ain't yoah's!"

"The hell it is not mine! I fathered it! It is my seed that grows within her! Damn it, Mattie, what nonsense are you concocting? No man has lain with Amber save myself. I am the only one!" Trent ran his fingers through his hair in exasperation. "Christ! This whole thing is getting out of hand!"

Then as her words penetrated his tired brain, Trent whirled around and stared at Mattie in confusion. For the first time, uncertainty assailed him.

"What are you trying to tell me? Did Amber tell you it is not my child she carries?" When he received no reply, he demanded, "Answer me, Mattie!"

"Nawsuh, Miz Amber ain't nevah tole me nuthin' but de trufe. She ain't nevah ben wif no othah man. But jes' 'cause ya spilled yo seed inta her womb, dat don' gib ya no right—"

"*No Right?* I have *every* right! I made Amber mine that night aboard the *Mér Fleur. Mine*, Mattie! And the child is mine, too! He will know that I, Trent Darnell LeBlanc, am his father! He will be a LeBlanc and will carry the name with pride. Never will he want for anything!"

"An' Miz Amber? Whut 'bout her?" Mattie asked, "Wheah do she fit in, Massah, aftah de chile is borned? Will ya still want 'er heah?"

"Hell, yes! The child is not the sole reason for keeping Amber with me! Even if she were not carrying my child I would want her with me. I am giving her a home, clothing, whatever she wishes. She, too, will want for nothing!"

"Won't she, Mastah?" Mattie asked in a hushed voice.

"What else could she possibly ask for? Travinwood is one of the finest mansions in or about New Orleans. I have wealth, land, a fine ship. She and my child will be well cared for. What is mine is theirs!"

"Den ya plan ta keep Miz Amber heah fer always? At Travinwood? Dat be yer plan?" Mattie questioned closely. "Ya plan fer da chile and Miz Amber ta mak dey home heah forevah?"

"Of course! Amber will live here, she will raise my son here. Mattie, one day Travinwood will belong to my son," Trent assured her.

"Why ya so certain de chile be goin' ta be a male chile?"

"I have no doubt that Amber will bear me a son. If not the first-born, then the next!" Trent stated confidently.

"De nex', Massah? Den ya plan on moah babes?"

"Well, why not? It is bound to happen. Amber will be with me always, she will share my bed and my life here at Travinwood. Yes, there will be other children." Trent laughed happily, and his blue eyes danced as he added, "Never thought I would want children!" His face brightened at the thought of his own children playing on the grounds of Travinwood, of hearing happy laughter ringing through the halls. He smiled a lazy, one-sided smile.

"Massah, yo face is lit up lak de sun comin' frum behin' de cloud an' ah sho hates ta put out de light in yo eyes, but ah gotta tell ya dat thangs ain't a-gonna be lak ya want 'em. Dey jes' ain't!" Mattie told him, shaking her gray head sadly.

"And just tell me. Why not?"

"Well, suh, fer one thang, Miz Amber, she don' wanta stay heah. An' whin ya talkin' 'bout 'rights,' she have moah right ta de chile den ya hab, Massah. She carries it in her belly an' she be da one dat gonna bear it. Ain't nobody kin say dat she ain't de chile's mothah. But he won' be no LeBlanc! He will be a Kensin'ton, da bastahd chile of Trent LeBlanc. De babe will carry de kin name o' Miz Amber. Ya will hab no lawful right ta 'im, Massah, 'cause he be borned outa wedlock. Ya cain't claim 'im an' whin ya lose Miz Amber, ya lose da chile."

"Like hell! Oh, no, I will have Amber! And I will have my child and all the rights that go with them! You can count on it!" Trent boasted.

"An' how ya gonna do dat, suh?"

Trent saw the gravity and the earnestness with which Mattie was speaking, and again he felt uncertain. Never before had he doubted his ability to have things his way. Now he was not so sure.

"How, Massah?" Mattie persisted.

The annoying thought that Mattie could be right about all this bothered Trent. He paced the floor thoughtfully and the worry grew. The possibility of all she had said gnawed at him, and he began to see the likelihood of her reasoning. The thought of losing Amber and his child was more than he could accept, and in desperation he turned to old Mattie, his hands spread in a pleading gesture.

"All right, Mattie. You seem to have all the answers. Now just what do you suggest that I do about this damnable situation? Help me solve this problem, Mattie, as you have helped so many times before!" His plea wrung her heart.

"Massah, it be simple. All ya gotta do is mak Miz Amber a LeBlanc! An' ta do dat, ya hafta marry her."

"Marry her?" Trent stared in amazement. "Why, I never thought of that!" He threw back his head and laughed loudly. His relief was apparent. Of course that was the answer, he thought, although he had sworn that no woman would ever snare Trent LeBlanc! But had he not told Jason that night in Havana that Amber owned his very soul? Had she not, in truth, 'snared' him on the night he first lay with her?

The memory of that night flooded Trent's mind, and he remembered that he had rescued Amber from her drunken pursuers for reasons of gallantry. Then he remembered his remorse after he had stolen her virtue, his tenderness in attempting to make amends. Close behind this came the memory of her terrible temper and her barbed tongue. He chuckled softly at the thought of their many nights together and realized that he would never be free of her hold on him.

So, he reasoned, by God, if it takes marriage to assure him that he would not lose Amber, so be it!

Mattie had stood silently while her master pondered over their conversation. At length Trent strode to the doorway and, stopping on the threshold, turned to say,

"You are right, Mattie! Amber will be up and around tomorrow and I shall tell her that we will be married. And not a word from you, Mattie, understand? You see, I have never failed to get what I want, and I have no intention of failing now!"

"How can you be so damned sure that the child I carry is yours, Trent LeBlanc?" Amber stormed. Hands on her hips, her small chin thrust forward, she defied him, her green eyes never wavering from the deep blue ones which stared back at her. "There were other men on board the *Mér Fleur,* you know. You cannot be so sure—"

"Oh, no! No, little one! I will not play that game with you," Trent smiled the lazy half-smile that Amber knew so well. That smile had dominated her, had often infuriated her, and could sometimes melt her heart.

Shaking his head, Trent went on, "There is not a man aboard the *Mér Fleur* who would have dared to touch you, kitten. Not one!" As Amber opened her lips to speak she was stopped by a casual wave of LeBlanc's hand as he continued, "Oh, I am quite certain that some would have liked to, but they valued their lives too much to do so. Good God, Amber, do you not know by now that not one of my men would have dared to touch *my woman?"*

Trent smiled and stepped close to Amber. He cradled her face in his hands and stroked her cheeks with his thumbs.

"I am sure, just as *you* are, my sweet, that you were untouched. I am certain that it was I who was the first! And there has been no other, so why try to say different, kitten? The child is mine, Amber, and it shall bear my name. He will be born a 'LeBlanc,' the name to which he is entitled!"

"But I do not want to marry you!" Amber cried in distress. "I do not wish to be your wife! I can take care of myself and

my child without your help! My baby does not need your fine
name!" she said haughtily, pulling free of Trent.

"*You* do not want! *You* do not wish! Blast it, woman, I did
not ask what *you* wanted! What *your* wishes were! By God, I
said that you are going to marry me! You will be my wife!
And you will do as I say! Have you not yet learned that you
have no choice in these matters?" LeBlanc rasped, his face an
angry red. "My son will know that I am his father! So give in,
Amber, and realize that there is not one damned thing you
can do about it!"

"*No!* No, I will not marry you!" Amber shouted in rage,
tears swimming in her green eyes. "I do not love you! I loathe
you! Hear me! Never will I do it!" Her small foot stamped the
floor savagely.

"The hell you will not! Never is a long, long time, Amber,
and it will seem even longer while you are locked in this
room. And that is just where you will be until you submit to
my—shall we say 'request'? Think about it, my dear." The
words and his tone of voice were as much in contrast as an
iron fist in a velvet glove.

For a moment Amber stood uncertainly. Surely, she
thought, he will not lock me in this room! Then she remembered how he had locked her in his cabin while she was
aboard the *Mér Fleur*. It had seemed to be his favorite
method of forcing her to submit to the inevitable, to accept
the fact that he was lord and master! But not this time, she
thought, not this time!

"Well," Trent broke into her thoughts, "I see that you are
beginning to understand the situation as it is! So I shall
proceed with the arrangements. I must make the announce-
ment and contact Father Dupré about th—"

Amber's poignant cry cut into Trent's words.

There was a brief silence, but it was only the calm before
the storm.

"It will not work, Trent LeBlanc!" Amber said furiously.
"I shall stay in this damned room forever, stay here until I
die! But I will not marry you! Hear me, LeBlanc, and hear
me well! I shall die first!" Her words were low and menacing.

Trent stared unbelievingly. He had been so certain that she
would yield under his pressure that he was completely taken
aback by her fierce obstinacy and her rebelliousness. Face it,

LeBlanc, he thought, it is difficult for you to believe that a woman, *any* woman, would refuse you. Your ego has been badly bruised.

Spinning on his heel, Trent strode to the door. He paused in the doorway and flung over his shoulder, "You will let me know when you are ready to accede to my demand." Then he stepped from the room, locking the door behind him.

"Never!" The word was hurled at the closed door, and she heard LeBlanc's mocking laughter as it rang down the hall.

Chapter Ten

AMBER WAS FACED WITH A PROBLEM SHE COULD NOT SOLVE. SHE paced the length of the room in frustration and confusion. It had been three days since LeBlanc had issued his ultimatum and stalked from the room, locking the door behind him. Three days! The walls had begun to close in on her, and she had seen no one save Trent, Mattie, and Neva.

Mattie and Neva took turns bringing a tray at mealtimes. At least, Amber thought angrily, he is not starving me, too! A few times Neva had been allowed to sit and visit while Amber ate her meals. Otherwise, she spent her days and nights with nothing more to do than read, eat, and sleep.

Trent had made a habit of coming to bed very late, and in the mornings he rose early, thereby curtailing the time she could have spent with him. He would whistle happily as he dressed for the day and sometimes, looking out the window, would say cheerfully, "Beautiful day! Fine day for riding!" One morning he had said, "I have to go into town for a few hours. Is there anything you would like me to bring you?" This seemed unnecessarily cruel to Amber, as he knew that she would have been thrilled to accompany him into New

Orleans. After all, she had only seen the town briefly when they arrived from Havana.

At night Amber could hear voices in the dining room or study downstairs. Laughter rang out, and the clear tinkle of glass and silverware drifted up the stairs. How she longed to be a part of the activity! She was miserable.

"Damn you, Trent LeBlanc!" Amber flung at the locked door. "Damn, damn, damn!" She spun around, snatched up a volume by Shakespeare, and flopped down in the leather wing chair, absently leafing through the pages.

So he has done as he threatened, Amber thought heatedly. And he will leave me in this "prison" until I give in! Of course it will be *me* who will be forced to yield, she further thought, her anger rising. The arrogant, lordly Master Trent LeBlanc, the high and mighty, has *never* given in to anything or anybody! Had he not told her long ago that it was he who was the stronger? That it was he who would always win? And had he not been proven right?

"Ohhhh," Amber groaned aloud. "I hate you, Trent LeBlanc! You will pay for this, pay for all that you have done to me!" She vowed vengefully, through clenched teeth, *"I shall see to it!"*

Amber made her decision as she gritted out those words, "I shall see to it!"

When Neva came to remove Amber's lunch tray, she noted that the food had remained untouched. She made no comment, knowing that her friend was highly agitated. Amber also spoke no word until Neva had reached the door with the laden tray.

"Neva!"

"Yes, Miss Amber?" The girl was touched by the loneliness and the urgency in the call.

"Neva, please tell Trent that I wish to speak with him."

"Yes, miss. He has just come in from riding, and I will inform him of your wish." Neva stepped into the hallway, then turned to inquire, "Are you all right, miss?"

"No, but I never expect to be 'all right' so long as I am forced to bend to the Master's wishes! One would think that I have no mind of my own!"

Neva hastily retreated, not wishing to be drawn into further discussion on this matter. "I shall send Captain Trent at once," she said as she departed.

With head bowed and small hands lying lifelessly in her lap, Amber had to admit defeat. Once more the "master" had won!

After a time Amber sighed deeply and rose to her feet.

Trent seemed to be taking his time in responding to her summons, and she felt sure that this was just another method of reminding Amber that he was in command of the situation. Never mind, she thought, this will give me a little more time to gather courage to face the inevitable!

When Amber finally heard the scrape of the key in the lock she looked up to see Trent stride in, handsomely clad in a tanned deerskin coat lined with wolf's fur and with a wolf fur collar. The long sleeves were trimmed with a narrow fringe, his breeches and knee boots were made of the same tanned buckskin.

He made a striking figure as he moved to the bed with a slow, animal-like grace, tossing his gloves and riding crop aside. Trent sat down on the bed, then casually leaned back, supporting his weight with his elbows as he studied Amber questioningly.

Amber made no move, nor did she speak. How handsome he is, she thought, how masculine! Why was it that his very presence could send her heart pounding, the blood rushing in her veins, and make her forget her anger, she pondered. Trent smelled of man and of the out-of-doors. The musky, sensual scent made Amber weak, almost giddy. Through the opening of his shirt, which was unbuttoned halfway down the front, she saw the dark mat of hair on his chest glistening with tiny beads of sweat.

Trent's black hair was wild and unruly from his ride, and Amber felt the urge to sweep back a stray curl which had fallen over his brow. Then she became aware of his laughing sapphire eyes as they roamed over her freely, mentally undressing her.

Amber blushed uncomfortably, brining a slow, lazy smile to Trent's full lips. God, but she turned his blood to fire! The very sight of her caused his senses to reel, his self-control to lapse, and his desire for her was overwhelming.

His voice husky with emotion, Trent asked, "You wish to

speak with me, madam?" His blue gaze lingered on Amber's lips, lips that were lush and inviting, lips which held the promise of unlimited, abandoned passion.

"Yes," Amber answered softly, "there is something I must tell you." She was finding it difficult to speak with Trent looking at her so intimately. Her pulse quickened and her cheeks felt aflame. Damn you for having this power over me, she thought. Damn you for awakening desire within me!

"Well?" Trent broke into her thoughts and his eyes locked with hers.

"I have come to a decision!" Amber blurted, not quite knowing how to put into words that she really had no choice. She actually had not made a decision and was only submitting to his will, as he had known that she would do. Yet her pride would not allow her to meekly surrender so she must speak as if she had given the matter much thought and had arrived at her own decision.

"And what might that decision be, kitten?" Trent stood from the bed, relieving himself of his coat. He pulled his shirt free from his breeches, slowly unfastening the few remaining buttons. His deep blue gaze never left Amber.

Amber found her attention drawn to the strong, bronzed body which was being undressed before her. Tranquilized by Trent's being and his proximity, she did not reply. She could never think with Trent so close, but it was even more difficult with him standing there near-naked. Amber's emerald eyes took in every lean line, every curve and muscle of his frame.

Pleased with the gleam of desire in Amber's bright eyes, Trent announced, "It is yours for the taking!" He grinned in self-satisfaction, knowing full well that she wanted him.

"W-What?" Amber asked, disconcerted.

"My body! It is yours for the taking, little one!"

"Do not be absurd, Trent LeBlanc! I have no use for you *or* for your body, though you may find it hard to believe, you haughty toad!" Amber shot at him hotly, her face a mask of embarrassment.

"Ah, pshaw! And here I thought you had called me for an afternoon tumble!" He sighed exaggeratedly, pretending great disappointment. "I could have sworn that I recognized a growing flame of lust in your eyes, kitten."

"You are mistaken, sir!" Amber assured him coldly. "I

have only asked you here to inform you that I accept your terms."

"Oh?" Trent raised one dark brow in surprise before a pleased look settled over his handsome features.

"Although I cannot truly be of sound mind to make such a decision, but in order to prevent myself from going completely insane in this room—" Amber hesitated. Then, her head held proudly and her chin tilted determinedly, she took a long breath and finished with a rush of words. "I agree to marry you."

Trent remained quiet. As the silence grew, Amber stepped over to the fireplace and nudged a smoldering coal that had fallen from the gate into place. Folding her arms across her breast, she stood staring into the dancing flames.

When Trent still made no reply, Amber spoke in extreme agitation.

"I wish you to understand that I have reached this decision strictly because I have no other choice. Make no mistake about it, Trent LeBlanc, this marriage is to come about *only* due to the fact that *you* decree that it do so!"

Trent's broad shoulders began to shake as a deep rumble of laughter began within his chest and broke from his lips.

"It did not take you as long to comply as I had predicted!" he commented approvingly. "That is a good indication, kitten, that you are indeed learning submission!" He chuckled in appreciation.

"Oh, you arrogant bastard!" Amber stormed. "You—you damned, pompous—"

She got no further with her furious outburst. Amber was suddenly seized by a painful, powerful grip and found herself crushed against Trent's hard, bare chest. His hold tightened, his fingers of steel seemed to dig into her small wrist as he rasped through clenched teeth,

"If you swear at me once more, Amber, just once more, I will beat you within an inch of your sweet life!"

Amber stared up at the brilliant sapphire eyes, now dangerously dark with anger. She flinched at the warning which they held so plainly. Struggling to free herself, she felt Trent's grasp close even more securely around her.

"Do you hear, Amber?" His words grated against her ear.

"Just swear at me once more and I shall put the bloody fear of hell in you! *Comprens?*"

"Yes," came Amber's choked whisper as tears stung her eyes.

"I did not hear you!"

"*Yes!* Damn you, yes!" Amber hissed with venom.

"By God, Amber, you asked for it!" Trent roared. He picked her up roughly and stalked across the room.

Throwing her unceremoniously upon the bed, Trent lifted Amber's full skirt, exposing her firm, round buttocks. His hand swept upward, then descended, meeting the soft, white flesh with a loud, stinging splat.

Amber cried out in both rage and pain.

Again Trent raised his hand to strike, but when he saw the ugly red welt that marred Amber's smooth, tender bottom, his hand stopped in midair. Beneath the hand which held her body against the bed, Trent felt Amber trembling. Her low whimper tore at his heart.

Instantly remorse swept over LeBlanc. God! She could make him so damned angry one minute, then melt his heart in the next.

Sighing heavily, Trent sank to the bed and lifted Amber onto his lap. Cradling her in his arms, he held her close as she quietly wept.

It was a beautiful day in late September, that day of Amber's marriage to LeBlanc. The sun shown brightly, and puffs of soft white clouds floated across the clear blue sky. The trees were arrayed with leaves of varying colors—red, orange, yellow, and green. The cool nip of autumn braced the air, a much different kind of day from that early spring day in London when Amber had fled from the church and the proposed marriage to Sir Michael.

But this time Amber had no place to run. *This* marriage was going to take place—LeBlanc would see that it did! For the second time, Amber thought, I am being forced into a marriage that is not of my choosing. However, she had yielded once again to Trent's will, and she knew that she had no recourse.

Amber stood before the full-length mirror while Neva

fastened the last of the tiny satin-covered buttons of the wedding gown. Who was the young woman whose face stared back at her? Who was this girl dressed in the ivory-colored satin gown? And why was she so sad?

What am I doing here? Amber mused. I would have been far better off in London, better to have married Sir Michael. But no, she thought bitterly, I panicked and fled, thinking I should be allowed to live my life as I wished.

Smoothing the soft fabric along her hips, Amber studied the beauty of her gown. The low scoop of the neckline revealed the fullness of her bust, the bodice boasted tiny tucks edged with delicate lace. The full skirt was gathered across the front, the back was of narrow, folded pleats that swept into a long train. The sleeves were full, gathered onto a band of ice-blue velvet at the wrists. Embroidery of the same blue velvet trimmed the neck, waist and hem. Delicate crewels of baby roses in ice-blue dotted the skirt.

Amber's emerald-green eyes slowly appraised her mirrored image from the tips of her small satin slippers to her coppery ringlets, caressed by a blue ribbon from which escaped whispers of tresses to frame her child-like face with its pouting rosebud lips.

"My goodness, but you are lovely, miss!" Neva voiced happily as she sat back on the bed to admire Amber. "The Captain will be right proud of his bride."

Amber sighed deeply and turned from the mirror.

"This is not my wish, Neva. It is not what I want at all."

"Whyever not, Miss Amber?" Neva asked in undisguised surprise. "Why, I would be walking on air if it was me that was going to marry the Captain! Gawd, but he is the handsomest man I ever did see!" Clasping her hands to her heart, Neva pretended to swoon.

Amber failed to see any humor in the situation and only looked at her young friend wordlessly.

Neva tried again.

"If you do not mind my saying so, miss, I think you are daft!" she stated flatly. "You oughta be glad the Captain wants to marry you. You told me from your own lips that you love him, so why do you not want to marry him?"

"That was a long time ago, Neva," Amber replied wearliy. "I no longer love him. It is not my choice, this marriage. You know that! He is forcing me into it, just as he has consistently forced his will upon me from the beginning! And the *only* reason Trent is marrying me is because of the child!" she said bitterly. "That is not a good reason to marry. One should marry for love, Neva, and for nothing less!"

"But you *do* love the Captain, miss, no matter what you say! I *know* you do and I believe he loves you, too. Why, if you ask me—"

"I did not ask you, Neva!" Amber snapped, "And I do not care to continue this discussion!"

"'Scuse me, miss," Neva said. Clamping her mouth closed, she shook her head in bewilderment, wondering what the future held for Amber and LeBlanc.

There was a troubled silence between the two friends, then they heard old Mattie's heavy footsteps outside the door.

"Miz Amber," Mattie called, at the same time rapping the door. "It be de time ta go down."

Amber seemed to freeze, and her lovely face paled as she clutched the back of a nearby chair. Neva moved swiftly to the door and opened it to the old servant.

"Dey say ta cum fetch ya, Miz Amber," Mattie said, peering over Neva's shoulder at her mistress. "Mistah Jason, he be heah ta walk ya down de stairs."

"Thank you, Mattie," Amber replied in a low voice. "Please, first give me a minute alone. Then I shall be along."

Without a word Neva motioned to Mattie to follow as she slipped from the room. She felt instinctively that this was a moment when no one could help her friend, a time when Amber must become reconciled with this reality.

Meanwhile, Amber had again turned to the mirror. For a long moment she stared at her reflection, then, catching her lower lip between her teeth and drawing a deep, uneven breath, she turned and walked slowly into the hallway.

Descending the stairs on Jason's arm, Amber felt as if she would faint. Her heart thudded wildly in her breast, and she imagined that she could hear its loud drumming.

LeBlanc stood at the foot of the staircase watching Amber's slow, graceful descent. Handsomely dressed in a cutaway waistcoat of rich blue velvet graced with elaborate gold silk embroidery, LeBlanc nervously pulled at the wide ruffle which fell from the cuff of his light blue shirt. A white velvet

vest, also embroidered with gold silk, dark blue breeches and
shiny black leather knee boots completed the bridegroom's
attire. He wore no cravat as his silk shirt was adorned with a
ruffled front.

As Amber's foot touched the last step, Trent reached for
her. Taking her small hand from Jason's arm, he placed it
within the crook of his own. With his forefinger beneath her
chin, Trent tilted Amber's head slightly upward. Burning
sapphire eyes met vivid green ones.

Tears were swimming in her eyes, and her voice trembled as
Amber softly implored,

"Please," the word was a plea, "Please, Trent! Do not
make me do this!"

"Did I not say that you would marry me, Amber? And did
you not agree?"

With those words, LeBlanc led Amber into the library.

The next few days passed swiftly for Amber Lynn Kensington LeBlanc. She experienced grave misgivings about the
marriage and felt a vague uneasiness about the future.
Although she had declared to Neva that she no longer loved
Trent, Amber freely admitted to herself that, in truth, she
did!

But the certainty that LeBlanc had married her only
because of the child tore at Amber's heart. Had she been
given even the slightest indication that he wished to marry her
for herself, Amber thought, or if she could have the meager
hope that one day he would learn to love her, then she could
have felt better about the situation. But the word "love" was
not in LeBlanc's vocabulary, she thought bitterly.

Chapter Eleven

HURRIED FOOTSTEPS SOUNDED IN THE HALL, AND LEBLANC, seated at his desk in the library, looked up expectantly. The door swung open without ceremony, and young Rual burst into the room.

"I came as soon as I heard," the lad panted. "I knew that you would want to know." The words came out somewhat jerkily as Rual drew his breath in gasps in his excitement. "It was not at all as Lafitte thought it would be!"

Trent had sprung to his feet and with great concern, asked, "Lafitte? What do you mean? What is it you have learned, Rual? Has something happened to Jean?"

"No, Cap'n, but his island! Barataria! It has been taken! The news is all over town!" Rual stopped to catch his breath, then continued, "Colonel Ross and Commodore Patterson assembled forces and attacked Barataria!"

"What! Rual, are you absolutely certain of this?"

"Yes, sir, I am certain. I heard the whole story from some of Patterson's men. They are celebrating down at the Water-front Inn. Dominique You was taken, along with some others. He surrendered, sir, they say he never even fired on them!" Rual was agog with excitement.

"Of course not! Dominique would never fire on an American vessel," was Trent's reply as he sank back into his chair, shaking his head as he attempted to understand the reason for an attack on Lafitte and his island.

Then, "What about Jean, Rual? Is he all right?"

"Don't know nothin' about him, sir. Neither him nor his brother was found. Dominique You said they left the island and left him in charge. He was expecting the British for some reason, and when he spotted ships approaching the island he had his men readying to fire on them. That was when he realized that the vessels were flying American flags.

"He ordered his men to set fire to the Barataria ships and warehouses, then told them to scatter. Hundreds of Baratarians escaped through the bayous in boats before Patterson landed and took the island."

Rual was quite breathless, and when he paused, Trent prodded,

"Is that all you learned?"

"No, sir, Cap'n. Dominique You and the others that were captured were all taken and jailed in the Cabildo when they reached New Orleans. Patterson has charged them with piracy. The Lafitte brothers don't even know about it. Or maybe they have heard and they're hiding someplace," Rual concluded.

LeBlanc sat thoughtfully tapping his pen on the desk top. After a time he reached forward to draw a sheet of paper toward him and began to write. When he had finished, he folded the paper and placed it in an envelope, then sealed it with drops of wax from a lighted candle. Handing the letter to Rual, Trent gave him instructions.

"Take this to Number 39 Canal Street. You will be met at the door by a woman, Miss Percy. Tell her that you are my man and that this note must get to Simmons. Tell her to send it by Jema. Ride the white mare, she has good footing and can travel fast. On your way, my man. It is a very important mission I am sending you on, and I am depending on you!"

"Yes, sir!" Rual tucked the letter inside his shirt and hastened from the room. As he left, LeBlanc heard him repeating his instructions to himself, "39 Canal . . . Miss Percy . . . Simmons . . . Jema . . ."

Trent called for Kane to saddle Satan and bring him around to the front door. Mattie was instructed to fill a saddlebag with provisions. Then Trent dashed up the stairs. When he returned he was clad in buckskin breeches, shirt, and riding boots. A hunting knife and a pistol were in his belt, he carried a rifle in his hand, and a riding coat was thrown over his shoulder.

"I expect to be gone for at least two days, Mattie. I am leaving Miss Amber in your care, and she is not to leave her room. Those are orders, do you understand?" Trent's voice was firm, edged with steel.

"Yassuh, Massah Trent. But ya be keerful, now. Ah knows ya be up ta sumpin'! Jes' be sho ya come back heah safe, ya heah?"

"Of course I will be back, Mattie. It will take a lot to get rid of the 'likes of me,' as you say." He patted the servant's hand as she extended it to give him his saddlebag. "Tell Miss Amber that I shall see her in a few days. She was sleeping when I went up to change."

"Yassuh, ah will. An' don'cha worry none, ol' Mattie'll tak good keer uv yo lady fer ya."

Outside, Trent slid his rifle into the saddle holster, tied down a bedroll, and swung to Satan's back.

A quick thrust from Trent's boot heel sent Satan galloping toward the woods which led deep into the back swamps of the Louisiana bayous, his master sitting straight and tall in the saddle.

Satan's steps were sure as he walked slowly over the marshy ground. Gray fingers of moss hung from the trees, the dark mass choking the life from their branches. A damp, eerie haze claimed the very air, and only the faintest glimmer of moonlight fought through the maze of haunting timbers before being smothered in the gloom below. The ghostly cries of night creatures echoed deep into the swamp.

LeBlanc listened for any sounds not those of the bayou. Halting his steed in dark shadow, he cupped his hands over his mouth and gave a ghastly, inhuman cry. He listened. Repeated the cry. Moments passed, then LeBlanc eased Satan forward and stopped again. There came an answering

call. He repeated the uncanny wail. Again it was acknowledged. Slowly he nudged the animal along the boggy path
toward the sound. Then he called in a low voice, "It is I,
LeBlanc. I come alone."

"*Oui*, you speak true, *mon bon ami!* We have been
watching you for some miles," came the reply.

Suddenly a man appeared from the dense mist. As the man
approached him, LeBlanc dismounted.

"I have been expecting you, Trent," came the low greeting.

"I trust that you have not waited long, for I only learned
this day of the attack on Barataria," Trent answered.

"*Oui!* I, myself, only learned of it some few hours ago,"
replied Jean Lafitte. "Some of my men came to me in New
Orleans with the information. When I learned of the attack,
I came here to wait for those who were fortunate to escape. Now tell me, *mon ami*, what you know of the situation."

"Only that the island was taken by Ross and Patterson.
Dominique and those captured are being held in the Cabildo.
When I heard the news, I came straight here to see if you
needed my help."

"My thanks, but there is really nothing that you can do.
Remember, Trent, you are a government agent. *Non, mon
bon ami*, I must not ask your help. You see, the British want
New Orleans. And when they attempt to take her, Claiborne
and the great Jackson will need me and my 'band of pirates,'
as we are called," Lafitte spoke knowingly.

"Yes, you are no doubt right about that. But remember,
Jean, I am your friend as well as a government agent, and my
wish is to help, if you will allow me," Trent assured Lafitte
with sincerity.

"You must return home, *mon ami*, and do not worry about
me. It would be sure trouble for you if it were known that you
had been here." Lafitte's voice held concern for his friend.
"Go, *bon ami*, I will contact you if I find myself in need of
your services. For now, all I need is to know that I have your
friendship."

"That you do! And that you shall always have, Jean. I will
go, now."

The two men shook hands with a firm grasp, which spoke volumes to each.

LeBlanc placed his booted foot into the stirrup and gracefully swung his lithesome frame astride Satan's back.

"God go with you until we meet again." Trent's voice floated back as he disappeared into the frothy coldness of the swamp.

Chapter Twelve

A COLD GRAY MIST CLOSED IN, AND DAMP CLOAKS OF FOG HUNG overhead as cloud-like masses swirled and hovered just above the ground. Awesome shadows of threatening danger lurked, ready to pounce upon its victim.

A great warrior sat astride a mighty black stallion as a beautiful maiden danced about him. She was dressed in gossamer white veils, her long, blue-black hair flowed freely, and her crimson lips beckoned to the handsome warrior in a lover's song. The maiden's skin glistened smooth and silky in the pale moonlight, and her haunting eyes were as the color of fire.

The warrior watched as the dark beauty danced her alluring dance. When she had finished, she moved gracefully forward and stood before him. Lifting her eyes to his, she smiled enticingly and began to open her bodice, exposing the willingness of her body. Reaching out, she took his hand and placed it to the warmth of her bosom. The warrior ran strong, willing fingers hungrily over the soft flesh. The maiden parted her moist lips, and he leaned forward to accept her kiss.

From the fair-haired maiden, who stood in the shadows watching, there came a wail. The cry was torn from her lips and penetrated the silence, echoing through the swamp. Fear twisted in her heart, and she ran swiftly toward the warrior. But before she reached him, his lips met those of the dark-haired maiden who, at his touch, changed into the form of a great, black, two-headed serpent. Terror sprang into the warrior's vivid blue eyes, and he tried to pull free as the serpent slid slowly about his strong, handsome frame.

With each step that she took, the fair maiden's feet bogged deep into the murkiness of the mire as she desperately attempted to reach the warrior. She watched as the serpent began to squeeze the life from him. Mournful cries came from the fair maiden, and tears ran down her cheeks. Her eyes met those of the handsome warrior, and, as she stared, she saw the blue of his eyes fade. Then he fell silently from his great black steed and met the ground soundlessly.

The mighty warrior was dead.

The serpent released the still form and again became the beautiful, dark-haired maiden. With a sneer on her lips, she turned and looked at the fair-haired maiden and gave forth a shrill peal of cruel laughter.

The stallion fled, the dark-haired maiden danced into the gray mist, and the fair-haired maiden fell to her knees beside the fallen warrior. Gently cradling his head in her arms, she rocked back and forth, her tears bathing his face. The swamp echoed her haunting cries.

Amber awoke with the mournful cries, "No, no, dear God, no!" filling the room, and she clapped her hands over her ears to drown them out before she realized that the screams were her own. The warning wail from the fair maiden and the mocking laughter of the dark one rang through her mind.

Suddenly Mattie was at her side, and Amber, her trembling body drenched in cold sweat, clung to the faithful old servant. The thin cotton gown was twisted about Amber's body much as the serpent was twisted about the warrior as he died.

"Trent!" Amber cried. "Oh, Mattie, it is Trent! He is hurt! He is in trouble!"

"Now, chile, ya jes' had a bad dream," Mattie attempted to calm Amber. "Ah'm heah now, an' ah'm gonna mak everthin' awright, ya'll see," she crooned as she rocked Amber in her arms.

Closing her eyes tightly, Amber willed the bad dream to

go away. But even with her eyes closed she could still see the deep blue eyes of the warrior with the shadows of death playing across them. Trent's eyes! Her heart cried out.

"No, Mattie! You do not understand! I saw him! Trent is in danger!" She stifled a sob, then went on. "Oh, God! Mattie, he could even be dead! You have to believe me!" Amber begged, tears flowing down her cheeks.

The faint whinny of a horse met their ears and Amber bolted from the bed. Flinging open the veranda doors, she ran to the balcony and looked down over the railing.

Morgan and Jason, both men clad only in breeches, stood on the stone drive below.

As Amber's eyes adjusted to the darkness of the outside world she saw the black steed approaching. Her heart leaped in her breast and the breath caught in her throat for there was no rider.

Satan was alone.

The twenty-four hours since Satan had returned, alone, to Travinwood had been hectic ones. The entire household had been in near panic. Servants had been seen surreptitiously wiping tell-tale eyes while still others had wept unrestrainedly. All had gone about their tasks as usual except the men, who had joined in the search for the Master of Travinwood.

Jason and Drake had organized search parties, and Rual had ridden to the *Mér Fleur* to alert the crew that their Captain was missing and to see if they had received any word from him.

Morgan walked the floor of the great entry hall like a caged animal, muttering to himself. He bitterly resented the fact that he was no longer a young man and could not ride out with the others to scour the area, seeking out the young master.

"Morgan," the name was called out softly. The old man turned to see his faithful wife approach him, tears brimming in her brown eyes.

"Mattie," Morgan responded as he stepped to meet her. "Ya gotta be strong 'case anythin's happn'ed ta de Massah. If'n he don' git back awright, Miz Amber gonna need ya, 'spesh'ly if'n dey don' fin' 'im alive—" The man's voice broke, and he closed his long arms around Mattie. They clung together, the two loyal old servants, and Mattie's shoulders shook as she buried her face against Morgan's breast.

"Now, now, Mattie," Morgan attempted to console her. "Miz Amber gonna be needin' us all. Dat babe she carryin', he need us, too. De Massah, he'd want it dat way. An' it'll be up ta us ta tak keer of dem bofe."

Neither Mattie nor Morgan was aware that Amber had been standing at the top of the staircase and had witnessed their grief, her heart breaking for them as well as for herself. Suddenly she realized that Morgan spoke as if he had given up hope for Trent's safe return, as if he might be dead! Tears burned her eyes and she felt sick.

"*No!*" The high-pitched, heart-rending scream came from above them. The two old servants looked up, startled. They realized that Amber had heard the words Morgan had spoken.

"*No! No! No!* Trent *is* coming back! He *will* be all right! He will! He must!" the distraught girl shouted, her fist raised as she beat the air. Her small body shook uncontrollably, and her face was ashen.

Mattie and Morgan mounted the stairs, Morgan reaching the landing first.

"Miz Amber, ma'am, ah—"

"Shut up, Morgan, do you hear? Just shut up! I will not hear you! Trent is not dead! I need him, our baby needs him!" Amber had become hysterical. "I love him, Morgan! Dear God, I love him! I cannot lose him!"

Mattie had reached the landing and was standing with tears streaming down her wrinkled, brown face. She could not bear the stricken look in the young mistress's eyes, green eyes that had darkened with pain until they looked almost black.

"Tell him, Mattie," Amber begged. "Tell Morgan that Trent is all right!"

When Mattie only stood weeping helplessly, Amber cried shrilly, "*Tell him, Mattie!*" Then she fell in a dead faint.

Morgan lifted the fallen Amber and carried her into the Master's bedroom. With Mattie's help he settled the girl in the large bed, then hurried from the room to dispatch someone with a message to Doctor Holmes.

Mattie sat beside Amber until Doctor Holmes arrived, then hovered in the hallway while he examined her mistress. When the door opened and the little doctor stepped out, Mattie looked at him imploringly.

"Doctah, is she gonna be awright?"

"Yes, Mattie, it is just the shock of LeBlanc's disappearance. She will be fine, physically, but somehow I do not feel that she is responding properly. It is as if she does not hear me. She will answer no question, nor will she speak to me. She is just lying there, staring at the ceiling. I have seen this type of shock before, and it will just take time for her to come around to accepting the situation, whatever it may be."

"Doctah, whut kin ah do fer Miz Amber?" Mattie asked in concern.

"Well, there is nothing any of us can do at the moment. As I said, it is a matter of time. Now, Mattie, is it possible that you could prepare a room for me? I intend to stay close by for a few hours."

"Yassuh, Doctah Holmes, ah sho kin!" Mattie assured him. "An' if'n Miz Amber don' need ya, den de Mastah, he jes' might, whin dey bring 'im home."

As she spoke Mattie led Doctor Holmes to a room across the hall from Amber.

"Dis heah room's close an' don' need no preparin', Doctah. Ol' Mattie, she gonna keep things ready 'roun heah. Don' nevah know whin dese rooms gonna be needed." Mattie had busied herself with opening the window and turning down the bed as she talked. Now she turned to the door with a final word, "If'n ya need anything durin' de night, call fer Kane. He be sleepin' on a pallet jes' outside Miz Amber's doah, case she calls."

The door opened slowly, soundlessly. A gentle breeze stirred the curtains at the open window; the murmur of rustling leaves and a faint, lonesome melody whispered among the trees.

The drone of hushed voices rose from downstairs, and dusty, pale rays of moonlight filtered through the veranda doors. In the hearth the fire crackled as the flames licked the logs.

Amber sat in the middle of the large four-poster bed, her unbound copper hair falling down her back and over her smooth shoulders. In her small hands was clutched Trent's blue silk robe as she held it to her breast. She breathed in the lingering scent of leather and tobacco mingled with a manly scent that was Trent's own.

The warm glow from the fireplace danced over the room causing shadows to flicker across the walls. Amber stared sorrowfully and unseeingly into the flames, tears streaming down her pale cheeks.

"Please, dear God!" she whispered brokenly. "Please let Trent be safe!"

To LeBlanc, standing in the duskiness of the room, Amber had never looked more beautiful. Her soft, pure beauty made his heart pound in his breast. He knew that the flowing tears were for him. Afraid for Trent, Amber was praying for his safety. He was deeply touched at the knowledge that Amber could have such profound feelings for him.

Trent remembered how Amber had cursed him, slapped him, wished him dead, how she had sworn repeatedly that she hated him. A tender smile touched his lips as he thought to what lengths Amber had gone to cover her true emotions. Did she, after all, truly care for him? Did she love him? He swallowed hard as he realized how very much he wished that she might.

LeBlanc moved toward the bed to stand before Amber. As his shadow fell across her, Amber started and raised her head, meeting the warm, passionate gaze of Trent's brilliant sapphire eyes.

Amber's dark green eyes widened and she quickly came to her knees, arms outstretched.

"Trent!" she choked, lips trembling. "Oh, Trent!"

LeBlanc pulled Amber into his embrace, crushing her to his breast as if he would never let her go.

"Amber . . . Amber . . ." he whispered, his voice almost a moan. His lips found hers, and he kissed her with tender passion. A consuming need swept over him, not quite like any emotion he had ever experienced.

They clung together while Amber wept and Trent soothed her, calming her fears. He is alive! her heart screamed, he is alive! He has come home and he is safe! And Trent held her securely in his strong arms, the arms for which she had longed, had needed. She silently thanked God, burying her head against Trent's broad chest.

Then Amber began to laugh and to cry at the same time. "You are alive!" she shrilled happily. "Oh, thank God you are alive! They have been searching for days. Days! Oh, Trent, you have had us all so worried! Poor Mattie! And Morgan! They have mourned so for you! They feared that you were dead!"

Amber turned tear-bright eyes up at Trent. Cupping her now-flushed face in his large hand, he gazed into the depths of two dark green pools from which tears still escaped.

"And you, little one? What about you?" Trent queried. "Were you worried, as well? Have you mourned for me, believing me to be dead?"

"No! I told them! I told all of them! I knew that you were not dead. I would have known!" Amber's fingers trembled as she reached out and touched Trent's unshaven cheek. "I would have known," she whispered.

Amber wanted to tell Trent that had he met his death she would have known it in her heart because she loved him so deeply, but she could not. Oh, Trent! My love! My life! How very much I love you, she groaned inwardly. Will the time ever come that you will return my love? Will I ever know your love as I so desperately wish to?

LeBlanc released Amber only long enough to seat himself on the side of the bed, then he swept her into his arms and settled her upon his lap. As the firelight touched him, Amber stared at Trent's face, which had, up to now, been in deep shadow. Above his right eye was a deep gash, and the flesh lay open and bruised. Dried blood had matted his dark eyebrow, and his face was bloodstained.

"My God, Trent, you are hurt!" Amber cried.

"Oh, that!" was Trent's simple reply. Then, raising his hand and gently touching his brow, he flinched. "'Tis naught, madame, but a scratch." LeBlanc smiled at the horrified look on Amber's face.

"A scratch!" Amber gasped, jumping to her feet. She turned to face Trent, her arms akimbo and her breast heaving in indignation. "How dare you, Trent LeBlanc! How dare you sit there so—so damned calm, so—unconcerned! You act as if you had just come in from a leisurely outing! Oh, but you are absolutely insufferable!" she ground out between clenched teeth.

Oh, but she was lovely when she was angry, Trent thought. He had not expected Amber to become enraged at his words. He had dismissed the wound as being of little or no importance in order to avoid further upsetting her.

"Your temper is showing, kitten. And you know that it is not good for you to become fretted in your condition," Trent said evenly. He pulled off his boots and lay back on the bed. "I am exhausted, my sweet. I have been trudging through that damnable swamp all day. Now come help me with my clothes and welcome your weary husband home."

"You are insane!" Amber snapped.

"Oh, I think not," came Trent's lazy drawl.

"But you are injured, Trent—"

"True."

"—and you need the care of a physician. Doctor Holmes—"

"I fear the good doctor cannot cure what ails me," LeBlanc chuckled. "Now, come here, wife!" He reached for Amber's hand and pulled her onto the bed with him.

Amber lay sleeping, her head resting on Trent's broad chest while his strong arms encircled her petite frame. LeBlanc watched through half-closed lids as, in her sleep, she snuggled closer to the warmth and security of his body. Smiling lazily, Trent brushed a kiss across Amber's brow, his lips lingering at her temple. She gave a sound of contentment which, to LeBlanc's ears, sounded very much like the purr of a kitten.

Confident that his words would not be heard, Trent whispered gently,

"I shall not fall in love alone, Amber! I shall be taking you with me! I love you more than life, little one, I just have not the courage to love alone. But one day you will love me, I will see that you do! And then—" The words trailed off and LeBlanc brought Amber's hand to his lips, kissing the tips of her slender fingers. He toyed with the gold band on her third finger as he breathed, "Then, Amber, I shall speak of my love!"

Trent held his breath as Amber stirred. Had she heard his whispered confession, he wondered. But she did not awake, she only nestled contentedly against him as her enticing lips formed his name.

Was it possible that she would take him with her into her dreams, Trent wondered. For her to speak his name in such a manner sent his heart pounding, his blood racing like a fire within his body. This was his woman! His wife! He must never lose her. He would never share Amber, nor her love, with another. I will kill any man who dares the attempt to take you from me, he groaned inwardly. I will kill any man who dares even to touch you!

LeBlanc cradled Amber close in his arms. And with her in his heart and his thoughts, as well as in his arms, he soon fell into a deep and untroubled sleep.

Chapter Thirteen

"*ALIVE?*" THE SHOCKED WORD WAS FORCED FROM BETWEEN tight lips. "But how can that be?"

"It seems that your man only grazed him! He walked out of the swamp on his own two feet, arriving at Travinwood sometime after midnight." The man's answer was followed by an amused chuckle before he continued. "Although tired, dirty, and bleeding, the Great LeBlanc took not the time to inform his household that he was alive and safe. He simply entered the house unobserved, going straight upstairs to the warm bed and soft arms of his lady!" He coughed discreetly. "So I have been told, of course."

"Alive!" The word was a dull whisper.

"Very much so! This Amber Kensington LeBlanc must be some woman! For a wounded man, after fighting his way through the muck and the snakes of those infernal Louisiana swamps—and in the dark of night, I might add—to seek her bed . . . There is no wonder that you were jealous, Kathleen!"

"Jealous! Nonsense! Jealous of that—that little bitch?" Kathleen's laugh held no humor. "Never! Devon, my darling, you have never seen this woman or you would see the jest of that ridiculous statement!''

"Ridiculous, is it? Come, Kathleen. I have seen the way you react when there is another beautiful woman on the scene. And your sullenness since your call at Travinwood. Furthermore, you have been preoccupied with your desire for revenge against LeBlanc. All this clearly indicates extreme jealousy."

Kathleen did not speak, but her rising anger was evident by the fierce clenching of her fists and the rapid rise and fall of her breast as her breath came unevenly.

"God, but she must be a beauty!" Lord Devon went on. "Why, with that fool LeBlanc refusing to die, crawling back from the swamp to her, and with your dreadful behavior . . . Well! I can only say that I cannot wait to meet this 'Amber' person!" The words and his tone denoted deep interest in Amber.

"Get out!" Kathleen shouted in rage. "Ling! Ling, show Lord Devon to the door," she said to the small Chinese houseman who answered her call.

"Never mind, my dear," Lord Devon murmured, picking up his hat and cape from a nearby chair. "I should have remembered your temperament when your plans go awry."

Ling opened the door for Lord Devon as he left the parlor. In the doorway Devon turned to the enraged Kathleen and said in parting, "Since I find that my presence here is not wanted, I think I shall pay a call to Travinwood. It has been much too long. And there is a possibility that I will be fortunate enough to meet the new Mistress of Travinwood."

Devon tipped his hat at a jaunty angle and followed Ling to the front door.

At the sound of the heavy door closing behind him, Kathleen spoke aloud to the empty room, "Tread carefully, Devon, lest you, too, become my adversary!"

Then she rose and began to pace the length of the room, her thoughts coursing through her mind.

Kathleen Fulton had been intrigued by the tales of Trent LeBlanc that she had heard from the time her father had purchased Heritage Manor, the estate adjoining Travinwood. The Fultons had moved there during the time Trent had been at sea. The story was that Ashton LeBlanc had taken his young son, thirteen-year-old Trent, on a voyage to France. During the return voyage their vessel had been attacked by pirates, Ashton LeBlanc had been killed, and his young son taken captive. Trent LeBlanc had been reared with the pirate band but had never forgotten Travinwood, his home. He survived the years at sea with the pirates and lived with one goal in mind—that one day he would return to Travinwood.

Some seven years later the pirate vessel was attacked by other pirates, and following a long, bloody battle Trent LeBlanc had regained consciousness to find the ship drifting aimlessly. Upon investigation he learned that he was the only survivor. The deck was littered with bodies, many of them unknown to him, obviously pirates from the attacking vessel.

As he attempted to help any who might have been only wounded, Trent came upon the inert figure of his captain who, gasping his final breaths, had managed to ask, "Does any man survive, boy?" Trent had dropped to his knee beside the dying man and replied, "Only you and I, sir." Whereupon the captain had sworn, "You must be the son of Satan to have survived this massacre." The man had coughed and blood had gushed from his mouth, then he had spoken weakly but clearly, "The ship is yours, son. You have earned her," and closed his eyes in death.

The crippled vessel with her masts broken, her sails tattered, drifted through the night. On the following morning the ship cut through a heavy gray fog as if guided by unseen hands and found her way to a small island in the Caribbean Sea. Trent LeBlanc, clad all in black, stood in the ship's bow, his hands clasped behind his back. It was as if the vessel were steered without a ship's wheel but by some supernatural faculty possessed by LeBlanc.

After arranging for burial of the dead and making repairs to the vessel, LeBlanc had hired a small crew and set sail for New Orleans, the stronghold of his ship laden with booty now belonging to him.

So Trent LeBlanc had returned home to find that his mother had died some two years earlier and that he, at age twenty, was not only master of his own ship but owner and master of Travinwood.

And he had met Kathleen, the pert young beauty from

Heritage Manor. She learned that Trent had been devoted to his mother and that hearing of her death had plunged him into the depths of grief and loneliness. Kathleen had taken advantage of this and had made a point of being nearby whenever Trent felt the need for conversation and companionship.

In the meantime Kathleen had begun to scheme and to lay her plans to become the mistress of Travinwood. She pressed her advantage, and it did not take her long to find her way into LeBlanc's bed.

Ashton LeBlanc had not believed in slavery, and each slave that he purchased had been given the choice of freedom and making his own way or of remaining at Travinwood as paid workers.

The plantation had flourished, due partly to the hard work of the loyal and grateful ex-slaves who had never known anything other than cruelty from their masters. With the help of the family attorney, Marcus Eden, Casey Reed had done a commendable job of managing the plantation after Ashton's death.

Upon Trent's return, Casey had promptly relinquished all responsibility of Travinwood and had gone happily off to sea. Trent had watched him go and had felt a great sense of longing to go with him. Seven years at sea had made young LeBlanc love her ever-changing moods, her calm and her storms. It almost seemed to him that salt water, not blood, ran in his veins.

After a few months' stay at Travinwood, Trent became restless and admitted to himself that never would he overcome his passion for the sea, never would he be happy until he returned to her.

He then decided that the inheritance from his father should be used strictly to maintain the plantation and to care for its people and began to plan his own future. He already owned a ship and crew, he loved the sea, the booty he had "inherited" from the pirates would serve as assets, so why not begin his own shipping business, he had pondered.

In the eleven years since, Trent LeBlanc had built up a shipping empire. His name and his reputation were known on both sides of the Atlantic as well as in the Mediterranean and the southern waters of the new colonies.

During these years Trent had returned annually to Travinwood for a few weeks in order to keep a finger on the pulse of the plantation and to transact any business matters which needed his attention.

And one of the "matters" which always demanded his attention was Kathleen Fulton. She had never given up her dream of becoming mistress of Travinwood and used the time between Trent's visits to devise new methods by which she might trap him into marriage. But to no avail. She was merely a diversion for LeBlanc, a convenience, a plaything.

"Eleven long years!" Kathleen fumed as she paced the parlor floor. "And for what? Never did he commit himself in any way! Never was he at all serious about me! Always his parting words were, 'Until next time.' And, fool that I was, I kept laying my plans for the future, for the time that I, Kathleen Fulton, would be Madame Trent LeBlanc, Mistress of Travinwood. Oooh, how could I?"

Beating her fist in her hand, Kathleen pursued her thoughts right up to the day she had been at Madame Dunlap's dress shop and had overheard a conversation between Madame and that young woman.

"I am sorry, miss," Madame had said, "please make my apology to Captain LeBlanc. But the fabric which the Captain specified was not available in the shade of blue which he requested. The wedding gown is most beautiful, and I feel certain that the Captain's lady will be most pleased."

Kathleen had moved closer in order to better observe the gown and not to miss any of the conversation, while appearing to browse through the bolts of fabric which lay on the counter.

What a blow it had been to her to learn that LeBlanc was to be married! And *not* to Kathleen! To whom, then? Surely not that copper-haired creature whom she had seen barefoot and clad in boy's clothing? Her answer was not long in coming.

"Oh, Madame," breathed the unknown girl, "the gown is indeed lovely! And it will look beautiful on Miss Amber!" She turned her glowing eyes toward Madame Dunlap and continued. "You have not had the pleasure of knowing our Miss Amber, Madame, but you would love her. And the beauty of such a gown could only be equaled by Miss Amber's own loveliness!"

Jealousy had torn at Kathleen, and she had angrily swept from the shop. The need for revenge had gnawed at her until she had made definite plans for vengeance by the means of disposing of LeBlanc. If she, Kathleen Fulton, were to be deprived of Trent, then so would "our Miss Amber," she had thought with satisfaction.

But somehow her attempt had failed. How could it be? she wondered. What could have happened? And it had all seemed so simple!

Kathleen and her favored black buck, Breaker, had been returning from an afternoon ride and a round of unspeakable love play when they had observed the master of Travinwood riding toward the swamp. Breaker knew of Kathleen's plot for he was to play the major role therein.

"We will find a place and a time," Kathleen had said, "a time when least expected. Then you, Breaker, will dispose of LeBlanc. No one will be the wiser, for a man like LeBlanc has many enemies."

And that particular day had seemed ideal, Kathleen fumed. LeBlanc had been riding into the bayou . . . alone . . . there would be no one to see what happened. The time was right, the place would be perfect! So she had sent the black man after him.

"The time is now!" she had exulted. "Use the rifle and aim well! I want the bastard dead!" Kathleen had pulled a rifle from her saddle holster, and then Breaker had turned his horse to follow LeBlanc while Kathleen continued on her way home, confident that Breaker would do the job. Confident that her ex-lover, Trent LeBlanc, would be no more!

But it had not happend. LeBlanc was still alive and, most likely, right now was in the arms of the beautiful Amber. Not for long, Kathleen vowed, not for long! She turned and stormed out of the house and toward the stables, calling as she ran.

"Breaker!"

At the sound of breaking china and the high shriek, Trent opened his eyes and stared at a wide-eyed Mattie who stood trembling in the doorway. Amber woke with a start and sat bolt upright, the sheet clutched to her breast.

"Good morning, Mattie," Trent said in a lazy, unconcerned drawl. "Am I to assume that that was coffee?" He indicated the mishap on the floor by allowing his blue gaze to casually roam over the assortment. The silver serving tray lay to one side, a china cup and saucer were in pieces of varying sizes. Steam rose from the black liquid pool that was flowing from a broken pot.

"Trent!" Amber scolded, a hint of laughter in her soft voice. "You have frightened poor Mattie."

"Yes, it would seem so," Trent chuckled and looked at the old servant. She had neither moved, nor had she uttered a sound aside from her shocked scream.

"Mattie?" Trent gave a short whistle and snapped his fingers loudly at the woman. "Mattie, are you all right?"

Slowly nodding her grizzled head, Mattie stammered, "Y-yassuh, ol' Mattie she jes' fine, Massah Trent." The words were so faint that they could barely be heard. Then tears began to spill from her dark eyes as she said more clearly, "Massah, we—we though ya wus daid—we thought we'd nevah see ya agin'." At the thought, Mattie choked then continued, "Lawd, Massah, we thought—"

"Well, Mattie, as you can see for yourself, I am very much alive. I am in my bed . . . with my wife . . . as I have been for some hours now!" LeBlanc replied happily. "Now do not look so sad. You may inform the household that their Master is safely home." As an afterthought, Trent added, "I do not wish to frighten anyone else."

"Yassuh." Mattie stooped to clear the wreckage from the floor, but Trent stopped her.

"That can wait, Mattie. Right now I would like a little more time alone with my wife. A little later you may bring more coffee and prepare a bath for me."

Still somewhat stunned, Mattie shook her graying head and mumbled, "Yassuh." As she pulled the door closed, Trent called out.

"And Mattie! Knock next time!"

"Oh, Trent, you were awful!" Amber reproached. "You are a bully and—" She did not finish for Trent pressed her back down on the bed, covering her body with his own.

"Oh? You did not think me so awful earlier, kitten. You did not think me to be a bully. It seems that my actions *then*, pleased you. Or do you not remember?" Trent said huskily, cupping her bare breast with a gentle hand.

"I remember," Amber whispered as Trent's lips claimed hers.

Chapter Fourteen

"TOO LONG," AMBER GASPED AS SHE URGED MOON ON, BRINGing the mare to a brisk pace. "Oh, Kane, Master Trent will be furious! We have been out far too long!"

The young boy said nothing, only dug his heels into his mount coaxing the animal to keep up.

Amber released a weary sigh as she caught sight of Travinwood.

"Almost there!" she announced happily.

The two riders hurried into the yard. Amber reined to an abrupt stop and swung down from Moon's broad back. As her feet touched the ground she turned quickly, too quickly, and collided with a broad solid chest. Strong arms caught Amber as she stumbled, steadying her. Then a deep masculine voice spoke.

"Steady there, miss. Are you all right?"

"Y-yes, I am fine." Amber stared up into the handsome face of the stranger, her eyes meeting dark, wintry green eyes that were regarding her through half-closed lids. In a trice Amber had noted that the man was about the same height as Trent, broad-shouldered, deep-chested, an intelligent face

209

with a large, straight nose and high forehead. He was strangely attractive, handsome in an intriguing way.

"I did not see you, sir," Amber continued, still somewhat shaken by the unexpected collision. "I am sorry that I ran into you."

"Not I!" came the smooth reply. The stranger allowed his gaze to freely scan the arrestingly beautiful woman who stood before him. Emerald green eyes sparkled in a most exciting way, and her soft, golden cheeks were now tinted with a pink glow. Her coppery hair was wind-blown, and tousled curls tumbled down her back.

Although dressed as she was in breeches, vest, jacket, and knee boots, all made of soft, fawn-colored buckskin, the man summed Amber up as enchanting, most desirable and far more beautiful than he could ever have imagined.

God! No wonder Kathleen Fulton was in such a state, he thought. And no wonder LeBlanc had married this woman! He no longer thought LeBlanc a fool, indeed LeBlanc had been most fortunate to have found such a beauty as this! And smart enough to secure this woman to him by marrying her.

He chuckled to himself as he mused, Kathleen, my dear, there was never a contest. Amber LeBlanc has won all the way and you were never even in the running. And at that moment he decided that he, too, wanted Amber!

"Are you a guest here at Travinwood, Miss—ah—"

"Amber. Amber Lynn Kensington—well, LeBlanc, now," she supplied her name when he hesitated. "I married Trent LeBlanc, Master of Travinwood, only a few days ago."

"I am sorry," and it sounded as if he really meant it.

"For what, sir?" Amber asked, puzzled.

"Oh, I was merely hoping that you were a guest, not LeBlanc's new wife. Damn my luck!—er—I beg your pardon, what I meant was—"

"What he meant was that if you were not my wife he would make an attempt to sway your interest in his direction!" The deep, scornful voice cut in on the stranger's words.

Amber whirled about to see Trent striding toward them. Was it anger which darkened his blue eyes, she wondered. Then she returned her attention to the unknown man, puzzled at what she read in his cloudy green eyes.

"Afternoon, LeBlanc."

Amber's eyes flashed to her husband, who merely acknowledged the greeting with a curt nod, his blue stare never straying from the man at her side. She shivered as she felt a current of hostility, loathing and—hate? Yes, hate—between the two men which was frightening. It was apparent that they were not friends, so why was this man at Travinwood? Why had he come and what did he want?

"Congratulations on your marriage, LeBlanc! I never thought you had it in you—to marry, that is." The newcomer extended his white-gloved hand to LeBlanc, who made no move to accept it. The stranger's green eyes hardened and narrowed dangerously as his hand dropped slowly to his side. Amber watched the scene anxiously, her bright eyes darting from one man to the other.

"Why are you at Travinwood, Devon?" LeBlanc asked bluntly.

"I am somewhat familiar with the swamps, and when I heard that you were missing I thought to join in the search, my friend," Lord Devon replied smoothly. He hoped to assuage LeBlanc's irritation at his, Devon's, unwelcome presence at Travinwood and, at the same time, to impress Amber with his so-called good intentions.

Amber started at the enraged, obscene oath that burst from Trent's mouth. She clapped both hands over her ears for a moment, then removed them cautiously.

"You take me for a fool, Devon?" Trent was saying harshly. "Think not that I am! You are lacking in wit if you think that I do not see through your unconvincing show of concern," LeBlanc snorted contemptuously.

Trent's lips pressed into a hard, thin line, his eyes narrowed, and Amber saw the muscles twitch in his jaw. She sensed that LeBlanc was fighting the urge to strike the man.

"Never again call me 'friend,' Devon," rasped LeBlanc. "The word is false upon your lying tongue. A man such as you knows not the meaning of 'friend,' and it angers me to hear you use it!"

"You go too far, LeBlanc!" Lord Devon snapped, his handsome face reddened with anger.

"Do I, now!" Trent drawled. The corners of his mouth

tilted upward, and a mischievous glint danced in his sapphire eyes as he stepped forward.

Dear God! Was the man daft? Would he actually challenge LeBlanc? Amber knew the situation to be getting quite out of hand. Turning to her husband, she placed her hand in his, saying,

"I know not the controversy, my husband, between you and this man. But can it not be settled at another time?" Amber's eyes implored Trent as she continued, "Trent, please! I do not like the course this exchange is taking!"

Trent looked down, his gaze impaled by soft, emerald eyes that held a silent plea. Amber's small hand trembled within his grasp, and LeBlanc reached down, gently placing a finger to her quivering lips and said tenderly,

"You are right, little one, I did not mean to distress you. Another time will please me well!" Raising his head he spoke to Lord Devon.

"Be thankful, Devon, that my wife delays the confrontation which you and I shall eventually have!"

Without a backward glance, LeBlanc guided Amber to the front door and into the house, leaving Lord Devon where he stood, his anger rising.

As the great door closed behind them, Amber questioned, "Who is that man, Trent, and why do you dislike him so?" Trent remained silent as they continued their way into the library.

Amber tried again.

"He seemed so nice, such a gentleman. He is English, is he not? I could tell by his speech."

"Yes, he is English," Trent answered reluctantly, "but he is no gentleman, and I will not have the man in my house or around my wife! Let us speak no more of him, Amber!"

LeBlanc seemed adamant and unyielding on the subject, but it served only to intensify Amber's curiosity about the handsome stranger whom Trent had called Devon. Was it because of LeBlanc's very obvious dislike for the man that she wanted to know more about him? she wondered. What was the mystery involved here? Why the open animosity between the two men? Was it possible that they were once rivals? If so, who had won? And then, inevitably, the question—who was the woman? Amber felt a sudden sting of jealousy.

She thoughtfully regarded Trent as he angrily splashed brandy into a crystal goblet, sloshing the liquid carelessly over the tilted side of the glass. No matter, Amber reflected, he was not going to tell her anything about the man, Devon, but she determined to find someone who would. Perhaps, and she suddenly stifled a giggle, perhaps this Devon was a man of whom Trent was jealous! Perhaps the infamous, arrogant Master Trent LeBlanc had a flaw after all. Amber chuckled softly at the thought.

"Amber!" LeBlanc's sharp voice broke into her private thoughts.

"You need not yell, Trent, I am right here! And I am not the slightest bit deaf!" Amber responded haughtily.

"My pardon, madam! It is that I had called your name three times before and you did not answer. Only then did I raise my voice," Trent said coldly. He admitted to himself that he was irritated at Amber's earlier interest in Lord Devon as well as the fact that she was apparently absorbed in her own, faraway musings. And those musings, he decided, included Devon! Well, he would be damned if he would let it bother him!

"Go dress for dinner, Amber!" LeBlanc snapped. "We have guests coming."

Amber looked at Trent in surprise. The tone of his voice was unusually sharp. She knew that he was angry, knew that the man, Devon, was the reason for his irritability. Aware that Trent's dark blue gaze was upon her, Amber curtseyed in an exaggerated manner, smiled pleasantly, and with a flippant toss of her head left the room. LeBlanc watched the seductive swing of her shapely hips as she ascended the curving staircase.

Amber had finished dressing and was tucking the last wayward curl into place when a knock came upon her bedroom door.

"Miz Amber, may ah cum in?" came Mattie's muffled voice from the other side of the heavy door.

"Of course, Mattie," Amber answered, and as Mattie

entered, the girl turned from the mirror to ask, "How many guests will be here?"

"Foah, Miz Amber. Dey be Mistah Casey an' a Mistah Simmons frum New Orleans. An' Massah Trent, he told Mistah Jason an' Mistah Monrow ta join 'em."

"And Miss Neva? Did you tell her what time dinner would be served?"

"Yassum, ah tole Miz Neva dat dinnah wus gonna be at eight 'steada seben 'cause dey'd be guests. But she said ta tell ya dat she weren't agonna be a-cummin' ta dinnah." Mattie's voice showed concern as well as curiosity.

"But why would she say that, Mattie? Miss Neva always has dinner with Master Trent and me. Is she ill?" Amber was puzzled.

"No'm, she ain't sick. Leastways she weren't when ah first seen her." Mattie paused as if in deep thought, then continued, "Wusn't 'til ah mentioned Mistah Casey's name. Den she went all pale an' put 'er hands ta her breast an' in a real shaky kin' a-voice, she says, 'Mattie, please tell Miz Amber dat ah won't be a-joinin' 'em fer dinnah.' Den she run up dem dare stairs lak de ole debil hisself wus aftah her!"

"Thank you, Mattie, I shall go see what is wrong with her. Please set a place for Miss Neva. I shall try to persuade her to come to dinner." Amber had started for the door but stopped on the threshold. "Mattie, have Mister Casey and Mister Simmons arrived?"

"Yassum, Mistah Casey in de liberry wid Mastah Trent. But Mistah Simmons, he gonna be a little late. An' ah done sent Kane ta fetch Mistah Jason and Mistah Monrow frum de carriage house."

Neva paced the floor in agitation. "I cannot go down, I cannot face him! Oh, what am I to do?" she questioned herself aloud. In the midst of her confusion, Neva heard a knock on her door.

"Neva?" Amber called from the hallway. "Neva, it is I, Amber. May I come in?"

When the door was opened, Amber entered the room and looked anxiously at her friend. "Mattie told me that you would not be down for dinner. Are you not feeling well?"

"I am well, Miss Amber. Only I cannot come to dinner."

"And pray why not?" Amber queried, "If you are well, then why should you not wish to join us at dinner?"

"You are having guests, miss." Neva paused, trying to find an answer which would satisfy Amber. "You see, I do not belong at your table when you are entertaining." She sincerely hoped that this reply would suffice.

"Nonsense! Neva, you know that you are always welcome at my table! Now you just get dressed and I shall wait for you. We will go down together!"

"But I cannot!" Neva wailed as she threw herself across her bed. "Oh, Miss Amber, I just cannot!"

"Neva," Amber began and, sitting on the side of the bed, she reached out to lay her hand on Neva's quivering shoulder. "Neva, my dear! Why are you so distressed? Please! You can tell me, I am your friend. We have no secrets."

"Oh, Miss Amber!" Neva cried as she turned to Amber, tears streaming down her flushed cheeks. "It is that I cannot face him! I just cannot!"

"Face *him*? But whom is it that you cannot face? Surely not Trent! Has he said something to you that was upsetting? Did you two have words?"

"Oh, no, miss! The Captain, he has always been most kind. No, Miss Amber, it is not the Captain!" Neva assured her friend.

"Then tell me, Neva! Is it Jason?" Neva shook her head. "Monrow?" Amber pressed. Again came only the shake of Neva's head. "You must tell me, Neva! If I am to help, I must know!"

Neva wiped her eyes with the back of her hand. Amber brushed a stray curl from the girl's damp brow.

"If someone hurt you, Neva, I must know. If one of Trent's men has hurt you—"

"No! It was not one of the Captain's men, miss. And no on has hurt me!"

"Then what is all this about?" Amber asked irritably. Her patience had begun to wear thin.

"It is Casey Reed, miss!" Neva managed to say.

"Casey Reed?" Amber was taken aback. "I do not understand. Neva, do you know Captain Reed?"

"Yes, miss."

"How do you know him? And from where?" Amber asked, puzzled. When Neva made no reply, Amber continued, "This Captain Reed. Did he hurt you at one time? If so—"

"Oh, no! No! He has not hurt me, Miss Amber! Why, he does not even know me!" Neva answered, causing Amber more confusion.

"I do not understand, Neva. Perhaps you should start from the beginning." Amber was aware that she would have to press the girl for an explanation.

There was a moment of silence, then Amber said, "I am waiting!"

Drawing a deep, uneven breath, Neva began her story.

"I have known of Captain Reed for a very long time, just as I have known of Captain LeBlanc."

As Neva paused, Amber spoke in surprise, "What? You knew Trent before?"

"No, miss, not really. You see, both Captain LeBlanc and Captain Reed were well known in Havana," Neva replied, her voice thoughtful, as if she were remembering some long ago time. "It was Captain Reed's ship that brought my mother and me to Havana six years ago. We came from England to join my father. I was quite young, only fourteen, and I fell madly in love with Captain Reed. He was so handsome, so kind—" Neva broke off and glanced at Amber. "You must think me daft!"

"No, no. Go on, Neva," Amber encouraged.

"Well, when we reached Havana, I knew that I would never see him again. In my childish mind I thought it was the end of the world." Neva raised pleading eyes to Amber as she questioned, "Miss Amber, have you ever just looked at a man, perhaps passed one on the street, and known instinctively that he was the right man for you?"

Amber could not answer. She was remembering the night in London when Trent had rescued her and had carried her to his ship. She had felt a faint stirring of emotions, but at that time of confusion she had been unable to interpret her feelings. She had been afraid, and, when Trent had raped her, she had felt that she hated him. But yes, she had felt an emotion other than hatred, and, yes, it had been very much as Neva had described.

"It can happen, Miss Amber," Neva was saying. "It happened like that with my mother and I have heard many girls say the same. But I did not believe it until it happened to me! Two years later I saw him again and knew that I still loved him. But I was too young for such a man. I was only sixteen . . . skinny . . . flat-chested—"

"Neva!" Amber scolded.

"Well, it is true! I was!" Neva protested. Then she grew thoughtful and her eyes had a faraway expression as she reminisced. "I would slip down to the docks every afternoon and watch him as he walked about on the deck of his ship. I listened to his deep, rumbling voice and dreamed that he was mine. Fancied that he loved me. But he never noticed me. Then he was gone again.

"It was another year before he returned to Havana, the same time that the *Mér Fleur* was docked there. That was the first time I saw Captain LeBlanc and I thought him to be very handsome. But it was Casey Reed that I wanted. He of whom I dreamed foolish dreams and over whom I cried myself to sleep at night. I saw the pretty young women who visited him on his ship, flirted with him, hung on him in taverns, and followed him about the streets.

"Oh, there were many who followed Captain LeBlanc and visited him on his ship, but he would have nothing to do with most of them. And Captain LeBlanc never went to Madame La Roy's, although Casey did. Madame La Roy's is a whorehouse on the waterfront," Neva explained.

"Can we just ignore the parts about Trent? Just tell me about Casey Reed."

"Forgive me, Miss Amber. Anyway, Captain Reed sailed again, and I have not seen him for three years. I never saw Captain LeBlanc again until that day at the auction. Although I must say my heart plumb near stopped beating when you called his name and then, again, when I saw him in the warehouse."

There was a brief silence as the two girls remembered their shared experience and their gallant rescue. Then Amber was jolted back to the present as Neva sprang to her feet.

"But I never thought to see Captain Reed again, never!"

Twisting her hands in agitation Neva implored, "Oh, Miss Amber, what am I to do? I cannot go down there! I cannot sit at the same table with him! I would just die! I know I would!"

"You will do nothing of the kind," Amber retorted. "Now sit here beside me and listen."

Neva stood uncertainly, then did as Amber bade. Taking Neva's hand in hers, Amber spoke in a calm, matter-of-fact voice, her tone commanding thoughtful consideration to her words.

"You tell me that you have loved Casey Reed for years. You also tell me that he never noticed you. This means, to me, that he does not know you, that he has never met you. Is this correct?" Neva nodded her head vigorously, and Amber continued. "So, when you go down to dinner, Captain Casey Reed will meet Miss Neva Lawson, an attractive young woman, and *not* the fourteen-year-old child whom he may, or may not, remember."

Seeing that she had Neva's full attention, Amber pressed her advantage.

"Do you not see that you are no longer a child? That you are no longer 'skinny,' nor are you 'flat-chested.' You are a woman, and a very pretty one. Do not give up now, not after loving Casey for all these years. Do not run, nor hide like a frightened pup. For if you do, I shall be most ashamed of you.

"Now get yourself up, fix your face, and put on that lovely deep-rose velvet gown that Madame Dunlap made for you. Then gracefully walk down those stairs with all the confidence and assurance of the beautiful woman you truly are. And if you do not win Captain Reed's heart, then he has none."

Neva smiled timidly, rose, and crossed to the wardrobe for the velvet gown. Seeing the hope in Neva's eyes, Amber nodded with satisfaction.

"There is one other matter about which I wish to speak with you."

Neva turned expectantly as Amber went on.

"My name is 'Amber' and there is no need for the 'Miss.' If you will recall, I have asked this of you once before. We are friends—equals—and you must realize this fact. From this moment forward, you will call me 'Amber,' for I call you 'Neva'!"

Although it sounded like an order, Amber's sweet smile took any sting from the words which had been spoken in genuine friendship.

Chapter Fifteen

THE FRONT HALL WAS FILLED WITH THE SAVORY AROMA OF roasting game, sweet potatoes, and fresh-baked bread. As Amber wandered into the dining room Mattie was placing two large platters of roast duck on the long table, which had been draped with a snowy white damask cloth edged with lace. Matching napkins were encircled by silver rings on which the letter "L" was engraved.

Amber's mouth watered at the orange dressing, green pea pods smothered in rich butter sauce, fried okra, and sweet golden corn. She noted that the place settings were of the finest china, white and powder-blue, harmonizing with the color and formality of the elegant room. Tall crystal goblets sparkled with clarity and luster as the candlelight was caught and reflected. The highly polished silver gleamed richly.

As a finishing touch, a centerpiece of yellow roses and white mums clustered snugly among delicate, soft green ferns resting in an oblong silver bowl. It was apparent that extra-special effort had been made for these dinner guests.

"Oh, Mattie, everything is so lovely!" Amber praised the servant. "The food smells simply wonderful and the table—well, it's really the most beautiful table I have ever seen!"

"De Massah, he say mak' de place dis way, so's ah do jes' dat! He say he want dis ta be a real nice dinner pardy, dis be fer you, Miz Amber," Mattie told her, a wide smile on her aging face.

"For me? But I thought Trent was having guests."

"Miz Amber, de Massah he wantin' ta show ya off! Chile, ya real special to 'im."

So Trent had made these arrangements for her, Amber mused, had told Mattie to make the place nice, special—for her! He never ceased to amaze her. Would she ever really know him, she wondered with a weary sigh, this man she both loved and hated, whose moods were as complex as her own!

"Miz Amber," Mattie's voice broke into her thoughts, "Mistah Jason and Mistah Monrow, dey not gonna be a-joinin' ya fer dinnah. Kane say dey say ta tell de Massah . . ." The old woman paused and stroked her chin in perplexity. "Sumpin' ta do wif' gubber—gubberment, or sumpin' lak dat."

"Government?" Amber supplied.

"Yassum, dat's de word! Anyhow, ah done gib de Massah de message."

Amber thanked the woman for seeing that Trent received the message and wandered thoughtfully from the room, pondering over what the two men were up to and what the "gubberment" had to do with their missing dinner. She certainly hoped that they were not courting danger—government, indeed!

"By damn! You're in love with the girl!" Casey Reed blurted and his roar of laughter filled the library. LeBlanc, crossing the room to hand his guest a brandy, stopped in his tracks.

"Love! I love *no* woman!" Trent's voice held a tinge of unpleasantness. Handing the snifter to Casey, he stated bluntly, "I have not the time to court such feeble notions!" With a dry chuckle, he added, "I am immune!"

"Immune, hell!" Casey expostulated. "No man is immune! Love is not a weakness, Trent! There is no shame attached to being in love!" He rolled his smoky-gray eyes heavenward. "My God, to be in love with a woman—*truly* in love—is a wondrous thing. Granted, it is a fearful thing, as well. We men—all of us brave, arrogant bastards—are afraid of love!"

Casey took an ample gulp of his brandy as if to bolster his courage to speak what ordinarily would be difficult words for him, then continued,

"Now love, to a woman . . ." The words trailed off and he sighed heavily, staring down into his now empty glass. "Love, to a woman, now that's a completely different story. It's in her very being, her soul lives for love!"

"Christ, Casey! You sound like a damned preacher! Shut up and drink your brandy!" Trent snapped.

"I seem to be out of brandy," Reed replied.

"That figures!" LeBlanc reached for the decanter and replenished Casey's glass with a healthy shot of the brownish liquid.

His nerves and composure were on the verge of breaking. Why in bloody hell had he told Casey about the encounter with Devon and his rage at Amber's apparent interest in the man? Why had he felt that Reed could, or would, help?

Of course he was in love with Amber, Trent acknowledged to himself, and it was a new and heady experience. But he was not about to admit it to *anyone,* he thought grimly.

And, of course, he had not liked the interest that Amber had shown in Devon and all the damned questions. Amber was *his,* and he had told Casey so, which was what had brought about this whole blasted conversation.

Casey Reed was not a man to let an interesting matter drop before it had reached a conclusion satisfactory to himself. Now he watched LeBlanc closely, smiling covertly. Oh, Trent, my friend, he thought, not only do you love this Amber but you are terribly jealous, as well. Love and jealousy—two things which you have never before encountered nor been forced to cope with!

Casey silently enjoyed LeBlanc's discomfiture for a few minutes, then fired his next shot,

"So what if Amber *has* taken a fancy to Lord Devon. Why should *you* care, if you do not love the woman?"

"Damn it, Casey, leave it be!" Trent began to pace the room like a caged animal. One hand rubbed the back of his neck, the other held a threatening grip on his snifter.

Damned if Reed was going to help matters, he fumed. The man understood nothing of what Trent was feeling. All Casey could do was deal out his superior knowledge of men and women, spout his wisdom of love! Why, one would almost think—

LeBlanc's pacing steps came to a sudden halt, and, turning, he looked at his friend and asked simply,

"Just how is it, Casey, that you know so much on the subject of love?"

"I have been there," came the soft admission as Reed intently studied the slender stem on his crystal glass.

"You!" Trent looked shocked as he dropped to the arm of a nearby chair. "Surely you jest!"

"No, no jest, I assure you. I've never before admitted it to anyone," Casey began slowly. "A pretty little thing she was, too. It's been near seven years since last I saw her."

"Why so long? If you love this woman, why do you not have her with you? Why has it been these many years?" Trent asked in genuine concern. It was unbelievable that Reed had loved and had not kept the woman at his side, had allowed the years to separate them.

"She was only a child. But a lovely child who would one day be a beautiful woman. I was a man who had his life well ahead of him and, as you so aptly put it, I had 'not the time to court such feeble notions.'"

Trent ignored the acid comment and persisted, "Where is she now? Do you know where to find her?"

"She was in Havana all those years. Recently I had made up my mind to go back and find her." Casey killed his brandy in a quick gulp and set the empty glass on a small table. He stood, walked over to the window, and stared out unseeingly. "When I got back to Havana she was gone! Sold!" The words were full of hurt and angry frustration.

"I am sorry, my friend, truly I am. I had no idea!"

"Of course, you did not. I never told you," Reed told him, turning from the window. "That is why I think it so important that you face your love for Amber. If *I* had faced up to the truth I would have my Neva today!"

Trent's body became alert, his blue eyes locked with those of Casey. Neva! The name was not that common! And

Havana! God, could it be that here in this very house, right now in a room upstairs—

"'Neva,' a lovely name. What was her surname, did you know?" he asked casually, though watching the other man closely.

"Lawson. Her surname was Lawson," Reed told him, returning to his chair and dropping into it with a heavy sigh. "Well, I will be damned! Casey, you are not going to believe this—"

"Pardon me, am I intruding?" Amber's soft voice came from the doorway, and both men turned to face her. Casey stood as Trent crossed to Amber.

"No, no," LeBlac assured her. He took her small hand in his and led her across the room for introductions. Casey would soon learn what he had been about to tell him, he reasoned, and the sight of Neva would be much more effective than mere words.

"Amber, my dear, this is Casey Reed, captain of the vessel *Sea Dog* and a very dear friend of mine."

"Captain," Amber smiled, raising her hand to the tall man before her.

"Make it 'Casey,' please!" he replied, then bowed and placed a kiss upon her hand. His lips lingered a bit too long, Trent thought jealously, and at the sound of LeBlanc impatiently clearing his throat Casey slowly released Amber's hand.

"'Casey,' it shall be," Amber assured sweetly and graced Reed with one of her rare smiles that made Trent wish it had been for *him*.

Amber was secretly pleased that LeBlanc showed open dislike for the fact that her hand had been ardently kissed by his friend. It was something she had seen earlier, the annoyance displayed when another man showed an interest in her.

"Sweet Amber," Casey began daringly. "I may call you 'Amber'?"

"Of course, if I am to call you 'Casey,'" she answered with another smile as she sat in the chair Reed had vacated. She watched the play of emotions dance across Trent's handsome face and smiled inwardly.

"You are far lovelier than any of the rumors have reported!" Casey, too, was enjoying the byplay, and his suave manner came to the fore, as always with a beautiful woman. "Too many young ladies in New Orleans have long hoped to capture LeBlanc for themselves and none ever succeeded. And then you—"

"I am sure that Amber cares not what the local gossipmongers have had to say," Trent broke in, uncomfortable with the trend of the conversation.

"Oh, but *darling,* I *do!*" Amber flashed Trent a disarming smile.

Darling? Mon Dieu! This is too much, LeBlanc thought. What was she up to? What game was she playing? He could see the mischief waltzing in her emerald eyes.

"Please, Captain—I mean, *Casey,*" Amber fluttered her gold-fringed lashes boldly at Reed. "Do go on!"

Oh, this is too much! Trent groaned silently and said mockingly,

"Yes, Captain—I mean, Casey, do go on!" He seated himself on the arm of Amber's chair and handed her a snifter half-filled with brandy.

Unperturbed, Reed continued, "Well, every man that knows or has known Trent LeBlanc had long ago decided that he would never get married!"

Amber's soft, "Indeed?" amused Casey.

"Yes. And his marriage, to be honest, has caused quite a stir!"

"I am sure!" she purred.

Casey laughed heartily and helped himself to another brandy as he went on, "It was—ah—well, sudden!"

"Quite!"

"And very much a surprise to all concerned," Reed mused aloud.

"Very true!"

LeBlanc had not spoken during this exchange between Amber and Casey, had only watched and listened with some amusement.

"Tell me, Amber," Reed was saying, "how is it that LeBlanc was so lucky as to find you? And fortunate enough to marry you, as well?" When the girl seemed hesitant to speak, he urged, "You are among friends, you can tell *me!*"

There was more than a hint of humor in his voice as he added, "I know his reputation with—

"No, wait! Let me guess! You did not willingly come all the way from London. Right?" Casey's gray-blue eyes were laughing as they met the stormy blue eyes of LeBlanc.

Unknown to Amber, Casey was well aware of the whole story for he had played an important part in it. He had got word to her Uncle Edward that she was safe and had taken him the money he had so desperately needed. Trent was angered that Casey would use his knowledge for his own humor and to thrust the sword a little deeper in LeBlanc's side.

"And this scoundrel saw you—wanted you—and carried you off, kicking and screaming, against your will!" Reed concluded with a roar of laughter.

"Casey, you do not know just how close to the truth you are!" Amber's soft lips curved into a shy smile as she saw Trent stiffen and change his position on her chair arm. "Why, if you *really* knew—"

"Amber!" came Trent's angry warning.

"Yes, darling?" Again she purred the word "darling."

"I do not believe that our guest would be interested in the details of our courtship!"

"Courtship?" she countered sweetly, observing the boiling anger in his eyes. "Oh, yes. You mean our memorable meeting and all the rest."

"Well, you do look happy," Casey remarked as he watched the battle of wills between the two. "And Trent does not beat you—or *does* he?"

"Oh, no! That is, so long as I do what is expected of me, as his wife," Amber said breathlessly. "But he is not always an easy man to live with, nor to please."

"I am sure you speak the truth. He has always been a man concerned with himself and his own pleasures and possessions. What is his, is *his!* A very demanding man, LeBlanc."

"How true!" Amber agreed and patted Trent's knee lovingly. "How very true!"

"Amber!" Trent warned again. Then in a controlled voice he said, "You will close your pretty mouth, if you please!"

"But I do not please!" she argued in honeyed tones and

raised her hand to stroke Trent's cheek, her green eyes full of devilment. "You cannot beat me here, my husband. Not in front of our guest!"

"Do not be so sure!" he smiled lazily, catching her hand in the warmth of his own.

"Why, Trent! You would!" Amber gasped, her other hand flying to her breast in mock fright. "You—you would beat me for speaking my mind? You would beat me for this reason?"

"I can think of several other reasons!" Trent shot back in a clipped voice.

"Well, he will not beat you while *I* am here!" Simmons spoke from the doorway. "Trent LeBlanc, you will quit bullying your wife!" The man crossed to Amber and took both her hands in his and kissed them softly. "My dear, I have heard all about you and have so wanted to meet you!"

At that moment, Mattie announced dinner and so ended the battle of words and threat of beatings.

Amber showed Simmons his place at the large table and turned to Reed.

"And you, Casey, may sit there," she waved a slim hand toward a chair at one side of the table where two place settings had been laid. We have a houseguest who will be joining us shortly."

"Male, or otherwise?" Simmons wisecracked, his short fingers busily stuffing his napkin into the collar of his pale brown shirt.

"That, sir, is *my* secret," she replied with a smile as she turned to Trent. "And you, my husband, may carve the duck while I see what is keeping our mystery guest."

As Amber left the dining room Trent stood from his chair and, with a murmured "Excuse me," followed his wife into the hallway. He caught up with her at the bottom of the staircase.

"Amber, what are you up to?" he asked, mounting the stairs behind her.

"Oh, just a little matchmaking."

"Matchmaking? Amber, wait! There is something you do not know. It is about Neva and—"

"And Casey? I *do* know!"

"You know? But how?" Trent wanted to know. Had Amber overheard his conversation with Reed? Sweet Christ! he hoped not!

"Neva told me," she was saying as they stopped at the girl's door. "She was not coming down to dinner when she learned that Casey was here as a guest, so I had a talk with her." Amber turned to Trent, her green eyes bright with excitement. "Oh, Trent, it is all so unbelievable! Neva has been in love with Casey since she was a child, loved him from afar, so to speak! Now he is here and she has the chance to win his love."

"There will be no need for her to try to win Casey's love—"

"And just pray tell me why not?" Amber flared hotly. "You would have me to believe that your Casey Reed is as untouchable as you? That the man is like the steel of a blade . . . cold . . . hard . . . unbending?" Her lovely face flushed an angry red as she blurted, "Oh, why should a woman waste her time? Why should she hurt with her love for a man?"

"That is not what I meant, my wife! It was not that, at all." The words were low, almost choked. Amber's words had found their mark as surely as if she had plunged a dagger into him. Her aim had been sure, and he had received the blow of her meaning.

"Then, *what,* Trent? What *did* you mean?"

"Casey loves Neva, already. He had come to this realization and had gone after her only to learn that she was gone—had been sold. He has loved her just as deeply as she has loved him, and neither of them are aware of the love of the other. And now he has lost all hope of finding her, of ever having her love."

Just as I have lost all hope of having your love, he wanted to tell her. Just as I have lost any hope of finding you, finding that part of you that you keep so carefully out of my reach. Oh, Amber, my life, can you not see my love for you? A love that is such bittersweet pain within my being? A love that I cannot openly admit until I am sure that you can have that same love for me? My darling, a part of me dies a little each day that I do not have your love.

Amber had stood quietly listening to the story as Casey had

told it to Trent. She had heard him say that he knew of Casey's love for Neva and was happy beyond words that Neva's love would be freely returned. How she wished with all her heart, with every breath, that Trent loved *her*. Her heart was breaking, her love would never be realized, never be fulfilled.

What was there in the depths of LeBlanc's sapphire gaze? What mystery lurked within his seemingly cold heart? She knew there was a warmth there, she had felt it reach out to her. Often it had caressed her. How she wanted that heart to love her, the man to need her as she loved and needed him. She wanted to be so deeply seated within Trent's heart that it would beat with love for her, ache for her. She needed his breath to mingle with her own, to breathe, to love, to live as one.

"Amber," her name was a whisper upon his lips as they met hers. They were warm and sweet, causing fire to lick with urgency along her stomach and thighs. She raised her arms and encircled his strong neck, answering his kiss with force. All was lost . . . the guests downstairs . . . the beautiful dinner . . . Neva . . . all that mattered was Trent and his lips against hers . . . the yearning she felt for him.

His hands roamed her soft form. He pressed her against the wall, his own need growing, his thighs strong and unyielding along her own. Trent's grip tightened about her, his lips trailed fire along her neck and shoulder.

"Amber, my wife, my beauty!" His husky whisper stirred her even more. "I cannot bear to have you want another." His blue eyes met hers, searching her face. "Tell me you will never want another. Please, only want me!"

"Trent, I—"

Dear God! She had come close to telling him that she loved him. The words were on the tip of her tongue. She would *never* want anyone else. Not ever! There was no wanting another man the way she wanted Trent LeBlanc. Did he not know this? Could he not see?

She had to break free of those eyes, those knowing eyes that would be able to read her every thought and see that her heart, her love, her very soul was in her eyes.

"Trent, I could never want another," she admitted shakingly. "None other could be to me what you are or could beckon my body as does yours. I am your wife! I belong to you!"

With a ragged groan Trent took her lips. He was pleased with her answer, pleased that she wanted no other. God, but he wanted her, wanted her *now* without any waiting. Wanted her hands on his flesh, her body next to his without the hindrance of clothing.

His fingers pulled at the tiny buttons of Amber's dress.

"Trent!" she breathed. "Our guests! Have you forgotten them?"

"Damn! If Simmons were not down there—" He broke off and a lazy smile formed on his lips. "To hell with Simmons!" His fingers again fumbled at the buttons. "God, I need you, wife!"

"No, Trent, wait!" Amber's hand closed over his. She knew that she must be sensible even if he was not. They had friends waiting downstairs, and Simmons was of great importance, that much she knew from the times she had heard his name mentioned. No, they could not just leave their dinner guests and merely disappear into their bedroom to make love.

"Trent, believe me. I want you as well, but . . ."

LeBlanc's fingers stilled. "You are right," he said flatly and brushed his fingertips slowly across the tender mounds that rose above Amber's tight-fitting bodice. "I shall return to our guests, and you see what is keeping Neva."

He leaned forward and placed a kiss upon her parted lips, his teeth tugging lightly at the soft inner flesh. His tongue played lazily about the corners of her mouth, and Amber was once again lost.

But Trent did not linger. He stood upright, stepped away from her, and said in a tight voice,

"Do not tempt me, my beauty, or I shall sweep you into my arms and head straight to our bedroom and never give another thought as to who is in this house!"

And with that he turned, walked down the hallway and descended the stairs to the dining room below.

"Gentlemen, Miss Neva Lawson!" Amber announced as she and the girl entered the large dining room.

Trent stood as they approached, placing his napkin upon the table.

Simmons rose slowly to his feet, an appreciative smile on his face.

Casey had just taken a sizable gulp of brandy and began to choke as the amber liquid threatened to squeeze the breath from him. His handsome face was beet-red, and he was coughing in spasms as he beat one hand on his chest in an effort to clear the fiery liquor from his windpipe.

Amber stifled a giggle and walked to the man who was apparently on the verge of collapse.

"Casey, are you all right?" she questioned in feigned concern, beating Reed on the back.

"Fine—I'm fine," he managed in a strangled voice.

He raised smoky-gray eyes to Neva, who was calmly seating herself in the chair beside him. She was more beautiful than he had remembered and a woman grown! But what was she doing here? She had been sold! At least that was the information he had received when he had gone to Havana to find her.

Casey regained his composure and sat back in his seat, completely at a loss for words. Here was his love, the love he had thought was lost forever. In his heart he thanked God that she was real and safe in LeBlanc's home. He would learn the details as to why, how, and when later. Right now he only wanted to feast his eyes upon her, content just to be near her.

The evening had gone very well. The lovely dinner which Mattie had prepared was enjoyed to the utmost by everyone. The men had returned to the library, and Neva and Amber had retired to the small sitting room.

While Neva busied herself with some needle work, Amber tried to read but found it impossible to concentrate on the reading matter. Her mind was on the earlier scene in the upstairs hallway. She could still feel Trent's arms about her, the taste of his lips lingered on her own.

What had come over him, there in the shadows? she wondered. There had been a strange feeling between them, a force that seemed to come from nowhere drawing them into such a closeness that she had wanted to confess her love for him, to let him know how she felt and *had* felt for a long time.

But she had failed to do so. She could not tell him, she had been too afraid of his reaction.

"Amber?" Neva's soft voice startled her and Amber jumped, so lost in her thoughts she had been that she had not realized that the girl had been speaking to her.

"Y-yes?" she responded.

"I was just saying, did you not think it very strange, the way Captain Reed behaved at dinner?"

"Strange? How do you mean, 'strange'?"

"I do not rightly know," Neva admitted. "It was—well, it was just—*odd*. The look in his eyes and his actions when we first came into the dining room, as if he were shocked at the sight of me. And later, all through dinner, I felt his gaze upon me. Oh, I was much too frightened to look directly at him, but I could feel him staring at me!"

Neva sighed and put away her sewing, folding her hands in her lap before she went on.

"I do not think he likes me very much." Her voice quivered slightly. "He never really saw me before—as a woman, I mean—so I do not know why I should think he would look at me, really *see* me, *now!*" She was silent for a brief time, seemingly lost in her own thoughts, then, "I should never have let you talk me into going to your dinner party. It only served to show me how very much I still love Captain Reed and the fact that he will never see me as a woman!"

"Neva, you are blind! And so is your Captain Reed!" Amber laughed and closed her book. "Do you not know that the man is in love with you? That he was so frightened of you and of his love that he could not look at you without going pale? Yet he could scarcely keep his eyes off you!"

"Frightened? Of me? What ever do you mean? Please, Amber, do not tease me. I—I cannot bear it!"

"I am not teasing you, my dear. Casey Reed is deeply in love with you and has been for many years. He told this to Trent just this very evening. He did not know you were here, nor that we knew you. He had no way of knowing. He confided to Trent that he had long been in love with a young woman and when he mentioned her name, you can only imagine Trent's amazement!"

Amber related the story as Trent had told it to her.

Neva was thrilled, her face alight with happiness. Her

dream had come true, she was loved even as she loved! It was unbelievable! But how could she let Casey know that she loved him, that she was aware of his love for her?

"One does not just walk into a room and say, 'Casey Reed, I love you!'" she told Amber, laughingly.

"Oh, but one *does!*" Amber said firmly. "You walk right into that library, put your arms around his neck and say, 'Casey Reed, I love you!' Just like that!"

"I—I cannot do that!" Neva was aghast, her eyes wide with wonder that Amber would think that she could do such a brazen thing!

"And why not?" Amber demanded.

"Because—because a lady would *never* do such an outrageous thing! 'Just like that.'" She snapped her fingers, emphasizing her words. "Not something like—like telling a man that you *love* him!"

"*I* would!" Amber stated emphatically. "I would do it if I were sure that that man loved *me!* I would not chance losing him because I was too proud to speak up, to admit my love!"

Oh, just listen to you, Amber LeBlanc, she taunted herself, listen to what you are saying. The words are pretty and they are filled with emotion. But you know very well that you could lose Trent because of your own fear and pride. You can tell Neva how to do it and what she should say, urge her to admit her love for Casey. So why can you not do the same?

Because it's different for her, Amber answered her own question. I know that Casey Reed loves Neva, he freely spoke of his love for her. And if ever Trent should speak his love for me, then I, too, will admit the love I have for him! But only when I am sure!

Neva sat in silence, her head bowed and her hands clasped tightly together.

"Well?" Amber prompted quietly, yet insistently.

Neva raised her head to look at her friend. How she wished that she were as strong as Amber, as sure of herself. Amber was honest, straightforward and seemed to fear nothing.

Apparently arriving at a decision, Neva drew a deep breath and stood from her chair.

"This is truly what you would do, Amber? You would be bold enough to tell the man you love him?"

"Yes!" Amber confirmed her reply with a vigorous nod of her head and smiled reassuringly at the other girl.

As Neva moved slowly toward the library door, Amber rose quickly and followed her.

Chapter Sixteen

"DAMNED BRITISH!" SIMMONS EXPOSTULATED. "ENEMY SQUAD-rons roam at will about Pea Island. Raiding parties burned Frenchtown to the ground—and Havre de Grace. They are inhuman, that is what they are! Burning . . . prowling . . . killing and pillaging! They must be stopped!"

"Do you have a plan?" Casey asked as he poured Simmons a brandy. "If so, let us hear it."

"No, no plan," Simmons sighed wearily and shook his gray head. "I wish I did. Jackson is rarin' to meet up with 'em. This war is personal to him. Not just because the British are fighting the Americans, either." He took a drink of his brandy, licked his lips, and continued:

"It goes back to when he was a boy. Andy was taken prisoner by the British during the Revolutionary War. He was struck by a British officer for refusing to polish the man's boots. The officer laid the flat of a saber across his cheek. Andy was never one to forget an injury, he has been anti-British ever since. Guess I would be, too," Simmons finished with a snort.

"Well, I believe Jackson can get the job done," LeBlanc

opined as he leaned his lanky frame against the doorjamb. "He is good, fights well. And he knows what he is doing. We need a man like that."

"I agree with you, Trent. But if the British march on New Orleans, they shall have me to deal with," Casey boasted. "This is my home and I will be damned if I will just let the bastards walk in and take her!"

"Hold on, Casey! They aren't here, yet," Simmons told him.

"No, but they are damned close. Why, the sons of bitches were in the Bay of Barataria some weeks back and they still sail our waters. How damned much closer do you want them to get?" Casey shouted angrily.

"Casey is right, Dan, they *are* too close. They are up to something, and my intuition tells me we will know what it is, very soon," LeBlanc voiced calmly. "Lafitte warned Claiborne about an attack on New Orleans. He had received a letter from Havana describing the arrival there of a small expedition under the command of a Captain Percy and—uh—Nicholls, Colonel Nicholls. The expedition was destined for Pensacola.

"The letter went on to relate their plans to raise the Indians, secure Mobile, and march against New Orleans. The writer is also persuaded that the entire Creek nation is joining forces with the British troops, and he added that, although the force was small, strong reinforcements were expected from Bermuda. Lafitte forwarded the letter to Blanque in New Orleans. He later wrote a letter to Claiborne and again offered the services of his men, as well as himself." LeBlanc concluded with, "Whether or not Claiborne believed him, I do not know."

"Well, he had damned well *better!*" Casey's voice was raised in anger. "The man is a fool if he does not believe!"

"I am sorry to interrupt, gentlemen," Neva's soft voice drifted across the library.

All three men turned toward the door, and Neva took a few uncertain steps into the room, her dark eyes meeting the gray ones of Casey Reed. Amber stood closely behind her, and suddenly Neva turned to her friend, as if for encouragement.

Amber motioned her forward and whispered, "Go on! It will be all right!"

"Captain Reed," Neva began nervously, "I—I wish to speak with you."

Reed came toward her, his hand outstretched to take her hand in his.

"Of course, Miss Lawson. What may I do for you?" he asked as he led her to a chair.

When Neva neither spoke nor seated herself, Amber breathlessly suggested that perhaps the two of them should go out onto the terrace. She knew that the girl's self-confidence was ebbing and that it was frightening to her to tell Casey that she loved him. It would be much easier for her to do so without an audience. Besides, it was a very private matter.

As Casey and Neva passed through the French doors to the terrace, Trent moved to Amber's side.

"What is that all about?" he questioned, a knowing smile on his lips.

"Looks like love to me!" Simmons declared with a chuckle. "Our man could not keep his eyes off that little woman all evening." He winked wickedly at Amber and added, "Ah, to be young and in love!"

The older man joined LeBlanc and Amber at the terrace doors, and the three watched unashamedly as Casey and Neva stopped and turned to face each other. Casey seemed to be watching the girl closely, his eyes intent upon her upturned face.

Then Neva bowed her head slightly, her fingers laced together nervously, and the observers at the doorway could hear the soft murmur of her voice.

Casey did not interrupt, and when the girl finished speaking she drew a heavy breath and slowly raised tear-bright eyes to the man towering over her. Still the man made no move, nor did he speak. Neva's lips moved and she caught her underlip with her teeth as she turned from Reed, the luminous moonlight catching and reflecting a tear as it coursed down her pale cheek.

For another moment Casey stood motionless, then suddenly his body seemed to shudder and a broad smile spread across his face. He reached out and grasped Neva's trembling shoulders and ever so gently pulled her close in his arms. His lips were at her ear as he spoke, and the three spectators could only hear the rise and fall of his voice.

Whatever words he had uttered had an instant effect upon Neva. Her slender arms crept about Casey's neck and a happy laugh escaped her lips. Reed was laughing softly, and, lifting her small frame clear of the ground, he took her lips in a deep, satisfying kiss as Neva clung to him, her face radiant in the full moonlight.

With a heavy sigh Amber turned, right into Trent's arms. They encircled her, gently bringing her closer into his embrace. She longed for him to declare his love for her. After watching Casey's and Neva's love unfold before them, there under the brilliant moon, surely the words would not be hard for him to find.

You tell *him!* her heart screamed. Tell him that you love him! But she could not, she would not do as she had advised Neva. Amber shivered at the thought that she might never hear those words from Trent's lips, that she might never say them herself.

LeBlanc moved her from him, his blue eyes scanning her face. She was crying, the tears falling like silent rain. He ran his thumb tenderly across her cheek, wiping a tear away.

"Why the tears, Amber?" he asked softly, his gaze hot upon her.

"I—I am so happy," Amber choked. "So happy for th—them. They are so very much in love and—and to love someone so deeply is quite beautiful. I am truly elated that they have found each other."

LeBlanc and Simmons had retired to the study while Neva and Casey sat, talking quietly, in the parlor. Amber had made her excuses and sought the privacy of her room.

She lay across the large bed which she shared with Trent, recalling the scene between Neva and Casey, and the memory made her heart ache dully. It had been beautiful—the two finding each other, admitting their mutual love!

With a weary sigh Amber moved from the bed and crossed to the balcony door, stepping out into the cool night. The yearning for Trent's love lay heavy on her heart. She loved him so very deeply, loved him with every fiber of her being, and longed to have that love returned.

She leaned against the wrought-iron railing and stared out into the quiet night. Only a faint, wintry breeze stirred about the veranda, and the golden glow of moonlight stole softly across the gardens below.

How she had grown to love Travinwood and all its beauty. She no longer missed England, for this was home and she would never, *could* never, think of it otherwise. Of course, she missed Uncle Edward and Aunt Alice and often wondered if she would ever see them again. She wondered if they were all right and if they had settled their business with Sir Michael. But Trent had assured her that everything would be all right, that he would see to it and would let them know that Amber was safe and happy.

How this had been accomplished she did not know, but she was positive that it had been done. Trent LeBlanc was trustworthy, and his words of assurance had spared her hours of worry about the only two loved ones she had.

"You have a life here now, Amber," Trent had told her. "You need not worry about England. This is your home! Here, in America . . . here at Travinwood . . . with me! Don't look back, stop mourning over your blasted England and everything will be fine!"

She had assured him that she no longer missed England, had attempted to erase any doubts that she would try to return there, that she would leave him. It had not been an easy task for many times he would repeat his lecture, a steely edge in his tone, a tightness in his voice.

Amber often wondered if Trent feared losing her, if that loss would mean something more, something deeper, than she could understand.

"I will never let you go, Amber! Never!" How many times had he spoken those words? How often she had returned after a long walk or a ride to find Trent out watching for her or saddling Satan, ready to go after her! At those times she imagined she read relief on his darkly handsome face when he saw that she was home.

The man was a mystery, he confused and puzzled her with his actions. And his words, "I will find you! No matter where you go, how far you run, Amber, I will come after you and bring you back!"

She did not doubt his words. He had come after her before, had found her. But why? Why was he so adamant? Sure, the unborn child was important to him for she knew he wanted his child. That was why he had married her, had forced her to stay with him. And she had loved both Trent and their child enough to share Trent's life, his country.

Her life at Travinwood had been good. She had made friends, loved Mattie and her family which, in a strange way, was hers. Trent had teased her about the "Southern drawl" that was creeping into her voice. She smiled, remembering the many hours she had spent with Kane while the young boy coached her, insisting that she draw out her r's, d's, and so on. He had taught her some slang words and pointed out the times when she would clip her words, like the proper *"Eng-lush-mon,"* as Kane had pronounced it.

Amber's heart would soar when Trent would take notice, laugh at her usage of some word, and tell her that she would "be an American, yet!" And she felt that he was honestly pleased.

The sudden throaty rumble of LeBlanc's laughter from the study below drifted upward to meet her ears, and Amber's heart lurched slightly. Such a deep, rich laugh he had, she thought fondly, and she wrapped her arms about her, wishing they were the arms of her husband.

She listened and could hear the low, vibrant tones of Trent's voice echoing through the house. The sound of the Master's voice reaching out, settling, resting on that which belonged to him. Even the faint murmur of that voice sent a warmth pulsating through her, quickening her breath. The rich, velvety sound had a strange effect on her and always had. It stirred an exciting emotion within her; the husky tone strongly aroused her.

Amber had long since stopped fighting her emotions and Trent's power over her. She was *his*—in name . . . in heart . . . in soul . . . in body! She knew that she would never love another, never belong to any man other than Trent LeBlanc! And yes, she admitted, she *did* belong to him, as he had so often told her. He wanted her, desired her, and needed her, Amber reasoned, and if that was his way of loving her, then she would accept it. She would willingly give him her body, her love, even her soul, and pray that one day he would come to truly love her for herself.

Suddenly a movement caught her eye. She stood motionless, her fingers tightly gripping the railing and her green gaze intent on the apparition beyond the rose garden. The shadowy form slipped about in the darkness, making a stealthy approach toward the house. Who was out there?

For a moment Amber could not find the power to move, her legs anchored her, not allowing her to move from her spot on the veranda. Then she pressed her frame deeper into the shadows, scarcely breathing.

The dark figure crept soundlessly through the garden, inching closer and closer. Amber's heart pounded wildly in her breast, the palms of her hands became cold and clammy. She should call out for someone! No, that would alert the prowler that he had been seen. But she should warn Trent that someone was out there, and the intruder must not get away before it could be learned what devilment was afoot.

Silently Amber slid along the wall, keeping well in the shadows until she reached the bedroom. Quickly she lifted the lid of Trent's sea trunk and rummaged through the contents until her slender fingers touched one of his pocket pistols. Tucking it into the pocket of her robe, she stepped from her slippers and returned to the upper gallery. She walked across the wide veranda, her bare feet soundless on the tiled flooring.

Reaching out over the balustrade, Amber took a secure hold on the wooden lattice which clung to the side of the house. Then she carefully placed one foot, then the other on the makeshift ladder, climbed easily downward and jumped lightly to the ground.

She moved furtively around the corner of the house where the shadowy figure had disappeared and pulled the pistol from her pocket, a sure grip on the weapon.

There it was, the figure, a massive bulk of a man looming near the study door. Amber saw a flash of metal in the moonlight and knew that he, too, held a weapon. Was he there to rob, to kill?

From where she stood, Amber could see LeBlanc sitting on the edge of his desk, his back to the door. The man tried the doorknob, it moved freely in his hand and he stepped closer. He pushed the door open a few inches and took careful aim with his pistol.

A shot rang out . . . the sharp sound of shattering glass echoed into the night followed closely by a shrill scream . . . there was a dull thud as the intruder fell to the floor.

Amber stood motionless, her feet braced slightly apart, her spine straight and both hands holding the smoking pistol.

"My God!" came a stunned voice from within the study, then there were other voices, all talking at once.

Slowly expelling a deep breath, Amber raised her eyes to see Trent as he stepped through the French doors and over the still figure on the ground.

"Sweet Christ!" LeBlanc gasped, looking at Amber. She stood there clothed in a silk gown and wrap of milk-white, barefoot, her copper hair in a mass of childish curls and the pistol clasped tightly in both small hands.

"He—he was going to shoot you," she whispered, dropping her hands to her sides. "I watched him approach the house. I did not dare call out lest I frighten him away." With a quick, indrawn breath, she explained, "I found your pistol and climbed down the trellis and—"

"You *what?*" Trent roared.

"I took the pistol and climbed down the trellis," she repeated dutifully.

"Mon Dieu! Amber, are you daft? Have you forgotten that you are with child? What in God's name do you mean, doing such things? You could have been severely injured!" he raged, his face an angry red. "What will you do next? Damn you, Amber, you are not to go climbing down trell—"

"But he would have killed you, Trent!" she stormed hotly. "He had a pistol aimed at your back! He—he would have pulled the trigger and blown a damned hole in you! You were an easy target, Trent LeBlanc, and if I had not climbed down that—that blasted trellis, you would not be alive right now to yell at me!"

Amber moved past Trent hurriedly, brushing at the tears that clouded her vision and heedless of the broken glass that lay scattered upon the terrace.

She heard Trent's warning too late. The glass bit into the soft flesh of her foot and a startled cry of pain escaped her lips. She was swept effortlessly into LeBlanc's arms, and as he entered the study the slivers of glass crunched beneath his booted feet. Once again he stepped over the prone body of the would-be assassin.

Trent sat on the sofa holding Amber on his lap as his gentle fingers tenderly removed the fragment of glass protruding from her foot.

Neva crossed the room and knelt at their side, handing Trent a wispy handkerchief.

"Oh, Amber," she wailed. "We—we were just entering the study when Casey saw that man at the door!" The girl's voice was shaken. "Before we could warn Captain Trent—oh, when the shot—I thought—"

"Well, except for my wife," Trent began, smiling down at Amber, "it could have been *me* lying over there."

Amber glanced toward the door and saw Simmons and Casey lifting the man to a chair. She heard a low moan and realized that she had not killed him.

Morgan rushed into the room, concern on his kind face. Mattie was close behind him, carrying a bowl of water and a cloth.

"Miz Amber, honey, is ya awright?" she asked. "Is she hurt, Massah? Oh, ah'd neber forgib mysef if'n enythang wus ta happ'n ta 'er."

"I am fine, Mattie," Amber replied reassuringly. "There really is no need to worry yourself."

A painful cough brought their attention to the other side of the room. Trent rose and set Amber on the sofa so that Mattie could attend her mistress's injury. He strolled across the study to where the wounded man was half-sitting, half-lying, in the leather chair. Amber could just make out the murmured words of the culprit as Trent questioned him.

"With what purpose did you come here tonight?" Trent demanded harshly, towering over the defenseless man. Then he grasped the man's collar and pulled him upright in the chair, smiling grimly as his captive paled noticeably and coughed deep in his chest.

"Who sent you?" LeBlanc shouted, a strong grip on the blood-stained shirt. When there still was no answer, Trent swore loudly and flung the man backward where he cowered, staring with frightened eyes.

The stranger moaned, pressing a hand to his shoulder and

gritting his teeth against the pain. He looked down to see his hand filling with his own blood and spilling slowly through his fingers.

"I am dying!" he gasped pitifully.

"It would seem so," LeBlanc confirmed unfeelingly.

"But—but I do not wish to die!" he cried, attempting to sit up.

"Neither was it *my* wish to die, yet you were not concerned about my wishes when you were about to take *my* life," Trent told him matter-of-factly. With a wave of his hand toward Amber, he added, "If not for my wife, I would have received the bullet that you were ready to plant in my back!"

"Your wife?" Dark eyes swept to Amber. "It was—was she who shot me?"

"It was," LeBlanc assented proudly.

"Trent, I think it wise that Mattie take Amber upstairs," Casey told him in a low voice. "She looks quite pale."

"Yes, of course." Trent went to Amber and again lifted her in his arms. As he left the room, he spoke over his shoulder, "Casey, see if you and Simmons can get any information out of our 'guest' while I see Amber to our room."

LeBlanc paused in the doorway, casting a deadly look at the would-be killer before he added bluntly,

"If he should choose not to talk and if he is not dead when I return, I shall see if I cannot assist in putting him out of his misery!"

With those menacing words LeBlanc strode from the room, leaving both Casey and a smiling Simmons regarding the man whose eyes were wide and pleading as his words began spilling forth, accompanied by an occasional gasping cough.

Chapter Seventeen

AMBER TOSSED RESTLESSLY IN THE WIDE BED, FINDING IT difficult to sleep. The night was long and empty without Trent lying next to her. She had become accustomed to his strong arms clasped about her, his brawny frame molded along hers, wrapping her in a cocoon of warmth, his breath faintly fanning her neck as he slept peacefully.

Without him, she was spending a restless night, her thoughts dominated by the events of the evening.

Simmons and Casey had learned something from the man whom she had shot. The information must have been of great importance for, soon after LeBlanc had left her to rejoin the men downstairs, she heard him call out to Morgan to ready the carriage and saddle Satan.

Amber had watched from her balcony as the men carried the wounded intruder outside and loaded him in the carriage. Simmons had climbed inside with the man, and Casey had taken the reins at the driver's seat. Trent had mounted Satan, and all had headed for town at a fast pace.

Later, Neva had come to look in on Amber and had told her that the men had gone into New Orleans and that they would not return tonight. In fact, there was a possibility that they would not be back for two or three days.

When Amber pressed her for more information, Neva could only shake her dark head and repeat what she had already told her. Then Amber had asked if the man was still alive and had been assured that he was indeed alive, although bleeding profusely. Captain Trent had said that he would see that the man had a doctor as soon as they reached town, Neva told her.

Amber's stomach fluttered slightly, and she placed her hand over her gently rounding belly. The first stirrings had begun some days ago. Her child was growing, Trent's seed flourishing within her body. Only a woman who has experienced this miracle could understand her thrill, comprehend her joy. She carried within her a living part of the man she loved, a gift of their coming together as one. Trent's child nestled below her bosom, his little heart beat with her own, he drew nourishment from her body. She would bear this child in love and with pride.

"If only your father loved me," Amber whispered brokenly into the darkness. "If he loved me as I love him, it would all be so perfect."

Rising from the bed, Amber reached for her silk wrap and slipped her arms into the wide sleeves, the fabric cool against her flesh. She lit a candle and, crossing to the washstand, poured water from a pitcher into the large bowl and washed her face.

Then she sat on the stool before her mirror and brushed her hair with long, even strokes. After a time she stopped and sat looking into the mirror.

"I wonder," she mused, a faint smile on her lips. "Will your hair be as black as a raven's wing, like your father's? Will you possess his temper and confidence? And have his eyes, that are the rich color of the sapphire stone? Will you walk with his assured stride and ride a sturdy mount as gracefully as he?"

She sighed, once more placing a hand lightly to her belly, and spoke again,

"Whether you be son or daughter of Trent LeBlanc, I believe you will have all your father's traits!"

Now feeling more relaxed, Amber snuffed the candle and returned to bed to drift into slumber and dreams.

"Good mornin', Miz Amber!"

Mattie's cheerful voice penetrated Amber's sleep-drugged consciousness.

"Hit sho be a purty day out," the servant conversed as she thrust aside the drapes and opened the veranda doors. Drawing a long, deep breath, she went on. "Jes' smell dat! Da breeze's plum full uv da scent uv wintah roses!"

Only the slightest movement came from the large bed, assuring the old servant that someone lay hidden among the covers. Then there came a muffled groan of protest from beneath an oversized pillow.

"Now, Miz Amber," Mattie clucked, hands on her broad hips and her gray head cocked to one side. Her brown eyes rested lovingly on her young mistress. "Ah's got ya sum hot tea an' sum fresh baked biscuits wiff' yo fav'rit jam." Walking to the bed, she eased back the covers and, in a voice close to a whisper, said, "Honey, ah eben snuck ya a helpin' uv ma homemade honeybutter, knowin' da Massah wusn' heah. Now, don' dat jes' mak' yo mouf watah?"

Another groan sounded and a mass of coppery tresses appeared as a small hand slowly drug the fluffy, cotton pillow from Amber's head. Mattie chuckled in amusement at the young girl whose face was still buried under the sheet.

Amber turned her head to one side as she removed the covering, her eyes tightly closed against the golden brilliance of sunlight spilling into the room.

"Oh, Mattie!" came a drowsy mumble, and first one emerald eye was revealed, then the other, and gold-tipped lashes parted then were immediately squinted as the green orbs adjusted to the brightness of the day.

Amber sat up, pushing her silky, copper mane away from her face to fall carelessly about her shoulders. She yawned luxuriously, stretching her arms high above her head. Lacing her fingers together, she arched her slender back.

"Mattie, you spoil me shamelessly," Amber accused, smiling sweetly at the faithful servant.

"Yassum, ah sho do!" Mattie agreed honestly with a wide

grin as she bent to place the silver tea tray upon the pillow which the girl had positioned on her lap. "Dey ain't nuffin' ol' Mattie wouldn' do fer ya, miss."

Suddenly her eyes clouded, and Mattie studied her mistress closely.

"Ya sho gib us a fright las' night, Miz Amber! Lawd! Dat man mighta shot ya if'n he'd a-saw ya!" She rolled her brown eyes heavenward, clasping her hands together as if in prayer. "Don' ya eber do dat agin, miss! Da Massah, he wus awful upset 'bout ya takin' a chance lak dat!"

"Mattie, if I had *not* taken that chance, Trent would have been killed!" Amber earnestly defended her action. "I—I would not have been able to go on, to *live*, had anything happened to him!" A tear trailed slowly down her cheek, and she held a white-knuckled grip on her teacup. "I thought not of danger to myself when I climbed down that trellis—only of him! I took a chance, yes. But because I did so, Trent is alive!"

"Ah knows, miss, ah knows." The servant stroked Amber's bowed head soothingly. "An' da Massah, he knows, too. An' he be grateful fer what ya done."

"Well, he failed to relay that gratitude, Mattie!" Amber replied resentfully, brushing sudden tears from her eyes. "He—he yelled at me as if I were a troublesome child!"

"Da Massah, he do hab a tempah, miss, an' he wusn' a-thankin' 'bout nuffin' but yo safety," Mattie assured her softly. "Ya be 'is wife and ya a-carryin' 'is babe. It be right fer 'im ta be concerned."

Amber did not answer. She knew Mattie was right, and there would be no point in pursuing the conversation.

The old servant admonished her to have her tea and biscuits and left the room.

As she sipped her tea, Amber's mind focused on Trent's attitude toward her pregnancy. He had become more and more solicitous of her as the weeks went by, repeatedly warning her to take care of herself, to eat properly, to get enough rest, and on and on. The man was worse than Mattie with her clucking like a mother hen.

Recently, Trent had forbade her to ride Moon, "or any other horse!" If she wanted to ride, he had told her, then Kane or Morgan would take her for a leisurely drive in the carriage. Besides, he had further advised, it would do her more good to walk. But even when she went for a walk someone was to accompany her.

Amber had considered Trent LeBlanc to be overbearing before she was with child, she reflected. But now! God, the man was impossible! She wished that he would not be so anxious about her—after all, she was not the first woman to ever bear a child! And she had told Trent as much. She smiled at the memory of that day. . . .

She had asked Kane to saddle Moon, and as she neared the stables the boy had emerged, leading Satan. Before she could ask why he had not brought Moon, Trent strode across the grounds with a clipped, "Thank you, Kane," and took the reins, saying, "Now, run give your father my message." As the young lad ran toward the house, Trent's deep voice rang out, "And Miss Amber will not be needing Moon!"

Amber had stood transfixed, her anger rising as Trent strolled toward her. Pulling herself up to her full height, her green eyes blazing and her hands on her hips, she demanded,

"And just *why* will I not be needing Moon?"

"Because, my dear wife, one does not need a horse when one does not ride!" He had stressed each word.

"But—"

"You are with child, Amber! Though it seems that I must constantly remind you of the fact. There will be no more riding, save in the carriage, until after my child is born!" he told her firmly.

"You need not remind me of anything, Trent LeBlanc," she had snapped heatedly. "I am fully aware of my condition! And aware of the person responsible for my condition!"

Trent made no comment as he calmly adjusted Satan's saddle. Ignoring Amber's outburst only served to further infuriate her.

"I am not the only woman to ever bear a child, Trent!" she announced belligerently and turned toward the house.

A slow, lazy smile spread across LeBlanc's countenance and he drawled,

"But you are the only woman to ever bear *my* child!"

The comment caused Amber to turn on her heel to face her arrogant husband, and her heated words tumbled out in a rush, her voice high and shrill.

"And that fact gives Trent LeBlanc the right to dictate to me, to—to tell me when to eat . . . when to sleep . . . when to breathe!"

Angry green eyes clashed with deep blue ones. Amber's heart beat wildly, and her breath caught sharply in her throat as she read the danger lurking in Trent's gaze. He was holding a tight rein on his temper as he stepped forward. Then, as if he had suddenly changed his mind about whatever he had been about to do or say, he had swung his lithe body astride Satan, secured the reins in his capable fingers and spoke tersely,

"You *belong* to me, Amber! *That* gives me my rights!"

And with a gentle slap of the reins he rode off in a regal manner, leaving a furious Amber who stood watching the horse and its master out of sight down the red dirt road.

Her thoughts returned to the present, but the remembering had angered Amber anew. She was not a child, she was a woman! A woman fully capable of making her own decisions. She would *not* be treated like an invalid! And she was not a weak, fragile creature who must be handled carefully for fear that she would break! She was strong, healthy, and tired of being molly-coddled!

Amber looked out at the bright morning. The sun shone high in blue skies, beckoning her to freedom. Trent was not here to prevent her indulging in an early morning ride.

She placed the breakfast tray on the bedside table and, flinging back the covers, rose from the bed to remove her nightgown. She dressed quickly, humming tunelessly. She would have Kane saddle Moon, Amber decided, and she would ride about the grounds and steal away down by the lake.

There would be no harm in such an innocent outing, she reasoned, and she would keep Moon at a gentle trot, a slow pace. She needed this time, Amber declared to herself, and she would have it! If Trent found out, it would already be done. He would scold, of course, but she had grown quite accustomed to being scolded!

Amber sat perched atop a large rock, her bare feet dangling in the cold waters of the lake. She watched her reflection, the image wobbly, swaying back and forth as the gentle ripple of waves drifted across the water. Birds soared overhead, their high, shrill singing was carried on the crisp December breeze. The wind whistled a different kind of song as it fluttered across the land and played about the trees, and the sun beamed down, attempting to blanket the earth with its warmth.

It was a timeless place, a place of boundless beauty. Amber often came here to this special place, to this haven by the lake. To her it was a hideaway, a sanctuary where she could spend endless hours without any intrusion.

Suddenly she wanted to wade out into her private lake. The fact that it was the middle of December did not matter. Amber shucked her cape and eased off the rock and, step by step, walked into the chilly water enjoying the breathless shock, the icy sting that claimed her limbs and caused the blood to surge through her veins.

It had been a temptation that she could not deny herself, and she waded further out, letting the shimmering waters engulf her. She tilted her head back and allowed her body to float slowly upward, the waves carrying her at will, relaxing her body, her mind. She was unmindful of the cool, winter day.

But as a deep chill began to claim her body, Amber shivered and headed back to the bank. She sat on the large rock and drew her cape about her, snuggling deep within its warm folds. She slipped her breeches off and wrung them with numbing fingers, then pulled them back on. Unbuttoning her blouse, she struggled out of it, still clasping her cape about her shoulders, and twisted the water-soaked garment tightly.

Finding it difficult to don the damp, clinging blouse with the cape about her, Amber shrugged the cumbersome cloak from her shoulders and let it fall to the rock behind her. Hurriedly she put on the blouse and had begun to button it when a sharp, snapping sound startled her, and she stood abruptly, the cape sliding to the ground.

"Sorry I startled you," came the low voice of Lord Devon as he stepped into view. "You made such a striking picture," he went on throatily, his eyes devouring Amber's wet-clad figure. "Are you aware of your rare beauty?"

She blushed uncomfortably, aware only that the man had

observed her in her state of undress. He surely had stood
there for some time, and the knowledge both angered and
embarrassed her.

"You might have let one know of your presence, sir!" she
said haughtily as she retrieved her cape from the ground and
wrapped it around her. "It was not gentlemanly to stand from
sight and watch me!" As Devon chuckled low in his throat,
she added, "I find no humor in what I said!"

"Perhaps I am not a gentleman," Devon suggested, raising
a dark brow. "What man would simply turn his back upon a
beautiful woman standing bare and unshameful before him?"

"I was not standing before you," Amber stormed, sweeping the cloud of wet, russet hair from her eyes. "This is
private property, Lord Devon! You have no right to be here,
no right to come upon me and watch me!"

She moved past him to where Moon stood waiting, but
before she could mount, Devon's hand shot out and clasped
her upper arm in a painful grip.

"Does a woman of LeBlanc's think herself to be above
me?" he hissed through gritted teeth. "If so, think again!"

His anger frightened Amber, she wanted no quarrel with
this man. She did not even know him! Had only met him
briefly! And in her condition she would hardly be able to
defend herself. She feared for her unborn child, for herself.

"That was not at all what I was implying, sir," she began in
a soft voice. Her emerald eyes locked with the cool green eyes
of Devon. Amber smiled and his hold eased about her arm.
"You—you frightened me, Lord Devon, and embarrassed me
greatly." She took a deep shuddering breath and placed her
hand over the hand that held her. "You see, I am not
supposed to be here—rather I am not to be riding. My
husband has forbidden me that pleasure until our child is
born. And I thought it was he who had come upon me and
was frightened of what his anger would be, yet when it was
not Trent but a stranger, well . . ."

"I understand," Devon told her in a light tone. "I know of
LeBlanc's anger. So you are with child?" he asked, his glance
moving to her abdomen.

"Yes."

"You carry the child well, keeping your shape, your
slimness. I would not have guessed."

Amber was frightened by his gaze upon her, the huskiness in his voice. She moved from him.

"You are much too beautiful for LeBlanc," Devon announced as his free hand cupped her chin, tilting her face upward to his. "You need a man, Amber, a man who will worship you and pleasure you. I could be that man."

With those words his head descended, his mouth covering hers. The kiss was not unpleasant, but his lips were overly warm and his tongue seemed to choke her. Amber pushed against his chest in an effort to break the kiss. Devon's arms embraced her, roughly crushing her against him. She struggled within his grasp, forcing her lips free of his.

"Let me go!" she whispered thickly. "Let go!" She kicked blindly with her bare foot as she fought his hold. Her feeble attempt only amused him.

"I like fight in a woman!" Devon said with admiration. "The fight makes the conquest more exciting, more fulfilling."

Surely this man would not dare to take her against her will! she thought fleetingly. Not here! Dear God, no! Please give me the strength to ward off his attack! Why would he do this? Was his hatred of Trent so strong that he would take his enemy's wife? Rape her? Sweet Christ! Would he kill her? She had to do something! Protect herself!

"Please," came her choked plea and she stopped struggling. "Please, let me go." When he made no move to free her, Amber whimpered, "Y-you are hurting me." Her eyes filled with tears and she blinked, causing them to spill over.

"It is not my wish to hurt you, Amber." Devon assured her quietly, almost gently. Then he smiled wickedly and asked, "Do you love your husband, Amber? Does your heart rejoice at the thought of bearing his heir?"

The sudden change in him confused, yet warned her that he was up to something. Why this course of questioning?

"Your answer!" he demanded shortly, tightening his clasp about her.

"I love the child I carry," she began. "I shall be proud to bear my child."

"You would protect it with your life? Do anything to assure the child's safety?"

"Of course!"

"What about the safety of LeBlanc? Your husband's life?" Devon asked smugly, already sure of her answer. "Is your love for him as strong, as deep?"

"Yes." Amber cried desperately. "Yes, my love for him is as strong!"

"I believe, Amber, that we will get along just fine." He murmured and released her. "You will do as I bid, my lovely, all in the name of love." Boldly he ran a finger along her throat, letting it rest between the swells of her breast. Amber stood motionless, her eyes intent upon his face inches away from her. "I shall have a most enjoyable time, I think," he laughed maliciously.

"Wh-what do you want from me?" her voice broke as she asked the question, and she swallowed with difficulty as she awaited the dreaded answer.

Devon studied her closely. LeBlanc had chosen well, he thought jealously. This woman was not only beautiful, she was strong although she had fear. She was loyal and she loved the son of a bitch! So bitter was his dislike for Trent LeBlanc, so deep his hatred, that Devon would do anything to hurt him. Go to any length to get to the man, to one day have the pleasure of killing him.

"It would please me greatly to kill LeBlanc," he told Amber flatly, a cold smile on his thin lips. "He has been a source of irritation to me for some time now. But the time is not yet. I have use for him. I need information that only he can supply, and with your help I shall obtain that information. I can take your man's life at any time, and I will not hesitate to do so if you do not cooperate. I know his whereabouts, even at this moment.

"LeBlanc will not be returning home tonight, of that I am certain. This will give you and me the time needed in which I will set down some rules and arrangements that you will follow. It would be much easier if you were not so beautiful, Amber, yet at the same time it makes my job more interesting. Business first and pleasure later," he said suggestively. "I will call on you tonight about half past seven. Then I will tell you what you are to do. And, Amber, you are not to tell anyone of this meeting, and do not think that once you are away and back at Travinwood that you are safe. For if you should make that mistake, LeBlanc might meet with an accident."

At Amber's sudden intake of breath and the concern in her eyes, Devon knew he had made his point. He would have her eating out of his hand, doing his every bidding, if she feared for LeBlanc's safety.

"He may be lucky enough to escape with his life, but I am afraid that his dark good looks may suffer," he concluded with a demonic chuckle.

Amber paced the length of the large parlor, her mind dwelling on the distasteful encounter of that morning. What had she gotten into? What vengeful plans had Lord Devon made for Trent? How could she help her husband? How could she warn him without harming him?

Oh, why had she gone out today? If she had to ride, why had she gone alone? Had Trent feared that something like this would happen? Was he aware that Devon or someone else might harm her? What was she to do?

The loud pounding of the door knocker sounded, causing Amber to jump. Her nerves were raw, her emotions high. She glanced at the clock on the mantel, it showed the hour to be the time Devon had said to expect him. She stood in the middle of the room, staring at the door.

"Miz Amber, dey is a Lord Devon dat wish ta see ya," Mattie announced from the doorway. "He say you wus espectin' 'im."

"Yes, Mattie, please show him in," Amber told the servant in a tight voice and moved to a winged-back chair.

Lord Devon entered the room followed by Mattie. The servant was puzzled. She had caught the undercurrent in her young mistress's voice and had noted earlier that she seemed upset about something. In fact, Amber had been downright jittery all day. Was this man a friend or an enemy? Mattie wondered in concern. What did he have to do with the miss? Why was he here?

Devon looked at Amber seated in the leather chair. God, but she was a beauty! Her hair was the color of russet gold, glowing in the light of the fireplace. And her eyes were the stunning green color of the jewel called emerald. Shaking himself mentally, he glanced over his shoulder at the old servant hovering just inside the door and then back at Amber, his eyes narrowing slightly.

Reading the look in Devon's eyes, Amber turned to Mattie, saying,

"That will be all, Mattie. Please close the door as you leave, Lord Devon and I have a private matter to discuss."

Mattie hesitated for the briefest moment, then mumbled, "Yassum," and did as her mistress had bid.

Devon seated himself on the sofa opposite Amber and regarded her for several long moments. She had not spoken, only sat rigidly, her small hands clasped in her lap and staring unflinchingly at him. Devon read the distaste in her open glare.

"Mind if I have a drink?" he asked stiffly. Amber made no move, nor did she reply. Devon shifted in his chair, sensing that there was something very disturbing about Amber. There was a stillness about her, a cool silence. It was unnerving, and for a brief moment he experienced a quake of impending danger. He stood and walked to the liquor cabinet and helped himself to a drink. Taking a healthy gulp he began his recital.

"Amber Lynn Kensington, daughter of Tamra and Kiles Albert Kensington II, born July 21, 1795. At age seven your parents were killed in a carriage accident when it overturned during an attack by highwaymen. You were taken in by your uncle, Edward Kensington, and his wife Alice."

Still Amber said nothing, and after a pause, Devon went on,

"There you stayed until July of this year when you were to marry one, Sir James Michael Windom. A very wealthy man, I understand. I have heard of him and his fortune. You may be wondering how it is that I have access to this information?" he asked the still silent Amber. "Well, shall we say, 'I have my ways,' as your infamous husband would say. Oh, and I have something here that may be of some interest to you," Devon commented, and, reaching into his coat, he brought forth a folded portion of a newspaper.

"I have a newsclipping from a London paper. After reading the story I made some inquiries, thus learning a great deal more than I expected."

He walked over to Amber and handed her the clipping. "The picture does not do you justice, you are far more beautiful." She took the article, first studying her picture, then began to read the bold black print.

MISSING
FIANCÉE OF PROMINENT AND WEALTHY SIR JAMES MICHAEL WINDOM

The disappearance of Amber Lynn Kensington, niece of Edward J. Kensington of Kensington Imports and fiancée of the well-known Sir Michael Windom has caused a citywide stir. She was to have wed Sir Michael yesterday afternoon at the Holy Christian Chapel and was last seen by the family coachman when he drove Miss Kensington to the chapel around two o'clock. Miss Kensington is small in stature, about five feet three. She has dark green eyes, auburn hair, and bears no scars or identifying marks. Anyone who has seen Miss Kensington or knows of her whereabouts should contact Sir Michael, Edward Kensington, or the London Authorities at once. A reward has been posted.

When she had finished reading the clipping she handed it back to Lord Devon, her eyes meeting his as steadily as they had before. The intensity of those green eyes chilled him and caused a tingling sensation on the back of his neck.

"You have nothing to say?" he asked testily.

"Do you expect this reward? Is that why you have shown me the clipping?" she queried. "The news article is many months old. I am now married to Trent, and he has long since informed my family that I am safe. The offer of a reward is no longer good!"

"I want no reward!" Devon snapped, crushed the paper in his hand, and threw it to the floor. "I want your cooperation! And I shall have it," he promised, taking his seat again on the sofa. He crossed his long legs and tossed down the remainder of his drink.

"My dear Amber, you and I are both English. You are aware that we are at war with the Americans!"

"What does that, and the news clipping, have to do with me?" Amber questioned somewhat uneasily.

"Everything! You are English and you are in America! You have married an American who, I might add, is a spy!"

Amber started at the word "spy". Trent was a lot of things, she thought, but not a spy. She did not believe it.

"I do not believe you! How can you say a thing like that? I know you hate Trent, as he does you. But to accuse him of being a spy!"

"I am not merely accusing LeBlanc. I know him to be just that! He, along with his friend Casey Reed. They both work for the government, for an agency straight from the President!"

"And how is it that you know this?" Amber pressed.

"Because I am a British agent!" he stated bluntly. "I was sent to America to find the leak in our British contacts. Someone here is intercepting our messages before they reach our Havana agents and again before reaching London head-quarters."

"And you believe that source to be Trent? Or Casey? No, this I do not believe!"

"Whether or not you believe it is of no importance. What you are going to do, is!" Devon said determinedly.

"Which is?"

"You will inform me of all LeBlanc's goings and comings. Where he goes, how long he was gone, who was with him, and any conversations you might overhear. You, Amber, are to relate to me the name and business of every visitor who comes to Travinwood!"

"I will not!" she protested heatedly, her green eyes smoldering. "I will not 'spy' on my husband! I—I—"

"Oh, but you shall, lovely Amber! And you will do so willingly. Have you not admitted your love for your husband, for the child you carry?" he reminded her acidly.

Amber's hand unconsciously went to her stomach in a protective manner. She watched Devon with wary eyes. This man had threatened her, just this morning. Had spoken of harm coming to Trent, even her child! It had not been a shallow threat, she realized with sudden clarity.

"It was a very close brush with death last evening for

LeBlanc," he reminded her. "Had it not been for someone coming to his aid . . ." He let the sentence drop in midair.

"An incident in which you no doubt had a hand!" Amber accused, her hands gripping the arms of her chair. "Sorry to have spoiled your plans, Lord Devon!" she said in a honey-sweet voice. "My only regret is that it was not your ruthless heart that my bullet found!"

Devon laughed evilly and leaned forward in his seat, his elbows resting upon his knees, his light green eyes impaling Amber.

"So it was *you!*" he said softly. "*You* saved LeBlanc from receiving his due! How very touching, such loyalty. Tell me, Amber, does the depths of that loyalty include Edward Kensington? His wife?"

"Of course! But what—"

"What does your uncle have to do with this?" Devon cut in smoothly. Leaning back, he made himself comfortable. "Everything! And how lucky for me that I ran across that clipping." He smiled cunningly. "Because you see, up until now, LeBlanc was unreachable. Damn bastard! I have honestly been tempted to believe those tales of him being the devil's own son! Death flirts all about him, yet never touches him!

"Then you, Amber, became our pawn. The son of a bitch finally had a weakness!" Devon slapped his knee and shook his finger at Amber. "LeBlanc fancied a beautiful woman he found in London, a woman he could not do without, could not leave behind. What he did not know was that the woman would open the doors that had long been closed. We shall have him right where we want him, thanks to his own unknown stupidity.

"And you ask what part Edward Kensington plays? He serves only as a bonus! Our security that had you not cared for LeBlanc, loved him enough to protect him—we knew our information would still be obtained!"

Lord Devon noted the puzzled expression on Amber's lovely face. "You see, your dear uncle and his wife will be taken prisoner by the British and shot for treason, if you do not cooperate!"

"*Treason?*" Amber shrilled the word in panic as she sprang from her chair.

"Exactly!"

"But they have done nothing wrong! They—Uncle Edward—"

Again Devon broke in smoothly, his voice cold, showing no emotion, "No? Then let me tell you a little story and perhaps you will understand." Rising, Devon again moved to the side of the room and poured another drink. He began slowly, as if choosing his words.

"One week after your mysterious disappearance, a known American agent arrived in London. His name—Captain Casey Reed, master of the American vessel *Sea Dog,* although she was sailing under the flag of Britain. This American agent was searching for Edward Kensington. After going to Kensington Imports, he learned that Edward was at home, that his niece was missing, and that he and his wife were so distraught over her disappearance that Edward had not been at his office since the girl had been missing.

"Reed was later seen entering the home of Kensington and reappeared some hours later. Now the story began to take shape." Devon smiled and returned to his seat. "It turns out that our Captain Reed not only is a spy but the near and dear friend of the infamous Captain LeBlanc, who had left London the week before on the same evening of the day of Miss Kensington's disappearance. And the missing lady ends up in New Orleans, married to LeBlanc! Coincidence? Perhaps, but the British would find this information very interesting, do you not think?"

"What I *think* is that you are despicable! You are a cold-hearted bastard! You would twist all that you know, feed whatever information, no matter how distorted, to your people in order to serve your purpose! You would hurt innocent people, kill if necessary! You are a loathesome pig, a disgrace to humanity!" Amber spat venomously.

"Now that you understand me and know that I will stop at nothing, I feel certain that I shall have your cooperation! Do not cross me, Amber! If you fear for those whom you love, you will take heed."

Devon rose from his seat and, looking down at Amber, told her flatly, "Your tasks start now! I will know everything! Understand?"

Amber made no reply, her gaze averted. She felt ill at the

sight of him! The man sickened her, he cared nothing for the human life! Had she a dagger she would surely thrust it deep within his cold heart! Amber had never hated as passionately as she did at this moment! The only thing that comforted her was the knowledge that one day LeBlanc would take the life of this hideous man. And, she smiled inwardly, if not Trent, she would do it herself!

"You are to meet me every two days in late afternoon, at Winter Rose Place. It was once a mansion as lovely as Travinwood. There is a small cottage that still stands. Winter Rose is beyond the ridge, by the lake. Our first meeting will be tomorrow. You will be there!" he stated unequivocally.

Amber said nothing. She sat motionlessly staring into the fireplace. Only the confirming nod of her head assured Devon that she would be there.

Chapter Eighteen

"No!" AMBER WHISPERED TO THE EMPTY ROOM. "IT IS NOT right! I will not be a party to Lord Devon's scheme, I will not!"

Yet as she spoke the words, she remembered his threats. He would surely bring harm to her—to Trent—to her loved ones. How could she beat Devon at his own game? She had to think—to plan!

An overpowering sense of wretchedness swept over her. She paced the length of the room, wringing her hands nervously, and, pausing at the French doors, she watched as the dusk of the evening slowly increased. It was the waiting—this damnable, watchful waiting, which was responsible for her gnawing anxiety, the feeling of suspense.

Where was Trent? What connection had he with the government? Was he in truth a spy, as Devon had accused? So many unanswered questions!

Well, Amber decided, whether or not he be an American agent, it mattered not. He was her husband and she loved him! She had adopted his country as her own, and the only loyalty she held for England was the love she had for her aunt and uncle! They were still there, and, as Devon had so cruelly pointed out, they could be harmed. So much lay in her hands, depending upon her ability to deal with Devon. Or outsmart him!

Four long, never-ending days had dragged by since Trent and the others rode away in the night, carrying with them the stranger who had attempted to kill her husband.

"Oh, Trent, my love!" she moaned softly. "I do not know what to do! How does one protect that which one loves at the risk of harming another beloved one?"

Pressing her clenched fists to her temples in frustration, Amber willed the dilemma to go away. If she could but stop her heart from breaking, stop the aching . . .

Two meetings with Lord Devon had been more than enough. The man was insufferable! If, in reality, he *did* know of Trent's whereabouts, why his insistence that she meet with him the day before and again, today? He must be aware that she had no news, nothing to report! Besides, she did not like the look in his pale green eyes, his open gaze upon her body gave her a feeling of uneasiness.

Still, it would do her no good to spend night after restless night fretting about the situation. Her health was beginning to suffer, she had slept very little and eaten less. She must think of her unborn child and of the harm which could be done to it. And, above all, she must hide her emotions from Trent and the others and act as if nothing unusual was going on, that nothing had happened out of the ordinary.

Amber returned to the bed, pulling back the covering. She slipped between the sheets and leaned over to snuff out the candle, then lay back in the darkness with a heavy sigh.

Somehow, some way, she would beat Devon! She would foil his ugly plans! No longer was she Amber Lynn Kensington, the young English miss! She was Amber LeBlanc, woman! Wife of the proud and infamous Captain Trent LeBlanc! And an American!

She had been brought here to this strange new world, this untamed land with its wilderness and untarnished beauty and had come to love everything about it and its people. Now she belonged here! And *wanted* to be here! There was no changing that love, that deep sense of belonging!

Smiling to herself, Amber snuggled deep into the bed covers, her murmured vow heard only by the silent night:

"You will not win, Lord Devon! I shall see to it that you do not!"

Amber felt a strong, yet tender grip about her shoulder as she was rolled gently to her side. Opening her eyes she stared straight into the deep blue eyes of her husband.

"Amber!" LeBlanc whispered her name softly as his mouth found hers. He kissed her with sweet abandon, his rock-hard body pressed urgently along hers. His hands moved slowly over her body, caressing her smooth flesh, his tongue lazily tracing the outline of her parted lips.

Once again her name was upon his lips as he moaned huskily,

"How I have missed you, Amber. The nights have been far too long and empty without you."

He was home! Trent held her safe within his strong arms and no one could hurt her, no one could touch her! Not while he held her protected and loved. He was her love, her life, and her strength.

"Trent," Amber managed between his kisses. "Please, never leave me again! Please tell me that you will always keep me safe!" she pleaded as she clung desperately to him.

Trent heard the urgency in her voice and he held her from him, his face filled with concern. Her words had been heartfelt, she had spoken them as if she feared something.

"Amber?" His hands cupped her flushed face, his thumb brushed away the tears that trailed unchecked along her cheeks. "Has something happened? Has someone harmed you?"

"No!" she denied quickly, shaking her head vigorously. "I—I am sorry, my husband. It is only that I have missed you so. I have not slept well. . . . I suppose I am overly tired."

Hopefully she had amended her lapse of discretion. She must not alarm him lest he learn of Devon's threats. For he would surely go after the man, and should Trent kill him, her aunt and uncle would no doubt pay with their lives. Devon's agents would see to that, she had been warned.

"Oh, would you listen to me," Amber laughed lightly. "I have never been known to indulge in fits of weakness—crying over mere trifles! Honestly, Trent, since I have been with child I have become a weak, whining woman! A—a female milksop!"

Her comment brought a roar of laughter from LeBlanc, and he rolled atop her, pressing her to the bed.

"You are many things, *ma* sweet, but a weak, whining milksop you are not! I have heard that when a woman is with child she goes through many changes, does things and says things that ordinarily she would not. It will last only a short time longer, kitten, then you shall be back to your old, impossible, unpredictable, lovely self!"

"I suppose you are right," she agreed meekly as Trent's fingers began to unbutton the tiny buttons at the throat of her nightgown.

He slipped the filmy garment from her shoulders as he pressed his hot lips against her creamy throat.

"I want you, wife—I need you!" The tenderness in his voice caused Amber to tremble with anticipation. "I can never get my fill of you, little one. I can only be denied your charms for a brief time, ever!"

Amber arched her body toward his as Trent caressed her aching breast. His moist lips trailed the length of her slender neck, across her smooth shoulders, and came to rest at the peaks of her jutting breasts. He kissed them gently, nibbling at their crests. She could feel his heated flesh against her own, feel the taut muscles of his thighs pressing along hers.

The gentle suction at her breasts brought a low throaty moan from Amber's lips. Trent's hands touched her hungrily, stroking the velvety skin, and naked desire claimed her, the unbanked fires mounting with each measured stroke, each intoxicating kiss.

"Amber, Amber . . ." his voice was thick, his breath hot upon her.

Her hands were upon him, returning the pleasure which he gave to her. Amber kissed him wantonly, the tip of her tongue drawing forth the sweetness of his kiss. Her hand slipped lower, resting at his manhood, and the act caused Trent to catch his breath sharply.

"Yes, little one, touch me! Yes . . ." he groaned, his husky voice at her ear.

Amber's hands moved over the smooth muscles of his

thighs, his buttocks. She was pleased with the excitement she could stir within LeBlanc, and his accelerated heart beat kept pace with her own. She moved against him, urging him on, beckoning him to take her, to fulfill her longing, to love her.

And when Trent took her it was with such sweet pleasure that it seemed to take her breath away. She rose to that plane of boundless ecstasy as wave after wave of stormy passion seized her.

As their bodies stilled and relaxed in a warm cocoon of mutual fulfillment, Trent whispered,

"Amber, you give me such satisfaction! You take pleasure even as you give it. I could want no more, my wife!"

She made no reply, only smiled into the haziness of the early morning light. How she loved this man! She nestled contentedly against him, enjoying the feel of his body next to hers. His arm rested possessively across her, his hand cupped her breast, and his warm breath softly stirred about her neck.

Closing her eyes, she invited sleep and soon fell into a satisfying, restful slumber.

"Are you going to sleep the entire day, wife?" LeBlanc's gruffly tender voice invaded her dreamless slumber. "Laziness is not a virtue, woman, nor will it be tolerated!"

Amber opened sleep-glazed eyes to see him towering above her, his dark blue eyes dancing with merriment, his tanned hands on his slim hips and his muscular legs braced slightly apart.

She blinked and her gaze focused on her husband who stood proud and naked before her. The sun shone on his bronzed skin, giving it a copper hue, a dark lock of his raven-black hair trailed over his brow, and the powerful muscles rippled beneath his tanned flesh.

He was perfect! Amber reflected. The man was an excellent specimen of the male species. A slow smile crossed her lovely face as she boldly observed him.

"Does something amuse you, wife?" he growled in mock disapproval.

"Amuse? No," she replied, her green eyes darkening. "Arouse, I should think would be the correct word!" she said brazenly, leaning forward to run the tip of her finger along his flat belly as she looked up at him.

"You are a wanton woman, Amber LeBlanc!" Trent scolded, catching her hand within his as it eased daringly close to his awakening manhood. "Had you not enough of your husband last night?"

"I shall never have enough of you, Trent LeBlanc," she purred, "and 'tis your own fault, sir! Had you not taken my innocence and made me a wanton woman, then I should not know what lust is!"

His rich, deep laughter rang out, and he sank to the bed, taking Amber in his arms.

"*Mon Dieu,* wife! I pray you do not tire of me before I reach the age of thirty and five! I anticipate many long years in your bed!" And his lips claimed hers in a searching kiss, his knee gently nudging her soft thighs apart.

At a loud knock on the door, LeBlanc swore softly and called out in a tight voice,

"Who is it?"

"Hit's Mattie, Massah," the old servant replied, her voice muffled by the heavy wooden door.

Trent eased away from Amber and pulled the bed sheet across them.

"Come in, Mattie," he called out. Then he smiled at Amber and whispered, "Later, *ma* sweet! You may rest assured that we shall resume this most delightful pastime, pursuing it to a satisfying conclusion!"

"Ah'm sorry, Massah, but de guests, dey be a-waitin' downstairs," Mattie told Trent, her dark eyes avoiding the two upon the rumpled bed. "Mistah Casey, he say ya'd want ta know w'en dey git heah."

"Thank you, Mattie. You may tell them to wait in the study," Trent instructed her. "Have Morgan bring in their baggage and take it to one of the guest rooms. You will know which one is most suitable."

"Yassah, ah'll do dat." As the servant turned to leave, she asked, "Ya all gon' be habbin' breakfus' in da dinin' room?"

"Yes, Mattie. And Amber and I will be down shortly to welcome our guests."

As the door closed behind the woman, Trent rose from the bed, donned his breeches and crossed to the washstand. He splashed water from the large bowl onto his face as he prepared to shave.

Amber had not moved from the bed. She sat staring at her husband in bewilderment. Who were their guests? she wondered. Was he not going to tell her who had arrived?

They had had no visitors since Simmons's arrival. At least she would have something to report to Devon, she thought bitterly, if his spies did not inform him before her meeting with him.

She rose to her knees in the middle of the bed and watched LeBlanc as he shaved, her mind wandering to the inevitable rendezvous which she would be forced to keep with the despicable Lord Devon.

After a few strokes of his razor, Trent looked at Amber through the mirror, his gaze first locking with her green eyes then sliding over her naked frame. Her copper hair fell about her silken shoulders in sensuous disarray, her breasts were full and tempting, and those smooth, velvety thighs, he remembered, had just moments ago been parted to him. Her softly rounded belly only enhanced her beauty.

"Amber, you would tempt the devil, himself!" he announced in a thick, throaty voice. "A man can only endure so much! I shall be most uncomfortable, as it is," he told her, glancing down at his breeches, meaningly.

Amber's gaze followed his and she saw the noticeable bulge straining against his tight black breeches.

"We have guests, little one, and I must attend them before I can attend to my own desires—and needs," LeBlanc concluded with a wolfish smile.

"Who are our guests, Trent? I was not aware that we were to have visitors," she told him as she left the bed and began to dress.

"It is a surprise, my lovely wife! A surprise which, I should think, will please you," he answered mysteriously. "Now, finish your toilette for I would prefer that we go down together."

He continued with his task and said nothing further, leaving Amber no more enlightened about their unexpected guests than before she asked about them.

Chapter Nineteen

AMBER AND TRENT DESCENDED THE STAIRCASE AND NEARED THE study. Her husband stopped before the closed door, took both her hands in his and said in a low tone,

"The surprise I have for you, *ma* sweet, I hope will make your being in America, your living here with me at Travinwood, a bit easier." He leaned down, placing a tender kiss on Amber's parted lips. "I only wish for you to be happy here, Amber. I wish for you never to find reason to want to leave."

Opening the study door, Trent stepped back and, with a wave of his hand, indicated that she should precede him.

Amber could not believe her eyes! Was her mind playing tricks? It just was not possible! She could not find her voice and tears filled her wide green eyes as she moved forward as if in a trance, both arms outstretched.

The tall, gray-haired man was the first to see the young woman as she entered the study. His choked sob caused his wife to turn quickly to see Amber slowly approaching them, and the older woman began to weep silently.

"Uncle Edward! Aunt Alice!" Amber cried joyously.

"My dear, beautiful child," came Edward Kensington's

broken whisper as he crossed to meet his beloved niece. He and his wife embraced the young woman whom they loved and had reared as their own.

Amber's pleasure was unsurpassed, but beyond the thrill of the moment, she knew a great relief that they were here! And deep gratitude toward the man who had made it possible!

Now her loved ones were safe from harm, she realized. Lord Devon and his men could not touch them! Trent had brought her family to her, and he would see that they were cared for and that they were safe.

Oh, but the world looked so much brighter, even through the tears of happiness which now flowed unchecked down her flushed cheeks.

Amber turned to see LeBlanc still standing in the open doorway watching the heart-wrenching scene with evident satisfaction. Could she ever love this arrogant man more than she did at this very moment? she wondered. Could you only love so much and no more? Or, in truth, were there really any boundaries to love? To the depths of caring, of needing?

She moved to him and raised both graceful arms, lacing her slender fingers behind his neck.

"Thank you, Trent," Amber breathed as she kissed him. "You have made me most happy, my husband. I do not have the words, I can only say that, at this moment, I am happier than I ever dreamed possible!"

"Married!" Amber shrilled excitedly, embracing her friend. "Oh, Neva, how wonderful! I had hoped that it would not take Casey long to ask you. I am so happy! And I truly have much to be happy about, so much for which to be thankful!"

"Yes, Captain Trent has made us *both* happy," Neva told her gratefully. "He saved me from the auction block, brought me here, gave me a home and—Casey! He is a good man, your husband."

"Yes," Amber readily agreed. "Yes, he is."

"My Casey, he is very much like him . . ." Neva paused, pondering. "There is something most strange about their friendship, I think."

"Strange? How do you mean, 'strange'?"

"I do not rightly know but I am certain there is *something*.

Like the way they talk about Travinwood and about Captain Trent's mother. And even the servants! They treat Casey far differently, with more respect, than the Captain's other friends. . . . Yes," with a confident nod of her dark head Neva finished, "yes, I am convinced that there is something that we do not know."

"Oh, Neva," Amber laughed indulgently at her friend. "You read mystery where there is none!"

"No, you are wrong about that. There is definitely something quite unusual about the two of them. Have you never noticed that, at times, they have the same expressions and that their mannerisms are most similar? And, although Captain Trent has a rare, rich laugh, Casey's laugh is suspiciously like it."

"You may be right, Neva. I have not been around Casey as much as you, so I may not have noticed the things you mention. But for the present, let us put aside the intrigue which our Captains have created and move on to more important matters—such as, planning your wedding!

"Aunt Alice will surely wish to help arrange the affair since she did not have the privilege of planning for *my* wedding—of course she *did*, but *that* wedding never took place! Now, when is the happy day?"

"Friday."

"Friday? B—but that is only three days away!" Amber stammered.

"Yes, I know," Neva told her with a pleased smile.

The days went by without incident. The household of Travinwood was ready for the wedding. Mattie had outdone herself with her baking and cooking, preparing a feast fit for royalty. The finest crystal, silver, and china had been brought out and the dining room prepared for the wedding dinner.

Amber, with the help of Aunt Alice and Mattie, had made certain that the Lawson–Reed wedding would be an affair long remembered in the town. Travinwood had not hosted such a magnificent function since Trent's mother was its mistress. Now the doors of LeBlanc's stately mansion would again be opened, for the Master and his lovely young bride were bringing back the sounds of gaiety, laughter, and music to Travinwood.

"Mattie?" Amber called from the staircase as the old servant plodded through the entry below. "Have you seen Master Trent?"

"No'm, him an' Mistah Casey, dey lef' sum time dis mornin', goin' inta town an' ah ain' seen neithah one uv 'em, since." As an afterthought, she added, "Kin ah do sump'n fer ya, Miz Amber?"

"No," she shook her head. "But, Mattie, I do want to tell you what an absolute marvel you are! The house looks lovely, the wedding feast will be perfection, and it is all because of you! Thank you for your efforts."

She graced the old woman with a rare smile and turned away toward her room, leaving a weary but beaming Mattie to her chores.

Entering her bedroom, Amber sat heavily on the wide bed, lost in her thoughts. Her meeting with Devon had not gone well. The man was incensed that LeBlanc had shrewdly evaded the London agents and had managed to spirit Edward and Alice Kensington out of England and brought them to New Orleans.

"This changes nothing!" he had stormed, his fists clenched tightly. "LeBlanc cannot be with each of you at all times, and you will do well, Amber, to remember that fact! I have men in places that you would never suspect, and they are watching Travinwood at all times!"

So, Amber fretted, she must still worry about her aunt and uncle, about Trent and herself. And tomorrow she would have to give Devon a list of the wedding and reception guests. She must also watch closely to see if Trent had any closed-door meetings with any of the guests and, if so, with whom and how long they had remained closeted.

And the black book! Lord Devon had ordered her to find a small black book which he told her was kept locked in the desk in Trent's study, a book which she had never ever seen!

Also, according to Devon, an envelope had been delivered to LeBlanc on the previous day, and she was expected to find and hand over that envelope and its contents tomorrow!

How in God's name was she to manage this, to obtain this material, these items of which she knew absolutely nothing! And what would happen if she were caught pilfering Trent's desk? She shivered at the thought of her husband's dark, narrowing eyes, his wrath were he to discover her spying.

Amber drew a deep, ragged breath and rose from the bed to dress in the bright green, velvet gown that Trent had brought to her on his last trip to New Orleans. The color accented the green of her eyes, the low, sweeping neckline emphasized her firm breasts, fine white lace edged the sleeves and the bodice and the full skirt fell gracefully to the floor. Only the barest hint of her rounding belly was noticeable.

Pulling her copper tresses away from her face, she secured them with a tortoiseshell comb at each side of her finely shaped head. Tiny, wispy curls escaped their confinement to trail lightly about her brow and temples.

As she stepped back to inspect her appearance in the floor-length mirror, the door opened to admit LeBlanc.

Closing the door behind him, Trent stood with his hands clasped behind his back, much as if he were standing on the deck of the *Mér Fleur*. His deep sapphire gaze roamed over Amber, a crooked smile settled on his handsome face.

"*Mon Dieu*, Madame LeBlanc! You are beautiful!" His tone was husky. "Of a truth, I have seen you more beautiful but once!"

"And when was that, Captain LeBlanc?" she asked teasingly.

"The day you became my wife!" Trent replied honestly.

Amber's heart lurched. The fact that he would speak of that day as a cherished memory—a tight little knot caught in her throat.

"Thank you, Trent, that was a lovely thing to say," she told him softly.

"I spoke only the truth, my beauty," he assured her as he moved to her side. He lifted a hand to her throat to stroke her slender neck, his fingers brushing lightly over her breasts. "I have something for you," he whispered. "Something to which your beauty alone can do justice."

Reaching into his coat he brought forth a black velvet box and handed it to Amber. She held the box without opening it, her gaze raised to her husband.

"Open it!" he gently urged, his eyes intent on her lovely face.

Slowly Amber lifted the lid to look inside. Her sharp intake of breath pleased LeBlanc. Her eyes sparkled the loveliest shade of green, and she caught her lower lip between small white teeth.

Resting on a bed of black velvet was the most exquisite necklace she had ever seen. A large, flawless emerald, shaped like a teardrop, twinkled up at her. The rare stone was surrounded by sparkling diamonds, and the droplet was attached to a fine, gold chain along which trailed small, winking diamonds. Elegant in its simplicity, the necklace bespoke LeBlanc's extravagance in the purchase of the costly gem.

"Oh, Trent! It—it is exquisite!" Amber breathed in awe. "I have never seen anything so beautiful! Never!"

"I am pleased that you like it," he told her as he removed the necklace from the case and unhooked the clasp of the gold chain. "The emerald matches the green of your eyes."

LeBlanc placed the treasure about her creamy throat and secured the clasp, then turned Amber toward the mirror so that she could behold the vision she created.

Her hand fluttered to the jewels about her neck and she whispered,

"Thank you, Trent!"

"That is all?" he asked mockingly, "A mere 'thank you'?"

Amber laughed happily and turned to him, her arms circling his neck. She pressed her soft body to his and kissed him deeply. His own arms tightened about her, and he crushed her close to his heart.

"Now, *that*, wife, was a sure sign of gratitude!" LeBlanc said thickly as the kiss ended and he kept her in his arms. "I believe that I shall bring home fine gifts quite often." He smiled and kissed the tip of her nose. "I enjoy your reaction when something pleases you."

Neva made a lovely bride and Casey was a proud groom. Amber and Trent had stood with them as the minister performed the ceremony. Mattie, seated at one side of the grand ballroom, cried quietly, wiping her tears on her white apron, and Morgan had stood beside his wife, patting her shoulder.

It had been a grand occasion with friends and neighbors driving for miles to attend the social function. And all was well at Travinwood this day.

Amber mingled with the guests, meeting her neighbors. Everyone spoke about the surprise of LeBlanc's marriage, yet expressed their pleasure in the fact and how nice it was to have a new mistress at Travinwood.

Occasionally Amber's gaze would meet with that of Trent across the crowded room, and he would smile or nod his dark head. He was so very handsome and stood taller than any man there, save Casey Reed.

How proud she was of her husband! She watched as the women hovered about him, hanging on his every word. He was friendly to all, yet impersonal, and was an ideal host. When a young woman would become too aggressive or flirtatious, Trent would politely excuse himself and move on to other guests.

And if a man stayed too long near Amber or appeared to monopolize her attention, she would soon find LeBlanc at her side, his arm possessively about her waist. No one could mistake the fact that Amber belonged to him and that Trent held this possession closely and protectively.

"How very much in love they are!" Amber overheard two women talking near the fireplace and assumed they were speaking of Casey and Neva. "He is so tall and handsome and she is beautiful! Such beauty is rare. LeBlanc chose well!"

At the mention of Trent, Amber realized that it was she and her husband who were being discussed, and her heart sang at the knowledge that these people believed that Le-Blanc truly loved his wife and had willingly chosen her for his life mate.

Amber's eyes scanned the room in search of Trent but he was not there. She had not noticed his departure but knew that she had not seen him for an overly long time. Remembering her pact with Devon, she set her drink on a low table and slipped out, leaving the host of laughing, chatting guests.

Kane sat on the marbled floor of the hallway, his feet tucked beneath him. He was eating a large slice of wedding cake, and Amber giggled at the sight of him. He grinned up at her, his brown face smudged with white icing.

"I do believe you are enjoying that cake, Kane."

"Yassum!" he agreed. "Massah Trent, he say ah kin hab all ah wants!"

"Well, do you not think that you should eat some proper food before you fill yourself with cake?" she asked softly.

"Ah laks cake, miss!" Kane replied with another wide grin.

"I see that you do," Amber laughed. Then, "Kane, have you seen Master Trent within the last few minutes?"

"Yassum, he be in da study."

She thanked him and went toward the study, a feeling of dread washing over her. The door was slightly ajar and she could hear the deep rumble of Trent's voice, but the din from the reception area prevented her from being able to understand his words.

Amber inched the door open a bit wider and peeked in to see LeBlanc standing with his back to the door, hands on his hips. He was angry, of that she was certain. The tone of his voice betrayed that fact.

From where she stood, Amber could not see the other person, did not know the identity of the recipient of her husband's wrath. Then someone, probably Morgan, closed the large double doors of the ballroom, confining the noise therein and Amber held her breath lest the occupants of the study realize she was there.

But they were too engrossed in their conversation to notice, to her relief! And at that moment she heard another voice. A woman!

"Darling, please understand!" the woman pleaded. "I only did it because I love you! And because you love me!"

LeBlanc walked toward the window, running his fingers through his dark hair exasperatedly, and Amber saw that it was Kathleen Fulton to whom he had been speaking.

Trent turned abruptly back to the woman, shaking his head.

"You just cannot see! Or is it that you do not *want* to see? I do *not* love you, Kathy!"

"Do you love her? That—that woman you married?"

"We will leave my wife out of this!" Trent countered. "My feelings for her are no concern of yours!"

Amber felt a stabbing pain somewhere in the region of her heart, and hot tears stung her eyes as she heard his words.

Why had she thought he would tell Kathleen that he did love his wife? Why did it hurt so deeply when he did not?

"You do not love her!" Kathleen accused, moving to Trent. "You cannot say the words to convince me! Oh, darling, do you not see—it is because you love *me!*" Throwing her arms around his neck, she kissed him, clung to him desperately.

LeBlanc reached up and, disengaging her arms from his neck, stood her away from him, his eyes a deep, stormy blue.

"Damn you, Kathleen! Must a man bodily throw you from his house to be rid of you?" he hissed through clenched teeth. *"I do not love you, woman! I never have and I never shall!"*

The words made her furious, humiliated her! She must not lose him, Kathleen thought in despair, she could not let years of planning be wasted!

"What about your son, Trent? What about Darnell?" she asked craftily.

Oh, God! Amber felt her knees weaken. She pressed her hands to her stomach where her child lay. She felt ill and suddenly faint. Kathleen had borne Trent's child! A child of which Amber had been unaware, and he had lied to her when he had said that she, Amber, was the only woman to bear a child of his!

When LeBlanc made no reply but stood staring down at the small blonde, Amber could come to only one conclusion— Trent knew the child was his but had chosen to deny its parentage and wanted nothing to do with it. But why? A man as proud as he would *have* to care about his own son!

As if her thoughts had been relayed to Kathleen, the woman choked,

"You have to care about your own child! Your own flesh and blood!" She reached for the man before her but Trent threw her hands from him in disgust.

"True! I would care about my child; my flesh and blood," he told her in a deadly tone, "I *would* care—if he were mine!"

Kathleen paled and twisted her hands nervously, watching LeBlanc closely.

"There is a child I shall love, a child I shall cherish," he continued. "That child rests now within my wife's womb. *My* child, *my* seed, Kathleen! And there is no doubt, has never been a doubt that it is mine. The child which Amber LeBlanc carries within her belly—*that* child I shall love!"

"Why would you deny that my son is your child? I do not understand!"

"Then I shall explain, Kathleen," Trent began patiently. "Darnell is not my son! This I know for I have never spilled my seed within you! I was, at all times, most careful for I cared not to father a child, not with you nor any other, save Amber.

"You attempted this deception once before, if you recall, and I would not go along with it. Later, you went to Casey with the same story, and when you could not convince him that the child was *his*, you have again turned to me!" LeBlanc laughed without mirth and crossed his arms over his broad chest. Raising one dark brow he asked, mockingly,

"Can you not find the father of your offspring? Poor Kathy! Will not one of your many lovers admit to being the sire?"

Kathleen remained silent but stared at him insolently.

With a heavy sigh, LeBlanc announced, "You have exhausted my patience, Kathleen. I want nothing more to do with you. Nothing! You came here today, to my home and to Casey's wedding, without benefit of invitation to either. I shall only tell you this once to leave this house. Should there be another time, I shall forget that I am a gentleman!"

As he turned to stalk from the room, Amber quickly slid into the shadows of the hall, and Trent strode into the corridor without seeing her. She could hear him cursing under his breath as he passed her and returned to the reception hall.

She waited for Kathleen to leave. Several minutes elapsed, and the woman had not emerged from the study. Stepping to the open door, Amber entered unobserved by the other woman who stood at Trent's desk, her hand swiftly shuffling about the papers which lay there.

"May I assist you in finding that which you seek?" Amber's quiet voice startled the woman, and she jumped guiltily, withdrawing her hand as if it had suddenly been burned.

"Oh, I—I was going to leave Trent a note," Kathleen explained as she left the desk and walked toward Amber. "So! We meet again," she said, her blue eyes hostile.

"Yes, it would seem so." Amber watched the blond woman closely, suspiciously. "I should be happy to fetch my husband, Miss Fulton, then you need not write a note." She turned as if to leave.

"You think you have won," Kathleen spat, grasping Amber's upper arm in a painful grip. "Well, you have not! And you shall *never* win! Trent LeBlanc does not love you! He has told me this. It is *me* he wants, *me* he loves. Where do you think he has been these last nights?" the woman snarled.

Amber made no reply and Kathleen sneered,

"He was with *me!* In my bed! Loving me!" At Amber's look of utter disbelief, the older woman laughed scornfully. "And do you know why? It was because he needed satisfaction—needed a woman who could appease his hunger. *I* am that woman!"

Amber jerked her arm free of the restraining hand, her green eyes dangerously dark, her breath uneven. She stepped very close to her antagonist and rasped,

"You are a damned, malicious liar, Kathleen Fulton! You are vile and conniving, you reek of the gutter! I know not my husband's whereabouts on the nights in question but what I *do* know is that *he was not with you!*"

Her angry emerald glare held Kathleen motionless, the voice cut like the sharp blade of a knife. There was cool danger within this small copper-haired spitfire, Kathleen realized uneasily, then Amber went on,

"Do you crave him so that you would lie and slander, even deceive Trent, to bed him? I am not as knowledgeable of men as you surely are, but I know quite enough to please mine! So much so, that he does not seek his pleasure elsewhere! And if *ever* I fail to fully satisfy him . . ."

She let the sentence drop, and the disdainful wave of her hand and curt nod of her head clearly indicated that, at that time, Kathleen would be welcome to LeBlanc!

Kathleen could only stare at her in speechless consternation.

"You are free to lure my husband to your bed *if* I fail to keep him in mine! And should you succeed in bedding him, while you lie with him and he between your thighs, know this! Of a certainty you will never truly have him! For, in the end, Trent will come home to *me!*" Amber stated confidently. Then she walked regally to the open door and swung it wider. "You will do well, Miss Fulton, to leave this house as my husband advised!"

Kathleen rushed past her, threatening over her shoulder,

"I shall not be bested! If I cannot have Trent LeBlanc, then neither shall you!"

Amber remained in the open doorway watching Kathleen's retreating figure. As the woman passed from her sight, Amber spoke aloud,

"We shall see about that, Kathleen Fulton! You will find that Amber LeBlanc will fight for that which belongs to her, as ruthlessly as does her husband!"

"Well spoken, little one!"

LeBlanc's velvety voice reached her ears, and she spun about to see him standing in the shadows where she had stood earlier. An amused smile lit his face and he came toward her, moving gracefully.

"Trent! I—I did not know—"

"That your husband was witness to your confrontation with his one-time mistress?" He chuckled deeply. "No, I rather think you were unaware of my august presence," he teased. "You are a little wildcat, wife! Truly the kitten has claws! She purrs as she lies with her mate and bares her claws when another she-cat comes prowling around!"

Trent took the embarrassed Amber in his arms and kissed her thoroughly, molding her to the length of his hard body.

"You were right, you know!" His words were low and intimate. "You please me as no other woman could. The hunger I feel can only be gratified by you! I want no other, Amber! And it shall be thus, always!"

Chapter Twenty

AMBER AND MATTIE STOOD IN THE FOYER. GREEN EYES AND brown ones were raised to observe LeBlanc gingerly descending the stairs, one strong bronzed hand clutching the mahogany bannister for support. The other hand held his pounding head with great care, bracing it against the slightest movement. Walking with slow, studied steps he carefully watched his booted feet lest they falter.

Reaching the dining room, Trent gripped the back of his chair then hesitantly lowered himself onto it. A faint moan escaped his lips.

The two women had followed him, and raising red-rimmed blue eyes, he gave them a weak, lopsided grin, but it quickly faded. His dark hair was unruly, his face ashen. He gripped the edge of the table, his knuckles whitening as he tried in vain to steady his head and body.

"Coffee, Mattie, please!" he ordered gruffly.

Amber had taken her place at the table and sat wide-eyed, her upper lip caught between her teeth in a desperate attempt to hold back the threatening laughter. Then in a light, cheerful voice, she chimed,

"Good morning, Trent!"

"What is so damned good about it, madame?" he grunted discontentedly.

"Why, *everything!* Just look out there!" She rose and with a sweep of her hand drew back the blue and white curtains covering the wide window. The bright sunlight rushed in, spraying the room with its golden light.

Trent flinched and closed his eyes tightly, staying the intruding brightness. The woman had no compassion, he groaned, none at all.

"Is it not the most beautiful day?" Amber continued happily, a sly, mischievous grin on her face.

"If you say so!" he muttered, lowering his head to cradle it in both hands. He opened one eye and looked at his wife. How was it that she could be so chipper? Why was it that her lovely head was not pounding as was his? He knew that she had had more to drink than customary at the reception. She surely must feel the after-effects. He could hold his liquor better than most, and here he sat, his head spinning. So why did she look so damned undisturbed!

"Trent!" Amber's voice broke into his thoughts. "It is such a beautiful day that I should love to go riding. Kane went into town with Morgan this morning and Jason and Rual are at the ship. Would you mind terribly to go with me? Unless, of course, you will allow me to ride alone. I would be most careful!"

"You will go nowhere alone, Amber!"

"Good! Then you will go with me!"

"Did I say that?" he questioned in surprise.

"Trent, you would have me stay here just because you do not feel up to an outing?" She frowned, her face clouded, and she looked very disappointed.

"Who said I did not feel up to it?" Trent's voice was raised. "Damn it, Amber, I feel fine!"

She walked to him and rested her hand upon his brow.

"You do not look so fine," she commented, a hint of amusement in her voice. "I do not think I have ever seen you thus. And I do not like your pallor. Are you coming down with something?"

"Hell, no!" he snapped. "I am as fit as ever I was. Christ!" He flung his hands in the air in defeat. "Go dress for your ride, madame, and I will drive you in the carriage."

"Oh, thank you, Trent!" she shrilled, causing Trent's head to come near exploding. Then she placed a quick kiss on his lips. "I shan't be but a moment."

Amber rushed from the room and hurried up the stairs. She heard her husband telling Mattie to have one of the stable boys ready the carriage. She sighed with relief at the thought that she would not have to go to her meeting with Devon.

She would have Trent drive her down to the lake and about the grounds, and Devon or his spies would see them together. Later, when she next had to meet him, she would explain that she had been unable to leave the house for Trent was there and that at her attempt to go out he had insisted that he take her on her outing. This would give her a few days to find the black book and the envelope!

"Is something disturbing you, Amber?" Trent asked as he lifted her from the carriage and set her to the ground.

"Of course not! Why do you ask?" She feared that her actions had alerted him that something was bothering her. She must be more careful!

"You seem preoccupied, that is all," he replied, watching her closely. "Are you not feeling well these last days? Has the babe been giving you discomfort?"

"No, I am fine! It must be the excitement of the wedding and reception. I—I did have more spirits than usual and in my condition . . ." She paused and patted her abdomen. "Your child, I fear, does not care for liquor as does his father."

LeBlanc laughed heartily at her comment. Retrieving a blanket from the carriage he spread it on the ground. The two relaxed by the lake in the bright sunshine, content in each other's arms.

They talked of the wedding and of Trent's parents. He told her of his days with the pirates and that fateful night of the attack which had left the ship in his command at an early age. He related how he had made his life and fortune, aside from the inheritance left by his parents.

Then they spoke of their child and planned for its future.

It was a beautiful day and one Amber would always remember. For this day she had learned much about the man she loved. LeBlanc had bared his soul to her, had shared with her his past and spoke of a future which included her.

She could almost believe that Trent loved her, just a little. As she lay sheltered in his arms and listened to his beloved voice she vowed that she would one day have his love, a love as deep as her own!

This man was her life, and the babe that she carried would be a bridge by which she could reach his love. For Trent would love his child, he had told Kathleen as much. And for him to love his child, he would surely learn to love its mother—the woman who gave birth to his child.

"Are you cold, little one?" Trent asked worriedly and tightened his arms more securely about her.

"A little," she admitted, pleased with the concern in his tone and his protectiveness for her. "I would stay here forever," Amber murmured, looking up into his face. "Just like this—in your arms, by this beautiful lake." Then she whispered, "Trent, if I am still here at Travinwood when I die, I should want to be buried there, just beyond the lake by that tree." She pointed at the spot to which she referred.

Her reference to death jolted Trent and the words, "if I am still here at Travinwood," startled him. Of course she would be here! There was no place she would be other than here at Travinwood with him, with their children! He would be nothing without her at his side, without having her to love. And if she should die! Sweet God in Heaven! He would not allow it! She was his life! Amber was the very core of his soul. He would not be able to live without her! Her whispered words tore at his heart. Never had he allowed the thought of being without her to enter his mind!

"Do not speak so, Amber!" His voice was tight and strained as his blue eyes held her. He drew a shuddering breath and crushed her to him. "I forbid you to speak thus, ever again!"

He held her close, so close that she could feel the rapid beat of his heart beneath her cheek.

Amber slipped along the darkened hallway. The house was deadly quiet and only the chill winter breeze stirred outside. Its almost mournful sound caused her to shiver with apprehension. She was uneasy about her task, but when she did not meet Devon this afternoon he had sent a message ordering her to produce the items he had requested by the following morning. Should she fail to do so, she had been warned, something dreadful would befall a member of Travinwood!

She inched her way along the corridor, her bare feet soundless on the cool marbled floor, and felt her way down the staircase. Upon reaching the downstairs hall she lit a candle and walked cautiously for fear she might disturb and alarm the household.

As Amber neared the library she heard low voices and glanced down to see light streaming from beneath the door and she stopped in her tracks, staring at the closed door in perplexity.

Early this afternoon one of Trent's crewmen had come to the house with a message from Drake Monrow that the Captain was needed at the ship. LeBlanc had left immediately and Simmons had accompanied him. Trent had told her not to wait up, for he may stay the night aboard the *Mér Fleur* and return early tomorrow morning. She had not heard them return so she was not sure who could be behind that closed door.

She drew closer and paused to listen.

"New Orleans is protected on all sides by water," came Simmons's voice. "To invade her, the British would have to force a passage of the Mississippi!"

"A risky undertaking," replied a strange voice. "Very risky!"

The voice was not familiar, it held a thick accent—French, she guessed.

"You say the Mississippi is a risk, then they will have to find some unprotected bayou or river." That was Trent's voice.

"They are being secured!" Simmons assured him. "Jackson has ordered another battery at Fort St. Philip. This, he is confident, will prevent any attack from that quarter. He also strengthened the batteries elsewhere and blocked the main bayou out of Lake Pontchartrain."

"The last message from Gates was that gunboats patrol Lake Borgne. We are ready for the sons-of-bitches and on the alert for any landing attempts by the British!" LeBlanc stated, then added, "The bastards really are going to attempt to take New Orleans!"

"Jackson has *ma* services!" Again the strange voice spoke. "This I have told him."

"And he will accept it, my friend!" declared Trent. "He needs you and your men, needs their skills with the big cannon and he knows this."

"What about your men, Jean? Will they fight?" Simmons wanted to know.

"The Baratarians remain loyal to me! They will fight!"

Baratarians . . . island . . . Jean . . . French accent! The man was Jean Lafitte! The infamous pirate, Amber realized. And the men were discussing war maneuvers, locations of their artillery, and an advance on New Orleans!

So Trent *did* work for the government and, from what she had just heard, he was deeply involved! She could not relate this to Devon! She would not!

Devon be damned! She would find LeBlanc's black book only to hide it elsewhere so that if any of Devon's agents should try to find it, it would not be where Devon had known it to be. And the envelope! She would find and destroy that!

Moving from the library door she hurried down the hall to Trent's study. She could do what must be done while Trent was otherwise diverted. Then she would steal back upstairs and into bed before he came to their room for the night.

Opening the door she tiptoed into the darkened room, lighted only by the low-burning fire in the fireplace. Amber went straight to the desk and set her candle down. She sank into the large leather chair and pulled open the top drawer.

After searching through it she found nothing and moved on to the next. Again, nothing! The final drawer held only ledgers and receipts for purchases at Travinwood.

Amber lifted a large ledger from the drawer to search beneath it. Her heart stopped in her breast as her green gaze fell upon a black book. But it was a *big* book and she released the breath that she held as she read the gold lettering. Holy Bible. Setting aside the ledger, she lifted the Bible to her lap, her fingers slowly flipping the worn pages.

The Book fell open near the middle to the family records. Amber scanned the names with interest. Under 'Deaths' the last entry was that of Trent's beloved mother. Turning to 'Marriages' she saw her own name and Trent's and the date of their marriage. But there had been one even later entry and her gaze widened as she read 'Casey Ross Reed and Neva Lawson'!

Amber quickly turned to the page headed 'Births' and there she saw Casey's name and the date of his birth. Beneath his name, in a feminine handwriting, were the words 'natural son of Trisa Reed LeBlanc.'

Neva had been right! There *was* something the girls had not known about the two Captains. They were brothers! But why was the fact not known? Surely Mattie knew! And Morgan! The old servants had been here when Travinwood was built so that meant that they, too, guarded the secret! But why it should be a secret puzzled Amber.

Placing the Bible back in its place and the ledger over it, she closed the drawer. As she rose to her feet, something fell from her lap and fluttered to the floor. Amber bent to pick up the object. The envelope! She knew instinctively that it was the one Devon wanted. It must have fallen from the Bible!

Looking closely she found no addressee on the outside and, turning it over, she found that the wax seal had been broken. Slowly she drew the papers out, unfolded them and, sinking back into the chair, began to read.

It was a list of strategic points in the New Orleans area and by each location there were initials. The next page listed more locations and initials but none were familiar to her. The last page was a list which apparently was for London because she did recognize the names of the localities.

Amber was certain that this paper was key information as to where agents were stationed and the initials must be those of the contacts. No wonder Devon sought this paper!

Tucking the document deep into her pocket, she leaped from the chair and rushed to the door. She remembered that she had left her candle and turned back for it. She had just lifted it from the desk when suddenly she had the uncanny feeling that she was not alone. She smothered the cry which rose in her throat and her eyes searched the dimness of the room, focusing on the terrace doors. They were slightly ajar. From the corner of her eye she caught a movement and wheeled about to see a man moving with catlike tread toward her.

"I will take that, miss! You have saved me a search!" He extended his large, hairy hand.

"No!" Amber backed away from him.

"I said to hand it over! I should not like to hurt you!" he snarled.

"Take one step closer and I shall set it aflame!" she threatened as she drew the envelope from her pocket and held it daringly close to the candle flame.

The man stopped his advance.

"Now, miss," he whined. "Why would you do a thing like that?" And he edged closer as he spoke.

"Not another step! I do not make idle threats!" Amber snapped, stepping back. The man followed. "I mean it!" she told him. The man merely laughed and, with a sudden move, was almost upon her.

Amber touched the envelope to the candle's flame as she retreated from his reach. He made a dive for her and she fell to the floor as they both scrambled for possession of the burning paper. Her determination that the man must not be allowed to get the papers gave her added strength and Amber somehow managed to reach the fireplace. She flung the singed documents into the low flames and watched with relief as they ignited with a brief flash of burning light.

The intruder swore vividly and reached across her, his hand groping into the licking flames but the desired papers quickly curled into ashes.

Amber had rolled free of his heavy weight and now she struggled to her feet. But before she could run, the man had seized her in his powerful grip, his hand over her mouth to prevent her scream.

"I will kill you for that!" he gritted.

Amber bit down hard on the hand loosely covering her mouth. Her attacker yelled, jerking his smarting hand away. Amber screamed! A blood-curdling sound that rang through the house and echoed along the halls!

Then came a sickening blow to her skull, she heard a whimper that must have been her own and the urgent sound of running feet before she met the floor and darkness engulfed her.

Amber drifted along atop a fluffy, white cloud. Her body was weightless and she breathed the cool, refreshing air. She was free! No cares, no worries! She never wanted to go back down there, she thought, looking down on the young woman lying there in the white-sheeted bed. The lovely face of the sleeping woman was as pale as the milky sheets tucked about her. Why would she want to go back there, Amber asked herself, where people were so unhappy?

Why was the old servant woman crying? Why was the grizzle-haired man at the old woman's side, praying? It was all so strange. And there in the doorway a young black boy hovered. He, too, was weeping.

Kneeling at the bedside of the sleeping girl was a darkly handsome man. His head was bent and his hands were tenderly clasping the young woman's fragile hands. What was it that the man whispered? "Come back"? Yes, that was it. He had whispered in desperation, his lips close to her ear, "Come back! Please! You must not leave me, my love!"

Amber's heart went out to the strong man who knelt there beside his beloved. How he must love her, she thought.

If she went down there, could she help those grieving people? Would she be welcome or would she be intruding on their private grief?

Again the man called to the woman in an emotion-filled voice. He was pleading with her to open her eyes, to look at him. But the girl slept on, heedless of his urgent plea.

Amber decided that she must do something to help. These people were suffering, the handsome man was in profound anguish.

Slipping from her lofty perch upon the soft cloud, Amber floated effortlessly downward, drifting slowly nearer the sleeping woman.

"Please, my darling! Please open your eyes!" Trent pleaded brokenly as he stroked her pale brow. "Please, Amber!"

"Massah?"

Trent lifted his stricken eyes to the faithful old servant.

"Miz Amber, she jes' *gotta* hear ya!" Mattie told him, her tears falling like rain down her cheeks. Her shoulders shook uncontrollably. "Da Mistress—we cain't do wif out her! She—she be too much lubbed! An' da babe, too!"

"We will not give up, Mattie! I shall sit at her bedside until she comes back to us! The doctor says that she must *want* to return, she must have the will to fight! And, damn it, I will not give her up!"

Why was Trent raising his voice to Mattie? Amber wondered. His voice seemed overly loud in her ear. God! Her head hurt and his loud, drumming voice was not helping the throbbing in her head. If he were to yell once more, she would tell him to go elsewhere to do his ranting!

"Amber!"

There he goes, again. Why must he insist on calling her name every time she drifted into sleep? The man had no consideration and this angered her.

"Amber! Please—"

"Damn you, Trent LeBlanc," Amber spoke just above a whisper. "Must you yell at me? Can you not allow a person to sleep?"

LeBlanc leaped to his feet with a joyful shout. Mattie began praising the good Lord along with Morgan, and Kane danced up and down, shouting to the top of his strong, young lungs!

There was just no use trying to sleep in this house! Of this, Amber was certain.

"Amber, my darling!" Trent knelt and clasped her to him, kissing her tenderly. "I feared that you had left me!"

"Left you?" she questioned as he eased her back upon the bed.

Suddenly it all came back. The night in the study . . . the intruder . . . the envelope . . . the crushing blow to her head!

"Oh, Trent!" Amber cried, reaching out to him.

LeBlanc eased himself to the bed, cradling her in his arms.

"Shhh, it is all right, little one!" he soothed. "I am here and no one will harm you."

The child! Amber thought in sudden panic. Dear, sweet God! Please!

"Have I—did I— Please, God, no!"

Pushing Trent's arms away, Amber's hands flew to her middle, her eyes wide and frightened.

"My baby!" she choked. "Is my baby—"

"It is all right, Amber. The child is fine!" LeBlanc reassured her, and once again he gathered her into the warmth and security of his strong embrace as she wept quietly.

"All is well, my darling! All is well!"

Turning to Mattie, LeBlanc instructed her,

"Please tell the others that Miss Amber has regained consciousness and is improved. The Kensingtons must be informed immediately. Even if they are sleeping, Mattie, wake them and relay the good news. Then you and your family must get some much-needed rest. I shall remain here and I will see to my wife."

Mattie gave him a wide smile and nodded her graying head. Taking Morgan's outstretched hand, she walked with him to the door to join Kane, and the faithful three left the room, closing the door softly behind them.

"Relax, *ma* sweet," Trent whispered to Amber as he stood from the bed.

Wearily he undressed and pulled back the covers. He joined her in the wide bed and, reaching out, pulled her close to him. He snuffed out the candle, leaving the room in peaceful darkness.

"Sleep, little one! I shall not leave you."

"Trent, how long have I—" Amber began softly.

"Three days!" he answered tiredly. "Three damn long days! And I never left you once during that time, my darling! Not once . . ." His words trailed into silence.

His deep, rhythmic breathing told Amber that her beloved husband had fallen asleep even as he spoke. He must be utterly exhausted, she thought, as she, too, drifted into peaceful slumber.

When she awoke the next morning her room was flooded with sunlight, and she lay listening to the sounds of her beloved Travinwood. For a few restful minutes she felt absolutely at peace with the world.

Then the sudden thought of Lord Devon intruded on her serenity, and she caught her breath in agitation. She knew that soon Trent would question her about the night of her attack. How much could she tell him, she wondered?

As if he divined her thoughts, Trent entered the room. He was fully clothed and looked as if he had been awake for hours.

"What time is it?" Amber asked.

"Nearly noon, little one! Have you slept well?"

"Very well, thank you."

"Damn it, Amber! I have not the time nor the patience for

idle chatter!" He dragged a chair to the bedside and sat heavily on it. "A lot has been going on these last weeks. Most of it I was vaguely aware of, the rest I learned through your delirium. All this, plus information gained from my own inquiries, has helped me to piece together a clear picture of the situation in which you have been deeply involved and grossly misused!"

"Trent, I—"

"No, let me continue," LeBlanc broke in. "You have learned that I am an American agent. Of this fact I am proud! It is an honor to be chosen to serve one's country in such a capacity. With the aid of fellow agents, we have achieved great progress in the building of our country. There are those who would grind us beneath their heel, would take from us our hard-won freedom. This must not happen!

"The blood of many men has been spilled upon this rich earth, fighting to retain our rights. In America a man is master of all he possesses, and this is as it should be! There is much more, little one, that you may not understand at the moment. But suffice it to say that I am doing what I must!

"The intruder whom you shot was also an agent. But he was an enemy agent sent by the British to eliminate me, to hinder the work which I was doing, along with Simmons and Casey."

At Amber's look of surprise, Trent nodded his head.

"Yes, Simmons and Casey are also American agents. We have worked together for many months, with Simmons as our leader."

Amber had listened in silence throughout LeBlanc's account of the activities of his recent past.

"I am well aware that your attack was the result of your attempt to protect me. The assailant has been apprehended and has confessed much, including his reason for invading this house.

"Although we know that Lord Devon is deeply involved in espionage we plan to allow him to remain at large. He is but a spoke in the wheel of a large conspiracy and he will eventually lead us straight to his superiors. He is being watched, as you were!"

"I was watched? But, by whom?" Amber asked in surprise.

"It matters not, little one. But you were followed to each of your meetings with Devon and were never in great danger for my man would have prevented such. My only wish is that you had confided in me so that I could have assured you of your safety. I could not do so as long as you felt that secrecy was your security.

"I know of Devon's threats, which is one reason that your aunt and uncle are at Travinwood. Now, I must ask your help. Tomorrow you must send a message to Devon that you have acquired the little black book which he is most anxious to receive. You will inform him that I will not be here, that I am driving your aunt and uncle into town. Make a definite appointment with him, ask him to come here to Travinwood as you will be alone. He will understand your not meeting him at the usual place due to your accident.

"Can you, *will* you do this, Amber?" LeBlanc concluded.

"I will!" she answered.

Trent pushed his chair aside and moved to the bed. He lifted Amber's hands, pressing his lips to first one palm, then the other.

"Would to God that I need not ask this of you! But—"

"I understand, Trent, and I shall be most happy to help in such a worthy cause. America is *my* country now, and Travinwood my home!"

Pleased with her response, LeBlanc embraced Amber. He had longed to hear those words from her lips. Moreover, he wanted her to verbally admit her love for him. She had shown a love for him through her loyalty, her desire to protect him. She had shown it in her possessiveness and confidence during her heated confrontation with Kathleen. In her unconscious state she had whispered his name, prior to slipping into the deep coma.

But she had never said, "I love you" and this was what he wanted most to hear. Would she ever say those words?

"Trent?" Her voice brought him back from his wonderings.

"Yes, *ma* sweet?"

"You have told me much. But one thing you have kept from me. Your family Bible—I found it in your desk that night—Casey is your brother. Why the secrecy?"

"Because we are both government agents, as I have explained. Had our enemies known of the relationship they would have used one of us against the other. Threatening us as they threatened you, knowing that neither of us would have allowed harm to come to the other. It was for this reason, Amber, and for none other.

"I love my brother. We had the same, dear mother. Although we were apart for many years, he never gave up hope that I was alive and would one day return to Travinwood. As you know, we are very close. And now each of us has a lovely wife and we can be a family, again. But for now we must be most cautious lest we bring harm to our loved ones. This war will soon be over, and with its termination, freedom will no longer be threatened.

"Now, little one. You must rest in bed through this day for you will need your strength for your last meeting with Devon on the morrow."

"But, Trent," she protested, "I feel fine. I should like to have my breakfast and walk in the gardens!"

"If that is your wish, my wife, then it shall be as you say. I will send Mattie to help you dress and she will accompany you on your walk. See to it that you remain close to the house for you are not as strong as you think. Do not overtire."

He kissed her once again and left her to dress.

Chapter Twenty-one

AMBER HAD GONE OVER THE PLAN WITH TRENT, STEP BY STEP. She was to wait for Devon in the library . . . the black book would be hidden behind a specific book on the bookshelf . . . shortly after Devon's arrival Amber would retrieve the book . . . she was to pretend to be reluctant to hand it over to him, lest he be suspicious that it was too easy to obtain . . . she was to try to bargain with him . . . then she was to hand it over. . . .

Casey and his bride had returned from their trip to New Orleans, and Casey was to accompany LeBlanc and the Kensingtons into town. They had left in the carriage, and Trent was to double back by the back roads to be in command of the men stationed in strategic places about the estate. Every man knew his post, and Amber was to have no fear.

The meeting between herself and Devon was set for eight o'clock that evening, and Amber looked at the large clock in the hall, reading the time to be half past the hour of five. She sighed heavily. Christ! She prayed that all went as planned for she looked forward to Devon's capture. She felt that only then would he be out of her life and no longer would she be at his mercy and be subjected to his insults and threats.

Amber paced the floor, her mind going over the plans for the evening.

LeBlanc and Casey left Edward and his wife at the home of friends and went to meet Simmons. They sat in the back of the smoke-filled tavern discussing the plans for the evening. The book which Amber was to deliver to Devon was a fake, filled with codes and numbers, locations, and dates which would appear to be authentic but which Devon would have no way of understanding. And when he left Travinwood, Devon would be closely followed and, if all went as planned, he would lead them to the leader of the conspiracy against the American government. The American agents would move in and nab their prize.

"Relax, Trent!" Casey told his brother. "Amber is not a weakling. She is not like most women, she has spirit. You know she is quite capable of taking care of herself!"

"But she is with child, Casey! She is not as capable as she was before that. *Mon Dieu!*" LeBlanc ran his fingers through his hair. "Would that I had not asked this of her! Should she be harmed—"

"That little woman of yours is tougher than you think, LeBlanc!" Simmons broke in. "She is a fighter! You have seen her wield a cutlass, fire a pistol . . . I have heard the story of the battle at sea where she fought at your side, saving your hide and others!" He chuckled, then said, "I do not think I should worry. Amber is brave and intelligent! I envy you, man! Lord, but I do!"

"Dan is right, Trent! Amber is smart and bold as hell! She will do fine!"

At that moment a young lad walked in and stopped at the bar to ask where he could find Captain LeBlanc. The bartender pointed a pudgy finger in their direction, and the boy rushed over, sweeping his cap from his fair head.

"Cap'n LeBlanc?" His light-blue eyes darted from one to the other as he reached their table, waiting for LeBlanc to identify himself.

"I am LeBlanc," Trent answered.

"A message for you, sir." The youngster handed over a slip of paper.

LeBlanc took the message and reached to sweep up a coin from the table and placed the silver in the hand of the boy.

The lad smiled his thanks and ran out the door as Trent's blue eyes scanned the message. It was from an informant and, leaning back in his chair, booted feet upon the table edge, he read the note aloud to Simmons and Casey.

It seemed that the writer of the note had vital information for Trent and wished to meet him at Arbor Branch Saloon at half past five. LeBlanc glanced at the clock on the wall above the bar and noted that, if he hurried, he would reach the Arbor Branch in time for the meeting.

Trent hastily rose from his chair and threw his cape about his wide shoulders, saying,

"I must hurry if I make this meeting. Casey, you must take my place in the plans for the evening at Travinwood. I shall return straight home and see you both there."

Amber stopped her nervous pacing at the peal of the door knocker. She turned after a few moments to see Devon strolling arrogantly through the library door. Amber glanced at the clock and noted that Devon was quite early for their meeting and hoped that the timing would not disrupt the well-laid plans.

She played for time, making small talk until Devon demanded that she give him the book. She went through the motions of being reluctant as she had been instructed, then grudgingly handed it over.

Amber watched the man as he flipped the pages, smiling in satisfaction at his accomplishment.

Amber had decided to remain completely silent after giving Devon the book so that he would not linger for further conversation. After a time she decided that he should go and she walked toward the door, indicating that the meeting was over.

"It is a shame that we cannot indulge in the pleasures which your husband, at this very moment, is enjoying."

Devon's words stopped Amber's progress across the room.

"What do you mean?" she asked sharply.

"What I mean, my dear Amber, is that Trent has joined forces with Kathleen—perhaps not 'joined forces,' but I would definitely say that he has *joined* her in a bout of lovemaking." He chuckled maliciously at the expression on Amber's face. "You are shocked!"

Amber's brain was whirling. What had happened to their plans? And what was she expected to do, now?

"So, you do not believe this of your wonderful husband?" Devon asked smugly. "You are not dimwitted, Amber, not by any means. Trent is a man! All men, married or not, find pleasure elsewhere!"

"Trent does not! I trust him, as he does me!" she answered calmly. "Believe what you will, Devon, for your opinion does not matter to me." She turned back to the door and added, "I think it is time for you to leave!"

"Oh, no! The fun has just begun. Besides, LeBlanc will not be home for some time, if at all. I told you, Amber, your saintly husband is being well entertained elsewhere."

"You may leave!" she stated flatly. She could not think with him there. "Get out or I shall have you thrown out!"

"And who will throw me out? You are alone, Amber. I have had it checked out, and no one is here save for the girl, Neva, an old man and woman servants, and your little black shadow that makes himself a nuisance by tagging along after you, everywhere you go. No, I shall not be leaving just yet, Amber. Not until I get that for which I came!" Devon crossed the room and, reaching for Amber, crushed her against him, searching for her lips. "The book was not my sole purpose in coming here!"

"Let go of me!" Amber screamed. "Are you crazy? Trent will kill you for daring to touch me! Let go!" Amber struggled within his grasp. Devon laughed as he pulled her down on the sofa, falling heavily upon her.

"I do not fear Trent LeBlanc!" Devon ground out. "I do not fear a dead man!" At Amber's shocked look, Devon laughed, saying, "That is right! Dead!"

With a brutal movement Amber brought her knee upward, meeting Devon's groin. An agonized wail came forth from Devon's mouth, he doubled over in pain rolling to the floor. Amber leaped from the sofa, but before she could run, her ankle was seized and she found herself being dragged to the floor.

Devon, despite his pain, was upon her once more, Amber

screamed out and he brought his hand down with a ruthless blow to the side of her face. Her head jerked back, slamming against the floor. Bright, multicolored lights seemed to flash before her eyes and she became dizzy.

She fought Devon and cursed him. He brought a backhand across her mouth, splitting her lip. Devon pulled her to her feet and Amber broke away, running behind the desk. Her eyes searched the room, coming to rest on two crossed rapiers mounted on a silver shield which hung on the far wall.

She ran to the rapiers and snatched one from its cradle. "Now!" she hissed. "Now, who is the weakling? Which of us holds the weapon?" Devon stopped his advance abruptly, his eyes wide with surprise. "I will kill you, Devon! You killed Trent and now I shall kill you!"

"Amber, my God!" came Casey's shocked voice from the doorway. "We heard you scream and—" His words died as he saw Amber, rapier in hand, her gown torn at the hem and shoulder, blood oozing from her lip. Then his gaze turned to Devon who stood in front of her. Casey, pistol in hand, stepped toward them only to halt at Amber's shrill cry.

"*No!* Leave be, Casey!" she bit out bitterly. "This is *my* fight!"

"Amber!" Casey came closer.

"I said, *leave be!*" her voice rang with steel. "He came here for something and I shall see that he gets it! If I do not succeed, then, and *only* then, are you to interfere!" And with that she advanced on Lord Devon. "It will not be as easy to rape me as you thought, Devon. And how well you will know this when I am done with you."

Amber circled Devon slowly, "What is wrong, sir? You no longer like the game?" Amber taunted as she moved threateningly closer with each calculated step. She was trapping her victim with worthy assurance and without him knowing the better. Amber stalked Devon until his broad back was flat against the wall and he had no place to go. She was ready to strike.

"He killed Trent!" she spat out. "You bastard, I shall glory in spilling your blood! Do you want it to be a quick kill, Devon? Or a slow painful death?" She pressed the tip of the blade securely against the softness of his throat, the razor-sharp point drawing forth a tiny flow of blood.

Sweat beaded on his upper lip and brow, the salty droplets coursed down his face, stinging his eyes, but Devon made no move, he appeared not even to breathe. His pale green eyes were wide, unbelieving.

"Well? Your answer, sir!" she demanded icily. Her grip firm about the cup-like hilt of the rapier, she nudged the blade, the yielding flesh surrendering more blood. Devon spoke not a word, choking in his own saliva. He was afraid to swallow for fear that the movement would sink the rapier deeper within his throat.

"I assure you, Devon, that my method of dealing out death is not that which my husband's would have been! The wrath of Trent LeBlanc was well known! Greatly feared! And avoided by all! His law was his own and was severe! It was enforced with speed and strict demands!

"Trent was a ruthless and deadly man when angered. He was neither lenient nor merciful with those who took or misused that which belonged to LeBlanc! No, I am sure that if you are to befall the wrath of a LeBlanc you would much prefer it be *my* anger that you feel, rather than his! He taught me and taught me well, but I am still more lax than he would wish me to be, for I show more mercy than he ever would!"

Raising the rapier, Amber slowly and steadily ran the blade's tip along Devon's left cheek deep enough to be sure that it would leave its mark. Deep enough to be assured that once the wound healed it would scar and he would carry the mark always. Devon gritted his teeth against the stinging pain as he felt the warm blood trickle down his cheek and jaw.

"I have longed for this day to repay you for the torment you have caused me." Amber actually found herself enjoying punishing the man.

Dark green eyes held his and in their depths he stared at death. In that moment Devon knew that this slip of a woman, this beauty, would kill a man and never bat an eye.

When Amber had finished, she stepped back to admire her

handiwork. The rapier was back at Devon's throat. "Yes, I believe that will do for a start!" Amber laughed, a sound that made Devon's blood go cold and sent an eerie shiver up his spine.

"Come!" she invited happily. "Bear witness to a new feature you now exhibit with your handsomeness!"

Amber led Devon to a large gold-framed mirror which hung over the liquor cabinet. He stared aghast at the sight of his face. Her blade had formed a small, flawless "L" upon his cheek, the wet, warm blood seeping from it.

As Devon turned from the mirror with stricken eyes, Amber thrust the rapier deep within his chest. His eyes bulged, and without a sound he crumpled in a heap on the floor.

"What in God's name?" came a shocked voice from the doorway.

Amber spun about to see Trent entering the library, his blue eyes wide with disbelief.

"Trent!" Amber gasped and fainted dead away.

Amber moaned and slowly opened her eyes. Trent was at her side.

"Trent! I—I thought— Devon said you were dead!"

"Well, as you can see, I am alive and well!" He smiled at her. "Lord, woman! Will you ever stay out of trouble? I give you a fairly simple task to perform, and I return home to find you in the heat of battle, thrusting a rapier into a man's heart. A man who had apparently already suffered greatly at your hands."

"Trent," Amber began hesitantly, "I thought you were dead! I thought he had killed you!"

"And you killed Devon for that reason?" Trent was shocked. He had not thought that Amber would kill for him. But, he reasoned, he would have done the same for her.

"Will I ever tame you, little one?" Trent threw his hands up in defeat. "You are with child, yet you fight my battles, you indulge in war games and spying to protect me. You wield a pistol when a man attempts to take my life and kill with a rapier when you think me dead."

LeBlanc paced the room, shaking his dark head in wonderment. Then he stopped and looked at his wife.

"Amber, this must stop! I will not have the woman I love take such chances as you have!"

Amber's eyes widened and she stared at LeBlanc when she heard those words, "the woman I love." Was he saying that he loved her? Was he aware that he had spoken those words? Her heart was near bursting.

"Amber, are you listening to me?" Trent asked, towering over her.

"Yes, Trent," she lifted green eyes to his, her lips trembling.

"Are you going to cry, woman?"

Amber nodded her head, confirming her intention. But this time she would not be crying because he yelled at her.

"Damn it, Amber! I am not yelling at you because I *want* to, it is because I *have* to! It seems to be the only way I can get through to you!" Sighing heavily, he added, "I do not wish to make you cry."

"You said, 'the woman you love,'" Amber told him in a small voice.

Trent stared at her in awe. Yes, he remembered, he had said that. He had openly admitted his love. God, but he felt better! As if a heavy weight had been lifted from his shoulders, yet, at the same time, he felt apprehensive about her reaction to his declaration. Pray to God that Amber would love him in even a small way. He would ask nothing more than she could freely give.

Taking her hand in his, Trent said,

"Yes, Amber, that is what I said. Do you not know this? I have loved you for so very long!" He sighed deeply as he watched the play of emotion on her lovely face. What was she thinking, he wondered. What was she feeling, he wished to know.

"That night so long ago," LeBlanc began slowly, "in London a beautiful young woman stumbled at my feet and into my life. Until then I had not the time for love but with that first look into her emerald green eyes, I was lost. I knew not who you were, where you came from, but neither did I care.

"And then, later, as I held you in my arms, I knew that I could never—would never—let you go! I would never be free of you! I fell so deeply in love that night, my darling, so hopelessly in love! I knew that I could never live without you, could not leave you behind—so, I assured myself of always having you by taking you with me."

Amber had not spoken as he talked, drinking in his words. He loved her! Oh, but the words were beautiful! Love! It made so much difference!

Just as she was about to confess her love for him, Trent stood abruptly from the bed where he sat, to walk to the French doors. Crossing his arms over his broad chest, his dark head bowed low, he began, again,

"I know," his voice was husky, "that I took you against your will. I forced you from your home and from your loved ones, bringing you to a strange, new place. I cannot ask that you understand my actions, I can only say I did it because I love you deeply. This is something which I have never before felt for a woman, have never told a woman."

Silence claimed the room, and one could almost hear the darkness creeping in from the night.

"Amber, I truly wish for you to love me. I will give you the time, I will help you to learn to love me." It was almost a plea. "Do you think you could ever love me, Amber? Would you try?"

Amber left the bed, making her way on soundless feet to the tall, proud man standing in the shadows. Slipping her arms about his waist, she pressed her warm, wet cheek to his shoulder and whispered,

"I need not the time, nor need I learn. One who loves already needs no time, no teaching."

Trent held her from him, his dark blue eyes searching her uplifted face. He noted the tears on her cheeks, the smile on her lips.

"I love you, Trent LeBlanc," she spoke softly as she touched his cheek tenderly. "I could not speak my love before for fear you would not want it."

LeBlanc gathered her closely and as his lips claimed hers, he whispered,

"I love you, Amber, my love, my life! You alone fan the flames of my passion!"

Both LeBlanc and Amber knew that they had survived the battles of uncertainties, mistrust, and deceit of others to make a life meant for them, to share a lasting love and a destiny that began for both of them on a stormy night in London.

SHERYL FLOURNOY lives in Harlington, Texas, but does most of her writing on Padre Island. This is her third novel.